OATH OF HONOR

Acclaim for Radclyffe's Fiction

2010 RWA/FF&P Prism award winner *Secrets in the Stone* "is a strong, must read novel that will linger in the minds of readers long after the last page is turned."—*Just About Write*

Foreword Review Book of the Year finalist and IPPY silver medalist *Trauma Alert* "is hard to put down and it will sizzle in the reader's hands. The characters are hot, the sex scenes explicit and explosive, and the book is moved along by an interesting plot with well drawn secondary characters. The real star of this show is the attraction between the two characters, both of whom resist and then fall head over heels."—*Lambda Literary Reviews*

Lambda Literary Finalist *Best Lesbian Romance 2010* features "stories [that] are diverse in tone, style, and subject, making for more variety than in many, similar anthologies...well written, each containing a satisfying, surprising twist. Best Lesbian Romance series editor Radclyffe has assembled a respectable crop of 17 authors for this year's offering."—*Curve Magazine*

In **Benjamin Franklin Award finalist** *Desire by Starlight* "Radclyffe writes romance with such heart and her down-to-earth characters not only come to life but leap off the page until you feel like you know them. What Jenna and Gard feel for each other is not only a spark but an inferno and, as a reader, you will be washed away in this tumultuous romance until you can do nothing but succumb to it."—*Queer Magazine Online*

2010 Prism award winner and ForeWord Review Book of the Year Award finalist *Secrets in the Stone* is "so powerfully [written] that the worlds of these three women shimmer between reality and dreams...A strong, must read novel that will linger in the minds of readers long after the last page is turned."—*Just About Write*

Lambda Literary Award winner *Stolen Moments* "is a collection of steamy stories about women who just couldn't wait. It's sex when desire overrides reason, and it's incredibly hot!"—*On Our Backs*

Lambda Literary Award winner *Distant Shores, Silent Thunder* "weaves an intricate tapestry about passion and commitment between lovers. The story explores the fragile nature of trust and the sanctuary provided by loving relationships."—*Sapphic Reader*

Lambda Literary Award Finalist *Justice Served* delivers a "crisply written, fast-paced story with twists and turns and keeps us guessing until the final explosive ending."—*Independent Gay Writer*

Lambda Literary Award finalist *Turn Back Time* "is filled with wonderful love scenes, which are both tender and hot."—*MegaScene*

Applause for L.L. Raand's Midnight Hunters Series

"Raand has built a complex world inhabited by werewolves, vampires, and other paranormal beings...Raand has given her readers a complex plot filled with wonderful characters as well as insight into the hierarchy of Sylvan's pack and vampire clans. There are many plot twists and turns, as well as erotic sex scenes in this riveting novel that keep the pages flying until its satisfying conclusion."—*Just About Write*

"Once again, I am amazed at the storytelling ability of L.L. Raand aka Radclyffe. In *Blood Hunt*, she mixes high levels of sheer eroticism that will leave you squirming in your seat with an impeccable multi-character storyline all streaming together to form one great read." —*Queer Magazine Online*

"*The Midnight Hunt* has a gripping story to tell, and while there are also some truly erotic sex scenes, the story always takes precedence. This is a great read which is not easily put down nor easily forgotten."—*Just About Write*

"Are you sick of the same old hetero vampire/werewolf story plastered in every bookstore and at every movie theater? Well, I've got the cure to your werewolf fever. *The Midnight Hunt* is first in, what I hope is, a long-running series of fantasy erotica for L.L. Raand (aka Radclyffe)."—*Queer Magazine Online*

"Any reader familiar with Radclyffe's writing will recognize the author's style within *The Midnight Hunt*, yet at the same time it is most definitely a new direction. The author delivers an excellent story here, one that is engrossing from the very beginning. Raand has pieced together an intricate world, and provided just enough details for the reader to become enmeshed in the new world. The action moves quickly throughout the book and it's hard to put down."—*Three Dollar Bill Reviews*

By Radclyffe

Romances

Innocent Hearts

Promising Hearts

Love's Melody Lost

Love's Tender Warriors

Tomorrow's Promise

Love's Masquerade

shadowland

Passion's Bright Fury

Fated Love

Turn Back Time

When Dreams Tremble

The Lonely Hearts Club

Night Call

Secrets in the Stone

Desire by Starlight

Honor Series

Above All, Honor

Honor Bound

Love & Honor

Honor Guards

Honor Reclaimed

Honor Under Siege

Word of Honor

Justice Series

A Matter of Trust (prequel)

Shield of Justice

In Pursuit of Justice

Justice in the Shadows

Justice Served

Justice for All

The Provincetown Tales

Safe Harbor

Beyond the Breakwater

Distant Shores, Silent Thunder

Storms of Change

Winds of Fortune

Returning Tides

Sheltering Dunes

Visit us at www.boldstrokesbooks.com

OATH OF HONOR

by

RADCLY*f*FE

2012

THIS TRADE PAPERBACK ORIGINAL IS PUBLISHED BY
BOLD STROKES BOOKS, INC.
P.O. BOX 249
VALLEY FALLS, NY 12185

FIRST EDITION: JULY 2012

CREDITS

EDITORS: RUTH STERNGLANTZ AND STACIA SEAMAN
PRODUCTION DESIGN: STACIA SEAMAN
COVER DESIGN BY SHERI (GRAPHICARTIST2020@HOTMAIL.COM)

Acknowledgments

Some characters live on in the back of an author's mind, waiting for the right story to come along in which to make an appearance. The First Responders series is a group of stories linked by the theme of featuring those who serve on the "front lines": firefighters, law enforcement agents, medics, soldiers, environmental engineers, and many others. When I conceived of the idea of writing about the First Doctor, the physician assigned to the president of the United States, I instantly thought of the characters I had created in the Honor series as natural cast members, and thus this crossover novel was born. This is a stand-alone spin-off from the Honor series, with a new central main pairing, but I think those of you who know the Honor series will be happy to see a few old friends. Old friends or new, I hope you enjoy!

Thanks go to Sandy Lowe, for shouldering a gargantuan task with energy, enthusiasm, and remarkable calm; to author Nell Stark for close reading and expert advice; to Ruth Sternglantz for editing with insight and dedication; to Stacia Seaman, for being the one I count on in the final stretch; and to my first readers Connie, Eva, Jenny, and Paula for reading the early drafts and never failing to encourage.

Sheri shines, and the covers are always proof of that. Thanks for a great one.

And to Lee, who never falters—*Amo te*.

Radclyffe, 2012

For Lee, for patience, understanding, and belief

CHAPTER ONE

Wes glanced at her watch as she turned off the coast road onto the narrow causeway leading to Whitley Island. 1142. With luck, she wouldn't be late. Luck wasn't something she usually relied on. She believed in schedules and ran her life by the clock. Unfortunately, death had a way of interrupting even the most finely tuned schedules.

Until thirty-six hours ago, she'd been looking forward to spending her upcoming annual leave with her mother and sisters over Christmas, not dealing with a new job, no place to live, and no idea of what the next day would bring. She definitely hadn't planned on attending the wedding of the year.

All that had changed when she'd gotten a call informing her she was at the top of a very short list for a job most people in the navy, let alone the nation, had never even heard of. The anonymity of the position didn't bother her—in fact, she preferred working alone and was happy contributing behind the scenes. The next rung in her planned career ladder had been a professorship at the Uniformed Services University where she was stationed. She'd joined the navy because she'd needed the scholarship to go to medical school, and while she liked the structure, she was an academic at heart. She wanted to teach, take care of her patients, and let others wage war. She hadn't been sure she wanted a job that was going to throw her into close contact with the most powerful people in the world on a daily basis. She'd asked for a day to think it over—they'd given her four hours.

Heading into an unknown situation without the proper preparation made her wary. Order, discipline, and perseverance had brought her from her working-class neighborhood in South Philadelphia to the United States Naval Academy at Annapolis and finally to the National Military Medical Center in Bethesda. Knowing what she faced—in the ER, in the field, in life—kept her cool and in control. If she never relied on anyone or anything to run interference for her, she had no one to hold accountable for the outcome except herself.

She'd called her best friend Emory for advice—not just because she'd known Emory since they'd shared a cadaver at Penn, but because Emory knew intimately the landscape and the people Wes would be spending every moment of her life with for the next year, or maybe the next five.

"Are you kidding, Wes?" Emory had said when Wes reached her en route to the island. "It's an amazing opportunity. God, you'll have a front-and-center for events that might change the future of the whole world. And you'll be doing what you're trained to do."

"But I'm a teacher, not a clinician," she'd protested.

"Uh, excuse me—don't you teach trauma care to military medical personnel?"

"Yes, but—"

"And didn't you spend ten months supervising a field hospital—"

"Yes, but—"

"And—"

"Emory," Wes said patiently, "I suck at politics."

"Huh." Emory fell silent for a moment. "This is true."

"So—"

"Should I mention honor and duty and—"

Wes sighed. "No. I already considered that."

"And?"

And she'd said yes to this new job because to do otherwise seemed impossible. She'd rarely been faced with impossible decisions, and she wasn't sure yet how she felt about a situation she didn't control. Nevertheless, she'd called her boss, Rear Admiral Cal Wright, and said she was honored to accept, and he'd passed the word up the chain of command. Her final security interview wasn't scheduled until tomorrow, but she'd been told to liaise with her new unit today. Several teleconferenced interviews and a lot of rushed paperwork later, here she was.

Short of any more surprises, she'd be moving her hastily packed belongings to a government-provided apartment within walking distance of the White House as soon as she could arrange movers. Until then, she'd be in a hotel. She was used to moving at short notice, but she usually knew what she faced.

1155. In five minutes, she'd find out.

She slowed her rental car as a red pickup truck pulling a battered fishing boat on a rickety trailer edged onto the narrow two-lane in front of her. She could just make out a hard-packed-dirt boat ramp half-hidden in a narrow strip of pines separating the winding coast road from the pristine shore on the ocean side of the island. The pickup headed in the opposite direction, probably bound for the huge marina she'd passed a half mile back. The marina boatslips, marine offices, and waterside cabins that ringed a narrow-necked inlet were the only commercial development she'd seen since leaving the mainland.

Mentally she ran down the stats she'd received by e-mail that morning. Whitley Island was privately owned and home to one of the largest private military contractors in the nation. Tanner Whitley had inherited Whitley Industries on the death of her father over a decade before, and she'd expanded into government security as American geopolitics exploded globally. Personal info on Whitley was scant. She lived with a female naval officer, and from what Wes had seen of the island, industrialization had not followed Tanner Whitley home. The few visible private residences were separated by large tracts of untouched evergreen forests and set well back from the undulating shoreline along the Atlantic. The place was wild and beautiful, even snow-covered and frozen under the December winter.

As she'd been driving, the already scant signs of habitation gradually disappeared. When she reached the northern end of the island, the narrow road ended in a cul-de-sac bordering a wooded property. The drive leading up to a pair of closed ten-foot-high wrought-iron gates set into a natural stone wall was congested with signs of high-level security. Unmarked black SUVs with smoked windows lined the turnaround. A man and a woman, both in dark suits, monochromatic shirts, and dark glasses, stood side by side in front of the gates.

Squiggly radio feeds running from behind their left ears and steely expressions pegged them as security. The discreet lapel pins, conservative suits, and all-American good looks said federal agents. These weren't rent-a-cops or gun-for-hire mercenaries. The man was six foot four and on the lean side. Wes would have pegged him for a runner, except the broad shoulders and solid thighs that stretched his not-off-the-rack suit said serious weight training. The woman was maybe five-six or seven and looked toned and fit, but next to him, she looked downright delicate. Wes doubted she was. Her tailored jacket and pants, crisp white opened-collared shirt, and low-heeled black boots screamed style while being completely functional. Definitely professionals. Considering the event—Secret Service.

Neither of them moved as Wes parked behind a long line of empty vehicles, exited, and walked toward them, but she knew they were following her every step. She couldn't see their eyes behind the unnecessary shades. The sky was blanketed in a thick cover of gray clouds, and she doubted either of them had any trouble seeing in the flat midday light. Being able to observe without being observed was a power play. It probably worked on civilians.

"I'm Captain Wesley Masters," she said when she stopped a few feet away from them, stating the obvious, as the insignia on her dress blues, visible under her open topcoat, clearly indicated her rank. "I'm here to liaise with the Medical Unit."

"We know all the members of the WHMU," the woman said in a surprisingly full, smooth alto. No intonation. Not aggressive, not challenging, not interested. Just the facts, thank you, ma'am. "You're not on it."

Up close, Wes could see that what she had taken for glossy dark hair was actually a deep burgundy—as if the midnight sky was flaming. Barely tamed curls fell to below the crisp white collar and fanned artfully around what appeared to be a sharply drawn but distinctive face. She'd put the eyes at blue on a guess, but the opaque shades made it impossible to tell. The agent had a body under those clothes, despite the suit being cut, intentionally Wes would bet, to blunt her figure. The tailored lines couldn't hide the curves of her breasts and thighs—she was fit and flinty and quite attractively female. The guy with her still hadn't said anything. The redhead was in charge.

"Your intel is out-of-date, then," Wes said, and the agent stiffened perceptibly. "You might want to check with your boss." She turned her wrist slightly. 1159. One minute. "If you could do that promptly, I'd appreciate it."

One perfectly sculpted brow arched above the flat rim of the dark shades. "ID, please."

Wes slid her hand into the pocket of her topcoat and handed over her military ID card. She smiled. "Here you are."

The male agent's lips lifted in a faint smile. The woman's face remained blank. Beautiful and remote. Wes waited while the agent spoke softly into her wrist mic. A few seconds later, the agent held out her ID.

"You're cleared to enter, Captain."

The man turned to open the gate. Wes slid her ID back into her pocket. "Thank you, Agent…"

"Daniels, ma'am," Agent Daniels said formally. "An agent will meet you just inside the gate to escort you."

"Thank you," Wes said. "I'm sure I can find—"

"It's protocol. Captain."

"Understood." Wes stepped through the gates and they swung closed behind her. She had a lot to learn, and she was out of her element on every level. Hopefully the WHMU personnel would be a little more welcoming than Agent Daniels.

❖

"She the one?" Gary Brown asked as the gates swung closed behind the naval officer.

"Looks like it." Evyn scanned the approach road and the dense underbrush growing right up to the shoulders. The advance team had been on-site for four days and had locked down the north half of the island. Fire roads and beach-access lanes that might provide curious onlookers and those with more serious agendas a way to get close to Whitley Manor had been barricaded and were being patrolled by agents, on foot and ATV. A two-mile no-fly zone had been established around the island. As protective details went, this one was fairly close to ideal. One access road, no surrounding buildings with line of sight, and the only other approach by sea. They had the Coast Guard patrolling that. There was even an expansive lawn big enough and clear enough to accommodate Marine One, so no motorcade route to secure. The nearest hospital was a short helo ride away. All in all, today looked routine, but that wasn't a word in her vocabulary. Complacency bred error. And she didn't make mistakes.

"That was pretty fast," Gary said. "Getting her on board. O'Shaughnessy hasn't even been dead two days."

"It's not like they could leave the spot open," Evyn said darkly. Except why the hell the powers that be had gone outside to bring in a complete novice was beyond her. They already had a field-tested, experienced battle surgeon who could have stepped into O'Shaughnessy's shoes without a ripple in routine. Instead, they dropped an unknown into their lap. Hell, they hadn't even been briefed she was going to show up today.

"Is Pete pissed he got passed over?" Gary asked.

"You know Pete. He's a team player. But that job should've been his." Evyn could be mad for Pete if he wasn't going to be mad for himself. After all, that's what friends were for, and even though they'd only worked together two years, they were tight. They shared a near-maniacal need to win at everything, which had been obvious the first time they'd played cards on an overnight flight to some now-forgotten destination. She came by her competitiveness growing up in a family of super-achievers, he by being the first American-born child in a family of immigrants. Pete had to be disappointed he didn't get the job, but he didn't let on. So she'd be disappointed and pissed off for him. "Who knows what strings got pulled? It's a political appointment—probably someone somewhere knows someone who owed somebody a favor."

"Happens all the time on the Beltway," Gary said.

"Yeah, I know." She rarely paid attention to politics—who had time? And if this appointment hadn't affected her so personally and her job so intimately, she wouldn't have cared.

"Younger than I thought she'd be," Gary commented casually. "Kind of…interesting."

Evyn didn't react to his not-so-subtle probing. Hell. She couldn't argue. The captain was younger—and way hotter—than O'Shaughnessy. She still couldn't take in that O'Shaughnessy was dead. He'd only been in his early fifties and a good-looking fifty, still fit and trim. Ran five miles every day. Didn't smoke, hardly drank. Who would have expected him to drop dead in the gym? She'd figured his replacement would be closer to his age, not almost two decades younger, like Captain Wesley Masters. The navy doctor was a lot more than interesting too. She was five feet ten inches or so of sinewy grace, capped off by golden brown hair shot through with sunlight and wheat and cut a bit rough-and-tumble around her face and throat. The effect was a little casual and a lot sexy. And her eyes, even on a gray, overcast day, were heather green. Spring-kissed. Gorgeous. Evyn grimaced. She'd rather have to dislike someone who wasn't so damn good looking, but she'd manage.

"You know," Gary said, "it's probably not her fault she got tapped for the post."

"Never said it was," Evyn said sharply. Of course Gary would pick up on the slightest sign of attraction—the guy was a sponge when it came to reading people. Never missed anything. She had to stay on her toes all the time or he'd be watching the X-rated fantasies she occasionally played in her head to pass the time standing post.

"Just saying," he went on, "since we have to work together and all. Might be smart to play nice."

"You don't have to worry about that. I can work with her just fine. As long as no one expects us all to be one big happy family."

"Kind of works better when we are, considering..."

Evyn folded her arms across her chest and made another visual sweep of the area. "Then they should have given Pete the job. After all, he earned it."

❖

The Secret Service agent who escorted Wes to the building was silent as they strode up the meandering flagstone walkway between snow-filled sunken pools. The manor house rose suddenly from the late-morning mist, a sweeping three-story stone edifice sitting high above cascading dunes that fell away to the ocean's edge. A white-pillared wraparound veranda, which she imagined was the perfect place for summer entertaining, was empty now except for security posted at regular intervals along its perimeter. The muted rumble of voices carried through the carved wooden front doors as the agent opened them for her.

"Thank you," Wes said, stepping inside.

A white-jacketed valet appeared instantly at her side. "May I take your coat, Captain?"

She shrugged out of it, said, "Yes, thank you," and handed it over.

She continued down a wide hallway, following the murmur of conversation into a great room with soaring ceilings and one entire wall of glass that afforded a view of the island and ocean. The sliding glass doors to the veranda were closed now, but in the summer the sea breezes would fill the space. She glanced around, taking stock of the guests. She was surprised to see—or rather, *not* see—many dignitaries in attendance. Some of the quietly milling crowd was in uniform, but many wore civilian clothes. She didn't know much about the president's daughter, other than what most of the world knew—Blair Powell had been by her father's side on the campaign trail and, since his election, often stood in for him at political events where an official presence was required but the president himself was not needed. Blair was the unofficial first lady of the nation, and the nation loved her.

She was also a lesbian, and today was her wedding day.

CHAPTER TWO

Blair stepped into the hall with her father just as Cam and Cam's mother came out of the room opposite. Cam looked even more handsome than ever—which was saying a lot. Blair's stomach tightened as their eyes met. She'd seen Cam just the night before when they'd had a late-night supper with Tanner and Adrienne at Whitley Manor. She and Cam had slept apart the night before the wedding, agreeing the tradition added to the specialness of the occasion. Twelve hours or twelve days made no difference—every time they met after being apart, she was struck with the force of their connection. The air around her came alive and her heart beat faster. Cam's gaze held hers for an instant, as firmly and certainly as a caress, before moving to her father.

"Sir." Cam nodded to the president.

Blair's father said, "Morning, Cameron," and moved a few feet away to greet Cam's mother.

"Hello, darling," Blair said softly, sliding her hand down Cam's arm to clasp her fingers. They were warm and strong, fitting hers perfectly. Like Cam.

"Hi, baby," Cam murmured, stepping close.

"Any second thoughts?" Blair asked playfully, but some tiny part of her was still amazed Cam wanted her, body and soul, forever. Her head might have little niggling insecurities. But her heart never did. Cam always made her feel completely and totally loved.

"Not a one." Cam answered with absolute conviction and gave her a look that said she wanted to kiss her. For a fleeting second, Blair wondered if it wasn't too late to elope. When Cam got that smoky look in her eyes, all Blair wanted was Cam inside her. She supposed there was no way off the island without being noticed, though, and tried not to sigh in frustration. Cam's eyes sparkled with amusement and a promise. Blair smiled. Cam knew her too well.

"Okay—it was just a passing thought," Blair said. "I really am looking forward to this."

"You look beautiful." Cam lifted her hand to kiss her fingers.

"So do you." Blair was surprised to hear her voice shaking. The wedding was important for a lot of reasons, not all of them personal. She loved Cam and wanted to say so to the whole world. She wanted to wear Cam's ring and put hers on Cam's hand. But more was at stake today than just their private celebration. Even today, she was not just any woman. All her life she'd been her father's daughter, and she wouldn't change that no matter how hard the public scrutiny had been at times or how often she'd chafed under the restrictions. He was the president of the United States and his daughter was about to marry another woman—with his blessing. Their wedding was historic. Blair squeezed Cam's hand, putting everything but Cam from her mind. "Just to be clear, I want to spend the rest of my life with you."

"I'm yours, forever. Count on it."

"I do."

"I do too," Cam said.

"I'll see you downstairs, then, and we can say it again for the whole world to hear." Blair released Cam's hand and rejoined her father. "Ready, Daddy?"

"Absolutely," her father said.

Blair glanced back at Cam and raised her brow. "Commander?"

"Anything you say, Ms. Powell," Cam called after her.

Her steps as light as her heart, Blair laughed.

❖

"Wes!"

Wes spun around, caught sight of Emory Constantine hurrying toward her, and opened her arms. "Hi, Em."

"Hi yourself!" Emory's arms went around her neck and warm lips brushed her cheek. Emory hugged her hard.

"It's great to see you," Wes said gruffly, her throat tightening. Why was it so hard to keep in touch with the most important people in her life? She hadn't seen Emory for months, about as long as it had been since she'd been home. She missed Emory like family. Emory *was* family. Wes had acquaintances at work, colleagues she liked and respected, people she talked with every day. But no one she shared with. Emory, and her mother and her sisters, were the ones she trusted. "You look beautiful."

Wes stepped back, keeping Emory's hands in hers. Emory's shimmering blue dress brought out the highlights in her dark eyes and glossy shoulder-length black hair. She was, as always, utterly stunning while radiating complete confidence and self-assurance. Some people probably thought her ease, even when surrounded by some of the most influential people in the world, came from being lauded on the covers of *Time* and *People* for her lab's stem-cell breakthroughs, but Emory had been certain about everything as long as Wes had known her. Emory never lost sight of what she wanted, where she was headed, what she would accomplish. Wes loved her single-mindedness and total confidence. Emory had always said the same thing about her, but Wes suspected she only looked self-assured on the outside as a result of her height and her athletic build and the lessons she'd learned early in life— never show fear, never show weakness, and never, ever be ashamed of who she was. Poverty had a way of creating dignity; at least it had in her house. But she knew it was camouflage. Even all these years later, she still wondered where she fit in the world and was always aware of what she had to do to secure her place. Her work was her lifeline—her security and her satisfaction.

Emory brushed her hand over the fruit salad above Wes's heart, her fingertips making the ribbons and medals sway against the immaculate blue material a shade darker than Emory's dress. "Look who's talking. You're downright dashing in this uniform, Captain. I fear I might swoon."

Wes laughed, and a sandy-haired, sharp-eyed woman in a dark suit and coffee-colored shirt coughed discreetly at Emory's elbow, her body language possessive without being proprietary. "I'm standing right here, babe."

Emory's face lit up with an expression Wes had never seen there before. Pure joy. Emory grabbed the lanky newcomer around the waist and pulled her close. "Wes, this is Dana. She's my"—Emory glanced at Dana, an eyebrow raised—"fiancée?"

Dana laughed, a deep throaty chuckle. "Proposal accepted." She held out her hand to Wes. "Dana Barnett. I'm with Emory."

"Yes," Wes said. "I believe I've heard your name mentioned a time or two…hundred."

Dana grinned. "Same."

"Wes," Emory said, "I didn't expect to see you here. I thought you had interviews and all that."

"Circumstances are a little pressured," Wes said obliquely. Emory was her best friend, but her new job demanded discretion of the highest order. "Things are moving a bit faster than normal."

Emory's expression grew somber. "I was so sorry to hear about Leonard. What a tragedy."

"It was." Wes hadn't known Leonard O'Shaughnessy personally, but even though she dealt with death on a daily basis, sometimes the seeming unfairness of life defied rationalization. A sudden twist of fate could send so many lives, including her own, careening down paths never anticipated. She shook off the cloud of sadness. "My orders were to report promptly, so—"

Emory laughed. "Do they have any idea who they appointed? Dr. Punctuality herself."

"Probably not," Wes said, hoping someone somewhere had actually looked at her file, or this might be a very short posting.

"Well, it's wonderful to see you, and now that you'll be—" Emory broke off as a hushed "Oh!" escaped the crowd.

Wes followed her gaze. At the far end of the room, the wedding party descended the stairs. Oddly, no cameras flashed.

She'd been to a lot of weddings, including some extraordinarily elaborate ones. She would've expected the wedding of the daughter of the president of the United States to be a State affair. But then she thought about Blair Powell—despite her well-known public persona, there was very little about her private life in the public domain. Blair rarely gave interviews and avoided media glitz and paparazzi. Her romantic relationship with Cameron Roberts had created quite a bit of controversy in the national media news, but Blair had had very little to say other than to acknowledge the truth of the rumors. She might be the public face of the presidential family, but her personal life was a mystery.

The gathering today was small, considering the importance of the event, and Wes bet everyone there, with the exception of security, was a personal friend of the first family or Cameron Roberts's family. There were few foreign dignitaries, no Hollywood stars, no political pundits. Only ordinary people gathered to celebrate the special day of someone they loved.

For a moment, Wes felt like an intruder. She was used to boundaries—clear, solid ones. She was about to witness an extremely personal moment in the lives of strangers, without even the excuse of professional involvement to excuse her presence. Then she recognized a face at the far side of the room from the briefing documents she'd been given earlier. Dr. Peter Chang, the acting head of the White House Medical Unit. A bulky black leather bag sat by his right leg—a bag that carried a defibrillator, emergency resuscitation equipment, surgical instruments, and drugs. This gathering might appear to be an ordinary wedding, but it wasn't. Nothing about any event with the president in attendance was ordinary.

Chang was present along with a flight nurse and a physician's assistant to ensure the safety and welfare of the president of the United States—the duty Wes would be assuming within a matter of days. As the chief of the White House Medical Unit—her new posting—her charge was to ensure the health and welfare of every employee, visitor, and dignitary within the White House and grounds. But above all, her number one responsibility was to the president of the United States. In a crisis situation, he was her only patient, earning her the title of First Doctor of the United States. She'd have to get used to witnessing private moments as well as world-changing ones, since she would never be far from his side again. Where he went, she went.

Right now, President Andrew Powell looked like every other proud father she'd ever witnessed. He wore a dark blue suit, snowy white shirt, and red tie. His face still held a hint of summer tan, and his thick blond hair made him appear younger than his fifty years. Blair, her arm linked with her father's as they descended the staircase, had the same midnight blue eyes, although her hair was a deeper gold. Her full-length cream-colored dress, with its square-cut bodice and figure-hugging design, accentuated her svelte, athletic body. Her arms were sleek and muscular, her carriage confident and graceful. She was beautiful. Cameron Roberts was just behind her, holding the hand of a beautiful woman who looked very much like her. Marcea Casells, Roberts's mother. Roberts—tall, thick black hair brushed back from her face, intense charcoal eyes—was dressed formally in a gray morning coat, silver-gray pleated tuxedo shirt, and dark trousers with a satin stripe down the side. Her gaze followed Blair as if no one else was in the room.

At the bottom of the staircase, Blair and her father turned toward an area ringed with arrangements of wildflowers and white roses in front of the glass doors opening out onto the veranda. An army chaplain awaited them. The president moved a few steps away from his daughter, allowing Cameron Roberts to take her place by Blair's side. The guests filled the seats set up in one half of the room.

Wes made her way around the perimeter toward Peter Chang. She wasn't officially the head of the medical unit yet. Until her final security clearance, she was in limbo. She hadn't felt quite so displaced since the day her mother met her at the bus stop after school one late June day when she was eight and said they were moving in with her grandmother. They couldn't afford to live in the house she'd grown up in any longer. Wes pushed the uneasy feeling aside. She wasn't eight anymore, and she had learned since then that destiny was hers to determine.

Chang nodded to her when she stepped up beside him. He'd obviously been briefed too, but there was no time for conversation. The chaplain's deep voice filled the room.

Dearly beloved…

The president's daughter and Cameron Roberts faced each other, hands lightly clasped, eyes locked.

I, Blair Allison Powell, take you, Cameron Reed Roberts, to be my friend, my lover, the mother of my children, and my wife. I will be yours in times of plenty and in times of want, in times of sickness and in times of health, in times of joy and in times of sorrow, in times of failure and in times of triumph. I promise to cherish and respect you, to care for and protect you, to comfort and encourage you, and to stay with you, for all eternity.

A willowy blonde stepped to Blair's side, and Blair lifted a gleaming gold band from her palm. She lifted Cam's left hand and slid the ring securely on her third finger. *With this ring, I thee wed.*

Cameron Roberts's gaze never wavered from Blair's face, her voice ringing strong and clear. *I, Cameron Reed Roberts, take you, Blair Allison Powell, to be my friend, my lover, the mother of my children, and my wife. I will be yours in times of plenty and in times of want, in times of sickness and in times of health, in times of joy and in times of sorrow, in times of failure and in times of triumph. I promise to cherish and respect you, to care for and protect you, to comfort and encourage you, and to stay with you, for all eternity.*

Roberts accepted the matching ring from a young dark-haired woman who leaned on a plain wood cane, and slipped it onto Blair's finger. *With this ring, I thee wed.*

An anticipatory breath shuddered through the crowd. Six uniformed officers, the Guard of Honor, stepped in sync to form a path from the proceedings area, facing one another in a line, white-gloved hands on shining saber hilts.

By the power vested in me by the United States Army, the President of the United States, and the Commonwealth of...

The three male and three female officers drew their swords with a slick of steel, their blades raised and touching to form the Arch of Sabers.

...I pronounce you wed.

The couple kissed, the crowd clapped, and Wes turned to Peter Chang.

"I guess you know who I am."

Chang held out his hand. "Welcome to the hot zone, Captain."

Chapter Three

Hot zone. The term wasn't new to Wes, but somehow she didn't think Dr. Peter Chang was using it in the usual medical sense, meaning an area of contamination—typically bacterial or viral or chemical. In combat, the term referred to the region under fire. When teaching battlefield evacuation, Wes stressed that the hot zone was the area where the injured were still in the line of fire, and those charged to secure their safety would be too. Working in the hot zone was a way of life for a battlefield surgeon, and though her career path had been one of teaching, she'd done her tour at the front.

She hadn't had much time to think about the tactical aspects of her new job, and she wasn't sure who she should talk to about the specifics. One thing any team leader learned quickly was to keep their inexperience to themselves. She wasn't too proud to ask for help when she needed to know something, but she didn't plan to walk into her first day on the job acting like a rookie, either. No one needed to explain the critical nature of her assignment; she had only to look around the room. The president of the United States, his chief of staff, his military liaison, his daughter, her newly wedded partner, several ranking members of the cabinet, at least one member of the Joint Chiefs, the national security advisor, and the president's security chief were all gathered in one room. A strike against this location would effectively paralyze the government of the most powerful nation in the world. It wasn't her job to worry about the security of the nation, only the health, welfare, and safety of its leader.

Right now, that leader was dancing with his daughter, as any father of the bride would. Ushers and valets in crisp white jackets and black tuxedo pants had magically secreted the chairs somewhere out of sight. A four-piece band had set up adjacent to where the vows had been exchanged and was playing soft jazz. Waiters passed through the crowd with flutes of champagne on silver trays. The atmosphere was boisterous and relaxed. Wes didn't feel relaxed.

She might not have officially begun her duty, but she was all but signed-on-the-dotted-line, making every individual in this room her responsibility whether she carried the black field-trauma bag today or not. She wasn't here to socialize. She wasn't exactly sure why she was here, but as long as she was, she intended to work if necessary.

"What's the evacuation route to the nearest medical facility?" she asked Peter.

"There's a EC145 Eurocopter standing by. The closest level one trauma center is about a twenty-minute ride."

"Who flies it?"

"One of the marine pilots out of Andrews. He and our flight nurse are in the building."

"And you're in charge today?"

"Yes. We draw up the duty roster monthly, depending upon POTUS's itinerary and events scheduled at the House." Peter's expression grew somber. "Len was supposed to have this detail."

She wondered if Chang and the previous medical chief had been close friends, although their personal relationship didn't really matter. The death of a colleague, especially someone you worked with every day, was painful, and no words of sympathy were ever adequate. "I was sorry to hear of his death."

Peter nodded, watching the crowd. "Yeah. We all were."

"I've seen the team roster." Wes had been provided dossiers on all the members of the team—three docs, three flight nurses, three PAs. Not a huge group considering they covered the clinic for White House staffers, visitors, and guests, oversaw routine and urgent care for the president's and vice president's families, *and* accompanied the president on all scheduled and OTR trips. "That makes for some pretty intense scheduling."

"It can get hectic."

"We can pull personnel from Bethesda if we need to?"

Peter shifted slightly and met her gaze. "You can do pretty much anything you want to do, Captain. It's your show."

She searched his eyes, looking for resentment or resistance or challenge. He was in his late thirties, about her height, clean-shaven with a wiry build, and dressed in a navy suit, a plain pale blue shirt, and a thin black tie. His straight, glossy dark hair was precisely parted on the right side, and a thick shock fell over his forehead. His eyes were chocolate brown, steady and calm. Understated, composed, with a hint of reserve—he didn't know her, and she was now his boss. She'd need his cooperation, if not assistance, to make the transition a smooth one and to ensure the team continued to function at top efficiency. Too much was at stake for anything less. Taking a chance that professionalism would trump personal issues, she exposed her underbelly. "Who do I answer to, unofficially?"

The guy whose job she'd probably taken smiled. "Pretty much no one, except the president's chief of staff. Lucinda Washburn runs his schedule, which means she runs pretty much everything. If you need something that affects the president, ask her. Next in line is the head of his personal protection detail, Tom Turner." Peter scanned the room. "He's around here somewhere—tall, thin African American, about forty. He'll provide our weekly itinerary and general assignments, updated every morning at briefing."

At the mention of the Secret Service detail, Wes thought of Agent Daniels. She'd struck Wes as being a little humorless and a short step away from unfriendly—a lot like some of the military police she knew. Maybe that was just an occupational trait in closed groups with little regard for outsiders. "Where exactly do we fall in the chain of command?"

Peter waggled his hand. "We have to liaise with the Secret Service pretty intimately, because when he moves, they move, and we go with them."

"Separate but equal?"

He shrugged. "That's not exactly how they see it but, technically, yes. If a situation impacts his physical security, they carry the ball. If it has to do with his medical safety, we do."

"And if we disagree?"

He smiled for the barest second. "Depends on who has the biggest bark."

"Or bite?"

"That too."

Wes sighed inwardly. She hated politics. What the hell had she been thinking?

❖

Evyn made her way along the veranda to the rear of the house, where they'd set up their command post. After four hours outside in the wind and cold, she was ready for a cup of coffee or ten. She had no idea how much longer they'd be stuck out here in the ass-end of nowhere, but she was pretty sure she'd be outside again before they left. Departure time was fluid, depending on how long the postnuptial celebrations went on. It didn't matter much to her. Other than being outside in the damn cold, she didn't care how long she worked. The more she worked, the more overtime she made and the less free time she had to figure out how to fill until her next shift. There was only so much after-work socializing she could do with the other members of the detail, only so many movies she could watch while rattling around her apartment in Alexandria, and only so much clubbing she could take in search of a few hours' company.

There had been less and less of the last diversion lately. Sometimes the effort just didn't seem worth the payoff. She enjoyed the physical anticipation as she got dressed to go out and drove to one DC club or another. The tingle in her belly while she spent a few hours nursing a drink and scanning the room for possibilities kept her mind occupied too. Anything that got her adrenaline surging felt good, and it was hard to complain about sex in any fashion, but more and more when the night was done and she drove home alone after leaving some near stranger's bed at oh-dark-thirty, she felt dissatisfied. Physically sated maybe, but with the nagging feeling whatever she'd been hoping to find, she hadn't.

So on those more and more frequent nights when she was at loose ends, the best thing that could happen would be a text telling her the duty roster had changed once again and she had to report for an extra shift, or POTUS had decided on an early-morning run and they needed more bodies to go with him. She never minded.

A couple of her fellow agents were married, and they griped and grumbled about the frequent changes in the rotation, although not so loud anyone higher up could hear them. After all, they did have the premier protection detail. What could be more important than safeguarding POTUS? Some of them tried to have a normal life after hours. She wasn't one of them and never expected to be. She'd always wanted to do exactly what she was doing—she craved the stress and challenge and satisfaction of her work. Except for the damn cold.

Nodding to the agent huddled in his topcoat on the porch of the truly awesome house, she stamped her feet on the deck to clear the snow from her boots and pushed through the door into the big kitchen that took up half the rear of the house. Caterers and waiters and busboys bustled around, replacing half-empty champagne glasses with full ones, pulling trays of hot hors d'oeuvres from the oven, and sliding cold canapés from the refrigerator. A huge coffee urn sat on a sideboard with a stack of what looked like honest-to-God china cups next to it. No way was she drinking out of one of those. She grabbed one of the paper takeaway cups pushed back under one of the cabinets and filled it to the brim with hot black coffee. Carefully making her way around the party staff, she eased through the door into the dining room, where several agents observed video feeds from external cameras, watched computer monitors displaying overhead satellite images, and manned the radio COM center. Several greeted her, and she flicked a finger in their direction.

She shed her coat, tucked it into the closet at the far end of the room, and meandered down the hall toward the noisy celebration. The coffee was hot and strong and she sipped it appreciatively. Her fingers and toes started to warm. Maybe there was life beyond December after all. She stopped in an archway with a view of the great room and automatically scanned the space looking for the other agents. Finding them posted strategically around the perimeter, and satisfied all was as it should be, she leaned a shoulder against the archway and relaxed.

She knew everyone at the gathering, either personally, by sight, or from reviewing the guest list at the morning briefing. The only person out of place was the woman standing directly across the room from her. Captain Wesley Masters. Evyn would have noticed her under any circumstances—and who wouldn't? Her face was a striking combination of elegant angles and sweeping planes, her eyes that vivid sparkling green, her toned body showcased in the immaculate uniform. Uniforms really didn't do much for her, since she was surrounded by people wearing them all the time, but just the same, Masters looked good in hers. Very good. Lean hips, medium breasts, narrow waist, and slightly broader shoulders. Evyn didn't have to work hard to conjure up a fantasy of wrapping her legs around those tight hips and twisting her hands in those thick, sun-kissed locks. Instantly, she banished the image. Masters was not fantasy material. She was all too real and was probably going to be a pain in the ass.

POTUS was about to embark on his reelection campaign, which meant constant traveling, insane hours, unpredictable changes in the itinerary, and very real threats at every stop. It was game time, and no one, including the green medical officer across the room, was going to have the luxury of time to adjust to the new circumstances. Masters would have to hit the ground running, and hopefully she'd be able to absorb everything she needed to know in record time.

"Have you met the new WHMU chief yet?" a rumbling voice asked from beside her.

She turned toward Tom Turner, her boss and head of PPD. "Saw her when she came in. Surprise, surprise."

Tom winced. "You know how it is. Decisions get made, people forget to share."

"Uh-huh." Politics—same old BS. "Kind of rushed to just drop her in like this, don't you think? We never even had a briefing."

"I'm sure the other members of her team will brief her on the medical end of things," Tom went on.

Evyn sipped her coffee, watching Masters move away from Pete until she was standing alone at the edge of the crowd. Her face was composed, unreadable really, as she carefully focused on first one individual in the crowd then another, as if she was memorizing their faces. Maybe she was.

"She's never worked with a security detail before," Tom said. "She's going to need indoctrination."

"And pretty damn fast too," Evyn said absently, fascinated by the intense, absorbed expression on Masters's face. The fantasy in her head changed from the hot, anonymous body pressing down between her thighs to a glimpse of a captivatingly beautiful face leaning over her, fierce concentration in her green, green eyes. She imagined how it would feel to be the focus of all that intensity, and something fluttered under her rib cage. Her heart rate jumped and raced. Pulling her eyes away from the navy captain, she tried to capture the last few words Tom had said. No luck. "I'm sorry?"

"I'm assigning you as her unit liaison."

Evyn stiffened. "I'm sorry? Me?"

"She'll need basic training to know how the unit runs, how we communicate, protocols for various threat situations, and obviously, we'll need to evaluate how she's going to handle different types of medical threats and emergencies."

"And you expect me to be the one getting all this done?"

Tom smiled. "You're not complaining about a week or so off regular rotation, are you? Ought to be a slam dunk."

Evyn slid her eyes back to Wes Masters, who was no longer looking at the crowd. She was looking directly at Evyn, her expression assessing, thoughtful, inscrutable.

The fluttering in Evyn's belly coalesced into a hard, unsettling pulse of arousal. What the hell? She felt like prey instead of the predator, a definite role reversal and not a comfortable one. She held Masters's gaze and threw back a little heat of her own. Masters smiled, shook her head ever so slightly, and looked away.

The instant Masters was no longer studying her, Evyn wanted those green eyes back on her. Her skin burned from just a glance. She wouldn't try to imagine what a real touch would do to her—not while she was in public. That little fantasy would have to wait.

CHAPTER FOUR

Captain Masters." The president's chief of staff, an imposing, auburn-haired woman in her early fifties dressed in a deep green Versace suit, appeared next to Wes.

"Ms. Washburn," Wes replied, extending her hand. Among a room full of power players, this woman seemed surrounded by an aura of command befitting a four-star general. Wes resisted the urge to come to attention. "It's a pleasure to meet you."

"Likewise. I'm glad you were able to join us today."

"It's an honor." Wes had been ordered to attend, but this was a very special event and she felt privileged to witness it.

"I realize we're dropping you into the deep end, with very little notice, but circumstances being what they are, there was no choice. The president will be traveling extensively very shortly, and we must have the White House Medical Unit fully staffed and at peak efficiency." Lucinda sipped from a glass of sparkling water and regarded Wes steadily. Taking her measure.

"I'll do my best to get up to speed as quickly as possible."

"No doubt. Tom Turner, the special agent in charge of the president's security detail, will discuss interfacing with your unit."

"I'll look forward to it. I still have a clearance interview, but I was planning to report for duty as soon as that was completed."

"Actually," Lucinda said, "I can expedite that. The sooner you officially assume your post, the sooner we can assure a smooth and rapid transition. You drove out?"

"Yes," Wes said, unclear on the urgency of the transition, but recognizing an order when she heard it. "I flew in and rented a vehicle."

"Excellent. We'll have one of the staffers drive it back. You'll fly back with us on Marine One."

"Today?" Wes wasn't completely successful in keeping the surprise from her voice. She hadn't packed for an extended trip, although she had brought along her regulation uniform for the flight back to Maryland the next morning.

Lucinda smiled. "This afternoon, this evening, whenever Eagle decides to return to base. Problem?"

"Not at all," Wes said quickly. She'd just need to find a hotel in DC. The details she'd handle in the morning.

"Until then, enjoy yourself." With a nod, Lucinda turned to a man who had been patiently waiting nearby for a word with her. She greeted him by name and moved away, leaving Wes alone again.

Wes searched the opposite side of the room where she'd last seen Agent Daniels. She was gone, Wes noted, with a twinge of disappointment she couldn't explain any more than she could explain the brief and disconcerting glance they'd shared a few moments before. She'd been observing the guests, searching for clues to allegiances and hierarchy, studying the people the way she would study a map for an upcoming campaign. These were the players on the new stage of her life, and she needed to know where she fit.

When she'd first noticed the Secret Service agent, Daniels had been talking to another agent, her body language somewhere between annoyed and aggravated. Wes couldn't hear their conversation, but from what she could glean from Daniels's expression and the tension in her body, Daniels was unhappy about something. As she'd been watching her, Daniels had focused on her as if she could feel Wes's attention. Daniels was obviously aware that Wes had been studying her, and shot her a cocky look that held a hint of invitation, taking Wes off guard. Wes had seen the look a time or two, but never quite in this context. Forgetting to hide her reaction, she'd smiled at the audacity and declined the obvious invitation to come and find out more, if she dared.

She wasn't a coward, but neither was she fool enough to rush in where angels feared to tread. Agent Daniels was a beautiful puzzle she planned to leave safely unsolved.

The music changed to a waltz, and the president's daughter and her spouse moved toward the dance floor. Other guests joined them.

Feeling conspicuously out of place, Wes made her way to a nearby exit and retreated down a deserted hall in search of a quiet place to make arrangements for her trip to DC.

❖

Blair deposited an empty champagne glass on the tray of a passing waiter and turned to find Cam watching her. The look in Cam's eyes was contemplative, dark and serious. Blair moved through the crowd and grasped Cam's hand. "Dance with me."

Cam smiled. "I'd love to."

They found a quiet corner, and Blair wrapped her arms around Cam's neck, settling her face into the curve of Cam's shoulder. She fit her body into the long, tight planes of Cam's as she had thousands of times before and marveled that the sensation could still feel so new and exciting. And today, so very, very right. "I love you."

Cam brushed her mouth over Blair's temple. "I love you too. Today, maybe more than ever, and I never would have thought that possible."

Tears welled in Blair's eyes, and with anyone else, she would have been horrified, but she just turned her face against Cam's shoulder until the overwhelming surge of emotion passed. "I'm sorry we can't have a proper honeymoon."

Cam chuckled, sweeping one hand through Blair's hair and settling her fingers against the back of Blair's neck. "I don't need a honeymoon, Blair. Every second with you is my pleasure."

Blair surreptitiously nipped Cam's neck. "If you think sweet talk is going to get you anywhere, you're right."

"Good to know."

"This year is going to be crazy. With the war, the economy, and the conservatives screaming for a return to tradition, my father—"

"Andrew is going to be reelected." Cam's fingers played gently up and down the back of Blair's neck, a soothing, comforting rhythm laced with unswervable strength.

"I know he is. But this campaign is going to be more of a dogfight than it was the first time around, and I need to be there."

"Of course."

"I hate being away from you."

"I know. I hate it when my job pulls me away."

"You're awfully calm," Blair said, nuzzling Cam's neck. She kissed her throat softly. "What are you not telling me?"

The chuckle reverberated in Cam's chest again. Blair loved the feel of Cam's hands on her, the heat of Cam's body warming the cold places no other had ever touched. Desire welled within her, and she slid her hand inside Cam's jacket and brushed her fingers over Cam's chest. Cam's intake of breath was so swift and sharp, an arrow of sweet need struck inside her. Dangerous. She could forget what she was thinking, where she was, everything except wanting more. "Cam?"

Cam tightened her fingers on Blair's nape. She'd been hoping to avoid this conversation for a few more hours, but she'd never learned how to keep anything from Blair. The longer they were together, the worse she got at it. "I'm going to take a leave of absence so I can—"

"You are not."

"Andrew's reelection is just as important to me as it is to you," Cam said. "I'm going with you."

Blair took note of Cam's calm tone. Unruffled, unshakeable. The way she sounded when she was determined on a course she knew Blair would object to. Blair kept her voice down, barely.

"You are a deputy director of Homeland Security. Your job is critical. It's who you are, it's what you do. You're not taking time off to drag around the country on planes and trains and God knows what while my father gives reelection speeches, eating at fast food chains at four a.m. and fielding mud balls from hecklers in the audience." Blair poked a finger into Cam's chest. "You'd die of boredom in a week."

"I'm not going to be working crossword puzzles while all of this is going on," Cam said. "Lucinda will find something for me to do."

Blair braced her palm against Cam's chest and pushed back until she could meet Cam's eyes. "You already talked to her about this?"

Cam nodded.

"This might be the shortest marriage in history."

"As long as we make it through our wedding night." Then Cam's beautiful, sexy mouth curved upward, and Blair wanted to kiss her, which only made her angrier.

"Damn it, Cameron."

"I had to know what my options were before I could say anything to you. I had a feeling you might disagree—"

"Oh really? You did? How perceptive of you." Blair kissed her, not caring that half the room might be watching. "I could kill you."

"If that's any indication of your methods, I'll—"

"We're not done talking about this."

"We will." Cam kissed her back, slow enough and hard enough to drown Blair's anger. "But I want to be with you. Only and always you."

Blair sighed, surrendering to the need that never lessened, and rested her cheek against Cam's shoulder. "I guess it's a good thing I married you, then."

❖

Evyn had half an hour before she was due to relieve Gary on the gate. She found a quiet corner by a bank of windows in a long hallway at the rear of the house. Below her, the ocean roiled against the shore. The slashing whitecaps looked nothing like the warm crystalline waves that broke along the south Florida coast. These surges were gray and cold and hard, as merciless as the wind buffeting the dunes, freezing the blood—icing the bones.

"Stunning, isn't it?" Wesley Masters said from beside Evyn.

Evyn glimpsed Masters's face in profile, as starkly beautiful and commanding as the ocean below them, and she was anything but chilled—a flash of heat enveloped her and she had to catch her breath to stifle a gasp. Even a simple greeting was beyond her.

"Sorry," Masters said, stepping away. "I'm intruding."

"No," Evyn said quickly. "You're not at all. I was just…" She was at a loss to explain, having been caught in a contemplative moment that was so atypical of her she was embarrassed. Most of her daily conversation was with her fellow agents, talking about sports and office gossip and the latest movies—anything to pass the time before those intense moments when all that mattered was the constant search for danger, when a split-second's delay could be disastrous. In the off time, when the pressure was relieved, all she wanted was to let down her guard even a little—no demands, no obligations, no one to ask more than she could give. She waved a hand toward the window. "I was just…well, daydreaming."

Wes turned toward her, that intent expression in her eyes. "Were you?" She looked deep into Evyn's eyes for another second, as if she might find the memory of her imaginings still swimming beneath the surface. Then she turned to look back out at the ocean. "I've always thought the ocean held all the mysteries of life. I could watch it forever."

"Is that why you joined the navy?" Evyn asked, speaking softly so as not to shatter the strange sensation of having stepped slightly outside her life. She wanted to preserve this sheltered moment as long as possible and had no idea why.

Wes laughed shortly. "I suppose—that and I bought into the idea of traveling the world while doing the work I wanted. All that seems so whimsical now."

"You don't strike me as the whimsical type."

"No, I was always practical," Wes said, although there had been a time, long ago, before her father died—before everything changed— when she'd dreamed without boundaries. "I knew growing up I'd need to join the armed forces if I wanted an education. I chose the navy because of the sea."

"But you stayed in. You didn't have to."

"No, I could have left after I fulfilled my educational obligations, but the navy needs doctors and teachers, and I was comfortable."

"Is that what you do mostly, teach?" Evyn came back to earth as the sinking feeling in her stomach spread. Masters was not only green, she wasn't even a front-line medic.

"Yes," Wes said. "I'm an associate professor at the Uniformed Services University."

Evyn watched the frothing water climb higher on the sands, encroaching on the dunes, and digested that little detail. A professor. The choice of Wes Masters to replace O'Shaughnessy made even less sense, but then most government decisions were based on some complex rubric of politics, power maneuvering, and personal agendas. She should never have expected any of it to make sense. She looked at Masters, who was contemplating her again. "This duty is going to be a lot different than what you're used to."

A muscle bunched in Masters's jaw, but her expression remained calm, appraising. "I'm aware of that, Agent. I can assure you, I'll be up to the task."

"Oh, I'm certain of that," Evyn said. "Unless something changes, it's my job to see that you are."

Wes frowned. "I'm sorry? I don't understand."

"I don't really understand, either," Evyn said. "I don't understand why Peter Chang—" She broke off, sucked in a breath. She was about to lose her cool and complain about Peter being passed over to the last person who should know she had issues. She never made mistakes like that. "I've been assigned to orient you to the interface between the Presidential Protective Detail and the White House Medical Unit."

"I see."

Evyn sighed. Maybe it was the cold—three years, and she still wasn't used to the damn winters. Maybe it was the lack of sleep over the last few days. Maybe it was the unsettling, unwavering focus in Wes's eyes. But something was making her behave like a stranger to herself as well as an ass. "Look, I'm sorry, Captain. The weather seems to be affecting my mood. I'm usually not quite so surly—well, not after my first cup of coffee."

"No apologies necessary. And it's Wes," Wes said, seemingly willing to accept the change in subject. "Not a Northern girl?"

Evyn snorted. "Miami, born and bred."

"Ah," Wes said. "The winter can do funny things to your perceptions sometimes. Just remember, spring always follows."

"I'll try to keep that in mind when my ass is freezing off," Evyn muttered.

"If you think that's in danger of happening, you should come in out of the cold."

"I'll take that under advisement," Evyn said lightly, wondering if the warmth in Wes's gaze just might make the cold a little more bearable. A warning twinge flagged that as a dangerous line of thought, and she wisely squelched it. "We brief daily at zero seven hundred in PPD command center in the Old Executive Office Building. You should plan to be there as soon as you're officially on board. I imagine all the bullshi—paperwork and getting moved and such will take a few days."

"Actually, no. I'll be in DC tomorrow. I'm riding back on Marine One today."

Evyn narrowed her eyes. What the hell? Why hadn't Tom said

anything? She hated being out of the loop when anything affecting her job was at issue. "On whose authority?"

Wes's face shuttered closed. "Lucinda Washburn's."

Evyn bit back a comment—Lucinda's word was law at the House. Maybe Tom could shed some light on why the rush to get Masters to DC. "Good. You should make the briefing tomorrow, then."

"I'll do that. Then I have to meet my team."

"You can do that after we review our schedule for the orientation," Evyn said. "Unless we have an away trip or you have a medical emergency, you'll be detailed to me until further notice."

"Thank you, Agent. I'll report to you in the morning, then."

Wes turned and walked away and Evyn looked back out the window. Wes obviously was used to calling the shots, but PPD was running this show. She'd just have to get used to it. Twilight enveloped the island, turning the ocean black. The sensation of having slipped out of time faded and the normal chaos of Evyn's life crowded back in. She welcomed the tension and the wariness, feelings she understood.

Chapter Five

The wedding celebration wound down around 2000 hours, and after the good-byes had been said, Wes followed the group returning to Andrews with the president. While the president boarded Marine One along with Lucinda Washburn, his security chief, staff, and med unit, Wes ducked under the rotors and clambered up the stairs into the body of a nearby VH-60N Whitehawk helicopter, one of several helos identical to Marine One idling on a large expanse of cleared land behind Whitley Manor. On the flight back, the decoy helos would fly alongside Marine One in a complex aerial shell game of shifting positions to obscure which aircraft carried the president, in the event of an attack.

Wes glanced around, saluted a vice admiral already seated in the single seat directly behind the cockpit, and took one of the three seats on the bench along the wall. Two marines in full dress uniform boarded and sat beside her, followed by Evyn Daniels and the male agent who'd been at the gate with her earlier. As soon as they were strapped in, the helicopter lifted away, making conversation impossible. Evyn, in the jump seat directly across the narrow aisle from Wes, pulled a small electronic device from the pocket of her black trench coat and started to scroll.

Looking out the window next to Evyn, Wes watched the lights of Whitley Island growing fainter and finally disappearing beneath the low-lying cloud cover as the convoy headed out over water. Wes shifted her gaze from the night to Evyn, whose profile was softened by the dim glow of the cabin lights. Her burgundy hair fell forward over her cheek in loose, thick waves, and she absently pushed them away as she focused on the small screen in her hand. The movement was wholly unconscious and lent her an air of vulnerability Wes suspected she would disavow. A small frown line bisected the smooth skin between her arched reddish brown brows. She had that on-the-job look and was probably getting some kind of status report. She hadn't looked at Wes once. Annoyed that she didn't register on Evyn's radar and annoyed at herself for caring, Wes wondered which woman she'd met that day was the real Evyn Daniels.

USSS SA Evyn Daniels was obviously competent, dedicated, and all business—that much had been established with their first encounter at the gate. But Evyn was more than just a suit with a gun and badge. For a few moments when they'd stood at the windows overlooking the shore, they'd talked of things that went beyond aimless party chatter. They'd shared something of themselves, something Wes usually only did with family and close friends. With everyone else, she discussed cases and assignments—safe, common ground. She'd been the one to strike up the conversation with Evyn, also unlike her. But she'd been drawn to the faraway look on Evyn's face as she'd stood alone against a backdrop of sea and sand—looking remote and somehow sad. And very beautiful. Evyn had been easy to talk to, showing glimmers of humor and warmth, at least until the subject of Peter Chang had come up. Then Evyn had revealed a well of anger she'd quickly suppressed. When Wes had shifted the conversation to safe ground and the subject of business, she'd instantly missed their brief but unexpectedly intense connection.

Evyn's slip when Chang was mentioned made it pretty clear she didn't think Wes was the right person for her new job. Ordinarily Wes didn't concern herself with what anyone other than her commanding officers felt about her and her performance, but it bothered her that Evyn didn't believe she had earned the post. What Evyn thought mattered, personally and professionally, so she was going to have to prove to Evyn she was capable of the job. After all these years, she'd thought she was past that. She hadn't needed or wanted to prove herself to anyone in a long time.

The day had been full of surprises, mostly unwelcome ones. She hadn't felt so displaced since she'd left home for the Naval Academy and had been cut loose from her strongest support system as abruptly as a blade across her throat. At first, she'd missed her mother's unwavering belief in her and her sisters' humor so much she'd thought she might break. She hadn't broken. She'd reached inside herself and found their voices alive and strong in her heart. She'd adapted, she'd adjusted, and she'd triumphed. Now she was back in unknown waters, with no place to live, a new command, and, apparently, the need to prove herself to Evyn Daniels.

❖

Evyn's push was waiting at the House when the motorcade from Andrews pulled into the south drive. Tom had texted they'd debrief in the morning. As soon as POTUS was on his way into the residence, she was done. She headed toward the west gate and the Ellipse where she'd parked her car. Up ahead, she recognized Masters walking toward Pennsylvania Avenue. She hesitated, giving her time to get ahead of her. In the next second, she sped up, refusing to think about why.

"Hey," Evyn called, catching up to Wes at the corner. "You need a ride?"

Masters looked at her, clearly surprised, making Evyn feel like a bigger jerk for even thinking about leaving her to fend for herself in the middle of the night. But Wes made her so damn uncomfortable—she didn't know what she was doing. "I've got a car." Now there was a fairly brainless statement. "Let me take you."

"Thanks," Masters said. "I'm okay. I'll grab a cab. I'm just going across town to a hotel."

"It's almost twenty-three thirty, Captain. Not a great time of night to get a cab in this part of town, and definitely no time to be out and about alone."

Masters laughed. "It's Wes, remember? Do you think I need protection?"

Glad for the cover of dark to hide the flush that heated her cheeks, Evyn said, "I'm positive you don't. But I can't see any reason for you to freeze your ass off out here."

"It's twenty-five degrees," Wes pointed out. "Not that cold."

Evyn snorted and watched her breath frost in the air. Obviously, Wes was from somewhere north of the Mason-Dixon Line. "It's about fifty degrees colder than I like it."

Wes laughed harder, a deep, mellow sound that warmed Evyn's stomach in a totally unexpected and not unwelcome way.

"What are you doing up here, if you hate the winter so much?" Wes asked.

Evyn jammed her hands into the pockets of her coat. The conversation was verging on the personal, and she was out of her element in more ways than the weather. She didn't even talk about this sort of thing when she was trying to connect with a woman for the night. And this was twice in one day with Wes. She shrugged. "This is the detail I wanted, so the weather is part of the job."

"The president is something of a skier too, isn't he?"

"POTUS, his daughter—regular snow bunnies. It's unnatural." God, she hated those ski trips, not that she'd ever let on.

"Obviously, you love your job."

"Yeah," Evyn said, meaning it, but Wes didn't need to know that. Wes didn't need to know anything at all about her. Time to shut down the information highway.

"Are you hungry?" Wes asked.

"Uh—yeah, for me, it's dinnertime."

"Well, I left my quarters at zero six hundred this morning, and the only thing I've had all day is coffee and little things that look like food but are really just a tease."

Evyn grinned. "Hors d'oeuvres. I don't even think they count as food."

"How about dinner somewhere, then?"

"I could eat." Evyn had the sudden sensation she was walking into a landmine, but Wes was just smiling at her. Friendly. Just a simple meal between coworkers. Safe enough. "Okay. Sure."

"Good. You know the area. You pick the place, Agent."

"It's Evyn."

"Okay. Evyn."

"Come on, I can't feel my feet." Evyn led the way to her '57 T-Bird, keying the alarm as they approached.

"Nice car," Wes said.

"The last of the classic design. I inherited it from my older brother."

Wes shot her a concerned look.

"Not that way—Aaron is fine. He just decided the T-Bird wasn't dignified enough for a feeb."

"He's FBI?"

Evyn climbed behind the wheel and started the engine, waiting for Wes to belt up before backing out. "Yeah. The shame of our family, but we still love him."

"Ah, let me guess. Government service is a family thing?"

"You could say that." Evyn hesitated, impressed by and a little wary of Wes's ability to hear more than she said. She'd have to be careful around her. "My father's ATF, my aunt's IRS, my younger brother's ICE, and the next oldest went army. We've got a few more agencies covered with the cousins."

"That's a heavy legacy to inherit."

"Not so much." Evyn shrugged and turned onto Pennsylvania Avenue, passing by the House, leaving the glowing lights behind, and headed north toward Dupont Circle. The streets were dark, nearly deserted. "Wasn't hard for me—I always knew what I wanted to do."

"And you love it."

"Yeah I do, except—"

"—for the cold."

Laughing, Evyn looked over and tripped into Wes's eyes. Under the streetlights, the green of her eyes darkened to the deep hues of a hidden glade in the heart of the forest. Splinters of moonlight carved out the elegant arch of her cheekbones and pooled in the hollow of her throat. Jesus. She was beautiful. Fixing back on the street, she said tightly, "You want fancy, or plain, simple, and good?"

"I don't need frills," Wes said. "But good, yeah. That matters."

"Not one for show, is that it?" Casual, she could do casual. And distant. She needed distance. She had to train her, for Chrissake, and don't forget Peter. What the fuck was wrong with her?

"The only thing I care about," Wes said as Evyn turned up Connecticut, "is getting the job done."

"So how come you're teaching and not...you know, doing?" When silence ensued, she glanced over and figured from the rigid set of Wes's jaw she probably could have phrased that a little more diplomatically. Well, she'd wanted distance. Now she had it. How come it didn't feel so good? "Sorry. I take it that was an insult of some kind?"

Wes blew out a breath and eased back in her seat. "No, it's not an insult. I'm not ashamed to spend most of my time teaching. I do my share in covering the ER in rotation, but I have a certain knack for teaching and I like it. The way things have been going the last few years, more troops see combat. War has changed. New weapons and new ways of fighting mean new types of injuries. If our medics aren't fully prepared for the kinds of battlefield causalities they'll face, troops die. I figure this is the best way for me to see that doesn't happen."

"I get that," Evyn said softly.

"What you do is totally different," Wes said. "For you, it's a lot more personal."

"Personal?" Evyn gripped the wheel harder, uncomfortable with the shift of focus back to her. Her hold on the whole night was slipping. She should be on her way home to Alexandria to get some much-needed sleep. Or maybe she just needed some human contact of the sexual variety—too late for a club, but she still had a few women in her little black book who would take her call no matter how late. Instead of either safe option, she was on her way out to eat with a woman who lured her into unfamiliar territory so smoothly she never noticed until she was floundering for direction. "I, ah, don't know about personal. I'm doing my job. It's what I'm trained to do."

"True," Wes said, "but what you do in a split second has an immediate and critical impact. Whatever effect I might have is at a distance…months, possibly years later…when a young medical student or resident saves a life because of something I taught them."

"And that's enough for you?" Evyn couldn't help asking, although she knew she should be searching for some vacuous topic like the Redskins' standing in the playoffs. She pulled to the curb in front of Circa and swiveled on the seat to face Wes across the narrow divide. "Just taking on faith that down the line, somewhere, sometime…?"

"For me, it's the long game. I'm not looking for immediate gratification."

"Yeah, well." Evyn cut the engine. "I don't look much past the moment. Not in my nature."

"I guess that makes us different," Wes said quietly.

"Like night and day."

Chapter Six

Senator Franklin Russo glanced at the brass clock on his desk. Nine p.m. Headlights flickered through the trees along the approach road to his Idaho mountain retreat, alerting him to a vehicle arriving. Hooker was punctual. He expected that of those who worked for him. That and absolute, unquestioning loyalty.

The doorbell rang and a moment later a soft knock sounded on his study door.

"Come in."

The door swung open, and his personal aide Derek Sullivan, a thin young blond in khaki pants and a starched striped shirt, said, "Mr. Hooker is here, sir."

"Good. Have him come in."

A heavyset middle-aged man with a thick brown mustache flecked with gray strode in. His snow-crusted work boots left muddy streaks on the wide pine plank floors. His broad, rough face was ruddy from the subzero temperatures.

"Close the door, Derek," Franklin said, "and see that we're not disturbed."

"Yes, sir." Derek backed out and pulled the door shut.

"Hooker," Franklin said, "what do you have to report?" He didn't offer Hooker a seat. The man was a hired gun, muscle. Necessary, but not part of his inner circle. He paid him well, and that was all that mattered.

"I've got a contact with the connections we need in DC," Hooker said. "It won't be cheap."

"Money is not a factor," Franklin said, "but discretion is."

"You don't need to worry about that. He doesn't know who I'm working for. He doesn't want to know."

"All the better." Franklin leaned back in his leather swivel chair and steepled his hands in front of his chest, regarding Hooker carefully. His presidential campaign was gaining strength in the heartland, but Andrew Powell was a popular incumbent. He needed to cast doubt on Powell's ability to lead the country through increasingly troubled times. He needed insurance. This man promised it to him. "What about obtaining the material?"

"He'll set me up." Hooker shrugged. "But we might have to get in bed with the militia to accomplish the actual acquisition."

Franklin shook his head. "I don't like exposing ourselves to hotheads, and after the fiasco at Matheson's compound, the whole bunch of them are going to be under surveillance. I can't afford to be linked to them."

"That's what you hired me for—I'll run interference and make sure nothing blows back on you."

Hooker smiled, a slow just-short-of-ugly smile that set off warning blips on Franklin's radar. If Hooker hoped to put him in his debt, he was wrong. Throughout his rapid rise to power in the senate and on the path to winning the presidential nomination, he'd had to make deals and promise paybacks, but he was always careful not to give anyone leverage on him. He never let anyone other than Nora Fleming know the whole of his plans. Nora Fleming was more than his campaign manager. She was the only one who shared his vision—not his wife, not his children, not his staff. As the leader of the Patriot Party, he was running for president on a platform of reinstating traditional American values of family, morality, and religion. His family was an essential element of his image—but Nora was his true support.

"Just remember—plausible deniability," Franklin said. "We need a lot of distance between my campaign and the activities of these radicals."

"Not to worry. The inside man at Eugen Corp—"

Franklin held up his hand. "I don't want to know names or details. Just get it done."

"Of course."

"And when it's over, everyone involved needs to disappear."

Hooker winced as if Franklin had breached some unspoken rule about what could be spoken out loud. Franklin almost laughed. As if his security wasn't the best in the world. Even Andrew Powell's inner sanctum wasn't as secure as he thought.

"The only way to ensure secrecy is by guaranteeing silence," Franklin said softly. "I don't care how you do it."

"I'll take care of it," Hooker finally said. "And the targets?"

"I want the country to know Andrew Powell is not only soft on terrorism and foreign affairs, his whole government is soft. When the people see he can't protect them, even within our own borders, they'll make the right and logical choice at the polls." Franklin lifted a shoulder. "I want a public forum, with media coverage."

"Civilian casualties could backfire. Look at what happened in Oklahoma."

"The threat alone will be enough. And if there are casualties..." Franklin waved a hand. "McVeigh and Nichols were amateurs. Hotheads. That's exactly the reason I don't want to get involved with another one of these militia groups."

"You still need foot soldiers—more than that, you need followers who are willing to sacrifice for the cause. You don't have much choice."

"Then I want absolute containment. No breaches. No leaks. Nothing that ties us to them or the events."

"I understand." Hooker's eyes went flat. "You don't need to worry."

"If we time this right," Franklin said, "Powell's standing will plummet before his campaign even gets started. The groundswell of negative publicity will bury him."

"I'll keep you informed."

"Contact me by phone when you have more for me. Good night."

Hooker let himself out, and Franklin turned off his desk light, letting the room fall into shadow. Through half-closed eyes, he watched the dim glow of Hooker's taillights recede down the mountain into the darkness. He was forced to consort with unsavory characters in order to achieve his goals. That didn't bother him. His was the path of righteousness. Someone needed to take back control of the nation, to redirect America's course and restore her to greatness and power. Someone needed to remind Americans of the true path. Andrew Powell needed to be removed from office. His daughter, who Powell flaunted in the face of God-fearing people, was a sinner, even more so for her insistence on pushing her unholy relationship in the faces of good Americans. Blair Powell was becoming a national icon, and that too must end. He wouldn't rest until both were gone.

❖

"So," Evyn said, pushing her empty dishes aside and drawing her coffee cup nearer, "do you come from a family of doctors?"

Wes carefully placed her fork beside her plate and reached for her espresso. They'd spent most of the meal talking about the job—the daily briefings between PPD and the WHMU, coordinating schedules, protocol when POTUS traveled, security and medical preparation for potential threats—safe topics. This one wasn't so safe, and she was a little surprised that Evyn, who had maintained a cool professional distance all night, breached the neutral zone into something personal.

"Sorry," Evyn said with no inflection, "is that a sensitive subject?"

Wes shook her head. "No, it isn't. Sorry. I was just thinking." She waited while the server cleared their places. "I'm the middle child, more or less, of four, and the first in my family to go to college. My mother and father were blue-collar workers. My mother in the garment industry, my father on the docks. He died in an accident when I was six."

"Hey, I'm sorry. If this is—"

"No, that's okay. I have a great family. I grew up in my grandmother's house in South Philadelphia with my mother and my sisters. It was pretty crowded, but it was..." She thought about the shared bedrooms, the squabbles over the bathroom in the morning, the big wooden table in the sunny kitchen smelling of home-cooked food, counters crowded with dishes and everyone jostling for a place at the table. "It was noisy and warm and full of life." She smiled. "It was great." She looked up from her espresso. Evyn was staring at her as if she were a stranger. She wondered what she had just revealed and then realized it didn't matter. She had nothing to hide.

"You miss them," Evyn said softly.

"Every day." Wes's chest tightened, as much from the tenderness in Evyn's eyes as from the memories.

Evyn sipped her coffee. "Okay—not following in the family mold like me. Why did you want to be a doctor?"

Wes laughed. "You know, I practiced that answer a hundred times when I was applying to medical school, knowing I would be asked about it over and over again. I never did have a very good answer. I just knew I wanted to touch people. Make a difference somehow." She looked out across the empty restaurant. They were the last ones at a table, but the servers hadn't rushed them and none were in sight now. They were alone. She hadn't been alone with a woman in longer than she could remember. She didn't date—given her circumstances it wasn't that easy. She might not necessarily agree with all the navy's regulations, but she followed them. Most women she might have connected with were below her rank and off-limits. She sometimes thought that might be a convenient excuse, but then, what did that matter. If she was fooling anyone, it was only herself. No harm, no foul. And those rare nights when she was restless and vaguely unsettled, she went for a run until she was tired enough to sleep.

Wes caught herself up short. This wasn't a date, even if the whole evening was something out of the ordinary. Evyn was still watching her. What had Evyn asked? Oh, the "why a doctor?" question. She almost gave a stock reply, but the intensity of Evyn's gaze derailed her. "Maybe I thought if I made a difference in someone else's life, it would make mine mean more."

"Sounds like you got your wish, then. You're about to have a patient whose health affects the whole world." Evyn paused. "Does that make the job harder?"

"No," Wes said instantly. "If and when the time comes he's my patient—and hopefully that day never comes—I'll be taking care of Andrew Powell, not the president."

"His office doesn't intimidate you?"

"No, but Lucinda Washburn does," Wes said, laughing.

"You and everyone else." Evyn grinned.

"What about you? You said you always knew what you wanted to do?" For a few seconds, Wes thought Evyn wouldn't answer. Sometimes Evyn's face closed so quickly it was like watching shutters slam against a window in a storm. Then Evyn's posture relaxed and she smiled, and the shutters opened once again and sunlight streamed through. "Well, come on. In my family? Like there was really anything else to consider. Don't we all want to grow up like our heroes?"

"So who was yours?"

"Oh, my father, no question. He's big and blustery and solid and brave. I didn't get to be big, but I hope…" Even in the dim candlelight, her blush was apparent. "Never mind."

"You hope you're solid and brave?"

"Geez, forget I said that, will you?"

"I'll pretend I've forgotten, if you'd like."

"Okay," Evyn said, blowing out a breath. "Change of subject."

"Fair enough."

"So…what about…besides your mother and grandmother and sisters. Anyone else…close?"

"My grandmother passed on at the grand old age of ninety-six," Wes said, sorting through the obscure question and deciding Evyn was asking whether she was single or not. While trying to formulate an answer, she was saved by her phone signaling a text message. At this hour, it had to be important. "Excuse me."

She fished her phone out of her pocket and checked the message. "Someone keeps late hours. I've just been informed by the duty officer at the House to report at zero eight hundred tomorrow."

"WST."

"I'm sorry?" Wes shoved her phone back in her pocket.

"Washburn Standard Time. Which means pretty much any time."

"Well, I guess I'm going to get the last of my security clearance taken care of."

"Formality. You wouldn't be here if there was any question." Evyn rose. "I guess that's our signal to get moving."

"I suppose," Wes said, rising with a twinge of regret. She shrugged into her topcoat while Evyn sorted through bills and left money for the bill on the table. Out of habit, Wes reached over, lifted Evyn's black raincoat from the hook beside their booth, and held it open for her. Evyn hesitated, then turned and slid her arms into the coat.

"Thanks," Evyn said.

"You're welcome."

Evyn turned, her eyes finding Wes's. It was way too late to pretend they were just grabbing dinner, and with any other woman she wouldn't hesitate. But then Wes wasn't like any other woman she'd ever met. She should have kept her mouth shut, but words popped out. "Nightcap?"

Wes glanced left into the bar, mostly empty now, shortly before closing. She was oddly not tired, even though she'd been on the move for eighteen hours. She'd spent more time with Evyn than she had with anyone in months and hadn't even noticed the time passing. Maybe she should take that as a sign. She shook her head. "I'd like to, but I've got a really early morning tomorrow."

Evyn smiled crookedly. Saved. She should take that as a sign. "Yeah, me too." She started walking toward the door. "Where are you staying?"

Wes angled beside her, pushed the door open, and held it as Evyn passed through. "The Marriott across town."

"A hotel? You shouldn't be staying in a hotel. O'Shaughnessy had an apartment that came with the job."

Wes smiled at Evyn's indignation on her account. "I wasn't supposed to be here tonight at all, but Lucinda Washburn wanted me on-site. So here I am."

"Well, what she wants is law."

"I gathered." Wes fell into step as they walked toward the T-Bird down the block. "I don't usually get my orders at zero one hundred."

Evyn laughed, opened the driver's door, and slid in. Wes skirted around the other side and settled in the passenger seat. "You'll have to get used to that."

"The text orders, or the no-notice thing?" Wes clipped her seat belt and stretched her legs out under the dash.

Evyn started the car and pulled out. "Both. When she wants something done, it means now or five minutes ago."

"Sounds like it's pretty much twenty-four seven call. Feels like being a resident again."

"And here you thought you were getting this fancy title and a cushy job," Evyn teased.

Wes laughed. "I was hoping for a big corner office and a lot of fanfare."

"I'll just bet." Evyn glanced at her. "What were you really expecting?"

"Truthfully? I don't have a clue. Until a day and a half ago, I thought my next posting would be another academic position. All I know about this one is that I'm going to get to see the world, just like the recruiters always promised me."

"Don't get your hopes up." Evyn snorted. "It's a campaign year, remember? You're going to see so many cornfields and listen to so many boring speeches you're going to wish you were anywhere else doing anything else."

"Thanks for the inspirational speech. I can't wait."

"Sorry. I've been on the campaign trail in an election year. Prepare to be perpetually tired, poorly fed, and probably verbally abused."

"Got it. I imagine it's pretty tense for you."

"No more so than usual," Evyn said flatly.

"Right." Wes was getting used to the way Evyn deflected anything personal. Obviously, the Secret Service never showed weakness. Or maybe that was just Evyn. Wes wondered just how much that shield of invulnerability cost her and if she ever let down her defenses.

Evyn slowed at an intersection, turned right, and looked over at Wes. "It's tough, but exhilarating too, you know? Being right there. Being part of something big."

"I think I understand. I'm used to being behind the scenes. Observing."

"That's all about to change, Captain."

Wes stared at Evyn's profile, aglow in the moonlight. "I think it already has."

CHAPTER SEVEN

Here you go," Evyn said, lifting Wes's overnight bag out of the trunk.

"Thanks." Wes took it from her and slung the strap over her right shoulder. The T-Bird idled in the turnaround of the Marriott. The marquee lights over the entrance had been dimmed, leaving them in fractured shadow. The sliding glass doors behind them whooshed open, and a voice called, "Need help with bags?"

"I've got it, thanks," Wes said without turning around. Evyn stood a foot away, one hand resting on the edge of the open trunk lid. Wes searched for something more to say, but she didn't know where to start. The last few hours had been different than any time she'd ever spent with anyone. She'd had hundreds of meals with colleagues, in the hospital, on board ship, in the field. When those conversations ended, she moved on, rarely giving the oft-times pleasant but superficial encounters another thought. But she didn't want this evening to end. Her reaction was so foreign she couldn't sort out wishes from reality. How could she be uncomfortable and feel so energized at the same time?

She wasn't a spontaneous person—she was a planner, always prepared for any contingency, always following the most efficient path. She'd always known what she needed to do to achieve her goals. She'd learned from watching her mother deal with challenges head-on, working hard, never bowing before adversity or buckling under seemingly insurmountable odds. As long as she could remember, she'd looked forward, she'd worked toward the future. She didn't have a lot of practice living in the moment. "Thanks for the ride. And the… dinner."

"No problem." No subtle suggestion as to what came next resonated in Evyn's tone, but her gaze never strayed from Wes's.

"I'll see you tomorrow, then," Wes said, still not moving. Evyn hadn't moved either. Wes's skin tingled as if charged with current ready to snap. There was more—a next move she couldn't grasp, words just out of reach. Her nerves vibrated at the sensation of a bubble closing down around them, isolating them, a fragile gossamer barrier that held them suspended in their own world. She wondered if she turned and walked away if the bubble would burst and they would never again share an unguarded moment. She didn't want that to happen. She didn't have any choice. Tomorrow, everything would change. She had no choice but to fall back on what had always worked, on the one thing she could depend upon. Doing her duty, fulfilling her obligations. "I'll report to you after my interview."

"Unless POTUS goes off schedule, I'll be in the command center. Text me. I'll find you."

"Yes, I'll do that." Wes backed up and the shimmering enclosure shattered. Evyn slammed the trunk closed. They were agent and doctor again. "Good night."

"'Night," Evyn called, walking around to the driver's door. She slid in without another glance.

Wes turned and walked toward the waiting bellman.

"You have that, Captain?" the bellman said, pointing to her bag.

"Yes," Wes replied as the sound of the T-Bird's powerful engine faded behind her. "Everything's under control."

❖

Evyn made quick time through the nearly empty streets to I-495 and down to her condo in Alexandria, VA. She pulled into her slot in the residents' parking garage, grabbed her go bag, and took the stairs up to her third-floor, one-bedroom unit. When she let herself in, she was greeted with a plaintive and highly offended cry. "I haven't been gone that long, and I know you're not starving, so you might as well forget the theatrics."

A sinuous gray shadow eased around the counter that separated the big living room from the galley-style kitchen. Ricochet jumped up onto the back of the sofa and proceeded to ignore her. She dropped her bag by the closet holding the stacked washer-dryer, passed behind the couch on her way to the kitchen, and scooped up the cat. He didn't like it when she was away, but he liked attention too much to feign indifference and immediately began to rumble, a rollicking purr that vibrated into her chest. Absently, she rubbed her cheek against the top of his head and pulled the refrigerator door open. She extracted a bottle of Turbo Dog, popped the top on an old-style Coke bottle opener screwed to the wall underneath the adjacent cabinet, and took a long swallow. She checked the floor—his water and food bowls were full. She poked his lean belly. "Definitely not starving."

He kneaded her shoulder through her shirt as she ambled back into the living area and flopped on the couch. She didn't bother with the lights—she knew her way around the place in the semi-darkness. Propping her feet on the scarred and scraped oak coffee table she'd been carting around since college, she stared out the glass balcony doors and sipped her beer. Usually she watched a little aimless TV until she unwound enough to fall asleep, but tonight she had something else to occupy her—Wes Masters lingered in her mind.

"So," she said to Ricochet, "I met the new chief medical officer today. Very spit-and-polish shiny. Ought to be interesting to see how she fits in at the House." Ricochet curled up in a ball on her lap and proceeded to lick his paws. She traced a finger around the back of each ear and he continued to purr. "I'm supposed to bring her up to speed on protocol."

Ricochet paused in his washings, one paw elevated, and blinked at her.

"Yeah, yeah. I know. Not what I want to be doing." Evyn set the bottle on the wooden arm of the sofa and turned it slowly. Dinner had probably been a mistake. She'd gone on impulse because she didn't have anything better to do, and after a long day of travel and intermittent boredom, broken by moments of intense alertness, she'd still had energy to burn. And Wes Masters was intriguing. Why was she here, who was she really? Understandable curiosity there, and she never could pass up a good mystery. But the going out to dinner with her? What was that all about? She hadn't shared a meal with anyone other than fellow PPD agents in two years. She hadn't had a dinner date, or a movie date, or any other kind of date in a long time. She'd had encounters, conversations in bars, a little bit of sex—enough to keep her from thinking about the fact that she didn't really have a personal life—until tonight. Probably not the smartest thing to do, sharing personal stuff before she'd had a chance to assess her professionally. She should've said no.

"Why the hell did she even ask?" Evyn muttered. Ricochet didn't answer. "It's not like we have anything in common, and chances are we're going to run into the old 'whose responsibilities take precedence in event of emergency' pretty fast. I can't see her bending on much of anything."

Ricochet rolled onto his back, reminding her of priorities.

"I can be flexible," she said grumpily, rubbing his soft belly. "I'm just not, usually. Stick with what you know, right? Right?"

She didn't make mistakes with women because she never varied her pattern. Now she had, and she ought to be sorry. She wasn't, and that was worrisome.

❖

Wes woke before the alarm she'd set for 0600 and lay awake, waiting for the backup wake-up call she'd requested from the hotel operator when she'd finally hit the rack at 0200. She hadn't slept well, but she wasn't tired. She was used to broken sleep and catching what she could at odd hours. She still covered the ER often enough to keep in shape for the demands of emergency medicine. Good thing, because it sounded like her schedule was going to be anything but regular from now on. A buzz of excitement shot through her. She loved teaching, but she was looking forward to having boots on the ground again. Actually practicing what she preached, although her number one goal where her new job was concerned was to be certain she didn't have to. She couldn't wait to get a look at the WHMU emergency protocols. Maybe she'd been tapped for this job because her specialty was triage and emergency management. Whatever the reason, she'd find out pretty soon.

The bedside phone rang and she picked it up. "Good morning," a mechanical voice said, "this is your wake-up call…"

Wes set the phone back in the cradle and swung out of bed. Evyn's face surfaced in her mind, and she wondered if Evyn was still sleeping or if she was on her way to the House. She wondered how she'd slept and if she'd thought about their evening. She didn't stop to ask herself why she'd awakened thinking about a woman for the first time in her life. Instead, she resolutely put thoughts of Evyn aside and hit the shower.

Thirty minutes later, dressed in her regulation khakis, Wes grabbed a cup of Starbucks takeout coffee in the hotel lobby and took a cab to the White House. She walked around the Ellipse, familiarizing herself with the terrain. She'd never been inside the White House before but assumed the fastest way to wherever she needed to go would be via the West Wing, where the bulk of the offices were located. At 0730, she approached the northwest gate and gave her name to the officer on duty. "I have an appointment at zero eight hundred hours with Ms. Washburn."

"One moment, please." The White House Uniformed Division officer turned away and scanned a screen. A minute later he said, "You're cleared to enter. You'll want the elevator on your right. A staffer will meet you and take you up."

"Thank you."

Inside, Wes noted the sign for the emergency medical clinic in the Old Executive Office Building and walked past the hall to her new base until she found the elevators. She repeated her name and destination to the staffer in the elevator, and when she exited, another staffer escorted her to a waiting area. She sat and waited.

At 0805, a young intern approached. He looked to be about twenty-two, buttoned down, slightly frazzled, with a friendly smile. "Captain Masters?"

Wes stood. "That's right."

"Ms. Washburn sends her apologies for keeping you waiting. She's ready to see you now."

"Thank you." She followed him through an archway, down a hall, and into another small waiting area. He tapped on the heavy, carved walnut door and responded to something that only he could hear. He pushed open the door, and Wes entered Lucinda Washburn's office. The south lawn was visible opposite her through French doors framed by floor-to-ceiling white brocade drapes. The Oriental carpet under her feet looked expensive and old. A closed door on her left probably led into the Oval Office. Wes stood at parade rest in front of Ms. Washburn's desk while the chief of staff signed off on a call.

Lucinda replaced the handset, stood, and held out her hand. "Good to see you again, Captain. Hang your coat up over there, and have a seat."

Wes shrugged out of her topcoat and added it to several other winter coats on a wrought-iron coat tree just inside the door. She took one of the two leather chairs facing the desk and waited.

"Do you have any objections to taking a polygraph?"

"No, ma'am," Wes said, seeing that they were about to get directly down to business.

"Good. That's really the last of the formal security items." She shrugged. "Protocol only. Your record has already been reviewed."

Wes said nothing. She wouldn't be sitting there if her service record and probably everything that came in her life before that hadn't already been scrutinized in intimate detail. *Pro forma.*

"Have any questions?"

"No, ma'am."

Lucinda smiled. "I am not in the military, so you can dispense with the formalities. And feel free to speak. None of this is on the record."

"May I ask how I came to be considered for the position?"

"Of course." Lucinda gestured to a coffee urn and a row of plain white mugs sitting on a linen-draped sideboard. "Coffee?"

"Yes, please."

While Lucinda poured, she talked. "Obviously, Dr. O'Shaughnessy's death was unexpected. The position is a critical one, and with POTUS about to embark on a series of national and international movements, we need the White House Medical Unit to be at full staff."

"I understand." Wes waited for the rest of the story. The White House medical staff usually came from the military, and there were plenty of military physicians available. But she'd been short-listed. Not just short-listed but fast-tracked.

Lucinda handed her a cup of coffee and angled the adjacent chair to face Wes. When she sat, their knees were a few inches apart. "As you can imagine," Lucinda said calmly, "an election year is a volatile time for the nation and disruptive to both parties. Emotions run high."

"If there's something I need to know about the president's health, I assume it will be in his records, but if not, then I need to know…off the record."

Lucinda's eyes glinted as if she was pleased with Wes's statement.

"This isn't television. There's nothing we're hiding about the president's health. He has some food allergies which you will note in his chart, an old ligamentous injury to his right knee, and some annoying, but I'm told not dangerous, floaters in his right eye. Other than that, he is remarkably fit and healthy."

"Excellent. I will be reviewing his records today."

"We have excellent security," Lucinda went on, "and the president and I have total faith in his detail. In an election year, we always see an escalation in death threats."

Wes nodded. "I'll need to know the nature of the threats, the analysis of the threat level, and what the Secret Service containment policies are."

"You see," Lucinda said, smiling more broadly now, "you've just proved my point. We need someone in charge who knows how to approach these kinds of issues in a scientific fashion."

"Any physician should be able—"

"But not with the facility of someone whose job it has been to set up treatment, triage, and interventional protocols under battlefield conditions. That is a fairly unique skill."

"Do you expect an attack on POTUS?"

Lucinda sipped her coffee and finally said softly, "It isn't a question of *if* the president will be attacked, but *when*. That is the presumption we all work under, Captain Masters. As long as we believe that, we will be prepared for anything."

"I understand." Wes decided to push her luck. "And the current staff? Isn't it customary to advance members from within?"

Lucinda shrugged. "There is nothing customary in the White House, Captain. The guard changes every four to eight years, and many of the personnel change at the same time. The rules, if there are any, are almost totally dependent upon who occupies these rooms." Lucinda regarded her for a long moment, and Wes sat under her dissecting gaze calmly. "The White House Military Office is your counterpart, and they felt no internal candidate was qualified for the unique demands of this position at this point in time."

"I can assure you, Ms. Washburn," Wes said, "I am prepared."

"I'm very, very glad to hear that." Lucinda set her cup aside, and her expression took on the kind of intense focus Wes recognized from the field when an engagement was imminent.

Lucinda Washburn was about to tell her the real reason she'd been hired. Everything else was reasonable, but that about-to-do-battle glint in Lucinda's eyes said there was more.

"Need-to-know, Captain," Lucinda said softly.

"Yes, ma'am."

"We have a security breach, as yet unidentified, but we suspect the individual has intimate access to the president. You'll be with those closest to him every day."

"I'm not a security agent, I'm a doctor."

Lucinda smiled. "And as such, a trained observer."

Wes asked, "Who are the likely suspects?"

Lucinda drew a long breath and listed the limited pool of individuals with close, continuous access to the president. Evyn Daniels was one of them. Wes thought back to the hours they'd spent together the night before. If she'd had this information then, maybe she wouldn't have suggested dinner, even though she couldn't imagine Evyn betraying her country. But then, she didn't really know her at all. All she had to go on were nebulous feelings, and feelings had no place in her job.

"I'll be read in on any security updates?" Wes asked.

"Yes—need-to-know." Lucinda stood, indicating the interview was over. "Questions?"

"No, ma'am. I do have a request."

"Go ahead," Lucinda said, a note of curiosity in her tone.

"I'd like to see the autopsy file on Dr. O'Shaughnessy."

Lucinda's jaw tightened. "You'll have that today, Captain. As soon as the last of the paperwork is completed."

"Thank you."

Lucinda Washburn leaned across her desk and pushed a button on her phone. A voice came over the speaker. "Yes, ma'am?"

"Would you please let the agents know Captain Masters is ready?"

"Certainly."

Lucinda turned. "We'll get the polygraph out of the way, and that should be the end of the formalities."

"Yes, ma'am." Wes rose. "As I said, I'll be reviewing the president's chart today. I would like to examine him at his earliest convenience."

"Really?" Lucinda studied her. "Why? Everything is in his records."

"That may be, but if I'm going to be his doctor, I need to perform a baseline physical examination and make my own assessment."

"You don't trust your predecessor?"

"I don't know him," Wes said. "But in any case, I wouldn't presume to take care of someone I had never examined. It's not good medicine." She hesitated, seeing the consternation in Lucinda Washburn's eyes. She imagined the president was incredibly busy, and finding time to meet with her would probably be incredibly inconvenient. "In my experience, high-profile patients often get poor care. Physicians and everyone else involved are reluctant to inconvenience them. Things get overlooked. That's not fair to any patient, but it certainly is not appropriate for the president of the United States. In light of everything you've told me, it's imperative I judge his status for myself."

"I understand. I'll see that it's scheduled as soon as possible." Lucinda extended her hand and Wes took it. "Welcome to the House, Captain."

CHAPTER EIGHT

Evyn hadn't slept much in the last few days, and she needed a coffee refill to keep her focused during the routine after-review of the wedding detail and the rest of the uneventful morning briefing. Trying not to look distracted, she sloshed milk into her Starbucks venti cup, added the always-good coffee the valets kept fresh in their command center, and settled back at the conference table with the other members of the day shift. She wasn't herself and couldn't figure out what was off. Usually a brisk shower, a fast fantasy, and a hard orgasm cleared her head for the day, but this morning, she'd opened her eyes and immediately replayed the evening with Wes—and the details that came to mind had nothing to do with the job. She kept stumbling over the way Wes concentrated on her when they talked, as if they had all night, the way Wes smiled at something Evyn said, her eyes glowing. And her mouth—God, she had a killer mouth—full lips, broad smile, a tiny lift on the right side that gave her a hot, sexy, rakish look. Evyn's stomach tightened into a hard knot and a quick pulse beat between her thighs. She sucked in a breath. Whoa. Bad timing—where was that rush two hours ago when she could have taken care of it? She slugged her coffee, burned her tongue, and choked.

When she looked over, Gary was staring at her with laughter in his eyes. She tossed him a *get bent* look, and he smothered a grin. He always claimed he could read her mind, but she assured him he was wrong, remarking if he could, he'd be walking around with a perpetual boner and he should be so lucky.

Agents rose and started to leave the room, the midnight shift heading home and the rest to their posts. Evyn grabbed her black trench coat and coffee.

"Evyn," Tom Turner said. "Hang on a minute, will you."

"Sure." Evyn dropped her coat onto a chair and tossed the empty paper cup into a nearby wastebasket. Gary hesitated, glanced at Tom, and followed the rest out, muttering, "Catch you later," as he left.

When the room was empty, Tom closed the door and gestured for her to sit.

Her antennae went up. She couldn't think of anything she'd done that could be problematic. She wasn't the most senior member of PPD, but over the last year she'd sort of become Tom's unofficial sounding board. She'd sat in the right front seat of the follow-up car a time or two, and had taken the lead when POTUS traveled. That level of responsibility told her she was doing okay, or at least she thought she had been. She waited for Tom to start, banishing a mild case of nerves, a wholly atypical reaction for her.

"Are you set to bring Masters up to speed?" Tom sat across from her and leaned back in his chair.

"She's still clearing security but should be done sometime today. I'll meet with her later and set up a schedule." Evyn's pulse jittered at the mention of Wes's name, also unusual. She rarely showed a bump in her blood pressure or her pulse, even during simulated actions. She'd been preparing for this job since she was a kid, and she'd taught herself not to react when something hurt, or scared her, or excited her. She kept her cool. She wanted to be ice in an emergency. She usually was. But just a reference to Wes Masters had her composure melting around the edges. That couldn't be good. She needed to clamp a lid on that.

"I had a call from Averill Jensen before the briefing this morning," Tom said.

Evyn tensed at the mention of the president's security adviser. The USSS answered only to the Director of Homeland Security—on paper—but Jensen had sweeping authority in security matters. "About We—Captain Masters?"

"Indirectly."

Evyn couldn't believe there was an issue with Wes Masters. She'd only just met Wes, but she'd spent time with her, more personal time than she'd spent with anyone in years, except the agents who'd just left this room. And they hadn't just talked about business. They'd talked about life. Wes was solid. She was dedicated and focused, all the way through. Evyn clamped her molars together and kept her mouth shut. She needed to listen, and to do her job. Right now, the best thing she could do for Wes Masters was find out what the hell was going on.

"They went outside to bring her in," Tom said, "and on the face of it, that's not that unusual. What's unusual is that with O'Shaughnessy's sudden death, they didn't move someone up from inside as interim director while they put the nominees through the selection process."

"I know." Just a few hours with Wes had blunted some of Evyn's anger that Peter had been passed over, but she still didn't think it was right. Wes wasn't at fault for that, at least not as far as she knew. "Did somebody pull strings to get her appointed? Pressure someone? Is that it?"

"No." Tom's smooth brow wrinkled, which for him was akin to shouting. He was the epitome of control. He just didn't get rattled, especially if he was angry or frustrated. Something serious was going on if Tom was unsettled. "Masters was brought in *because* she's a qualified outsider. There seems to be some concern that we have a leak inside."

"A leak?" Evyn took a second to let that sink in. "You mean someone in the *House* is passing information?"

"Communications analysts have been pulling snippets from surveillance tapes—routine Internet sweeps—that suggest potentially hostile groups might know plans we haven't made public."

"Jesus," Evyn said. "And they think it's in the medical unit?"

"They don't know—could be anywhere—the medical unit, the West Wing, our group—"

"Us? Oh, come on, that's just not possible. At the very least, someone is talking who shouldn't be because they're damn idiots— which excludes all of us. Worst-case scenario, someone is working with domestic or foreign hostiles. And *that* sure as hell isn't one of us."

Tom stared at her. "You believe it and I believe it, but that doesn't mean everyone else does. Let's not forget Robert Hanssen. He went undetected for decades."

"We're not the FBI," Evyn said dismissively. *You believe it and I believe it...* "Wait a minute. You're not saying that Wes—Dr. Masters is looking at *us*?" Was that what prompted the dinner invitation and the prolonged after-dinner conversation? She remembered every word that had passed between them, and she couldn't remember Wes bringing up anything probative. All the same, the invitation had come out of nowhere. Her heart plummeted. "Hell."

"I doubt that—not her job description. All the same, we can't really be sure what we haven't been told." He grimaced, clearly not happy. "Given the threat level, Masters has to be aware of the situation."

"Well, we better be sure she's ready to carry the ball," Evyn said.

"That's your job. In the meantime, we need to button down everything on our end. I want you to watch communications carefully. Make sure our analysts are looking for anything, no matter how small, that gets picked up from sources under surveillance."

She nodded sharply. "You got it."

"She's due for a polygraph. Pick her up and take her over. Sit in on it."

"I'm not certified—"

"I know—Preston will run it. You can play backup."

"Yes, sir."

"And for now, all of this is just between us."

"Yes, sir," Evyn said softly. She didn't want to believe that anyone inside the White House could be compromising the president by inadvertently mishandling information. But to do it willfully? To her, there was no greater sin. Wes couldn't think her capable of that, could she?

❖

Wes left Lucinda's office and walked out into the waiting area. Evyn Daniels stood with a stone-faced man in a dark suit who regarded her with unsmiling eyes. Wes looked at Evyn. "Good morning, Agent Daniels."

"Captain," Evyn said politely, nothing but professional friendliness in her eyes. "This is Agent Preston."

Wes quickly squelched a wave of disappointment at the formal tone. Business as usual. Last night was a thing of the past, and after what Lucinda had just told her, business as usual was all there could be for her with anyone on the job. She wasn't here to make friends. She nodded to Preston. "You'll be doing the testing?"

"That's right," Preston said. "If you come this way, we'll tell you about it once we get settled."

Wes followed them down the hall and into a small room with several windows that looked out over another expanse of lawn studded with rose bushes. The room was crowded with a conference table, eight chairs, and a row of bookshelves underneath the window. A file cabinet stood in one corner and a polygraph machine rested in the center of the table. She sat down across from it. Evyn and Preston sat facing the machine.

"The way this works," Preston said, "is that the test is given in two parts—part one will cover some basic informational questions. Then we'll move on to part two with more focused questions. Have you ever had a polygraph?"

"No."

"Is there anything you want us to know now before we start the test?"

"I assume you're referring to anything which I feel would disqualify me for this position?"

Preston answered before Evyn. "We find it's best not to try to outthink or rationalize whether or not there is a right or wrong answer."

Evyn added, "Just answer each question to the best of your ability. If there's something in the past you think may hamper or confuse your answers, you should tell us. That will actually help us interpret the test to your benefit."

"There isn't." Wes hadn't expected to see Evyn until later, and this wasn't the way she had hoped their next encounter would come about, but Evyn was here to do her job and so was she. In a way, she was relieved. There could be no ambiguity about what was happening between them. Nothing. Only business.

"All right," Preston said. "We're going to go through some basic questions first."

Wes knew the basics of the polygraph. She understood that some questions were designed to elicit a yes-or-no answer, and those responses formed the baseline comparators for other answers. She also knew it was best not to try to figure out which questions were the critical comparators. "I'm ready."

Preston made some notes while Evyn connected the galvanic

skin recorder to Wes's right arm. Wes was aware of sweating slightly. Unusual for her. Even under the tensest conditions, she rarely perspired. She wasn't concerned about the test, but she couldn't shake the lingering connection she felt to Evyn Daniels, and the disorienting effect of her presence.

"All right, Dr. Masters," Preston said, making a mark on a scrolling roll of paper. "We're going to begin. Is your name Captain Wesley Masters?"

"Yes."

Preston alternated asking her routine questions—her term of service, her duty stations, her field experience—interspersed with pointed questions.

"Have you ever been arrested?"

"No."

"Have you ever used illegal drugs, recreationally or in conjunction with an assignment?"

"No."

"Have you ever met with foreign nationals hostile to the U.S.?"

"No."

"Have you ever met with known terrorists?"

"No."

"The Ku Klux Klan, the American Nazi Party, the American Christian Army?"

"No. No. No."

She answered no so many times she began to feel as if she was revealing she had no life outside her job. But then, she didn't.

Finally, Preston turned off the machine and Evyn sat back. She gave Wes the slightest smile, and for some reason, Wes's uneasiness disappeared.

"We'll let you know the results as soon as they've been analyzed," Preston said.

Wes rolled her shoulders and stretched her neck. "Good, thank you. I wonder if you could tell me how to get to the medical offices from here."

"I'll take you," Evyn said.

"And someplace to eat?"

Evyn glanced at her watch. "It's almost sixteen hundred. I'll show you a good place to get a late lunch."

"I don't have much time," Wes said, not wanting a repeat of the intimacy of the night before. She needed a buffer between them if the disappointment she'd experienced earlier was any indication of how strongly Evyn affected her.

"I'm sure your team can wait another forty-five minutes. POTUS isn't scheduled to leave the House today. Whatever activity there is in the clinic is already being handled by your staff. Lunch first. Then I'll take you over to meet your staff."

"Thank you," Wes said, realizing when she had been given an order in the form of a suggestion. She'd have to get used to that, since Evyn was in charge. And since part of Lucinda Washburn's unspoken message had been to assess those on the list, she'd best get on with her job. "Lunch it is."

CHAPTER NINE

Cam leaned against the doorway to Blair's studio in the house they'd purchased not far from Tanner and Adrienne's on Whitley Point. In the middle of winter this far north, sunset came early, and the late-day sun slanted low on the horizon. Diffuse golden light cast a halo around Blair's face as she concentrated on the canvas propped up on the easel in front of her. Her paint-spattered jeans rode low on her hips, and her faded black T-shirt with a silk-screened Andy Warhol slid up and down over the hollow of her spine as she captured the colors of the sea in gray, and green, and blue. A strip of skin two inches wide just above the waistband of her Luckys winked into view and disappeared to the rhythm of her brushstrokes in a hypnotic cadence that captured Cam's attention and made her throat go dry. She knew that spot—the sweet softness of the skin, the delicate ripple of bone beneath supple muscle, the breathy moans when her fingers dipped and stroked. She'd rested her hand in just that spot while they'd danced at their wedding.

She smiled. They hadn't really celebrated privately yet. By the time they'd said good-bye to the last of their guests, thanked Tanner and Adrienne for opening their home and putting up with the weeks of heightened security, and made it back to their place down island, they'd fallen into bed exhausted. After sleeping far later than usual, they'd both needed to unwind. Blair wanted to paint. Cam needed to move. Now she wanted nothing more than to be right where she was, looking at her wife.

"Have a good run?" Blair asked, touching a dab of purple to the swell of a wave.

"The beach is a bitch. I'd forgotten how much harder it is to run on sand."

"Tire you out?" Blair wiped her brush on a cloth and set it in a tray next to the easel and turned, her gaze slowly sliding from Cam's face down her body.

"Just getting started."

Blair smiled slowly. "You're all sweaty."

"Sorry about that." Cam fanned her fingers over the center of her chest, and Blair's eyes flared with heat, making her nipples tighten and pressure surge in her groin. "Stark made me promise I'd let her join me when her leg healed."

"Oh, I can just see that—I know she hates to run. You've been torturing her again by playing to her need to best the boss."

"Ex-boss. And all Secret Service agents are competitive by nature. I didn't have to play her at all."

Laughing, Blair crossed the room with the easy grace of a trained martial artist. She gripped the bottom of Cam's T-shirt and jerked it up and over Cam's head, tossing it onto the floor behind them. She leaned against Cam's body, pinning her against the doorjamb. "Well, I like you sweaty and you're going to need a shower anyhow—I'm going to get paint all over you."

Cam circled Blair's waist and gripped her ass, snugging Blair's hips into the vee of her pelvis. "Is it washable paint?"

"I might have to work on it." Blair nipped at Cam's chin and kissed her, molding her mouth to Cam's, teasing the seam of her lips with the tip of her tongue. "Rub a little here and there."

"Make sure you get a lot on me, then." Cam pulled her closer, enjoying the heat spreading through her belly, the rising beat of arousal, the anticipation of the pleasure to come. Blair's hands covered her breasts, thumbs lightly brushing her nipples, and she tilted her head back, giving Blair room to scrape her teeth down her throat. "Your mouth is so hot—God, Blair."

"You taste so good," Blair mumbled as she nipped and kissed her way to the hollow of Cam's throat. She licked the salty skin there and moaned softly.

Cam pulled the tie holding Blair's hair back, letting her thick waves fall free. She tangled her fingers in them, cupping the back of Blair's head, guiding Blair's mouth lower, to the curve of her breast. Blair's teeth closed over her nipple and Cam jerked. They were alone in that part of the house, but several of Blair's security agents were in the kitchen—and she was losing her grip more with every stroke of Blair's tongue. "Shower soon?"

"Mmm, in a minute," Blair whispered, licking a warm path down the underside of Cam's breast.

"Blair," Cam warned, her thighs starting to shake.

Blair laughed, pressing the flat of her hand to the center of Cam's belly, making slow, tight circles, knowing the motion would work Cam up even faster.

"You looked beautiful," Cam whispered, "standing over there in the sunlight."

Blair stilled, then raised her head, her blue eyes dark and questioning. "You always catch me off guard, Cam. You mean that, don't you."

"Every time I see you, I fall in love again."

"I believe you when you say those things. You make my heart melt."

Cam framed Blair's face and kissed her softly. Her body demanded Blair's hands, Blair's mouth, Blair's fingers, but her heart wanted nothing more than to hold Blair close with her last breath. "I love you. You're all I want."

"Cam." Blair's fingers trembled against Cam's skin. "I never thought I'd have this. You undo me."

The tears shimmering on Blair's lashes were Cam's undoing. She only wanted her love to make Blair smile. "Don't worry—I'll never tell."

Laughing, the hint of vulnerability erased by joy, Blair closed her eyes and rested her cheek against Cam's shoulder. "Good. I'd hate for my badass reputation to suffer."

Cam skimmed her hand under Blair's T-shirt and stroked her back. "Want to take that shower with me?"

Blair fingers skated lower, brushing softly between Cam's thighs. "Want me to finish what I started?"

"Oh yeah. Several times."

Laughing, Blair took Cam's hand and dragged her down the hall. "I'll see what I can do."

❖

"Five Guys?" Wes said when Evyn stopped in front of the red-and-white checkered burger joint.

"What? You don't like burgers? Are you a vegetarian?"

"No." Wes shook her head. "I think my coronaries can take it. A burger would be great."

"Well, these are great burgers." Evyn reached for the door but Wes was there first, pushing it open and waiting for her to pass. "You know that's very retro, right?"

"What?" Wes let the door close behind them and followed Evyn to the counter.

"Holding the door for a woman."

"Does it bother you?"

"Do you always do it?"

"If I don't have to knock someone down to get there first."

Evyn laughed. "Chivalry just comes naturally to you?"

"I don't know. Is that what you call it?"

Evyn almost said *I call it sexy*, but caught herself just in time. Wes really didn't know her actions were both charming and unusual, and that made what might have been annoying in someone else just plain attractive. "I guess you take the officer-and-a-gentleman thing seriously."

"I do."

"So you don't just rely on the uniform to turn heads?"

"Never did, really," Wes answered easily. The glint in Evyn's eyes made it hard to resist her good-natured teasing. "I'm not the head-turning type."

"Come again?" Evyn stared. Did the woman really not know how hot she was?

"What?"

"Never mind." Evyn took a mental step back. Fifteen minutes alone with Wes and they were already dancing around personal issues again. Maybe even flirting. Without her even realizing it. Without meaning to. Wes slid right through her usual barriers, and she couldn't have that. Especially not here, on the job, and especially not with Wes. "We don't have much time, so if you know what you want…"

"I'm good to order," Wes said, visibly drawing back.

Evyn supposed she'd been rude, but better that than familiar. So what if the cool curtain that fell between them chilled her more than the miserable weather outside.

They ordered, grabbed a table by the window, and waited for their number to be called. She started to rise when the server called their order, but Wes got to her feet.

"I'll get it. Ketchup on your fries?"

"What else?"

"Vinegar," Wes said.

"Blasphemy."

"You should try it."

Evyn leaned back in her chair and stared up at Wes, who stood looking down, amusement dancing in her eyes. Every single thing about her was attractive—the sharp profile, the long tight body, the devastating mouth. And she was close enough to being on the job to know what it meant to have no life to speak of—a schedule that changed at a moment's notice, travel plans she couldn't share, colleagues who knew her better than family. Or maybe who were her family. Wes Masters might just be the most interesting woman she'd ever met, and that was a big, big problem. She'd had a very brief and very ill-advised affair with another agent right after she'd been assigned to DC. They'd split up when her ex's ex returned from an assignment overseas and wasn't so ex any longer. Unfortunately, Evyn kept running into said ex on the job. That was painful at first and then just embarrassing. Then and there she'd decided to keep life simple—a total separation of work and play. Wes was upsetting her game plan. Add to that the whole breach in security issue, and the inadvisable became the impossible.

"I'll stick to the sure thing," Evyn said. "Ketchup, that is."

"Okay." Wes looked at her a second longer before disappearing to retrieve their food.

"Smooth—really smooth, Daniels." Evyn shredded her paper napkin and wondered what the hell Wes had just seen in her eyes.

"This is kind of scary," Wes said, pointing to the grease-stained brown paper bag filled with french fries as she sat down a minute later.

"Never took you for a coward." Evyn grabbed her double burger with cheese and bag of fries.

Wes just laughed and carefully tore the bag open. Fat golden fries spilled out. She plucked one up, dipped it in a little plastic container of vinegar, and ate it. "Good."

"Told you," Evyn said as she plowed through her food. "After this I'll take you over to the clinic—it's in the OEOB." At Wes's raised eyebrow she added, "Old Executive Office Building. You can sort out your schedule and whatnot today in terms of coverage. Tomorrow, you'll report to me at zero eight hundred."

"All right," Wes said, carefully rolling up the remains of the paper bag that had held her fries. "I need to take shifts in the clinic as soon as possible. I want to see how things work—how the team meshes."

"I understand. We'll have at least one away exercise. The rest of the sims we should be able to do at Beltsville."

"Come again?"

"Our training center."

"Gotcha. Assuming the polygraph results are okay."

Evyn lifted a shoulder. "I doubt there'll be any problem there. It had to be done, but you wouldn't have gotten this far if there was a question." She hesitated. "Those things are always tough."

"It's okay—I expected it to be intrusive. So I have no secrets left—I never really had many to begin with." Wes smiled but there was a hint of bitterness in her eyes.

Evyn wished Tom hadn't wanted her there—she didn't want to learn about Wes's life in a windowless room while she was hooked up to a machine that was set to gauge whether she was lying. She wanted to hear about Wes's family and her aspirations and the places she'd been over dinner and a bottle of wine. She wanted to know more about her, and there was that big, big problem staring her in the face again.

"Have you been assigned permanent quarters?" Evyn asked, steering the conversation onto safer ground.

"I don't know." Wes flicked the temporary ID she'd gotten at the gate that morning. "I'm not exactly official yet."

"We'll take care of that this afternoon."

"Thanks. I appreciate—"

"The sooner we get you settled," Evyn said, gathering up her trash and standing, "the sooner we can see how you'll do in the field."

"Sure."

"Let's get back."

Evyn turned away from the intensity of Wes's gaze. She'd have to learn to look at Wes without wanting to fall into those damn gorgeous green eyes.

CHAPTER TEN

Cam settled Blair into the crook of her arm and dragged the sheet over them. Blair's hair was still damp from the shower, and she ran her fingers through the loose tangles while Blair traced lazy circles on her belly. The heat of Blair's body against her skin stirred the blood in her depths—again. "This is better than spending time traveling somewhere for a honeymoon."

Blair raised her head and rested her chin on Cam's chest, her expression grave. "Anytime I get to spend every day with you is a honeymoon as far as I'm concerned."

"I know. For me too." The times they were alone, or as alone as they could be, with no schedules, no responsibilities, were rare. And she was about to ruin it.

"Lucinda called this morning just as I was about to go out for my run."

Blair stiffened, her fingers stilling. "Lucinda never calls unless there's a problem."

"She wants me temporarily assigned to White House security."

"Secret Service? Replacing Tom?"

"No," Cam said. "I'll report directly to Averill Jensen."

"I know they ramp up the detail when he's traveling, but there's more to this, isn't there? Something is going on. That's why you're coming with me on the campaign trail."

Cam pushed up against the pillows so she could look down into Blair's face. She wanted Blair to read her eyes, as only Blair could. "Yes and no."

Blair slapped Cam's stomach, a sharp little slap that was part annoyance, but still damn sexy. "Don't use government-speak with me. Just tell me what's going on."

"Lucinda thinks we might have a leak, someplace close to Andrew. She wants me to find out who it is."

"She wants you to go undercover because we have a spy?" Blair pulled away and sat cross-legged facing Cam. She kept her fingertips resting on Cam's bare belly. The sheet pooled at her waist. Her breasts rose firmly on her subtly muscled chest. Her eyes sparked. "Why you? What she's asking you to do is dangerous. Are you going to have backup inside? What if whoever it is finds out you're—"

"You buy there might be a leak?"

"If Lucinda says there's a leak, there's a leak. How close, really? She must have given you some idea."

"Close. Military aides, medical staff, security detail. Someone with intimate knowledge of Andrew's movements well in advance of anything even his staffers and the communications department know."

"I can't believe it. I know every one of them." Blair's face clouded. "Of course, I knew James Benjamin Harker too, and he stalked me for years."

Cam slid her fingers around the back of Blair's neck and soothed the tight bands of muscle with long slow caresses. "Hey. Your father is the most well-protected man in the world. Nothing is going to happen to him."

"Every time he steps outside that building, he's a target. God, even when he's inside, he's a target. Someone tried to fly a plane into the White House, Cam."

"I know. And so does everyone whose duty it is to protect him, and believe me, they're the best. You know that. He doesn't go anywhere that every contingency isn't prepared for. And in the worst-case scenario, he has a full medical team standing by. Hell, there's an operating room on Air Force One."

"I know, I know. It's just—to everyone else in the world he's POTUS, the most powerful man in the world. To me, he's my father."

Cam pulled Blair down into her arms and kissed her. Blair had lost her mother when she was a child. Andrew and she had been a team since then, Blair at his side as he'd risen from the governor's mansion to the White House. He was her father, her friend, and her greatest supporter. "I know, baby. I know."

"I'm glad Lucinda has you on this. I know he'll be even safer. She needs you there." Blair gripped Cam's shoulders and pulled Cam over on top of her. "But right now, so do I."

"Ah, Blair," Cam whispered, "you have me, anytime. Anywhere."

Cam kissed Blair's eyes, her mouth, her throat. Blair was restless beneath her, her legs clasping the backs of Cam's thighs, pulling their bodies tighter, fusing them. Cam slid her hand between their bodies and caressed Blair's breasts until her nipples tightened and her breasts tensed.

"Oh God, Cam," Blair whispered. "Inside me. I need you."

"Soon," Cam whispered, inching down, skating her mouth over Blair's breast, kissing her nipple, biting lightly. Blair arched, a small cry escaping, and Cam's head pounded. She wanted her, hungered for her. Blair was the strongest woman she'd ever known, and she let herself be vulnerable beneath Cam's hands, beneath her mouth. She opened herself, gave herself, and Cam had never felt so humbled. She kissed the center of Blair's abdomen, moving lower, slowly, covering every inch of skin with her fingers and her lips.

"Oh, you feel so good," Blair gasped. "I want you so bad when you make me wait."

"I need all of you. So much."

Blair's fingers came into her hair, caressing her, guiding her lower. "You do. You always do."

Cam eased Blair's thighs apart, kissing the soft skin first on one side, then the other, moving inward, nipping lightly, kissing the spots her teeth had teased. Blair's hips lifted to her, inviting her deeper. She lost all sense of time, of place, of anything other than Blair. Blair's hands on her shoulders, Blair's skin beneath her mouth, Blair closing around her fingers. Blair was everything—air, sun, joy, eternity.

"Now," Blair whispered. "Now."

Carefully, gently, Cam drew Blair's clitoris between her lips, closing her mouth over her, slipping inside until she filled her. She pressed inward even as she sucked her deeper. Blood pulsed, muscles quivered, and Blair was everywhere—in her mind and blood and soul.

"There—" Blair swelled in her mouth.

She guided her higher, stroking, sucking, drawing her ever closer until Blair's thighs tightened into steel bands. Blair jerked hard against Cam's mouth, a choked cry torn from her throat. Blair's orgasm rushed around her fingers, pulsed against her lips, filling her with wonder.

"Oh my God," Blair gasped.

Cam kissed her one last time and settled her cheek against the inside of Blair's thigh, softly caressing her belly. "I love you."

"You make me so happy."

"That's everything."

"Almost." Blair's fingers twisted in Cam's hair and tugged. "Almost everything—but not quite. Come up here."

❖

Hooker slid into a booth in the rear of the Chicago O'Hare Chili's and waited for the server to take his drink order before saying anything to the man seated across from him. Anyone watching them in the dimly lit restaurant, and no one was, would be unlikely to remember two guys on a layover, in rumpled clothes, faces obscured by shadows. When they were alone, he said, "This is getting expensive."

"Safer."

"Right. Next time make it someplace warmer."

"If it's inconvenient, I'm happy to quit."

Hooker snorted. "I'll just bet you are. But that's not the way it works. You've already gotten your down payment."

"Don't worry. I'm loyal to the cause."

Hooker shrugged. He didn't know what motivated the guy, and he didn't care. All he cared about was getting his part of the job done, and he needed this guy to do it. "Tell me what you have for me."

"A few changes to the upcoming schedule."

"Delays?" Hooker frowned. "We've already got a timetable—"

"I don't want to know anything about what you're planning."

"Don't worry, you won't." Hooker leaned back while the waitress slid a beer across the tabletop. "All right. Give it to me. Anything else?"

"There's been a change in personnel at the White House. The medical unit has a new chief."

"Not unexpected. What do we know about him?"

"Her."

"What do you mean?"

"Brought her in from outside."

"Oh. Okay." Hooker didn't like surprises, especially when they affected one of the key players. "What do we know about *her*?"

"Not very much yet. Seems to be a straightforward appointment—navy captain. Nothing unusual."

"She could be useful. See if we can get close."

"The place is like a fishbowl. We can't just go poking around."

"And we can't have a wild card in a game we've already started."

"I'll do what I can. They're calling my flight. Here."

A folded ten was pushed across the tabletop, and Hooker swept it up in his palm and shoved the bill into his pocket. He fingered the small memory disk free and pushed it farther down so he wouldn't accidently dislodge it along with the money. "What's on it?"

"The contact info. I'd rather you didn't contact me—"

"When we need something, you'll know."

Alone, Hooker finished his drink, pulled the ten from his pocket, and left it on the table. Grabbing the check the waitress had left, he headed for the register by the door. Russo might be right—this thing was so big they couldn't afford to leave any witnesses.

❖

"So what's the agenda," Wes asked as she and Evyn walked back to the House, "for boot camp?"

Evyn smiled. "You won't have to run an obstacle course."

"Good to know."

"We need to see how you'll mesh with our team in different threat scenarios. Everyone else in the WHMU has been on board at least eighteen months. Not only are you the new guy, you're the new chief. You'll be with POTUS around the clock most of the time he's away."

"I understand." Wes paused at a corner for the light to change. "I don't suppose you're going to tell me what the sims are first, are you."

"No."

"Even though you probably practice the same simulations at regular intervals anyhow."

"You're quick." Evyn shot her a searching glance. "Piss you off?"

"What? Being treated like a squid?"

"Let me guess—that's like the lowest of the low at Annapolis?"

Wes nodded. She'd played the game, paid her dues, and earned her rank. She might be out of her element here, but she was no squid. Yeah, she was annoyed, but she'd also learned not to be thrown off center by her emotions. "Not really."

"Good," Evyn said, not sounding totally convinced. "We're on the same side, after all."

Wes stopped walking, and Evyn turned to her, her brows drawing together in a question. "There's something you should know— something all the interviews and polygraphs in the world aren't going to tell you."

"Okay."

"Run your simulations, analyze the polygraph, psychoanalyze me if that's what will make everyone feel better, but I would never put a patient's life at risk. If I'm not right for this job—one hundred percent qualified, I won't need anyone to tell me. I'll know. I'll walk away."

"That makes you very unusual, Captain Masters," Evyn said softly. Passersby streamed by on either side of them. Their breath puffed out in the cold air, mingling and misting and drifting away in small white clouds. Evyn's gaze held hers. "No ego investment?"

Wes shook her head. "Plenty. If I can't do something well, I won't do it."

"A perfectionist."

"I hope not—that's an impossible goal. A realist, maybe."

Evyn smiled. "I guess our lives don't leave room for much else."

"No." A pang of unexpected sadness raced through Wes's chest, and for some reason, she thought of her family. She'd grown up with love—surrounded by warmth and joy and support, even though she'd also been on her own a lot. She still had that love and support, but there were times, late at night or first thing in the morning, when she ached for something she couldn't name. Or was afraid to. "Do you regret—I won't say the sacrifices, because I don't think of it that way. But you know—the job?"

"No," Evyn said quickly. "You?"

"No. And I guess we should get to it."

"Yes." Evyn resumed walking.

Wes worked on getting grounded in what was important. She wasn't used to being thrown off track by people. Even her friends had never been successful at pulling her away from her responsibilities. Emory was always pushing her to go out to parties and clubs when they'd been at school together, but she'd been all about the grades. Emory'd been a serious student too, and no party girl, but she'd never worried quite as much as Wes. She'd dated. At least casually. Wes had never cared about that. Still didn't.

"First stop is getting your permanent ID," Evyn said.

They showed their IDs to the officer at the west gate, and Evyn took her to the personnel office. The clerk handed Wes a laminated ID card depicting her photograph, name, and rank.

"Where in the OEOB is the clinic?" Wes asked Evyn when they left personnel.

"Down this hall." Evyn glanced at her watch. "Almost seventeen thirty. Probably only the night shift is here, but you can see them and check out your office."

"Thanks. I appreciate the walk around." Wes mentally noted the twists and turns as she matched Evyn's long strides. At the end of a deserted hall with white walls, gray tiles, and rows of closed doors on either side, Evyn took a right into another corridor lit by glaring overhead fluorescents. A small waiting area on one side was crammed with black metal folding chairs. Opposite that, four rooms with the letters A through D over their doors stood open and empty. Examination rooms. Beyond those, she could see into a large office with a desk piled high with charts. Probably the headquarters of the Admitting Officer of the Day.

"Well," Evyn said, "this is it."

"I can take it from here—I imagine you need to get back."

"I was done at fifteen hundred."

"Oh," Wes said, flashing back to their dinner of the night before. For one second she considered asking Evyn if she had plans for the evening and just as quickly came to her senses. She had work to do—a lot of it. And Evyn—well, anything with Evyn was best kept simple. Tomorrow Evyn would be evaluating her. "Have a good night, then."

"Right." Evyn paused, then smiled briskly. "You too. See you in the morning."

Wes watched her walk away until she realized what she was doing. Abruptly, she averted her gaze and went in search of her team. Why was simple suddenly so hard?

CHAPTER ELEVEN

Evyn shoved her hands in the pockets of her trench coat, hunched her shoulders against the wind, and hurried around the Ellipse to where she'd parked her car. That morning she'd been running late and grabbed the closest street spot she could find, but it felt like a mile now. A light snow had begun to fall, and she brushed the loose powder from her windshield with the sleeve of her coat. Snowflakes melted on her face and neck. She swore she could feel icy snowmelt trickling down her back, although she didn't actually think it was snowing hard enough for that to be happening. Shivering, she jumped into the front seat, started the engine, and turned the heat on high. Cold air blasted in her face, and she lunged to redirect the vents away from the driver's seat. The windows frosted over more with every exhalation, and a cloud of steam rolled up around the outside of the windows to envelop her, making her feel as if she might step out of the car and find herself in another world somewhere. Not that far a stretch—seeing as how this world certainly seemed turned upside down in the last forty-eight hours. She'd spent more alone time with Wes Masters than she'd spent with any woman, other than fellow agents, in the last year. She'd spent even more time thinking about her—like right now—than any of the women she'd slept with. Evyn flicked melting snow from her hair and considered going back inside to look for Wes—the storm was picking up and Wes didn't have a car. How would she get back—damn, she was doing it again, behaving like a player in someone else's life.

Captain Wes Masters did not need rescuing—and she was nobody's savior.

Uncomfortable with her own discomfort, Evyn pulled her cell phone out and punched the icon for contacts. She flicked a fingertip over the screen, scrolling through the list, surprised at the number of names she could no longer put with faces and how many more there were than she'd thought. What had she been doing the last eight years? She could name every one of her postings and list each of her on-the-job accomplishments, but she could barely remember half the women she had known at least well enough to get a phone number.

On the verge of closing the phone to escape any more forced retrospection, she spied a name she did recognize. She even knew her address. Quickly, before she could subject herself to the third degree as to exactly what she was doing, she highlighted the number and pressed Send. Pulling her coat even closer around herself as the heater warred with Mother Nature, she waited.

"Hello?"

"Hi, Louise? This is Evyn Daniels."

A second's pause made Evyn's stomach drop. Then, "Evyn? God, it's been what, a year?"

Evyn felt her face heat in the cold car. "Maybe not that long," she said quickly. "I've been traveling a lot. Out of town on business. I'm sorry I didn't—"

"Hey, that's no problem. I've been really busy myself. I landed a spot in one of the repertory theaters here in DC and I've been working steadily."

Evyn searched her memory for some hint of what Louise had told her about her acting career, but all she could remember is where they'd met—a spinoff party from one of the bigger lesbian circuit events—and where they'd ended up. In bed in Louise's apartment, urgent and sweaty and desperate for fulfillment. The night had morphed into three days, and then Evyn was back on rotation and life went on. And she'd never called, never even looked back. Until now. Feeling a bit like a jerk, she said, "I was wondering—I know it's short notice—but about tonight. Maybe we could—"

"Tonight?" She heard soft laughter. "Have you looked out the window? This is supposed to keep up all night. My super-exciting plans for the evening are to make some hot cider, sit in front of the television with Netflix and a bowl of popcorn, and turn in early."

"I guess I can't persuade you to change those exciting plans?"

"You might, if the evening included dinner, but the weath—"

"I'm already out. Dinner sounds like a good place to start." Evyn winced at her really bad come-on line. When had she gotten so shallow? She turned her wipers on and watched the thin blades bend and scrape while pushing against the half inch of heavy new snow. The snow was coming down harder now and the sidewalks were empty. Cars crawled by, their headlights dull cataracts behind a curtain of snow. In an hour, the city would be gridlocked. She ought to sack out in the down room in the OEOB instead of going anywhere. At least she'd get to work in the morning. "How about I pick you up in forty-five minutes. You pick the place."

"I've got an even better idea—if you're really going to come over here, then let's stay in. I'll cook."

"Oh, that's no fair. I don't want you to have to work." Hell, Louise was too nice and she *was* a jerk.

"I don't mind, if you don't mind something simple."

"Well, sure, but—" Evyn didn't want to drive home—not because of the storm, but because she didn't want to face brainless TV and an uninspired frozen dinner or the warmed-up pizza she'd had three days before. So she opted for company—nothing wrong with that on the surface, or there wouldn't have been if an evening with Louise wasn't just a way to keep her from sitting around thinking about Wes. And that was enough to push her to say, "Yes. Okay, great. I'd like that. I'll grab some wine—is that all right?"

"Perfect. I'll see you soon, and be careful out there."

"Always," Evyn said, knowing even as the words left her mouth she was bluffing. Careful wasn't really part of her modus operandi. She was a risk taker, the first to volunteer, the first to rise to a challenge. She wasn't being careful around Wes Masters, and she wasn't thinking about where she was headed. Not smart at all. Good thing she knew better than to let her private affairs bleed over into work. None of that had changed, and she didn't intend it to. Wes Masters was off-limits and staying that way.

❖

A thirty-something brunette in a crisp white shirt and sharply creased navy blue trousers walked out of the AOD's office with a stethoscope slung around her neck and stopped when she saw Wes. Saluting, she said, "Captain, I'm First Lieutenant Jennifer Pattee, a nurse with the WHMU."

"Lieutenant," Wes said, returning the salute. She was in uniform, the lieutenant wasn't, suggesting the WHMU was geared toward medicine and not military customs. She had no problem with that. "Captain Wes Masters."

"Yes, ma'am." The dark-haired woman smiled tentatively. "Welcome aboard, ma'am."

"Thank you. Are you the AOD?"

"Yes, ma'am. There's also a nurse, Major Mark Beecher, on duty. He just went to grab us some dinner."

"Just the two of you?"

"No, ma'am. Colonel Dunbar is the MD on call—he's backup and in the on-call suite right now."

"Quiet down here."

The lieutenant smiled, more widely this time. "Activity varies, ma'am. During the day, when the House is filled with visitors, staff, and legislators coming and going from the Hill, we get quite a lot of activity. In addition, there are several hundred full-time House staffers rotating around the clock, and we render medical care to all of them. Of course, during a State visit—" She broke off abruptly. "Sorry, I'm sure you know all this."

Wes made a decision on the spot. She'd learned early in life to take lessons from everyone, anywhere she could. On the front line, rank often lost its significance. She was in command of the WHMU, but that didn't mean she couldn't utilize every resource possible. "Actually, no. I haven't been read in on routine around here."

"Well then, I'm sure Peter—Commander Chang—or Colonel Dunbar will brief you. Commander Chang is off rotation right now. He had duty at the wedding."

"Yes, I met the commander briefly. If I'm not on-site," Wes said, "you and the others can reach me by voice or text anytime. I just wanted to get the lay of the land tonight. I won't be taking call for a few days yet."

"Care for a tour, then, Captain?"

"I would."

"This is the clinic area, obviously." Jennifer pivoted and swept her arm to take in the hallway. "As you can see, four exam rooms, a fully stocked treatment room, and the admitting office over here."

Wes followed the lieutenant from room to room, noting the treatment room with state-of-the-art monitors, instruments, anesthesia carts, and OR table. Enough to perform emergency surgery. "Are we approved for general anesthesia here?"

"Yes, ma'am. One person on every shift is anesthesia certified. We can handle any medical or surgical emergency that comes our way."

After they completed the circuit of the clinic area, Jennifer took Wes to a conference room that doubled as a lounge and poured them both steaming cups of coffee from a large stainless-steel urn.

"Thanks." Wes pulled out a chair at the long wooden table and Jennifer sat opposite her. "What's the protocol for evacuation?"

"If we needed to transport the president, Marine One would fly him to Bethesda. We also use George Washington and Howard."

"I want to review the protocols for medical and surgical emergencies. Are they available on a hard drive?"

"On the computer in Dr. O'Shaughnessy's—sorry, in your office."

Wes nodded. "I haven't had the official tour—is that down here too?"

"No." Jennifer colored. "Sorry. That's in the West Wing."

"Then I'll find it tomorrow."

Wes rose, disposed of her coffee cup, and picked up her coat. "I appreciate the introduction. How do I reach everyone to schedule a meeting?"

"All of our pagers, phone numbers, and addresses will be in your office. If there's anything you need, I'd be happy to help you."

"I appreciate that, Lieutenant. I'm sure you have more important duties."

"The unit is my duty, ma'am. I'm happy to help."

"Thanks."

Jennifer held her gaze, her dark eyes warmer than they had been earlier. "My pleasure, ma'am."

"Well," Wes said, "I'll see you tomorrow."

Jennifer saluted.

Wes returned the salute. "We can dispense with the formalities among ourselves, Lieutenant."

"Very good. Good night, Captain."

"Good night."

Wes followed the course she had taken with Evyn back to the exit. The night was dark, cold, and snowy. Buttoning her overcoat, she wondered briefly if Evyn was somewhere cursing the stormy weather. Wes didn't mind the snow—especially as it was falling. The pristine coating of white made the world look somehow innocent and hopeful, as if every possibility existed just around the corner. She walked toward Pennsylvania Avenue to find a cab, snowflakes melting on her face. An unfamiliar ache centered in her chest, different from the occasional bouts of restless uncertainty she usually shrugged off with work or a workout. Tonight the storm's beauty stirred a surge of melancholy, a wish for something she couldn't define. Uncertainty was a strange and disquieting sensation. She'd always been able to see exactly what the future held for her. She waved a cab down and jogged toward the idling vehicle, determined to throw off the odd mood.

Once inside, she gave him her hotel address and checked her phone. One message.

"Hey, Wes. It's Emory. Are you in DC? Call me."

Wes braced her feet as the cab slid around a corner, and punched in Emory's number. "Hello, Em? It's Wes."

"Hey. Where are you?"

"Right now, in a cab headed to my hotel in DC."

"You got there just in time for the storm." Emory laughed. "Listen, Dana is there now on assignment and I'm coming down soon. Let's get together."

"I'm not sure what my schedule is yet—"

"Aren't you the boss? Make sure you're off."

Wes laughed. "I think that might be a title in name only. Apparently, I have some on-the-job training to do first."

"Really? What's that about?"

"Just routine stuff."

"Huh, top-secret stuff, right?" Emory laughed again.

"You got it."

"Well, I want to see you. It's been way too long." A moment of silence, then, "I realized the other day how much I've missed you."

Wes's throat tightened. "Me too. I'll do my best to make it happen."

"I'll text you the when and where, when I confirm with Dana. I thought we'd do dinner and try this great jazz club I read about. Bring a date if—"

"If you don't mind a third wheel, I think I'll be stag."

"Dana knows quite a few single women in DC."

"Uh, no. I'm fine."

Emory sighed. "You're sure?"

"Very."

"Let me know if you change your mind. It's never too late for a little romance."

"For now I've got all I can handle with this new assignment. But I'll do my best to see you when you're here."

"Make it so, Captain Masters. See you soon."

"'Bye, Em."

Wes slid her phone back into her pocket and turned to watch the storm outside. The streets held only cabs and official-looking government vehicles—black stretch limos, SUVs, and Town Cars bearing emblems and flags of various embassies. She thought about what Emory had said about Dana. Emory had found love, but as much as she and Emory had shared, they were fundamentally different. Emory was brilliant—brilliant and driven—but she also came from an old, privileged family in Newport, Rhode Island. While Wes had been scrabbling for scholarships, Emory had already been part of the social and political world she would eventually join. Wes didn't begrudge her a single thing—Emory had earned all her acclaim. But her outlook was far more optimistic than Wes's had ever been.

Emory was wrong this time—sometimes it was too late for some things. Wes had never regretted the choices she'd made or the direction her life had taken. She still didn't. She just wished she could shake the constant sense that something was missing. She knew that wasn't true.

❖

"This was fabulous," Evyn said, carrying her plate and an armful of dishes into Louise's small but expensively appointed kitchen. "I can't imagine what you'd come up with when you actually have time to plan a meal. Thanks again."

Louise stacked the dishes on top of the dishwasher, rinsed her hands, and dried them on a bright red towel. She turned, her hips against the counter, and grasped Evyn's hand, pulling her forward until they were toe to toe, their bodies nearly brushing. "You'll have to come by again when I can really do it up."

Evyn's skin tingled from the heat of Louise's body so close to her own. She watched Louise's mouth move as she spoke, captivated by the moist, lush surface of her lips. Her lips were full and red and, as she recalled, very kissable. She raised her gaze and saw that Louise had been watching her, probably reading her mind. She grinned and Louise's smile widened.

Louise was attractive—shoulder-length pale blond hair, straight and perfectly styled, unlike Wes's windblown canvas of golden browns and summer highlights. Louise's eyes were mahogany, completely different than the intense green of Wes's. They looked nothing alike—Louise was sultry and sensuous, Wes was intensely sexual, physically commanding. And why was she thinking about Wes when another woman was sending her come-and-get-it signals?

She wasn't just off her game, she was completely without one. True, she hadn't really thought about any kind of date in weeks, maybe a few months, but it's not something you would forget. Bicycle riding and all that. She kissed Louise softly. "If that's an invitation to return, I accept."

"Good. But you're not leaving just yet." Louise tugged Evyn's shirt free from her pants and slid her hand underneath to skate her fingers over Evyn's belly.

Evyn's muscles contracted into a tight knot beneath the teasing caress. Her breath caught. Somewhere in the recesses of her mind, a voice warned her off, but she ignored it. She was single, after all, and this was what she knew. Louise scratched her nails rhythmically up and down the center of Evyn's abs and then dipped her fingers beneath the waistband of Evyn's pants. Evyn gripped the edge of the counter, her thighs trembling, and kissed her again.

After all, why not?

CHAPTER TWELVE

Wes woke up a little after 0500 and turned on the television. The city had received over six inches of snow during the night, and the mayor had declared a snow emergency. All federal offices were closed, but she didn't think that extended to the White House. She ordered a large pot of coffee and an American breakfast and showered while waiting for it to come up. She'd had an aide send her clothes down from her previous quarters, and they'd been waiting for her last night when she'd returned. She'd have the rest moved down when she had time.

In keeping with the less formal WHMU protocol, she dressed in tailored black pants, a thin black leather belt, low black boots, and an off-white open-collared shirt. At 0600 she flagged down a cab in front of the hotel and instructed the driver to drop her off at the northwest gate.

"You work there?" asked the cabbie, a friendly young woman with red-rimmed eyes. Judging by the empty coffee cups and fast-food wrappers in the front seat, she'd been driving all night.

"Yes," Wes said. "Long night?"

"Yeah, but the money is good so I'm not complaining." The cabbie maneuvered down the single cleared lane in the middle of a two-way street, swerving around abandoned cars and piles of snow. Fortunately, the streets were nearly deserted—snow-covered cars clogged intersections and narrow side streets. The trip usually took fifteen minutes. Today was closer to forty-five, but she was still early for her meeting with Evyn when the cabbie let her out.

"Thanks," Wes called. "Have a safe one."

"You too."

The cab's wheels spun, then caught, and the vehicle sluiced away. Wes nodded to the officer at the gate and showed her ID. "Can you point me to my office?"

"Ground floor, halfway down on the left."

"Thanks."

Wes hung her coat on the wooden rack inside the door, sat in the leather swivel chair behind the desk, and took stock. The room previously occupied by Len O'Shaughnessy had been cleared of personal effects and now resembled every duty office she'd ever seen—the bookcases and desk were wood, not metal, but even so, they had an institutional look to them. The nicely framed prints on the wall were generic renditions of American historical events that had taken place in the region surrounding the capital. The titles in the bookcases were standard medical classics—Harrison's *Principles of Internal Medicine*, Schwartz's *Principles of Surgery*, Chance's *Introduction to Biochemistry*. Next to them, white loose-leaf binders were neatly labeled with black script: trauma protocol, acute surgical conditions, medical emergencies, toxic exposure, poisoning, and so on down the line of emergency situations. She'd have to review them all.

The computer was running and she booted up. O'Shaughnessy's password had already been swept. Her name appeared with a prompt to enter a password. She chose one, repeated it as directed, and was in. She clicked a desktop icon for an e-mail program, and a list of e-mails appeared in the in-box. Generic messages appeared from various White House departments—the press corps, communications—and, at the very bottom, one from edaniels@uswh.org. She looked at the recipient and smiled at the wmasters@uswh.org. Apparently someone was taking care of the details. Hopefully they'd arrange for quarters for her soon. She opened Evyn's message.

> Good morning, Doc. I'll wait for you in the ready room—it's in the basement of the OEOB. Thought you might be running late due to the nasty weather. ED

Wes checked her watch. She still had time, but none of the other e-mails looked important. Since the WHMU was set to run without her until she officially took charge and entered the rotation, she had nothing else to do. *Good morning, Doc. I'll wait for you...*

A rush of unexpected pleasure warmed her. She closed the mail program, grabbed her coat, and went in search of the ready room, Evyn's slow smile playing through her mind.

❖

Evyn poured a cup of coffee and dropped onto a sofa opposite a widescreen TV in the ready room where she and the other agents hung out between shifts or while waiting for Eagle to go out. She had the place to herself and was glad of it. She wasn't feeling talkative and definitely didn't want to spar with Gary about where she'd spent the night or what she'd been doing. She hadn't had time to go home after waking up at Louise's to discover the city buried under snow. Fortunately, she'd had a change of clothes in her car—she always did—although the blue long-sleeved polo shirt and dark khakis weren't what she usually wore to work. Gary'd take one look at her and know she hadn't been home—he knew by now what she packed in her go bag.

She closed her eyes and tuned out the news anchor, leaving her alone with her thoughts. That was a mistake. Her internal third degree was almost as bad as Gary's would have been. She hadn't had a one-night stand in months, although maybe one-night stand wasn't accurate since it wasn't the first time she'd been with Louise. The whole evening had come out of nowhere, and she wasn't usually impulsive when it came to women. When she wanted company, she found it, but it was always planned. Not last night. Why had she stayed when her mind was only half in the moment? Louise didn't know her well enough to notice. At least she hoped Louise couldn't tell she'd drifted away a few times, very nearly starting to think of someone else before she'd caught herself. Hell. That was just low. She'd never done that before and didn't want a repeat.

The door opened and Wes Masters walked in, looking just as good out of her uniform as she had in it. She walked as if she was still wearing her dress blues—confidently, her expression unhurried, untroubled, and sure. Looking just as good as she had for the briefest moment last night when Evyn had imagined how that tight body would feel covering hers.

"Morning, Doc," Evyn said, feigning a cool she didn't feel, conscious of her own slightly rumpled appearance. At least her clothes were clean. Still, a niggle of unease burrowed in her belly, and she wondered if Wes could tell she'd come straight from a bed that wasn't hers. Not a one-night stand *exactly*, more like a legitimate date—second date, even—and she'd made plans to see Louise again later in the month, schedules permitting. Evyn's skin prickled at the thought. She didn't do repeats—well, she hadn't in a good long time—but Louise had been fun, sexy and passionate, and completely undemanding. When she'd said she had tickets to a holiday show and invited her to go, Evyn couldn't think of a single reason not to say yes. So she had.

"Have any trouble getting in this morning?" Wes asked.

Looking up with a start, Evyn stood, wondering how long she'd been daydreaming and if anything showed in her face. "No. You?"

"Got a cab. No problem." A faintly puzzled look crossed Wes's face and was quickly gone.

"Ready?" Evyn heard the curt tone in her voice and consciously relaxed her shoulders. Wes was too sharp not to pick up on her tension, and she didn't intend for Wes Masters to have an inkling of what was going on in her head.

"Absolutely. Can't wait to get started."

Evyn laughed at Wes's dry tone. The uneasy churning in her stomach disappeared and she smiled. "I'll just bet." She walked to the door and locked it. "Take your jacket off."

Watching Evyn sort through a gear box she'd placed on the table, Wes shrugged out of her jacket. "Shirt too?"

"Ah, no," Evyn said, busying herself untangling the lines for the earpiece and wrist mic Wes would need to wear. She hadn't thought of Wes naked for all of five minutes, and she'd really like to make it ten—years—or so before she had to squelch another image of Wes's tight body sliding over hers. Her thighs twitched. Hell. She held up the radio. "This clips on the back of your pants. Turn around."

Wes complied. "I'll be on your channel?"

"That's right."

Evyn secured the radio with the minimal amount of contact

possible. Even clothed, Wes had a great body. Unclothed, she'd be incredible. She smelled really good too—kind of woodsy and crisp, like the breeze on Whitley Island before the storm had rolled in. Clean, sharp, exciting. Evyn stepped away before her skin burst into flames. "That's it. You can dre—put your jacket on."

"That's it?"

"You need something else?" Evyn asked around the knot in her throat. Maybe she ought to move up her date with Louise. This hair-trigger arousal thing was new and damn annoying. A little regular sex might put a lid on it. "Ah...any questions?"

"Nope. The sooner we get started, the sooner we'll be done, right?"

"That's the theory." Evyn searched for a hint of resentment or anger or resistance but found only the cool, confident tones she'd come to associate with Wes's approach to everything. Her body cooled off and her head started working again. Game time. "Let's go test it."

"Where are we headed?" Wes asked, matching Evyn stride for stride as they left the ready room. A trio of black SUVs waited outside.

"The James J. Rowley Training Center—but we just call it Beltsville."

"What are we—"

"If you're not in the president's vehicle, you'll be one behind it," Evyn said as they climbed into the rear of the second car. "Ordinarily you'd have your own field-trauma kit, but you can use our FAT kit today."

"If I'm expected to use this equipment for any reason today," Wes said, "I'd like to see what's in it before we leave."

"You'll have what you need if anything comes up. You can customize your own later."

Evyn settled next to the big guy Wes had seen at Whitley Manor. He extended his hand. "Morning, Doc. I'm Gary Brown."

"Wes Masters." Wes shook hands and settled across from him and Evyn. The cloak-and-dagger treatment was already starting to get old and she'd just started. She understood she needed to know how PPD operated, but she didn't see why she needed to be in the dark. "So, will I have to pass the physical before I get to play with the big kids?"

Gary coughed and looked out the smoked-glass windows. To Wes's surprise, Evyn colored faintly.

"Can you?" Evyn asked.

As a matter of fact, she'd just had her annual re-quals and part of that had been a fitness eval, but that had to be in her records. Which Evyn had undoubtedly seen. "Well, I do spend an awful lot of my time at a desk, but pushing papers around can be pretty tiring."

Evyn grinned as if Wes's sarcasm pleased her. "No sit-ups for you today, Doc, but I hope you can run."

CHAPTER THIRTEEN

The first blast rocked the vehicle about forty-five minutes into the trip. All Wes could see out the window was a tree-lined road and a brilliant flash of orange somewhere ahead of them before a cloud of dust—or smoke—enveloped the SUV. The vehicle swerved hard right and she bounced against the door frame. Pain shot down her left arm. She grabbed for the medical kit at her feet with her other hand and held on.

"What's the situation?" she shouted over a series of deafening roars. The road beneath the heavy chassis vibrated.

"Rocket attack," Gary yelled back.

Evyn pressed her fingers to her earpiece. Her mouth was moving, but Wes couldn't make out the words. She jolted forward as the SUV jerked to a stop.

"Out, and stay with me," Evyn said, pushing the rear door open.

Gary went out the opposite door and Wes scrambled after Evyn, the FAT kit clenched in her fist. Acrid air stung her eyes and burned her throat. Her ears rang. She expected to find craters in the blacktop and wished for a flak jacket and helmet. Her heart pounded in her throat. Everything she knew about battle training flashed through her mind. She followed Evyn's path exactly, thinking about IEDs and severed limbs and crippling burns. Another flash overhead, another bang. Her pulse shot up and her belly writhed.

That couldn't be live ammo, these people weren't that crazy, but she ducked all the same at the sound of weapons fire. The lead car was stopped crosswise on the road, smoke coming from under its hood. Two men and a woman crowded around the rear door of the limo. Evyn ran to them and Wes pushed forward, nudging Evyn aside to get a look in the interior.

"POTUS is unconscious." A heavyset Asian man pointed to a man she didn't recognize—the president's stand-in—sprawled half-off the rear seat.

More explosions, more noise. Wes couldn't make out most of what was coming over her radio, and she shut the chaos out of her mind. Her only job right now was stabilizing her patient.

"Don't move him," Wes ordered, climbing into the back.

"We have to—we're not secure," the agent said.

"Not yet." Wes flipped the locks on the FAT kit and surveyed the contents. Two seconds later she spied the cervical collar and pulled it out. "Hold this."

"I got it," Evyn said, crouching next to Wes's left shoulder.

Wes handed Evyn the collar, yanked out her earpiece, and fitted the stethoscope to her ears. She checked for bilateral breath sounds, made sure his airway was clear, and did a fast visual survey of the victim. No other injuries. "I'll take the collar now, thanks."

She secured the collar and said, "Okay—let's go. You"—she pointed to the big agent—"stabilize his head and neck while we move him. Evyn, get three others on torso and limbs."

"We know the drill." Evyn backed out of the vehicle and Wes followed, keeping below the top line of the SUV to take advantage of what little cover she had.

Agents crowded around, Wes hoisted her med kit, and the evac team took off running.

❖

Wes gathered up her gear from the floor in the back of the ambulance and stowed it in the med kit. Her shoulder ached and her eyes were gritty, but her head buzzed pleasantly with the adrenaline rush that followed every trauma alert. The "president" was in the OR fifteen minutes after injury—or would have been if this weren't a drill. He'd been delivered stable and ready for emergency intervention. A by-the-book field evac—just the way she'd written it.

"You about ready?" Evyn said from behind her.

Wes closed the FAT kit. "All set." She hefted it, winced, and shifted it to her other hand.

"What's wrong?"

"Hmm? Oh, nothing. Jammed my shoulder a bit. It's noth—"

Evyn climbed into the rig and pointed to the narrow stretcher against the wall. "Sit."

"I'm fine." Wes laughed. "I'm the doctor, remem—"

"And I'm team leader. Sit."

Wes shut it and sat. No point getting into a pissing contest over who was in charge just yet. She kept quiet as Evyn helped her ease her jacket off and unclipped her radio.

"Can you unbutton your shirt?" Evyn asked, her gaze fixed somewhere past Wes's left shoulder.

"Sure." Wes loosened the top half of her shirt one-handed and tugged it free from her pants. She wore a tight silk tank beneath it and was suddenly aware of her nipples tightening. Great. "It's a bit cold in here—can we do this fast?"

"Where does it hurt?" Evyn ordered herself not to look down. The aisle was narrow, and she was practically kneeling between Wes's legs. If she leaned forward another inch their breasts would touch.

"Left shoulder joint. It's just stiff—nothing—"

"We're going to do this, so you can just suck it up," Evyn said.

"Fine."

Ever so carefully, Evyn drew the collar of Wes's shirt aside with two fingers, careful not to touch skin, until she could see her shoulder. "Big bruise."

"Feels like it."

Evyn rocked back on her heels as far as space would allow. "I'm going to range it. Tell me if it hurts."

"Go ahead." Wes watched Evyn's face while Evyn gently cupped her elbow and manipulated her shoulder. Evyn's eyes were storm-cloud blue, but her touch was sure and steady. A streak of dirt over her cheek made her look unexpectedly vulnerable, and Wes brushed it away before she had time to stop herself. Evyn flinched and Wes dropped her hand. "Shoulder's okay. Sore, but no worse than at rest."

"You'll need to ice it," Evyn said.

"I will. Thanks."

Evyn looked away. "You're welcome."

"That was a pretty impressive sim."

"You didn't seem too bothered by it." Evyn pushed to her feet and moved back to give Wes room to dress. She resisted the urge to ask her if she needed help. She didn't want to touch her again. Not at all.

Wes looked up at her. "Did you expect me to be?"

"Well, seeing as how you're a paper pusher and all." Evyn grinned, realized she was falling into the habit of bantering with Wes, and skidded away from the friendly exchange. Relaxing her guard around Wes was just too easy, and she couldn't afford to get familiar with her. Even if she wasn't supposed to be training her, there was the little matter of Wes probably being on Lucinda Washburn's private security payroll just now. Hell, for all she knew, Wes was evaluating *her*. And didn't that just throw cold water on her libido. "I'll meet you at the cars. We're done for today."

❖

They didn't speak on the trip back to the House, and Evyn disappeared as soon as they disembarked. Wes couldn't figure out what had put that cold distance in Evyn's eyes after the warmth that had been there just minutes before, and the more she thought about it, the more frustrated she became. She shouldn't care—didn't *want* to care. Since the idea of sitting around her hotel room until the next day waiting for her next exercise held no appeal, she went back to her office and spent the rest of the afternoon setting up a schedule to review various protocols with the team members. When she'd gotten everything organized to her satisfaction, she turned to the last detail on her list and made a call.

"This is Captain Masters," she said when a young man answered. "Is Ms. Washburn available?"

"One moment, Captain," he said pleasantly and put her on hold.

Lucinda answered. "What can I do for you, Captain?"

"I wanted to follow up on my request to schedule the president for a baseline physical examination."

"Yes, I have that on my list. Can you hold for a moment?"

"Of course."

A minute passed, and Lucinda returned. "Are you free right now?"

"Certainly."

"Five minutes in the clinic?" Lucinda said.

"I'll be waiting." Wes hurried to the clinic and commandeered the PA, a man she knew by name but hadn't formally met yet, to assist. "Hernandez, you've got the duty. Set up a room for a complete physical, will you? The president is on his way."

Hernandez, a navy corpsman, snapped to attention. "Yes, ma'am. And welcome aboard, ma'am."

"Thanks."

Three minutes later, the president arrived, followed by a military aide carrying nuclear codes in a secure briefcase. Wes saluted.

"Thank you for interrupting your schedule, sir."

The president returned her salute and extended his hand. "Good to meet you, Doctor."

She indicated an exam room. "Right in here, sir. This shouldn't take very long."

The military aide took a post just outside the door, his expression neutral. Hernandez had laid out equipment on the counter next to the exam table and had draped an ironed white gown on the end of the chair. He stood at attention to the left of the door.

"I'll leave you to change," Wes said and stepped out to wait until Hernandez signaled the president was ready. Two minutes later he called her in, and she quickly worked her way through the exam, checking vital signs, listening to heart and lungs, testing reflexes. Everything was fine, which she had anticipated.

"All set, sir," she said when she'd finished. She stepped out while Hernandez assisted the president, and returned when Hernandez called her.

"What's your verdict, Doctor?" the president asked as he knotted his tie.

"We'll want routine bloods again in four months and an EKG in six. But you're cleared for duty."

Andrew Powell smiled. "Glad to hear it. How are you finding the post so far?"

"I'm honored, sir."

"I promise it's not always this quiet."

She laughed. "In medicine, sir, quiet is not bad."

"True about my job too. What are you doing for the holidays?"

"I have the duty, sir."

The president opened the exam-room door and paused. "Well, be sure and make the staff Christmas party."

"I will. Thank you, sir."

"I'm sure I'll be seeing you again soon," he said.

"Yes, sir. Happy holidays, sir."

"Happy holidays, Captain Masters."

Wes stayed in the hall until he disappeared. Today she'd been part of a simulated rocket attack aimed at destroying this man and what he symbolized to the nation and the world. The idea that someone close to him might be a traitor made the urgency of her job even more acute. She understood—at least rationally—a little bit better why Evyn didn't yet trust her, and as much as she resisted the idea, she couldn't totally trust Evyn either.

CHAPTER FOURTEEN

E vyn woke with Ricochet draped on her left ear. "Get off."
Ricochet stretched, shifted, and settled around her forehead
like a fur hat. His belly reminded her of feathers dancing on her skin.
Feathers. Fingertips. Wes's thumb tracing over her cheek. A shot of
adrenaline spiking her pulse, her clit instantly hard. Her eyes jolted
open. "Hell."

She stared at the ceiling. Flat gray light. The weatherman had said
more snow was coming. More freezing cold. She wasn't cold now. She
kicked the covers off. Ricochet complained and stalked haughtily to
the bottom of the bed. Evyn touched her cheek and her clit did that
twitching thing it had done yesterday when Wes had touched her. Wes
made her so freaking hot—didn't mean a thing, though. Just good old
reflexes. Never mind the way Wes had looked at her when she'd been
moving her shoulder around—so serious, so *right there*. Wes looked at
her—looked into her, and okay, that freaked her out too. She'd grown
up in a houseful of men she wanted to be just like—tough, competitive
men who taught her to win. And any fear or uncertainty—and, God
forbid, tears—that cropped up along the way, she hid. And eventually
she didn't need to hide those things because she didn't feel them any
longer.

Except when Wes touched her, she felt the doors opening and light
leaking into the closed rooms where she kept her secrets. Not good.
Didn't matter, though. She had a handle on it. She slid her hand down
her belly. Had a hand on it too. She was hard all right, and wet, and
damn if she couldn't get Wes's scent out of her head. So she closed
her eyes and let the green of Wes's gaze and the piercing winter-bright
scent of her fill her mind as she came.

❖

"Morning," Wes said when she found Evyn in the ready room at 0730. A box, empty save for a lone white powdered doughnut, sat in the middle of the round table. Evyn was dressed for fieldwork again—khakis and a blue polo shirt with the USSS logo on the chest.

"Hi," Evyn said, rising abruptly and dumping the remains of her coffee in the sink. "Ready?"

"Another sim? Sure."

"Nope. Today we go live." Evyn raised her left wrist and said, "Team One, ready to move out."

Wes followed her out into the hall, waiting for Evyn to fill her in on what was happening. They'd reached the south exit before she finally asked, "Isn't it customary to brief me?"

"There is no customary." Evyn reached the door first and held it open. "The only thing you can count on in this detail is that plans always change. Today's already have."

"Am I the only medic?"

"You'll have the usual backup in the follow car."

Wes caught the door and followed Evyn outside. A limo idled with the three black SUVs on the circular drive. Gary waited by the open rear door of the first vehicle, sunglasses on, earbud just visible behind his left ear. He nodded briefly to Evyn, and Wes thought she saw his eyebrow quirk before his stony expression returned. Several other men and a woman stood waiting by the other vehicles, and the profiles of additional agents were visible inside each one. She hadn't expected so many people to be involved in a training scenario but said nothing. Evyn obviously wasn't planning to answer any of her questions.

"We'll be in the first follow car," Evyn said. "Eagle is on his way."

Wes hesitated. "I thought this was a training scenario."

Evyn met her gaze, no trace of humor in her eyes. "Did I give you that impression? This is as real as it gets."

Wes adjusted her expectations and reassessed the situation. "Then shouldn't I ride with the president?"

Evyn opened the rear door of the SUV directly behind the limo and gestured for Wes to climb in. "Under most circumstances, no. You're part of the secure package now—we need you out of the kill zone. You can't treat Eagle if you're dead."

"Makes sense," Wes muttered. She accepted the reasoning behind safeguarding the first responder, but in light of the sim the day before, she didn't like it. If the vehicles were separated or the president's vehicle took a direct hit, she wanted to be closer than she would be in a follow car.

Evyn must have read her displeasure, because she said, "If a threat arises, we'll do our jobs and you'll stay out of the way until needed."

"I know the protocol, Agent Daniels."

"Then we're all happy." Evyn pulled out her handheld and started flicking through screens. Conversation over.

Wes settled onto the black leather bench seat and watched out the window as a group emerged from the White House. She caught a fleeting glimpse of President Powell, flanked by four agents, striding briskly toward the limo. Seconds later, they pulled away and exited the South Grounds onto E Street. The streets had been plowed and snowbanks lined the curbs. Somewhere in front of them, motorcycle engines rumbled, probably a police escort clearing the way. Across from her, Evyn texted.

Wes wondered what would happen next, and when. The thrum of anxiety in her belly was probably something she was going to live with indefinitely. Every trip the president took outside the White House was akin to a military engagement. Danger was always imminent. Stress and uncertainty didn't bother her, as long as she knew she was prepared. And she planned to be.

Forty minutes later, the motorcade pulled off the highway onto a wide drive and stopped in front of a row of large stone buildings. Car doors slammed, and Wes saw the group from the first car moving inside. Evyn opened the door and said, "You'll stay here with one of the military aides. If you're needed, he'll inform you. I hope you brought something to read."

"It never occurred to me I'd need it."

Evyn laughed. "Oh, you'll have plenty of time to kill on this assignment. I recommend an e-reader. Travels easily and holds up well."

"I'll make a note of that."

Evyn closed the door and disappeared inside along with several other agents. Wes settled back to wait, watching out the window. No foot traffic. An occasional car passed along the drive. She wasn't sure where they were. The uncertainty heightened all her senses. Her pulse was a little faster than usual, and tension in the back of her neck indicated her blood pressure was probably slightly higher than normal too—nothing to worry about as long as the tension didn't escalate into anxiety, which blunted response time. A certain degree of stress augmented essential reflexes. She felt on edge but sharp. The way she needed to be.

An hour passed before the main doors of the building opened and Evyn walked out, followed by the president and a phalanx of agents. A blur of motion cut across Wes's field of vision, shouts erupted, the loud crack of gunfire shattered the quiet. Evyn crumpled, the president staggered, and Wes grabbed her FAT kit and bolted from the SUV along with a sea of agents from the other cars. Agents converged on the president, others swarmed a young man holding a pistol and dragged him to the ground. Wes raced up the sidewalk, scanning the injured, automatically triaging. Only those who would die without immediate attention could be treated. Those who would die despite emergency care and those who would survive without it were passed over.

Evyn lay on her back, eyes closed, the collar of her shirt soaked in blood. Neck or chest wound—likely fatal without urgent treatment. Another agent, a man she didn't recognize, curled on his side, clutching his abdomen. A second potential fatality. The agents with the president pushed past her toward the vehicle she'd just vacated. The president seemed to be moving under his own power—injury status unknown. Without medical treatment, Evyn and the other agent would likely die.

Wes stared at Evyn—she was still breathing, but for how long? Ignoring her instincts, ignoring all her training, she ran for the SUV with the president inside and jumped into the back. The doors slammed shut, tires screeched, and they jolted forward. The president was supine on the rear seat, and the duty nurse already had an oxygen mask on his face.

Bracing one arm against the side of the speeding vehicle, Wes dragged the FAT kit closer. "Status?"

"GSW to the leg," Thompson, the nurse, replied.

"You," Wes said to the closest agent, pulling gauze from the field trauma kit, "hold this over the wound, press hard."

"Yes, ma'am."

"Get us to the nearest trauma center." She didn't wait for an answer. After grabbing a stethoscope, she pushed closer and slid a hand behind the president's back to check for any wounds she couldn't see. Nothing else. The leg wound was the only injury, but in that area, if he didn't bleed out, he could lose his leg. She found an intravenous pack in the kit and tossed it to another agent. "Hold this up."

"Got it."

She quickly connected intravenous tubing to the bag, opened the line and let the fluid run down, and clamped it off. With scissors, she cut the president's coat and shirt sleeve up to the level of his shoulder and wrapped a tourniquet around his arm. As she unwrapped a large-bore intravenous catheter, an agent gripped her wrist.

"I think you can hold up there, Doc." He grinned. "Dave here is afraid of needles and we wouldn't want him to faint on us."

Thompson removed the O2 mask, and the agent playing the president grinned at her. He could pass for Andrew Powell at a distance, but this close, she could see he was younger and a little heavier. "How are you feeling, *Mr. President*?"

"I'm doing great, Doc. So are you." The presidential double pushed up on the seat and swatted at the man holding the compression dressing on his groin. "Let up there, will you? My toes are falling asleep."

The agent holding the gauze laughed, said something into his microphone, and the vehicle slowed. "Nice work, Doc. We'd be arriving at the trauma center about now with the president stabilized."

"What about the two we left behind?" Wes asked, thinking of Evyn and the blood running down her throat. Everything in her rebelled against leaving a dying patient in the field.

His grin faded. "They're not your concern."

"Understood." Methodically, Wes packed up her kit, the image of Evyn bleeding to death on the sidewalk burning in her mind. The next time she had to leave her behind might not be an exercise. She wasn't sure how to square that with her conscience, or her ethics, or her heart.

❖

"Nice job, Doc." Vince, the agent who had assisted Wes during the resuscitation of the "president," veered off toward the ready room, leaving Wes alone.

"Thanks," Wes called after him. She headed for the locker room to store her gear. After the exercise had ended, their SUV had turned around and followed the limo back to DC. She hadn't seen Evyn since she'd left her on the sidewalk, but if Evyn wanted her for anything else, she'd no doubt find her.

The locker room was empty, except for a navy blue polo shirt and khakis folded neatly on a bench in the center of the room. The shower ran in the adjoining room. Those clothes were most likely Evyn's. She'd seen a few other female agents in the halls, and they'd all been dressed the way Evyn usually was—in jackets and pants. She wanted Evyn's take on the morning's scenario, and she didn't want to spend the rest of the day with the mental image of Evyn bleeding out on the street. She knew it was all a fabrication, but on some instinctual, primitive level, she couldn't shake the uneasy feeling she'd let her die.

Wes leaned against the lockers and reran the incident again. She'd been doing that all the way back in the SUV while the agents relaxed, cracked jokes, and gossiped. Someone had speculated on where Evyn had spent the night of the storm, noting she'd turned up for work wearing her emergency change of clothes and they hadn't had an emergency. Wes tried to tune out the good-natured griping about some people having all the luck. If Evyn had spent the night with someone, it was no business of hers. She blocked the chatter the way she did the constant hum of voices during a trauma alert and concentrated on what she had done earlier, and why. She still wasn't happy with the choice she'd made, despite knowing she'd made the only choice open to her. And would make it again.

"You planning on taking a shower?" Evyn walked in with a white towel wrapped around her torso, covering her to mid-thigh. She pointed to a closet. "In there."

"No, I'm fine. I wasn't out there long enough to work up a sweat."

"I wish I had." Evyn opened a locker across from the pile of clothes on the bench and stowed a bath kit on the top shelf. "I froze my ass off lying on that sidewalk, and it was wet."

"And of course, there was the blood."

"Since it wasn't real, it wasn't even warm." Evyn glanced at Wes over her bare shoulder, loosened the towel, and let it drop to the floor. "You sound a little pissed."

Wes jerked her gaze up to Evyn's face, but not before she'd taken in the entire naked panorama of Evyn's back and backside. Smooth skin, toned muscles, all blending into inviting tanned curves. "Not exactly pissed. Just not sure of the point."

"I thought the point was obvious—GSW is still the most likely form of assault on POTUS." Evyn slid black panties from an open nylon bag inside the locker and pulled them on. They were cut high on the sides, accentuating the expanse of honed thigh from hip to knee.

"And do you really think if I'd been briefed beforehand, I would have reacted any differently?" Wes shook her head. "I'm sure you practice that scenario regularly—knowing what is coming—and without the benefit of simulated blood."

"You're right—we do. Dozens of times, for months, before we ever ride in a vehicle on PPD." Evyn grasped the khakis, pulled them on, and slipped the polo shirt over her naked chest. "You haven't."

Wes watched. Evyn didn't seem to mind, and pretending she wasn't watching would only make her interest even more apparent. Evyn was beautiful and looking at a beautiful woman came naturally. Pretending she didn't want to would be unnatural, and she wasn't any good at pretending. That's what bothered her about the morning. She had done the right thing and her instincts screamed otherwise. "Had it been real, you would have died out there."

"This is where I say something like, 'That's my job. You shouldn't worry about it.'" Evyn regarded her across the small room. "Do you believe that?"

"Yes, and I respect your bravery."

Evyn waved her off with a snort and tucked her shirt into her pants. She zipped and buttoned and sat down to fish socks and shoes out of her locker. "It's not a matter of bravery, it's a matter of training. When you've done it enough times, you don't think about it. Isn't that the way it is for you?"

Wes moved down the row of lockers, wanting to see Evyn's face as they talked. "Yes, that's exactly how it is for me. Only *my* training says I don't leave a seriously injured patient in the field when my attention could make the difference between life and death."

"You see," Evyn said lightly, "that's the whole point. Your training might get in the way, and we can't let that happen, can we?"

"You're purposely being obtuse."

Evyn grinned. "Is that painful? It sounds painful."

Wes smothered a laugh. Evyn was very, very good at deflecting the conversation from topics that touched on the personal. "Any emergency physician could have handled that situation this morning. And any ER doc—"

"But that is the point, isn't it, Dr. Masters?" Evyn stood, zipped her bag, and slung it over her shoulder. "You aren't just any doctor anymore, you are the First Doctor. Your training isn't going to prepare you for what you need to do, because you are not going to deal with mass casualties as long as you are the First Doctor. You're going to deal with one patient. No matter what else happens, you only have one patient."

Wes swallowed back a snarl. Cool reason was the only way to get through a head as hard as Evyn's. "Let's just say, theoretically, that my primary patient sustains a superficial wound to the shoulder. He could easily be transported safely to a level one trauma center and receive simple field care en route. All of you are trained in CPR and emergency medical management, right?"

Evyn nodded. "That's true. But what happens if on the way, he develops a drug reaction, or a second wound is discovered, a more serious one. That happened with Reagan after Hinckley's assassination attempt. What if he crashes and you aren't there?"

"You'd rather I let one of you die despite how unlikely the worst-case scenario is?"

"Bingo." Evyn pointed a finger at her. "That's it in a nutshell. We have to assume the worst-case scenario every time and act accordingly. And if you don't believe that, then you don't belong in your job."

"I guess you're going to decide that, aren't you?"

"Not all by myself," Evyn said, her voice losing its faintly teasing edge. "You admitted yourself, you're an academic—and it isn't a classroom out there."

"That's what this is really all about." Wes took a slow breath. "You don't think I should have this job, do you?"

"I didn't say that."

"Peter Chang would be your choice."

Evyn colored. "Not my call. That doesn't figure in the equation and never did."

"If the medical team feels the same way, it's a problem. I can't allow such a vital unit to be destabilized due to politics and personal loyalties."

"Look, those people are all military. They'll follow orders." Evyn sighed. "We're on the same side here, Wes. I just need to know you have a clear idea of what the game looks like before you get to play."

"Fair enough." Wes couldn't argue against being prepared. Evyn held all the cards, and for the most part, she agreed with Evyn's call. "What's in store for the next inning?"

Evyn just smiled and shook her head.

❖

Evyn shrugged into her windbreaker, grabbed her go bag, and headed out. She thought about stopping by Wes's office but vetoed the idea immediately. Her job was to see Wes got a crash course in the way PPD operated, and she wasn't about to apologize for the way she did it. If Wes was pissed about the way the sim had gone down—well, she'd just have to stay pissed. Not like they had to be best friends or anything.

"Evyn!"

Evyn spun around at the sound of the familiar voice. Speaking of friends. "Hey, Pete! You're back!"

"Yep." Pete wore a bulky down parka, and his straight black hair was covered by a dark watch cap. He pulled off his cap and ran slender fingers through his hair. "I picked a good time to take a few days' leave."

"Yeah—you missed the worst of the storm. You working tonight?"

He nodded. "Anything happening?"

"No, it's been quiet. Emily is shift leader tonight. She'll fill you in, but he's not scheduled for anything."

"Good. I could use a little time to catch up on paperwork." He looked around and moved closer. "How's the new chief settling in?"

Evyn thought about Wes leaning against the lockers while she dressed, and the way Wes's gaze occasionally glided over her body. She liked the direct way Wes had looked at her, as if she'd appreciated what she saw and wasn't going to hide the fact. There'd been nothing flirtatious or suggestive in Wes's behavior, but Wes had noticed her, and remembering the flicker of heat in Wes's eyes made Evyn's nipples harden. Glad to be wearing a coat, she said casually, "A little soon to tell. She's got the creds for the job."

"I know," Pete said. "I met her briefly at the wedding. She seems nice enough."

Nice. That wasn't exactly the word she would use to describe Wes Masters. Intense, focused, honest, uncompromising. She supposed those things made Wes nice, but they also made her incredibly attractive. And if that wasn't enough, she was gorgeous. The morning's fantasy popped back into her head. Okay—kill that picture right now. "How do you feel about her getting the job?"

Pete shrugged. "I don't mind not having to deal with the politics."

"That's very political of you." Evyn nudged his shoulder with hers.

"I don't know. I guess we'll just see how it works out."

"Yeah. I guess we will." Evyn waved good-bye and pushed out into the flat gray afternoon. As much as she liked Pete, she didn't want to see Wes fail. Right now, what she really wanted was to see Wes again. When she was around her, she felt electrified. All of her senses were so charged, she thought she might start humming. She hadn't been this keyed up during the night she'd spent with Louise. That had her worried. Whatever the strange effect Wes had on her, it was something she'd never experienced before. Reason enough to keep a safe distance. Fantasies, though, were harmless.

CHAPTER FIFTEEN

Lucinda dropped her pen on her desk as the door from the Oval Office opened and Andrew walked in, a little after eight a.m. She stood. "Mr. President. I—"

Andrew closed the door. "I'm alone, Luce. Don't get up."

Lucinda came around the front of her desk and gestured to the chairs on her way to the coffee credenza. "I thought you were in a budget meeting."

"I was, but we're not going to move on anything at this point. Richard wants to wait until after the Iowa caucuses. He thinks we may have more support than the numbers are showing right now."

"Well, Richard is the campaign manager and he knows numbers," Lucinda said, pouring them each a cup of coffee. She handed one to Andrew. "I think as soon as Russo starts showing his true colors, we'll see a huge swing from the independents in our direction."

"That would be the best-case scenario," Andrew said, accepting the cup as he leaned back in the chair, balancing the saucer on his knee. "Blair called this morning."

"Ah," Lucinda said, sitting beside him. "I briefed Cameron on the situation."

"Mmm, I gathered. Blair was a bit peeved she hadn't been read in."

Lucinda smiled and sipped the coffee. "Just a little bit peeved? She is mellowing."

Andrew laughed. "I don't think I'd use that word, but she's beginning to accept some of the politics."

"Do you think that's age, or is she just bowing to the inevitable?"

"Blair?" Andrew smiled, his voice warming. "You've known her all her life. Do you think she'll ever bow to anything?"

Lucinda pictured the wild teenager, and the angry young woman of just a few years ago, and the incredible, strong, focused adult Blair had become. "No, she will always take things by the throat. It's one of the things I love about her."

"Me too," Andrew said softly. "That's what I wanted to talk to you about."

Lucinda set her coffee cup on the edge of her desk and turned to face him fully. He was still as handsome as he had been when she'd joined him during his race for the governor's mansion almost two decades before. Clear-eyed and strong, with an inner kindness that had not been blunted by politics. "What's worrying you?"

"I tried to talk her out of coming along."

"I thought you might. I take it she disagreed?"

"Vociferously." Andrew sighed and loosened his tie. "I couldn't deny that her presence has always made a difference in my election campaigns. The public loves her, and she grabs the attention of the younger voters. They rally around her because she's so smart and strong and doesn't care who knows how she feels."

"She's her father's daughter in that."

"No small amount of that comes from you."

"And her mother," Lucinda said softly.

"Yes. And her mother."

"Blair won't run from danger, and unless we change our plans to bring Cameron inside, there's no way we'll convince Blair to stay home."

"We could do this without Cam," Andrew said. "I'm not happy about involving her either."

"Andrew," Lucinda said, "Cam is the perfect person to investigate the source of these leaks. She has no political affiliations, other than her loyalty to you. We can trust her completely. And she's very, very good."

"Jensen briefed me this morning. Although the threat level remains unchanged, the soft intel we're getting shows a heightened probability for hostile action."

Anxiety squeezed Lucinda's throat, but she kept her voice even. They'd faced the worst together—his wife's death, attempts on Blair's life, threats against the nation abroad and at home. She would never let her fear for him show. "All the more reason to start looking hard at those around you."

He stretched his arm out between their chairs and she took his hand, closing her fingers around his broad, strong palm. He squeezed gently.

"I knew you'd say that," Andrew said. "And I know you're right. I know you'll make sure nothing happens to her."

"Blair will be safe," Lucinda said firmly. No matter what she had to do, she would see that was true. "And so will you. You just concentrate on winning this election."

The president laughed. "Yes, ma'am."

❖

A tap sounded on Wes's partially open office door and she clicked closed the autopsy report on Len O'Shaughnessy. "Yes?"

The door swung open and Peter Chang appeared in the doorway. She knew from the duty roster he'd been on the night before. She also knew from her early-morning review of the night's logs there'd been no major emergencies. One of the chefs had sliced his hand and needed stitches, a delivery man was evaluated for a wrenched shoulder, and a staffer in the press room had come down for something to help with her stomach flu and learned she was pregnant.

"Commander, come in," Wes said.

"I just wanted to say hello," Peter said. "If you're busy, I don't want to interrupt."

"Just trying to get a handle on the operation. Have a seat."

Peter pulled a straight-backed wooden chair from against the wall in front of her desk and sat down. He was dressed in a tan blazer, light brown button-down cotton shirt, and khaki pants. His tie was thin and black with no pattern. Conservative. As close to a uniform as he could get without wearing one. Wes sympathized. She felt vaguely uncomfortable working out of uniform, especially when she passed military personnel and officers from the Uniformed Division of the Secret Service at every junction. Without the symbols of her rank that had come to define her, she felt displaced, a lot like she did in this strangely skewed new medical terrain.

"Anything I can help you with?" Peter said.

"You can tell me if you think there are any protocols that need updating or reviewing."

He shifted ever so slightly in his seat, a tell indicating her question had caught him off guard and made him a little uneasy. She couldn't imagine why the question would make him uncomfortable, but her radar pinged—something was off.

"I can't think of anything," Peter finally said. "I know Len—Dr. O'Shaughnessy—reviewed everything himself. Once in a while he'd update some of the pharmaceuticals used in emergency protocols, but he pretty much left the management of acute problems up to the team handling the presenting problem."

"So the same injury or medical condition might receive different treatment depending on which team handled it?"

Peter shifted again. "Well, management is pretty standard, so I don't think anyone really deviated much."

"How often does the team get together—for debriefings or case review?"

"Our schedules can be pretty irregular—we're not usually all around at the same time. For Len—well, you now—especially. When the president is traveling, Len almost always accompanied him, which might mean he was detached to the president for weeks at a time."

"Meaning there wasn't really any unit Q&A."

Peter hesitated. "Not per se, no."

"Okay, thanks. That's helpful." Wes could see right away that her idea of running a unit was completely different than the laissez-faire attitude of her predecessor, and probably his before him. No one would conceive of running an emergency room without standardized protocols that everyone adhered to, departmental review of case outcomes, and regular morbidity and mortality conferences. And yet this unit, which not only cared for some of the most important individuals in the world, but several hundred high-level staff and countless visitors, had only the barest degree of internal organization or accountability. She planned to change that and doubted anyone would be too happy about it. She leaned forward on her desk and folded her hands. "Anything else you think I should know?"

"No," Peter said quickly. "It's all standard stuff."

"Yes, well, I gather that around here, standard means pretty much a constant state of readiness."

"I guess that's true." He kneaded his jacket between his hands. "Like most things, there's a whole lot of preparing for situations that never happen."

"Let's hope that continues to be the case." Wes stood. "I should have a new rotation schedule available for everyone in approximately a week. Until then, everyone should continue with the rotations as previously posted. If I'm needed at any time, my pager is listed with the operators. I left my cell phone number on the board in the clinic AOD office last night. Otherwise, carry on."

He stood and saluted. "Yes, ma'am."

She returned the salute. "Not necessary in private."

"Hard habit to break."

She nodded. "Yes, I know."

Peter disappeared into the hall, and Wes sat back down behind her desk. He didn't seem to harbor any resentment, at least not outwardly. He did seem uneasy, though, but that might just be because he didn't know her, and she had taken the job that presumably he had wanted. Or maybe she was reading too much into the situation because Evyn thought Chang deserved the job and not her. Evyn.

She hadn't thought about her while she was working, but every time she stopped, snippets of their conversations would start up again in her mind. Along with that split second of gut-wrenching horror when she'd thought Evyn was mortally wounded. Evyn was so certain of what should be done and why. In order to do Evyn's job, that kind of mindset was probably necessary. She understood. She even agreed, while another part of her mind questioned.

All Wes could hope was that her orders never conflicted with her training, but ultimately, she would follow orders, regardless of the consequences to others. Even Evyn. She shied away from the idea of leaving Evyn wounded, without the care that might potentially save her life. She thought of Evyn's body fresh from the shower—sleek and smooth and strong. Beautiful. She was trained to read a person's body with her hands—to feel the presence of injury and disease in the disruption of the pattern of skin and muscle and bone. She experienced the world through her senses, and Evyn filled her senses. The whisper of Evyn's skin beneath her fingers that day in the ambulance left her wanting more. Seeing Evyn naked after her shower, she'd ached to trace the tantalizing curve along the edge of Evyn's shoulder blade down the slope of her back to the hollow above her hips. She'd imagined heat and supple—

"Captain?"

Wes jerked and looked across the room. Jennifer stood in the doorway, a half smile on her face. Her hair was down, a luxurious sweep of soft midnight waves. Today she wore forest-green pants and a V-neck sweater in a lighter shade of green. Low brown boots completed the outfit. Her figure was small but full, perfectly proportioned.

"Something I can help you with, Lieutenant?"

"A few of us are going out to eat at the end of shift. Would you like to come?"

Wes quickly considered the advisability of fraternizing with her new team. If she didn't go out with them, she might appear standoffish. If she did, she wouldn't know the players or the power structure. She didn't usually fraternize with colleagues, and socializing with team members before she'd taken firm command wasn't a good idea. And there was the glint of interest in Jennifer's eyes, no small matter. Wes had thought she'd noticed it the first time they'd met, and now she was sure of it. Jennifer's invitation might be a little bit more than unit camaraderie.

"Thanks, I'd like to, but I can't tonight," Wes said. "I've got a million things to review, and I'm still finding my way around this place."

"I understand," Jennifer said, disappointment clear in her voice. "Some other time, then?"

Wes smiled. "Yes. Definitely."

"Good. I'll let you get back to work." Jennifer backed up. "If you need help with the files—"

"I've got it for now. Thanks."

"See you then."

Jennifer turned and left, leaving Wes alone with charts and protocols, the stuff of her life she knew well—and thoughts of Evyn Daniels, something new and entirely different.

❖

The round white clock hanging behind the red Formica-topped counter sported a dented chrome rim resembling a hubcap and a faded

Harley symbol in the center. The black hands shaped like handlebars read six forty. Hooker's contact was ten minutes late.

He looked around the roadside diner, studying the faces. At six thirty on a weeknight, the place was nearly empty. The locals, mostly farmers, ate early, and the truckers wouldn't start arriving until midnight. The militia go-between who'd arranged the meet hadn't given him any info other than the location—he'd said the contact was spooked about dealing with an "outsider."

Who the hell knew what a bio-disposal technician looked like? Two guys in oil-stained work pants and denim shirts with the sleeves cut off midway up tattooed biceps sat at the counter slurping coffee and uttering occasional monosyllables while working through enormous steaks and mounds of potatoes. A young woman, barely in her twenties if that, slouched in a booth with a glass of tea and a red-and-white cardboard boat of fries slathered in cheese. She ate slowly, making each fry last three bites, as if the food might be her last for a while. Probably a runaway—her face was worn with fatigue, but her eyes were too focused for her to be a junkie. Two men in white open-collared shirts and dress pants occupied another booth—probably businessmen on the road. No one paid any attention to him. He finished his coffee, slid two bills on the counter, and walked outside.

The Georgia heat slapped him in the face, momentarily taking his breath away. The change from the biting cold in Chicago was disorienting. Like the diner, the gravel lot was mostly empty. A few cars clustered around the far corner of the restaurant, where someone sold ice cream from an open window. Several people, mostly women, stood in line with children in tow. No one paid any attention to him. He'd come all this way for nothing.

As he walked to his car, he glanced into the small grassy lot on the far side of the building. A brunette in a floral sundress and strappy sandals sat under a tree at a picnic bench, an ice-cream cone in her hand. She smiled at him, holding his gaze for just a second longer than was typical for a lone woman who wasn't a working girl. Hooker walked over.

"Good day for ice cream," he said.

"They make the best vanilla bean around here. You should try it."

"Maybe I will. I haven't had an ice-cream cone in a long time."

She was early thirties, eyes as black as her hair, small and pretty. Built too. No wedding ring. In fact, no distinguishing anything—no jewelry, no flash. Attractive, but not someone who would draw attention.

"Probably too cold up north for ice cream," she remarked, catching a line of vanilla dripping down the side of the cone.

The quick flick of her tongue caught him by surprise and his cock got hard. He shifted slightly to hide the fullness in his trousers. "You got that right. I guess this doesn't feel hot to you, though, does it?"

"No—this is the best weather of the year." She smiled. "Sit down, unless there's somewhere you have to be in a hurry."

"Not really."

"Just get in?"

"That's right."

"Here on business?"

He nodded.

"What is it that you do?"

"I buy and sell things," he said.

"I imagine you find all sorts of interesting things."

"You never know what you might come across."

"You're right. Sometimes things turn up you never expect." She bit into the cone and a fleck lingered on her lip.

He had the urge to suck it off. He spread his legs a little wider to give himself a little relief. Something about this woman had him juiced up, and that was unusual. He had no trouble enjoying himself with a woman when he wanted, but when he was on the job, he rarely got distracted. "I'm always on the lookout for unusual items."

"I might have something you're interested in. If you're looking for one-of-a-kind items."

"Really? Rare items are at the top of my list."

"Those things tend to be expensive, though."

"I never mind paying what something's worth."

"And then there's transportation, the authentication, all of those things figure in, don't they?" She crossed her legs, her sandal dangling from her toes. "What would you pay for something no one else could find, delivered in perfect condition? Something rare, unusual."

"Fully functional, one-of-a-kind?" Hooker leaned his arms back on the table and crossed his ankles, taking in the vehicles parked in the lot. None were close enough for audible scanning, and he didn't think their conversation could be picked up from the building. If she was wearing a wire, it was well hidden. Her clothes were tight enough that hiding the receiver would be difficult. Nothing he'd said could be incriminating, but he still needed to be careful. "I'm used to paying for the right product. Half a million isn't out of range."

She took another bite of her ice-cream cone. "Two."

"The item would have to be extraordinarily rare, in perfect condition, and, in order to avoid the competition trying to duplicate it, completely untraceable."

"Guaranteed."

"Then I think we can do business."

She smiled, her gaze slowly moving over his chest and down his body. He couldn't hide his erection and didn't bother.

"Now that I've had dessert," she said, "I'm ready for dinner. How about you?"

"My evening is free."

"Not anymore."

CHAPTER SIXTEEN

The phone rang at 0530 and Wes grabbed it before the second ring. "Hello?"

"We'll pick you up in half an hour," Evyn said. "Pack a go bag and wear field clothes."

"What would that be when I'm not wearing a uniform?"

Evyn laughed. "How about jeans and a shirt? And a light jacket. Oh—and pack for overnight."

"Doable. Anything else I should know?"

"Now, Doc," Evyn said, a teasing note in her voice. "Haven't you figured out the routine yet?"

"I'm ever hopeful."

"Good attitude. See you in thirty."

Evyn rang off and Wes hung up the phone. She'd been up for an hour, reading through some of the WHMU protocols she'd downloaded to a thumb drive and brought back to the hotel with her. She'd worked all evening and finally turned in at 0200—and couldn't sleep. She didn't usually have trouble sleeping, but she'd lain awake in the dark feeling a little like a fish out of water. The entire fabric of her professional life—which was her life—had shifted precipitously. She was still a doctor, still a naval officer, but she had been transported out of the highly structured world of military hierarchy into what felt like a new society where the rules weren't clear and no one was filling her in. To dispel the undercurrent of anxiety, she fell back on what she knew best—discipline, order, and medicine.

As she'd mentally run down the things she wanted to do to fine-tune the medical unit, her thoughts kept wandering off to Evyn. Snippets of their first encounter, their first meal, their first fight, their first touch kept jumping into her mind. Flashes of Evyn's faintly teasing smile, the challenge in her deep blue eyes, her certainty about her job—everything about her stirred her. Spending time with Evyn had been easy, natural. Exciting. And considering their positions and the specter of a security breach hanging over every member of the team, including Evyn, very ill-advised. No matter she couldn't imagine Evyn violating her oath, she needed to keep perspective, and the only way she could do that was by maintaining professional distance.

Finally, to distract herself from thoughts of Evyn and a disquieting buzz in her belly, she'd texted her youngest sister Denny, a night nursing supervisor at Methodist Hospital, who was usually able to chat when her patients were all asleep.

> *Hey, you busy?*
> *Got a minute. Why are you awake so late?*
> *New post. Can't shut off my head.*
> *Not like you. Something wrong?*
> *Nah. Not really. How's everyone?*
> *We're good. Miss you. You're going to make it home for*
>   *Christmas?*
> *not looking good miss you too*
> *will mail leftovers* ☺
> *can't wait* ☺
> *Gotta go. Call—call me. Don't stress. Love you.*

Her sister had provided enough diversion that she'd been able to fall asleep. But as she rode the elevator down to the lobby, her thoughts returned to Evyn. She looked forward to seeing her. Spending time with Evyn was exhilarating—in one moment Evyn was a highly trained professional, demanding and a little arrogant, in the next personable, funny, a little flirtatious. Wes never knew what to expect, and she always knew what to expect. She planned everything and lived by her plans. She'd just discovered uncertainty was damned exciting.

Right now, though, she'd settle for boring routine over a new test of her fitness for her post, but what she'd like and what she got were often different. She pushed through the revolving door and stepped out onto the sidewalk at precisely 0600. Ten seconds later, a black SUV pulled up and the rear door swung open. Wes walked over and saw Evyn in the back beside Gary. "Morning."

"Morning," Evyn said.

"Hi, Doc," Gary echoed.

Wes settled down across from Evyn and the vehicle pulled away.

Evyn pointed to the newspaper in her lap. "Want a section?"

Wes smiled and slid an e-reader from her pocket. "I took your advice and picked this up yesterday at one of the bookstores."

"Smart."

"What? Taking your advice or getting the reader?"

Evyn laughed. "Both."

Gary's gaze flicked back and forth between them, a glint of curiosity in his warm brown eyes. Wes opened the reader and selected the *Washington Post* app she'd downloaded the evening before. Skimming through the sections with a flick of her fingertip, she asked, "Where we going?"

"Kitty Hawk, North Carolina," Evyn replied, surprising Wes with an answer.

"That's a long ride." Wes tried to remember what was in Kitty Hawk besides a nearby Coast Guard station.

"We're not driving the entire way." Evyn folded the newspaper vertically, as if she was going to read it in sections like a subway rider.

"What's in Kitty Hawk?" Wes asked.

"Ocean," Evyn said.

Gary laughed.

"I didn't bring a suit."

"That's okay. The water's pretty warm this time of year."

"It's December," Wes pointed out.

"Believe it or not, water temperatures average over sixty degrees in December in that area. Something about the Gulf Stream." Evyn looked up from her newspaper, her eyes dancing. "You're a sailor. You're not afraid of a little water, are you?"

"Just because I'm in the navy doesn't mean I enjoy being cold and wet."

"I promise we won't let you drown, or freeze."

"I feel so much better. What are we doing?"

"Water block." Evyn went back to her newspaper.

"I gathered it had something to do with water. I don't suppose you could be any more specific?"

Evyn smiled above the newspaper. She was enjoying this, the power play, and Wes was too, even though Evyn wasn't playing by the rules Wes was used to. She followed the commands of others and expected her own orders to be obeyed without question. She understood and accepted the reasons why. The military was a huge organization whose effectiveness was dependent upon coordinated action and instantaneous response, a hierarchy that could only function if orders were immutable. Otherwise, chaos reigned, missions failed, and causalities resulted. Part of what made the system work was accurate intel and preparedness.

In contrast, Evyn gave her no operation details—Evyn not only didn't brief her, she purposefully kept her in the dark. Evyn was testing her without giving her the benefit of bringing her best game. She should have been pissed off, but she wasn't really. If she'd felt she was being set up to fail, she would have resisted, but she sensed no malice from Evyn, despite Evyn's friendship with Peter Chang. They were playing war games, a challenge Wes enjoyed, and she intended to prove herself. Evyn was enjoying herself too, and Wes liked being part of Evyn's pleasure. That was a thought she wasn't going to study too carefully right now. She settled back and scanned the news. The vehicle slowed and she looked up. Evyn was watching her, her expression contemplative.

Wes raised a brow. "What?"

"You look relaxed." Evyn sounded surprised.

"Shouldn't I be?"

"You're not annoyed any longer."

Wes smiled. "Would it do me any good?"

Evyn grinned. "No."

"Then why bother?"

"You're pretty sure of yourself."

Wes glanced at Gary, who stared straight ahead as if he were deaf and their conversation wasn't happening inches away. Maybe he really wasn't listening. Privacy took on a different meaning for these two, apparently. She shrugged. "All I can do is my best."

"Do you always bring your best game?"

Wes didn't do humble when it wasn't true. "Always."

"To everything?"

"Don't you?"

"Damn straight."

Wes laughed. "Then we're not so different."

"Maybe not," Evyn said softly.

The SUV slowed onto the airport exit, and Wes pocketed her e-reader. She grabbed her overnight bag, followed Evyn and Gary into the airport, and went through the line while they cleared their weapons with security. The flight got off on time, and one hundred and twenty-six minutes later, they landed in Charlotte.

When they walked outside, a sun-washed blonde climbed out of the driver's side of a white Ford Explorer and approached with long, graceful strides. She looked to be mid-thirties, tanned, and was dressed in light blue cotton pants and a long-sleeved white T-shirt with a logo over the left breast reading Ocean Rescue Center. "Agent Daniels, Agent Brown—good to see you again."

"Hi, Cord." Evyn indicated Wes. "Dr. Cordelia Williams, Dr. Wes Masters. Cord is an oceanographer and an environmental medical specialist."

Cord said, "Good to meet you."

"Same here," Wes said. "What came first—medicine or the sea?"

"Medicine—then I saw the light." Cord grinned and shepherded them toward the vehicle. "Glad the flight was on time for a change—we've got a lot planned. Weather report says breezy and unseasonably warm, but a cold front is moving up the coast. Good conditions for riptides."

Evyn grinned. "Sounds perfect."

"Does that mean no riptides?" Wes asked as she climbed into the back after Evyn. Gary rode shotgun.

"No, it generally means strong ones."

"Perfect all right," Wes muttered, and Evyn laughed softly.

The cargo space behind Wes was filled with gear smelling faintly of salt and sea—wetsuits, fins, personal flotation devices, a buoy with a short length of rope attached. Evyn saw her checking it out and her eyes twinkled.

"I love water exercises," Evyn said.

"You've been here before, obviously."

Evyn nodded. "Gary and I are both water-rescue certified. Cord is the supervisor for the training. We all train down here with her."

"You've probably checked my file—I'm pretty good at advanced lifesaving techniques."

Evyn laughed. "I don't doubt it. But when POTUS is in the water, we will be too. He likes to snorkel. If we need to evacuate from the water, that's a little bit different than what you're used to on shore."

"Hence all the water gear. You weren't kidding when you said water exercises."

"No. You're going to get wet today."

"Sounds like fun." Wes settled back and closed her eyes. "Sixty degrees is cold."

"We'll just have to make sure you work hard enough to stay warm."

Wes smiled. "Never doubted it."

❖

Blair grasped Cam's hand as they walked along the shoreline. The wind blew through Cam's hair, the mist from the water curling the ends as they lay on her neck, softening the sharp edge of her jaw, making her look younger, more vulnerable. Blair's chest tightened. She couldn't remember a time when she hadn't been with Cam—no, she didn't *want* to remember a time when she hadn't been with her. Before Cam, she'd thought she was as happy as anyone in her situation could be. She'd had moments of professional satisfaction, friends—Diane and Tanner—she cherished, but at the very core of her had been a seething sense of restlessness, of never quite fitting, of unsettled searching discontent.

Cameron Roberts, someone so much like her father, was the last woman in the world she would've chosen. She adored her father but had spent much of her life angry with him. Cam and her father were both so dedicated to their jobs, guided by goals and principles that were so clear to them, and both so willing to ignore their own needs. What she hadn't appreciated when she was young and had only learned after being with Cam was the personal cost that living by those goals and principles exacted from her father and Cam and others like them. What she had seen as selfishness had been exactly the opposite. Cam, like her father, was willing to forgo personal happiness, was willing to risk her life for what she believed. As much as Blair loved Cam, she couldn't bring herself to give Cam that one thing—her permission to sacrifice herself for Blair or her father or her country. She needed Cam to be more selfish than that. She was not willing to sacrifice her, no matter the cost.

"I love being here alone with you," Blair said. "You know that, don't you?"

"I know," Cam said, lightly swinging Blair's arm between them. "And I love you more than you think."

Blair caught her breath. "What are you talking about?" She couldn't imagine that Cam didn't know how much her love meant to her. How precious it was. How she woke up every morning a little bit in awe of how her life had changed, of how much more there was to cherish than she had ever imagined. If she had failed to let Cam know that, she'd failed the most important challenge of her life. "I know you love me. Your love means every—"

"That's not what I'm talking about." Cam lifted Blair's hand to her mouth, brushed her lips over the top of Blair's hand.

Her lips were warm, reminding Blair that she often didn't know she was cold until Cam's touch warmed her deeper than flesh. "Then what?"

"I won't do anything to destroy what we have, not even for my country. I took the job with Homeland Security because I thought I could make a difference there, that I could contribute something. But there was another reason—a more personal one." Cam smiled. "You. I know how pissed you'd be if I stayed on protection and put myself between a bullet and a protectee. I really hate it when you're pissed at me."

"Are you angry at me because I don't want you to die for someone else?"

"No." Cam faced ahead, her expression growing remote, and Blair knew she was looking back. Maybe as far back as her father's death, when she'd watched him die and hadn't been able to stop it. She wished she could go back to that time, to hold the twelve-year-old Cam, to comfort her as she'd never quite been able to comfort the adult woman she loved. But as much as she wished for that, she couldn't go back in time and erase the pain and abolish the disappointment. She could only go forward and love, and hope it made a difference.

"I'm a lot more selfish than you," Blair said. "I don't mind admitting I'm glad you're not doing protection anymore. I don't want to lose you. Couldn't bear to lose you."

"You know it's one in a—"

"Yes," Blair said sharply, "I know it's one in a million. And *you* know, if you're the one, that million doesn't matter."

Cam laughed softly. "We've been down this road before, and we don't need to re-travel it."

Blair sighed. "I'm sorry. I don't want to ruin our time together."

"Baby," Cam murmured, releasing Blair's hand and sliding her arm around her shoulders, drawing her close. "Nothing can ruin our time together. Are you worried about your father?"

Blair rested her cheek against Cam's shoulder. "Yes. It's hard, wanting him to be safe and not wanting you to be the one responsible for it."

"I'm not. That's Tom's job, and the rest of your father's detail. That's a big reason why I'm not doing protection anymore. I don't want you to have to choose between your father's safety or your own, and mine. I get that. But what Luce asked me to do isn't the same thing. I won't be primarily protection." Cam stopped, put her arms around Blair's waist, and kissed her softly. "All I'm going to do is tag along, keep my eyes and ears open, try to find out who has access to the information that's getting out. I'm looking for leaks, holes in the security network, I'm not *doing* security. You don't have to choose between us, Blair. I would never do that to you."

"I'm sorry," Blair said softly. "I know, I do, really."

"I know you're worried about your father. Nothing's going to happen to him. He's got the best people in the world around him. He'll be fine, so will we."

Blair threaded her arms around Cam's neck and kissed her. Her protective detail was somewhere nearby, pretending not to watch them while keeping them in sight, pretending they didn't see their private moments, while seeing everything in their path. Right now, she was more grateful for those agents than she'd ever been. Where she'd once thought they imprisoned her, she now understood they gave her freedom. "Sometimes, I feel like a selfish shit."

"Nothing could be further from the truth. You know what I think?" Cam said.

"What?"

"I think we should go back to DC a little bit earlier than we'd planned. Weather reports say another big storm is moving up the coast. We won't have to worry about flights if we leave tomorrow."

"You're sure? I mean, it's our honeymoon, sort of."

"We can have a sort of honeymoon in DC. I'm not sleeping at the White House, though."

"Oh, really? And I so love being there with the press corps, and the valets, and the officers in the halls."

Cam grasped Blair's hand and resumed walking. "I'm sorry, baby. There are some things I just can't give you."

Laughing, Blair fell into step. "That's okay, darling. I still adore you."

CHAPTER SEVENTEEN

Cord hadn't been kidding when she'd said there would be currents. Wes was a strong swimmer, but in a wetsuit and gear, pulling an inert body through the water against the swirling tides that wanted to drag her under took all her strength and concentration. The instructor assigned to play POTUS wasn't as big as Gary, but he was heavy. The third time she pulled him from beneath the surface, hooked an arm around his shoulder and over his chest, and kept him afloat while a Coast Guard helicopter dropped a rescue basket, her arms and legs were trembling and her heart hammered in her ears. Evyn circled in a dinghy nearby, waiting to assist in the transfer to the lift basket. When they got the patient secured, the helicopter lifted off, the churning wash from its rotors blasting her with icy froth. After the first time she'd gotten a faceful and nearly choked up a lung, she'd learned to turn her head away and keep her mouth closed. Wearily, she fought the water's relentless pull, threatening to carry her out to sea.

"How you doing?" Evyn called.

"Great!" She caught a wave wrong and coughed out a mouthful of brine.

"Head in. Take a break."

"Roger." Wes stroked toward shore while Evyn docked the dinghy on Cord's boat. When she made it in close enough, she stood up and waited for the rest of the team, letting the blue-green ocean swirl around her calves. Despite the painful trembling in her shoulders and thighs, she felt great. She'd managed to keep her patient alive, gotten him transferred to the medevac chopper, and avoided drowning. Not once but three times. She considered that a damn good day.

"Looked pretty good out there." Evyn jumped out of the boat into the surf beside her. She unzipped the neck of the wetsuit, and Wes caught a glimpse of smooth pale skin framed between her breasts.

"I feel like I've just run twenty miles with a full pack."

"Tough work. You did a lot better than a lot of first-timers."

"Thanks." Wes looked around at the small ORS building and the mostly empty beach. Gary stood talking to Cord and Jeff, the other rescue instructor, at the boat dock. "Anywhere nearby we can grab lunch? I'm buying. Gary and the others too."

"Jeff and Gary played football together in college," Evyn said, "so Gary will probably hang here with Cord and Jeff."

"Just you, then." When Evyn hesitated, Wes wondered if she'd broken yet another rule of training no one had bothered to inform her about.

"I know a little taco place not far from here," Evyn finally said. "Mexican okay with you?"

"Sounds great."

"Let's change, then, and get out of here. We'll need to be back at fourteen hundred for open-water rescue."

Wes sighed. "I'm going to need a lot of tacos."

❖

"'One' does not qualify as 'a lot of' tacos," Evyn said as Wes pushed her plate aside. They'd both dug in when lunch arrived and hadn't paused for more than casual remarks while devouring the very good food.

"If I have to be back in the water," Wes said, sipping iced tea, "I don't want to cramp."

"We'll have at least an hour until we get everything loaded up and out to the rendezvous point." The rest of the day ought to be a little easier than the morning, and so far Wes was acing the training. Not that Evyn was surprised. Wes was solid—uncomplaining, focused, fit. She'd handled the recovery drills with calm competence, the way she seemed to do everything. "How are you feeling?"

"Not bad for a desk jockey."

Recalling her not-so-subtle put-down of Wes's teaching creds, Evyn managed not to blush. She really hadn't made a very good first impression, not that she usually cared. With Wes, she did—but she couldn't very well apologize for speaking her mind. "Okay, so maybe I was wrong about you instructor types."

"The day isn't over," Wes said lightly. "Are you and Gary the only water-certified agents on the detail?"

"No. When POTUS is in or on the water, two water-certified agents are with him at all times. The medical staff usually remains on shore, available by radio."

"I prefer to be on the water—close by him," Wes said. "Being on shore is too far away."

Evyn nodded. "I agree. When possible, we'll set you up in the patrol boat."

"Good enough. What about general security?"

"We clear the airspace, the surrounding water, and the shore."

"And transport?"

"Usually Coast Guard, but again, depends on where we are and the location of the closest medical facilities."

Wes's phone buzzed and Wes slid it from her pocket to check the readout. She shook her head. "Sorry. My mother."

Evyn laughed. "Go ahead. I'll get the bill."

"I'll just tell her I'll catch her later." Wes tapped the screen to take the call. "Mom, I'm at work. I'll call you as soon as I can, probably tom—what? No, I'm fine. Denny exaggerates, you know that. Really. Nothing. I'll call you. I love you. I've got to go. 'Bye."

Color rose in Wes's face and Evyn hid her smile. The calm, unflappable doctor was embarrassed. "Mothers. They never get that we aren't always available to talk when we're working."

"Oh, she gets it. She just thinks whatever she has on her mind is more important."

Evyn laughed. "Isn't it?"

"Of course." Wes took the bill the waitress had left on the table stood and they walked to the cashier.

"Does she know about your new post?"

"Some—I didn't really have time to discuss it with her."

"Everything okay?" Evyn asked as casually as she could. She couldn't pretend she hadn't overheard the conversation, and while it was none of her business, she cared if Wes was having a problem. After all, personal issues affected performance, and Wes was not only a key part of the team now, it was her job to see she settled in smoothly. She might tell herself that, if she wanted to blow smoke in her own face. She cared if Wes had a problem because she didn't like the idea of Wes being unhappy. If Wes was unhappy, it most likely had something to do with the new job, and she was a big part of that new job.

"She's doing the mother thing."

"You mean the part where they try to get you to share? And as soon as you do they tell you all the ways you screwed up?"

"My mother usually doesn't pry," Wes held the door open while Evyn went through, "but my sister ratted me out. My fault—I forgot what a little tattletale she was when she was younger."

"You've got three, right? You're in the middle?"

"I'm in the upper middle—one older, two younger. Denise— Denny—she's the baby."

Evyn rounded to the driver's side of the Explorer and waited while Wes climbed in. "You all must be pretty close in age—didn't you say your father—sorry, never mind."

"My father died when I was six. There's about a year and a half to two years between the four of us."

"So what did your sister know that she immediately told your mother?" The street in front of the cantina was clear and Evyn pulled out.

"Nothing. Not really. I just happened to talk to her in the middle of the night—she's a nurse in Philadelphia. I maybe mentioned I was having trouble sleeping, but not because of any problem. Just"—Wes shrugged—"a lot of changes. That's all."

Evyn glanced at her, then back at the road. Wes looked a little tired, but they'd been hitting the exercises hard for hours. She was obviously in great physical shape—she looked as good in a wetsuit as she did in the jeans and long-sleeved T-shirt she'd walked out wearing that morning. Rangy and lean and strong. Evyn put that image aside. If Wes was having trouble adjusting, she ought to know. She wanted to know. She wondered if she was part of why Wes wasn't sleeping, and the idea didn't sit well. "This isn't what you expected, is it?"

"I had no idea what to expect."

"Very politic of you."

Evyn shot her another look and their eyes met. Wes had gorgeous eyes—the kind of crystal green that reminded her of summers in the park, of fresh-cut grass, of carefree pleasures. She had to drag herself away from her eyes and the memory of freer, simpler times. She stared at the road. "I don't know why it is, but every time we're together, we end up talking about stuff I never talk about with anyone else."

"Like what?" Wes said gently.

"Like…personal things. I know more about you and your family right now than I know about Gary, and he and I have been partners on and off for a couple of years."

"I know what you mean," Wes said.

"Got an explanation?" Evyn asked half playfully, but her heart stuttered, waiting for the answer. She hadn't meant to voice that crazy feeling of being totally exposed whenever she was alone with Wes and expected Wes to understand even less. Now she wasn't sure what she wanted to hear.

"Not yet," Wes said softly.

A wave of disappointment heavily laced with relief washed over her. Refocusing the conversation on something safe, she said, "So? What's keeping you up at night?"

Wes laughed. "You're as bad as my sisters."

"Wait till you get to know me better."

Wes laughed again. "Nothing, really. Just adjustment. I'm fine."

"Oh, I'm sure of that. You wouldn't be where you are if little things like having a new command dropped on you, transferring overnight to a new post, being put through an accelerated version of boot camp, and being charged with safeguarding POTUS threw you off."

"Well, when you put it like that," Wes said lightly, "I guess I am doing amazingly well."

"We'll see, Superdoc." Evyn pulled the rented Jeep into the small lot beside the rescue station and cut the engine. She turned in her seat to face Wes. "If there's something you want to talk about, I'm a pretty good listener."

"You are. You make it easy to talk."

The wind had picked up, and whitecaps raced across the water. Wes was studying her, in that completely focused way she had, and the attention was as exciting as the touch had been. She'd never been so aware of being alone with a woman in her life. They'd barely touched, and that had been totally innocent, but her blood sang with anticipation. She didn't get this keyed up with a woman she was about to sleep with.

Her system was primed with expectation for more than a touch, and nothing could be less likely to happen. "I hear a *but* coming."

A wry smile played over Wes's face. "Unfortunately, I think you'd probably end up ratting me out like Denny. Only not to my mother."

Evyn wanted to deny that, but she couldn't. "If I thought something would affect your performance, then I might have to."

"I'd expect you to," Wes said. "And before we go any further, I can tell you there's nothing about this situation that bothers me. I'm fine."

"I wasn't looking for ammunition against you, Wes." Evyn pulled herself back from a dangerous precipice. She'd crossed one of her own boundaries without even realizing it. Wes blurred all the lines for her between personal and professional with frightening ease, and that just couldn't happen. "We both have jobs to do."

"I know," Wes said. "And since we do, I appreciate the offer to talk, but I think we'll both do our jobs a lot better if we don't complicate things."

Wes was right and only repeating her own mantra—never get personally involved with someone at work. Evyn pushed open her door and a biting wind rushed in. "We're on exactly the same page."

❖

The patrol boat rocked on the swell as the winds gathered force. The blue sky had given way to gray thunderclouds above churning seas.

"We've got time for one run," Cord called from the wheel, "until things get too rough out here."

Evyn turned to Wes, who wore civilian clothes as she would on a regular detail. She and Gary were in wetsuits. "POTUS has a sailboat, and the maritime weather reports aren't always accurate. He could be caught out in this kind of blow. But this could get dicey."

"Wouldn't do much good to only train on calm seas," Wes shouted, the wind ruffling her hair. "Let's do it."

Evyn waved to Cord. "Go ahead."

Cord threw a water-rescue mannequin into the water and yelled, "Man overboard."

Evyn and Gary clambered onto the bulwark and dove into the

ocean. Even in the wetsuit, the first shock of frigid water on Evyn's face and exposed hands and feet made her stomach tighten. She cut through the sea toward the bobbing figure, fighting the surging tides and buffeting waves. The figure alternately rode the swells and disappeared beneath the troughs. Were this the real deal, they'd only have a minute or two to reach the president, less if he went off the boat as a result of some kind of injury. The water temperature, the tide, and the rough surf created a swiftly lethal combination. She and Gary reached the mannequin at the same time, and she grabbed it in a rescue carry and started back toward the boat. Gary kept pace beside her, ready to take over and spell her if she grew too tired fighting the currents and the cold. When they reached the side of the patrol boat, Wes and Cord lowered a litter over the side, and she and Gary secured the figure inside. Gary tugged on the line to signal they were ready, and the litter swung away and up. Evyn scrambled up the ladder with Gary right behind. By the time they reached the deck, Wes was already in full resuscitation mode, kneeling on the soaked surface, rapidly running through the emergency assessment protocol, the field-and-trauma bag beside her, Cord acting as her first assistant.

Jeff tossed Evyn a towel, and she rubbed water from her hair, watching Wes work. Every time she'd seen Wes in action, she'd been struck by the way Wes gave everything her full attention, her all, a hundred percent of the time. Evyn spent her days with powerful people, and she wasn't easily impressed, but that kind of fierce focus was incredibly exciting to watch. Wes issued orders without looking up from her patient, calm, sure, utterly in command. Wes personalized power in a way she'd never experienced before, and watching her, Evyn couldn't help but imagine what that kind of potent focus would feel like turned on her in an intimate moment. Her skin beneath the tight neoprene suit pebbled with excitement, and heat bloomed in the pit of her stomach. She'd rarely been the recipient of physical attention even half as forceful and was always content to take the lead in bed. Satisfying a woman was incredibly gratifying, and she hadn't been looking for more. A calm and quiet orgasm was just fine—only when she imagined being with Wes Masters, there was nothing calm or quiet about it. She felt the weight of Wes's body pinning her down, Wes's hands exploring her—not asking permission, her consent readily given. Her blood raced with the urge to open, to be known, to surrender. Nothing familiar about any of it, but so right. So damn right.

Beside her, Gary cleared his throat. She shot him a look. He was staring at her.

"What?"

"You looked...mesmerized. Where'd you go?"

"Nowhere." Evyn was glad her face was already red from the wind and the water, because heat rose through her. "Just watching the exercise."

"Ha ha. Watching a lot more than that."

"Shut up, Brown."

He laughed. "She's really pretty hot."

"Will you shut up," Evyn said through her teeth. Gary had a wife and three kids and was one of the few people on the detail who never fooled around, married or not. She didn't pass judgment on those who did. When you spent days on end, week after week, with the same people in the tensest situations imaginable, doing things you couldn't tell your friends and family, letting off steam together was only natural. Sometimes letting off steam took the shape of sweaty groping in a hotel room in some city on the way to or from the next point on a map.

"Just saying," Gary said.

"Well, don't."

The beat of helicopter rotors cut through the howling wind, and a Coast Guard medevac chopper appeared overhead.

"Transport's here," she called.

"One minute!" Wes pulled a neck immobilizer from her bag and eased it behind the figure's neck.

Evyn switched radio channels and advised the helicopter to lower their Stokes basket. The helo rocked above them in the wind, and the metal-mesh toboggan swung back and forth like a pendulum on its cables as it descended from the open belly. She and Gary went forward to guide the basket down.

"How does it look?" she asked Wes.

"First stage hypothermia, potential head and neck injury from impact on the water, and possible aspiration. His neck is stable, we've got the thermal blankets on, and I've started antibiotics. He needs a CAT scan upon arrival."

"Can we transfer?"

Wash kicked up from the rotors and sprayed Wes's back and face. She blinked the water away. "He's ready."

Evyn signaled the chopper to continue lowering the Stokes. A sharp gust of wind nearly knocked her off her feet. The chopper dipped and rose sharply, canting in the shifting air currents. A crack like a rifle shot cut through the air and the rear cable securing the basket snapped. The metal toboggan came crashing down. Evyn lunged for the flailing cable end as Wes crouched over the mannequin, shielding the figure from the careening basket. The end of the madly swinging metal carrier sliced the air, struck Wes in the shoulder, and knocked her out of the boat.

For one millisecond Evyn was completely paralyzed. The deck where Wes had knelt was empty. The surface of the sea was nothing but angry water. Wes was gone.

Evyn jumped up on the bulwark and dove over the side.

CHAPTER EIGHTEEN

The world spun crazily upside down. The light flickered rapidly and finally blinked out and all that was left was cold. Only pain and blood-stopping cold. Unseen hands dragged Wes deeper beneath the icy mantle, into a blackness that extinguished the last glimmer of illumination. Instinctively, she held her breath, struggling to orient herself in the surreal landscape of shock and panic. Her left arm wouldn't obey her. She kicked and flailed but her water-filled boots and sodden jeans weighed her down. Up and down held no meaning—she revolved in a world without substance. Her animal brain fled from the freezing darkness, away from the primeval terror engulfing her. Primitive reflexes kicked in, and she fought to return to the last place she'd felt light and heat. The surface.

She struggled upward, her chest burning, the pain so huge she hungered to suck in air to soothe the flames. She clamped her teeth shut, finally recognizing the water that entombed her, water that would provide no air, only sudden and swift death. With only her right arm and her clumsy legs to power her, she flailed and kicked and writhed her way toward the shimmer of light penetrating the gloom. Despair squeezed her throat closed.

She wasn't going to make it. Too far, too cold, too much pain. Blood thundered in her ears, her heart crashed wildly against the crushing pressure in her chest. Another second and instinct would overrule reason. She had to breathe. Breathe and end the torture.

Fury washed through her. She would not surrender. Her mind hazed, confusion dulled her senses. The cold bored deep inside her and bloomed into heat, suffusing her with blissful warmth. Another few seconds and the fear began to abate. She stopped thrashing. The vise around her chest tightened, and her battle slowed. Her arms and legs were so heavy. The sea—warmer now—enclosed her, streaming past her face like gentle fingers caressing her, welcoming her. She was so close to falling asleep, the cold forgotten.

A frigid blast of air hit her in the face and someone yelled into her ear, "Breathe, damn it. Breathe!"

Wes jerked and sucked in a lungful of air. She coughed and life returned to her arms and legs. Pins and needles shot into her fingers and toes. A knife blade of slicing pain pierced her chest. The cold returned with a vengeance. Enemies grasped at her, threatening to pull her back into the dark. She thrashed.

"Wes, it's Evyn! Don't fight me."

The darkness disappeared, gray sky flashed overhead. An arm gripped her chest—Evyn. Evyn was towing her. Evyn was not the enemy. Wes tried to kick her legs, but she couldn't move.

"Almost there," Evyn panted, her breath sounding harsh and labored. "Wes, keep breathing."

Wes sucked in another breath, coughed again. Her throat burned. "Evyn, what—"

"It's okay, we're almost to the boat." Evyn's voice was strained, tremulous.

The water was so cold. The shore was a distant blur. A whirlpool pulled at her legs. Riptide. Evyn's grip on her slipped, and Evyn cursed.

"You've got to hold on to me," Evyn shouted. "The current is against us."

"Don't let me pull you down." Wes tried to force her lethargic limbs to move. "I can swim."

"Shut up, Wes," Evyn grunted. "I'm not letting you go."

Wes was too tired, too cold, and in too much pain to argue. Water splashed into her mouth, and she needed all her strength to keep her head above the roiling waves. She had to trust Evyn. She did trust her.

A shadow loomed overhead. The boat.

"Let me lift you," Evyn ordered. "Don't fight me."

Icy metal scraped Wes's back as she was rolled into a narrow litter and strapped down. She spun in midair and the litter rappelled upward, jerking with each ratchet of the winch. Hands grabbed the basket and guided it onto the deck, voices tumbled over one another—a jumble of orders and phrases she thought she recognized but couldn't make sense of. "Evyn?"

"She's right here." A man's voice. Then, "Daniels, get below. You're blue."

Someone lifted Wes's left arm, and she groaned.

"Sorry." A woman's voice. She knew her. Who?

Wes fought to come back to herself. She opened her eyes, focused on the faces looking down at her. She knew them. Had to connect the names floating in her hazy mind.

"Do you know where you are?" the blonde asked. Blonde—hazel eyes. Worried eyes. Cord.

"I'm okay," Wes said, her voice sounding like a croak. "On board the ship. I'm okay."

"You're okay," Gary echoed, his face oddly white against the flat gray sky.

"Let me up." Wes struggled against the strap across her chest.

"Just take it easy." Evyn appeared next to Gary. "You took a swim, Doc. Let us check you out."

Above Evyn's left shoulder the helicopter slid into view, its belly open, the rescue basket angled in the portal. The basket—the basket swinging toward her. Toward her and the patient, her priority. "I remember going in. How's the patient?"

Evyn smiled crookedly. "Which one?"

"The president. The only one."

"He's fine." Evyn's mouth twisted and a shadow passed over her face—storm clouds in a summer sky. "How are you?"

"Left shoulder's getting a workout, but it's just banged up some. Swallowed a little water, feels like. I'm okay."

The radio crackled. Cord said, "Lower the Stokes."

Wes twisted her head, felt a restraint on her neck. "You can take this collar off. I'm fine."

"You are," Evyn said, her bloodless lips tinged with blue. "But we're going to transport you to the hospital—check you out."

"No way," Wes said, her voice stronger already. "I never lost consciousness. There's nothing they're going to find in the ER that I can't tell you right now—my shoulder is contused and I'm cold. Get me warm and I'll be fine."

"You're not in charge here, Dr. Masters," Evyn said sharply. She shivered violently and her eyes glazed before she blinked them back into focus.

"I'm the senior medical officer," Wes said. "And you're verging on hypothermia. Gary—she needs to get out of that wetsuit and get warmed up."

"Yes, ma'am," Gary said. "Evyn, you heard the captain. Get below and strip down. The extra thermals are in the bulkhead."

"Don't pull rank on me, Wes," Evyn said.

With her good hand, Wes unsnapped the buckle holding the band across her chest and pushed up until she was sitting in the litter. "I wouldn't need to if you listened to reason." Her head swirled, but she fought down a wave of nausea. Her shoulder ached, but sensation had returned to her fingers and her arm was moving again. Stiff and sore, but mobile. "I've had worse playing rugby."

"That's not in your personnel file."

Wes grinned. "Not everything is in there, don't you know that?"

Cord's voice cut through the rush of wind. "Let's finish this pissing contest onshore. Can I release the chopper?"

"Yes," Wes said, "as soon as the president is transferred up."

"You're going too," Evyn said.

"If I needed to go—which I don't—we'd wait for another chopper. POTUS is the priority. We do this by the book."

"The exercise is *over*."

"I'm not grandstanding, Evyn," Wes said quietly, holding Evyn's gaze, letting Evyn see for herself she was okay and thinking rationally. "I wouldn't risk it if I thought there was a bigger problem, but I want to end this mission on my feet."

The glacial blue of Evyn's eyes softened and she nodded to Cord. "Send up the president's litter." She crouched by Wes, her face all Wes could see. "But when we get back to land, I want to check you over myself."

"Deal." Wes pulled the thermal blanket they'd placed over her more tightly around her shoulders. "Go get out of that suit."

Evyn grinned weakly. "No argument."

Wes waited until Evyn disappeared down the hatch before saying to Gary, "Make sure she gets something hot into her. She expended a lot of energy out there."

Gary handed her a steaming thermos. "Tea. I'll get hers next."

"Thanks." Wes sipped the blessedly hot liquid and closed her eyes. The mission had very nearly been derailed by the accident, and when they wrote up the report, they'd have to explain exactly how that had happened—and who, if anyone, was responsible.

❖

"Showers are down the hall on the right," Cord said as the group hurried into the rescue station. She waved Jeff and Gary on and turned to Evyn and Wes. "The first order of business is for the two of you to get warmed up."

"Go ahead," Evyn said to Wes. "You feel steady enough?"

"Yes, I'm fine. Some heat and dry clothes and I'll be good to go. You need to hit the showers too, Agent Daniels."

"Gary went to get our gear from the car—I'll get it and be there in a second."

"All right. Thanks." Wes left quickly and Evyn squelched the urge to follow immediately.

The distance in Wes's voice was nearly as chilling as the water had been. Evyn couldn't tell if Wes's aloof reserve hid anger, pain, or criticism, but the wintery expression in Wes's eyes left her feeling abandoned. The stab of loneliness was as frightening as it was unexpected.

"You okay?" Cord said softly.

"What?" Evyn focused on Cord, read her concern. "Yeah. You weren't kidding about riptides. Freaking strong, and freaking cold."

"The weather's changing fast. We're in for a blow. Maritime reports say we're looking at snow up and down the coast."

"The water sure felt like it dropped twenty degrees."

"In some parts of the current, it probably had—cold water pulled up to the surface by changes in the wind and air pressure." Cord grimaced. "I'm really sorry I didn't call off the exercise earlier."

"Couldn't be anticipated—or helped," Evyn said, listening for the distant sound of the shower running. She really wanted to go back and check on Wes. She wasn't convinced Wes was as steady as she claimed. When she'd finally located her, the powerful current had been pulling Wes hard and fast out to sea. Wes had been spinning, sinking, and she hadn't been struggling. For a sickening, heart-stopping second, she'd thought she was too late. She couldn't remember ever being so terrified.

"You want me to get your gear?" Cord asked. "You're shivering."

"No." Evyn ignored the chill spreading along her bones. "As soon as I check with Gary, I'll shower."

Cord nodded. "I'll be in my office."

"Thanks, Cord." Evyn turned away, pretending she hadn't seen the questions, or the concern, in Cord's eyes. They'd gotten to be friends over the years since she'd first met Cord during her water-rescue certification. Back then, there'd been a tiny spark of interest, but time and distance had made friendship more feasible, and she was glad to have avoided the awkwardness that would have cropped up when they had to work together. Besides, a friendship with no complications was worth a lot more than a hot and heavy—and short-lived—affair. That's exactly what she should be looking for with Wes—a sound professional friendship, but she couldn't seem to get her head around that. When she'd seen Wes disappear into the water, the only thing she'd thought about was getting her to safety. She hadn't thought about the mission or protocol or the fact that they were in the middle of an exercise to rescue the president. None of that had mattered, and that was a big problem.

As if reading her thoughts, Gary walked up, set two gear bags beside her, and said, "Stop beating yourself up. What happened out there was an accident. You okay?"

"I'm okay." Evyn leaned against the wall inside the entrance to the rescue station. "Listen, you should get out of here if you're going to catch the flight home."

"What about you?"

"I'm going to be here a while. I need to check Wes over, and she needs to at least get some sleep before she flies. I'll rebook us on a flight out in the morning."

"You want me to stay?"

"You don't need to. Your wife will be happy if you make it home tonight, and you'll score with her for the next time you *can't* get home."

Gary smiled. "Damn sensitive of you...and I appreciate it." He paused. "You did right out there, Evyn—start to finish. Stop second-guessing yourself."

She shook her head. "I don't know, Gary. I wasn't thinking about anything at all—I just reacted. If I'd waited just a minute, she might have come right back up to the surface, Cord would've thrown her a lifeline, and we could've hauled her in. Then you and I could have gotten the president into the chopper, just the way it reads in the rulebook. Instead, I went over the side without a thought to POTUS."

"Jesus, Evyn, it was a training exercise and we had a team member overboard. I would've gone after her myself if you hadn't already done it."

"Would you? That's not the protocol and you know it. Our responsibility is first to the president, and then to the team. We took Wes through the same scenario with the shooting sim, expecting her to leave wounded agents on the ground."

"Oh, come on." Gary snorted. "Sure, there was an element of uncertainty during that sim, but she knew somewhere in her mind those agents weren't really in danger of bleeding to death. That makes it a whole lot easier than having someone get pulled into a riptide."

"Maybe," Evyn said, appreciating his efforts to make her feel better but not buying the excuse. She'd broken protocol—instinctively and against all her training.

"I'm telling you," Gary said, "I would've done exactly what you did."

"I didn't do it consciously, Gary. I didn't even register we were in the middle of a training exercise. My instincts are supposed to be different than that."

"You know what—we can hash this all out when we debrief. Right now you're standing there blue as a Smurf, shivering all over. You need to get in the shower. You can beat yourself up back in DC tomorrow."

"Look, I'm sorry," Evyn said. Taking her anger at herself out on Gary wasn't fair. Not his fault she'd abandoned her training—it was

Wes's. Every time Wes Masters figured into anything, she totally went off the rails.

"Forget it—it's been a hell of a day." Gary thumped her shoulder. "Go shower, will you?"

"Yeah." Evyn grabbed her go bag and Wes's, and pushed off the wall. "You better get started for the airport or you're not going to make it. Storm coming."

"You sure?"

"Yeah, I'll get us checked into a hotel, call Tom, and bring him up to speed."

"Okay. But I want to see you when you get back to DC before we debrief on this mission."

"Why?"

"So I can make sure you don't fall on your sword when it's not necessary."

Evyn laughed. "Deal."

She waved Gary toward the door and headed down the hall. She wouldn't fall on her sword, but she needed to get herself back on track. She needed to do the job and forget about Wes going into the water, forget about the panic that had hit her hard and filled her with terror when she thought she'd lost her.

❖

The locker room was unisex and small—a ten-by-ten-foot room with three narrow gray lockers against one wall, a few open shelves for gear and supplies above a bench opposite the lockers, a tiny closet with a toilet in the corner, and another slightly bigger closet with a doorless wooden shower stall. The water was still running in the shower when Evyn walked in, and the single horizontal foot-high window above the lockers was frosted with steam. She shed the canvas pants and hooded sweatshirt she'd pulled on out on the patrol boat, dropped them next to the bench, and grabbed a couple of white terry cloth towels from the shelf. By the thinness of the material, they'd been washed a lot of times, but they were clean and dry, and that was all she needed. The shower in the other room turned off.

"Need a towel?" she called.

"I got one, thanks," Wes called back.

Evyn wrapped a towel around her torso and waited for Wes to leave the shower. The already small room shrank further when Wes walked in, her wheat-gold hair bronzed by the water, hugging her scalp and fingering along her neck. Sparkling droplets beaded on her chest and rained in thin rivulets over the muscles of her upper abdomen. Her skin was goose bumped.

Evyn unfolded a towel and held it out. "You're cold. Cover your shoulders. You've got a pretty good bruise going there."

"Thanks. Looks worse than it feels." Wes rubbed her hair and draped the towel around her neck. "There's still plenty of hot water."

"Good, I'm ready for it. Your bag is over there." Evyn gestured to the bags she'd left at the end of the row of lockers. "I'll be out in a second."

She edged past Wes, a foot of space between them. Despite the lingering cold that had taken up permanent residence in her bones, she was anything but numb. Being close to Wes charged her muscles and flooded her blood with heat and expectation. She tugged off the towel, draped it over the side of the shower stall, and stepped inside, twisting the hot tap all the way open. She added a little cold but kept the water as close to steaming as she could stand, immersing her head, turning her face into the spray, desperately hoping to purge the image of Wes's body outlined by the thin cotton towel. Strong shoulders, sculpted arms, the swell of firm breasts, the stretch of abdomen and slight flare of thighs. She shuddered and braced her arms against the smooth tile wall. She let her head hang down while the heat beat against her neck and shoulders. She stayed there until the water started to cool and then twisted the taps closed. Briskly, she toweled her hair dry, finger-combed it, and wrapped the last dry towel around her chest. She strode back into the locker room, not looking in Wes's direction, and quickly pulled on dry jeans and a long-sleeved T-shirt. After donning thick wool socks and kicking into her boots, she turned to Wes, who had stretched out on the bench with an arm over her eyes. She might have been asleep.

Evyn smiled to herself. Wes was like every other first responder she'd ever known—able to sleep anywhere, anytime, under any conditions. She eased her emergency kit out of her go bag and crouched next to the bench. "You asleep?"

"No," Wes said quietly. "Just enjoying being warm."

"I know what you mean." Evyn pulled out a blood-pressure cuff and a stethoscope. "I want to check your BP."

Wes moved to unbutton her cuff, and Evyn brushed her hand aside. "I've got it."

She unbuttoned Wes's cuff and folded the sleeve up to her mid-upper arm. Wes's skin was lightly tanned, soft and smooth, the muscles beneath firm and finely etched. She didn't look at Wes's face as she wrapped the blood-pressure cuff around her biceps and checked her pressure. "Ninety over sixty. Is that usual for you?"

"A little low," Wes said, "but nothing worrisome."

"Uh-huh." Evyn wasn't about to argue, but she wasn't going to let Wes self-diagnose, either. She checked her pulse. Sixty, slow and steady, full and strong. Wes didn't just look to be in good shape, she was. "Do you run?"

"I row."

"It shows." Evyn pulled out a digital thermometer. "Put this under your tongue."

Wes moved her arm from over her eyes and turned her head to look at Evyn. Her eyebrows rose slightly as she eyed the thermometer. "I'm okay."

Fatigue shadowed her eyes, darkening the green to nearly black. Her lips were pale. She looked exhausted.

"Your vital signs are good, but you need fuel and rest." Evyn wagged the thermometer. "Under your tongue."

Wes grinned wryly and opened her mouth.

Evyn slid the thermometer in, and Wes slowly closed her lips around it. Her eyes held Evyn's, and Evyn felt heat rush to her face. Her thighs suddenly trembled, and she dropped onto her knees to steady herself. Hell, she couldn't even do something as simple as take Wes's temperature without starting to lose it. Well. She might be able to keep her cool if she didn't look at Wes's mouth and imagine those moist, sensuous lips closing around her. Wes put every one of her fantasies to shame—and scared the hell out of her. She swallowed hard and wondered if Wes could hear the tightness in her throat. Her heart nearly froze when Wes's hand moved toward her face.

Evyn stilled, feeling a little bit like a rabbit paralyzed at the sight of a predator drawing near. Wes's fingers grazed her cheek, slid down to her neck, and Evyn's breath caught in her throat.

"You've got a bruise," Wes murmured.

Evyn slipped the thermometer from between Wes's lips and pretended to stare at it. "Ninety-six. You're too cold."

"And your pulse is racing." Wes's fingertips rested over Evyn's carotid. "I bet if we took *your* blood pressure, it would be all over the place. You need some rest too, Agent Daniels."

Evyn wanted to move away from Wes's touch. And she wanted more of it. She wanted the fire streaming from Wes's fingertips to scorch through her, burning away fear and uncertainty and caution. She wanted to explode. Her stomach trembled. She licked her suddenly dry lips and eased away. "We both need a meal. Sit up, I want to check your pressure while you're upright. I'm not letting you walk out of here and have you fall down halfway to the vehicle."

"I appreciate your concern," Wes said quietly, "but I'm not a squid, you know."

Evyn laughed. "I know. But I bet it's been a long time since you've had that kind of dunking."

Sighing, Wes pushed upright. "True." She closed her eyes. "And I do have a little orthostatic hypotension."

Instantly, Evyn forgot about everything except making sure Wes was stable. She took her pressure again. "Seventy over fifty. You're a little dizzy, aren't you?"

"Just a little."

"Okay." Evyn rose briskly. "We're spending the night in Kitty Hawk. You're going to get some hot food into you and twelve hours' sleep."

Wes frowned. "I can sleep in DC. The trip back isn't that long."

"Sorry, I'm not taking a chance on you decompensating on an airplane. Food, sleep, home tomorrow."

"Should I ask who left you in charge?"

Wes sounded grumpy, which only proved she wasn't at the top of her game. Evyn had never seen her disgruntled by anything.

"I'm only in charge by default, Captain," Evyn said softly. "I set up that exercise. It's my fault you went in today. I'm going to see you make it home, safe and sound."

"That's bullshit. The cable snapped. It was an accident."

"It could've been worse." Evyn shuddered inwardly. Wes had been on her way down when she'd reached her. She couldn't even think about that without feeling as if pieces of her were going to tear apart and shatter like glass on the rocks. "No matter what you think, I need to take care of you right now."

Wes drew a sharp breath. "I'm not sure how good I'll be at that— being the patient, I mean."

"Not used to being taken care of?"

"Not really, no."

"No one special?" The silence stretched and Evyn waited for the shutters to close again. But Wes just searched her eyes, and Evyn was too tired and worried to hide whatever might show.

"No, no one."

"Then I guess I'm it tonight," Evyn said, trying for lightness.

"It might take some getting used to," Wes said softly. "I might not be any good at it."

"I doubt there's anything you aren't good at." Evyn packed her gear and bagged their wet clothes. She held out her hand to Wes. "Let's start practicing and see how you do."

Wes rose slowly from the bench, wavering ever so slightly. Evyn slid her arm around Wes's waist. "Okay?"

"Don't quite have my land legs yet." Wes let out an exasperated sigh and draped her arm over Evyn's shoulders. "Just give me a minute."

"Take all the time you need. We're not on a schedule tonight."

Wes's hand curved around Evyn's shoulder, the pressure of her fingers shooting tendrils of excitement through Evyn's chest. Her heart hammered and her legs quivered. She braced her muscles, hoping Wes couldn't feel her tremble. She planned on taking care of Wes and nothing more.

"Ready to get out of here?" Evyn asked.

"More than ready." Wes dropped her arm and stepped away. "I think I can make it on my own."

Evyn missed the contact instantly and said casually, "Never doubted it. Let's go find a room for the night."

Wes laughed softly. "More practice?"

"Uh…hell. You think maybe you could cut me some slack? My brain is a little numb here."

"Well, let's go get you warmed up."

Wes reached for the door and pushed it open, and Evyn wondered how the tables had been so neatly turned.

CHAPTER NINETEEN

The neon sign announcing the Bayside Motel blinked erratically, illuminating the L-shaped motor court in flashes of holiday red and green. A mud-spattered black Ford pickup truck and a low-slung eighties Cadillac convertible with big patches of rust-colored primer on the fenders were the only vehicles in the gravel lot. A light burned in the room closest to the road. A hand-painted sign propped in the streaked window proclaimed "Office."

"Looks like a hot-sheet motel," Wes said, laughing softly.

"Cord swears this place is clean and makes decent coffee," Evyn said.

"That's all we need, then." Wes didn't care where they bunked—she'd slept in worse places, including a tent in the Afghan mountains. Compared to that, this rated five stars.

Evyn pulled the rented Jeep into the lot just as the sun went down and the wind came up. "I'll run in and register."

When Evyn pushed open the door, the wind clattering through the branches of the red oaks surrounding the motel filled the Jeep with a sound like machine-gun fire. Wes jerked and her stomach lurched. She had been posted to a field hospital close enough to the front to hear the firefights ranging in the hills at night, her tent a poor shield against stray rounds. She'd rarely slept deeply, her body always primed to duck and cover. Even now, eighteen months later, she instinctively looked for cover when a car backfired or a door slammed. She hadn't been this jittery since she'd returned stateside. The afternoon's brief unscheduled swim shouldn't have thrown her equilibrium off so much—maybe her agitation was due to the lingering chill the steaming shower hadn't dispersed.

Leaning out the open door, Evyn peered up at the sky. "Cord said we might get snow, and I think it's arrived—blowing in fast. You should stay in the car until I get back. The last thing you need is to get wet again."

Wes reached across the seat and grabbed Evyn's sleeve, stopping her from climbing out. "You need to stay dry too." She handed her North Face jacket to Evyn, who had left the rescue station wearing only jeans and her T-shirt. "This has got a hood. Go ahead, take it."

"You sure?"

"The heater's blasting in here. I'm plenty warm. Plenty hungry too."

Evyn grinned. "Excellent prognostic sign. What do you think about pizza? There's a place across the street, and I doubt we'll get anything delivered out here tonight if a storm is coming."

"Sounds great. Since I already know you're not a vegetarian, I'll take pepperoni."

"Perfect. Mushrooms?"

"And black olives."

Evyn nodded approvingly. "Nailed it."

Wes laughed. "How about beer?"

"Sam Adams if I can't get any kind of microbrew?"

"You nailed it."

Laughing, Evyn jumped out, shrugged into Wes's jacket, and flipped up the hood. She slammed the door, shoved her hands in her pockets, and ran through the icy mix of rain and snow, her form briefly outlined by the headlights before she disappeared into the dark. Wes watched a few seconds longer, a strange foreboding churning inside as soon as Evyn vanished from sight. She clasped her hands and put them between her knees. She wasn't cold, but her fingers were icy. She wondered if that was her imagination. The temperature had fallen rapidly in the face of the approaching storm, but she was used to cold weather. She shivered and peered into the near-empty lot, a creeping unease making her twitch.

Evyn had left the headlights on, and the halos from the slanting beams seemed to be keeping the circle of darkness at bay. She'd never been afraid of the dark and didn't get spooked by unknown terrain. She was a naval officer and an emergency physician—she was trained to handle imminent danger. The headlights dimmed and the darkness drew closer. Her breath came a little faster and a heaviness pervaded her chest.

She closed her eyes and she was upside down again, swirling in an endless void that sucked her down into cold, dark silence. Gasping, she shot up straight and opened her eyes. Outside her fogged window, the snow fell thicker, a white blanket screening the world from view. She couldn't see the motel. She couldn't see where Evyn had gone. Evyn. Evyn was solid and real and warm. She fought the urge to get out of the car and look for her.

"Okay," Wes whispered aloud, "you know what this is. Fatigue, residual hypothermic confusion, delayed stress reaction. You're entitled to all of it—for an hour or so."

Cataloging her symptoms helped relieve the pressure in her chest some. She took a deep breath, heard the faint wheeze of constricted bronchioles. Evyn was right, she wasn't fit to fly. She needed to replenish the fuel she'd burned off while struggling against the killer current. She needed to sleep. Evyn had to be in nearly the same shape—she'd been in the water almost as long. And she'd fought the current for both of them.

The car door opened and Wes jumped. Evyn dropped into the seat beside her.

"Okay," Evyn said, wiping traces of melting snow from her cheeks with one hand. "I called over for pizza and they said it would be ready in fifteen. We can get settled and I'll run over and get it."

"Maybe we should forget that," Wes said, her voice sounding hoarse and foreign.

Evyn backed the Jeep out of the slot and headed farther into the lot. The long, low motel came into view again as she coasted forward. "Why? I thought you were hungry?"

Wes swiped at her forehead. She wasn't hot, but she was sweating. She wasn't cold, but she was shivering. "Sorry. I—"

"What's going on?" Evyn stopped in front of a green metal door just barely visible through the falling flakes. A cockeyed 12 made from white stick-on, glow-in-the-dark numbers identified the room.

She downshifted into neutral and pulled the parking brake, leaving the lights on. "You okay?"

"Yes—sorry. Just jumpy. Sorry."

Evyn rested her palm on the back of Wes's neck. Her fingers were hot as banked coals. "Nothing unusual. You had a hell of a shock earlier."

"So did you. You need to stay warm and eat and—"

"Hey," Evyn said. "That's all in the plan, Doc. You can relax. Really."

"I know. You're right. I'll be fine." Wes closed her eyes and let her head fall back into the secure cradle of Evyn's hand. Evyn's fingers glided up and down the muscles on either side of her spine, easing the tension, sending warmth through her. She sighed. "I don't think the weather is going to get any better. We ought to make a run for it."

"Let me get the door open and you get inside—keep dry," Evyn murmured, continuing the gentle massage. "I'll bring in our gear."

"I appreciate it, but I can help carry our stuff."

"This is the part where you practice letting me take care of you."

A tingle of unease skittered down Wes's spine—she'd been looking after her own needs most of her life, and her need for Evyn's touch, her presence, made her feel exposed and vulnerable. She didn't want Evyn's attention just because Evyn felt guilty. "None of this is your fault."

Evyn frowned. "I suck at connect-the-dots, and I'm missing this picture."

"You don't have to look after me because you feel responsible."

"Wow. Okay." Evyn's hand fell away. "I'll just let you fend for yourself, then—and when you finally do collapse—"

Beneath the edge of anger in Evyn's voice, Wes heard hurt. She didn't want to hurt her. She didn't want the cold distance between them that had nothing to do with the storm or the dark either. "So maybe that came out a little wrong. I guess I suck at the being taken care of thing. I had two little sisters who couldn't even remember our dad. Things were harder for them, and my mother had only so much energy to spread around between the four of us."

"Okay." Evyn's shoulders relaxed and the tightness around her mouth softened. The red highlights in her hair gleamed against the glow of snow cocooning them, an ethereal image that imprinted on Wes's brain. She was beautiful—not model perfect but strong and bold.

Wes wanted to erase the last vestiges of wariness in Evyn's gaze. She wanted to trace the line of her jaw, but instead she grazed her fingertips over the back of Evyn's hand where it rested on Evyn's knee. "Can we try that again?"

A moment passed and Wes held her breath. Evyn's hand turned over and their fingers entwined.

"How about we get you settled and I'll go for pizza?" Evyn asked.

The heavy weight crushing Wes's chest dissolved. Evyn's hand was warm and solid. She tightened her hold. "I'd like that."

❖

The day shift had all left hours ago, and the corridor outside the Level 4 isolation lab was deserted. Her footsteps fell soundlessly on the white tile floor as she made her way to the airlock at the end of the hall. She pressed her palm on the identification plate and leaned down for the retinal scan. The light above the passage flashed from red to green, and the hydraulic door slid open with a faint whoosh. She stepped into the UV chamber, the outer door behind her closed, and she slipped on a pair of protective glasses. When she input her entry code on the wall panel, a hum accompanied the pulse of UV, and the next door in the chain opened. She deposited her protective glasses on the shelf and passed into the inner isolation room, where she methodically went through the routine of testing her positive pressure protective suit— sealing the cuffs at ankles and wrists, zipping the neck, and attaching the air hose to the one-way valve in the center of the back. She twisted the dial and compressed air flowed in. The pressure on the wall gauge held steady at 1 atm. No leaks. She closed the inflow valve and opened the vents along the neck. Air hissed out. She was ready to go to work.

Removing her shoes, she carefully stepped into the bright yellow suit and, after closing the seals, pulled on the calf-high impervious rubber boots. She wore no jewelry to work, not even a watch. She'd only have to remove it—she couldn't risk any snag or tear that might violate the PPPS. Even a microscopic rent in the isolation suit could allow a contagion to enter, where it might be absorbed by her skin or inhaled into her respiratory system. The biological agents they worked with inside the BSL-4 lab were either highly transmissible or uniformly fatal or both. The suit was her only shield.

Once the suit was secure, she covered the fluid-resistant boots with disposable booties, fit the head shield into place, and pulled on her gloves. She wasn't concerned for her safety. She was always prepared for any emergency. Caution was a way of life for her, and she'd been trained since birth to be composed under extreme circumstances.

With a bulky gloved finger, she pressed the entrance code, and the chamber pressurized. The inner door opened and she stepped into the lab. She nodded to a colleague working at a nearby station, sequencing a variant of Ebola. After connecting an overhead airline to the suit's port, she made her way down the aisle, the line following behind her like a colorful yellow umbilicus. She'd volunteered for the night shift six months previously, establishing her routine, arriving a little early, leaving a little later. Her colleagues appreciated her diligence and her willingness to take the graveyard shift for longer than the usual mandatory rotations. At her station, she booted up her computer and retrieved the samples she planned to run on the gel plates that night, along with a second rack of tubes. Over the past six months she'd been carefully siphoning off micro-aliquots of avian flu stock, too tiny to be noticed by anyone else, until she had a single test tube half-full of one of the most virulent synthetic contagions ever produced.

When she left at the end of her shift, she'd slide the tube into a fold in her suit beneath her arm and secure it in place with a strip of the special adhesive they kept for emergency repairs if one of the suits should be accidentally torn. Like a tire patch, the instantly self-sealing adhesive would provide enough protection until the lab worker could get to the decontamination chamber. Tonight, the lifesaving material would allow her to secrete out a virus capable of killing thousands. She wasn't really interested in the deaths of thousands, however, only one.

President Andrew Powell stood for everything she despised—a spokesman for the rich, a defender of the privileged, a champion of those without morals or values. Her father had taught her and her brothers and sisters the right path, raising them to be survivors. He'd encouraged them to excel, schooling them at the camp with the children of other survivalists, setting them on the path to positions where they could someday make a difference. She'd always known she had a mission, and now she was going to fulfill it. She would help him make his message heard—America for Americans—and now that a leader had emerged, they would have a president who would speak for the righteous. She would help make that possible.

The digital clocks at the far end of the room simultaneously projected the time and date in New York City, Washington DC, Los Angeles, Hong Kong, Sydney, New Delhi, Berlin, London. Seven p.m. in Atlanta. Twelve more hours and the first stage of her mission would be complete. Soon the reclaiming of America would begin.

CHAPTER TWENTY

Evyn handed Wes the last slice of pizza. "You finish it."
"I'm stuffed." Wes sat on the bed with her back propped against the wall. Some of the shadows around her eyes had faded, but her cheeks were still hollow, and her fingers trembled slightly as she reached for a napkin.

"You need the carbs—eat." She hated seeing Wes hurt. Wes didn't complain—she wouldn't, and her attempt to feign normalcy only made Evyn want to punch something. She had to do something, even something mindless, or she'd do something they'd both regret. She stacked the remains of their meal—crumpled paper napkins, a couple of paper plates, the pizza box. "I'll take the empty box to the trash. The pizza was great, but I'd rather not smell the aftermath all night."

The room was generous by motel standards—two slightly larger than single beds separated by a two-drawer nightstand with a peeling brown lacquer finish. A goosenecked reading light, dusty shade askew, sat on the water-stained top. The bathroom had been carved out of the closet area—a small toilet jammed in next to the sink, a two-and-a-half square foot shower stall, and a solitary overhead light. The closet held a few bent wire hangers and nothing else. Neither she nor Wes had taken anything from their go bags other than toiletries.

"Need a hand?" Wes asked.

"I got it," Evyn said, not looking at Wes. She'd sat on the far end of the bed during their takeout dinner, a meal she'd shared a hundred times in a hundred nondescript rooms just like this one. She'd never been as grateful for the pizza box sitting open between them as she had been tonight, though—every time she looked at Wes and remembered the way she had looked slowly spinning deeper underwater, she wanted to touch her. Just to assure herself Wes was warm and safe.

She gathered the trash and stood. "Need anything?"

"Nope. I'm going to grab another shower."

"Still cold?"

Wes grinned wryly. "I'm not really sure. Feels that way, but it might just be my imagination."

Evyn checked the thermostat on the wall above the dresser, a vintage fifties maple affair with wooden knobs on the drawers and a rickety mirror. Seventy degrees. The room was toasty. Wes still wasn't fully recovered. "Take your time—use all the hot water if you need to. I'm good."

"Okay." Wes rose, glanced at the door. A frisson of anxiety shot along her nerve endings. She'd never minded being alone, but she didn't want Evyn to walk out that door. She'd paced the room during the ten minutes Evyn had been gone getting the pizza and hadn't been able to relax until Evyn appeared again, a spark of triumph in her eyes as she'd held the pizza box aloft like a trophy. She'd looked vibrant and vital and sexy. Wes clamped down on the surge of heat that tingled down her thighs. "So I'll see you in a few minutes."

"Right." Evyn reached behind her and fumbled for the doorknob, her gaze locked on Wes. "I'll be here."

Wes broke eye contact first and disappeared into the bathroom. A second later the water came on in the shower. Evyn imagined Wes sliding out of her clothes and stepping naked into the heat. She'd seen enough of Wes's body through that thin, damp white towel back in the locker room to have a pretty good idea of exactly what Wes would look like naked. Ordinarily she didn't have any problem populating her fantasies with women she knew, but she chased the enticing image of Wes's body from her mind. She didn't want to fantasize about her. What she wanted to do was kiss her. She almost had—would have, just then, if they'd been any closer. She had quite a lot of practice reading women's eyes, and she'd read desire in Wes's. All the same, she hadn't had such a bad idea in longer than she could remember. Sleeping with Louise when she hadn't been one hundred percent present didn't hold a candle to the insanity of kissing Wes.

Wes had had a serious shock just a few hours ago—had almost

drowned. She was vulnerable. Physically depleted. Battered and bruised. By her own admission, not really on top of her game. She didn't need Evyn coming on to her—she needed a solid night's sleep and probably a talk with someone about what had happened. Evyn wasn't one of those agents who found psych support to be intrusive or threatening. Her older sister was a psychologist and one of the best listeners she'd ever met. She'd learned when she was struggling with the kinds of identity issues all adolescents face that talking with her sister helped. And when she'd told Chris she was a lesbian, her sister had been cool. Hell, she talked to Gary when things got really hairy—when the stress and the insane schedules and the lack of a personal life started to make her crazy. She wanted Wes to get any help she needed—and making a move on her did not qualify as helping.

Evyn pulled on Wes's jacket, not so much because she wanted to keep dry in the still-falling snow but because she liked wearing it. An unusual intimacy for her—wearing someone else's clothes. Silly, but no one needed to know. The jacket was a little big. Wes's shoulders were a little wider, her arms a little longer, but she wasn't so much bigger their bodies wouldn't fit together seamlessly. Wes's breasts were just the right size for their torsos to meld perfectly, Wes's thighs just long and tight enough to wrap around hers with no space between them. The fist of want in her belly tightened, and she dashed outside, welcoming the blast of cold wind and icy snow. The storm had picked up. Two inches of wet powder covered the parking lot. No cars passed on the two-lane. The road remained unplowed.

After tossing the detritus into the open maw of the dented blue Dumpster tucked behind the end of the building, she ran back along the row of darkened rooms. She stamped her feet to clear the snow from her boots and jumped inside their room, shutting the cold night outside.

Wes stood in the middle of the room with a towel cinched above her breasts, leaving her upper chest, sculpted shoulders, and a lot of thigh exposed. A sliver of light slanted through the partially open bathroom door behind her, highlighting her strong curves and sinewy planes. The red-green glow of the motel sign flickered through the open slats on the blinds hanging on the single window beside the door, leaving Wes's face mostly in shadow. Evyn flashed again on the picture of Wes wrapped around her, nothing between them. Her skin tingled and heat flooded her core.

"Better?" Evyn backpedaled until her ass hit the wall. She couldn't read much in Wes's face, but she bet hers was easy to decipher. She'd had more control when she was fifteen than she did now.

"Yes," Wes said. "How is it outside?"

"Snowing pretty heavy." Evyn couldn't move. Couldn't take her eyes from Wes's face.

"Your hair is wet." Wes took a step closer, ran her fingers through the hair at Evyn's temples. "You should've put the hood up."

Evyn laughed shakily and rubbed her hair with a hand. "I thought I could outrun the snowflakes."

Wes laughed. "Why does that not surprise me? Do all federal agents think they're capable of superhuman feats?"

"Only the ones who are, like me." Evyn grinned, watching the smile reach Wes's eyes. She loved making her smile. Still, she looked strained, as if she'd been pulling doubles for a week. "How are you really feeling?"

Wes shrugged. "Like I had a really long day. Nothing some sleep won't cure. I'm not that out of practice working twenty-four on—I still cover the ER pretty regularly."

"Yeah, but you aren't usually physically accosted in the ER."

"I wasn't today either," Wes said gently. "I took a header off the boat—none too proud of that actually. I should have ducked. I saw it coming."

"For how long—a second?" Evyn shook her head. "You never had a chance."

"And neither did you." Wes brushed a loose curl away from the corner of Evyn's mouth. "You must have hit the water pretty hard to bruise your face."

"You hit a lot harder." A pulse beat rapidly in Wes's throat, matching the crazy rhythm of Evyn's heart. Evyn started to sweat. Wes was inches away. She wanted to touch her. "You should get dressed before you get chilled again."

"You should get undressed before you end up the same way." Wes reached out and unzipped the windbreaker. "I left a little hot water. You need it?"

"I'm good," Evyn said, never having made a less true statement in her life. She didn't know what she was, but it wasn't good. Turned on, desperate to ease the shadows Wes couldn't quite hide, aching to hold her. "Wes, I—"

"I want to get one thing clear," Wes said.

Evyn drew up short. Here it came. The no-fraternization-at-work speech. Her own rule, the one she should have been remembering, and the one she forgot every time Wes was within a mile of her. "You don't need to say anything. I agree with you."

Wes's eyebrows shot up. The corner of her mouth lifted. "Do you? I didn't realize you were psychic as well as superhuman."

"Another big bad federal agent skill," Evyn said as nonchalantly as she could manage. "Always a bad idea to complicate a working relationship. No need to go there."

"You're right, we do agree." Wes's tone was soft and serious, but her eyes were partly amused. "Although I was going to say that what happened out there this afternoon was an accident. No one could have predicted it. No matter who set up the exercise, no one was at fault for that cable snapping and me going overboard."

A hot surge of embarrassment flooded Evyn's belly. Hell, she couldn't have been more wrong about what Wes had intended to say, and now she'd tipped her hand and probably made a fool of herself. "I won't argue. Obviously I can't win."

"It's not about winning." Wes stroked the backs of her fingers over Evyn's cheek, just beneath the bruise. "How about just believing it?"

Wes's mouth was so close, all Evyn could do was watch her lips move and struggle to make sense of what she was saying. Her mind heard the words but her body translated them into something else. Want, desire, an unfamiliar need. "Wes. I'm a little off balance here."

"I know." Wes's voice was barely above a whisper. "So am I."

Evyn went completely still.

"You saved my life today and I'm grateful. I know you were doing your job, and I would've done the same." Wes watched the muscles along Evyn's jaw tighten. Evyn didn't like being thanked for doing what came naturally—and for what she saw as her responsibility. Wes got that—she felt the same. But she was grateful—not for being saved from drowning, but for a warm sure hand in the cold dark night, anchoring her when she'd thought she might lose her way. For the silent assurance that she would conquer her demons and come out the other side of the tunnel whole. Evyn had faith in her—and had offered her a shoulder when she'd needed to lean without once making her feel weak. She was much more than grateful—she was soothed in a place she'd never known she was hurt. "And just so you know, this isn't about that."

"What?" Evyn's eyes were huge blue lakes filled with questions.

Wes had only one answer. She leaned forward and kissed her.

CHAPTER TWENTY-ONE

Evyn didn't know what to do with her hands. Wes had just kissed her, and now Wes was inches away, covered in nothing but a towel. She could easily pluck the cotton aside and pull Wes's hot naked body in tight against her. With a little subtle dip and turn, she'd have Wes against the door and she'd be back in control again. She'd made that move a time or two—Seduction 101.

She didn't do anything, not even breathe. She just stood there with their lips softly touching, her head whirling, her heart threatening to explode inside her rib cage. Whatever this was, she didn't want to change a thing. She'd been kissed before, but this wasn't like any kiss she'd ever experienced. She knew about kisses—she was usually the one doing the kissing. Sometimes kisses were an exploration, feelers sent out to judge the wind direction, the water temperature, the chances for more than just a kiss. Sometimes they were a warm-up for the real contest—a stretch of muscles, a quick glance around the field, a mental review of the game plan. A kiss was never just a kiss but always a step toward something more. A brief stop on the way to the ultimate goal. Everything in her life was a goal to be achieved, a game to be won—even sex. Always, she needed to be the best. She took the lead whenever she could; she was a front-runner. The fastest way to come out on top was to always *be* on top—metaphorically or otherwise.

Tonight, she was totally without game. She couldn't see the playing field through a fog of desire more heady than any she'd ever experienced. She'd given up the lead without even knowing she had entered the race. Wes was in total control, something she'd never allowed since she was old enough to get around on her own two feet. In her home, in her world, competition was king. Everything from dinner-table conversation to backyard catch was a challenge. She'd been team captain on just about every sport she'd ever played, was at the top of every class, and only took orders on the job because she knew it was the quickest way to achieve a position to give the orders herself. Whatever game she played, she played to win. And here she was, following, without a plan, with no freaking idea what she was doing.

Wes's mouth moved away and she wanted to whimper. Hell, she *did* whimper.

"Now would be a good time to breathe," Wes murmured, her lips skimming Evyn's as she spoke.

"I don't think I need to," Evyn whispered. "I think your kiss might be all that's required."

Wes laughed and kissed her again. A little bit firmer this time. More certain. Wes's confidence grew and Evyn lost her grip. Still their bodies remained separated. The few inches of air between them vibrated through Evyn's clothes and into the heart of her. Wes's lips were smooth and hot, lush and full. Evyn eased the tip of her tongue forward, seeking just a tiny taste. When she did, Wes moaned deep in her throat and Evyn's muscles turned to jelly. She sagged against the wall, a groan unlike any she'd ever made escaping her throat. Then Wes's hands were on her shoulders, pinning her in place.

"Is this all right?" Wes asked, her mouth on Evyn's throat.

"Oh yeah," Evyn said. "Really, really all right." She grasped Wes's waist, holding her lightly, careful not to disrupt the cotton-towel barrier between them. Wes would take it off if she wanted, and if she didn't...*I'll probably die.* Beneath her fingers, Wes's body was firm and strong, like her. Evyn ached to touch more. "But what exactly is this we're doing?"

"Had to do it," Wes muttered, kissing her way down Evyn's throat. She'd reached for Evyn thinking she knew what she would find— strength and understanding. She'd been right, but there was so much more. So much more than she'd ever dreamed. Evyn tasted like winter— sharp and tangy—and underneath the wild rush, a sweetness like the promise of spring. Evyn's pulse raced beneath Wes's mouth, vibrating with power, drawing her deeper into the mystery that was Evyn. She'd never in her life taken a step she hadn't planned, and rarely, even in the midst of an emergency, made a decision when she hadn't anticipated the outcome. Now she was flying blind. Evyn felt too good, sounded too beautiful to turn from while she analyzed, deduced, outlined, and planned. "Don't know what's happening, but I can't stop."

Evyn tilted her head back against the wall, giving herself to Wes's mouth. "Then don't. Please, don't."

"There's something you should know," Wes murmured, pushing the jacket down Evyn's arms. She got distracted by the warm, soft skin at the base of Evyn's throat and left the jacket tethering Evyn's wrists behind her. "I love the way you taste."

"Your mouth is so hot." Evyn rolled her head restlessly from side to side. "You make me burn."

Wes pulled at the jacket, got it off somehow, and pushed Evyn's T-shirt up her torso—searching for flesh. She slid her palm over Evyn's belly and gasped at the quick contraction of muscles beneath her fingers. She loved feeling Evyn's body respond to her touch. She traced the edge of Evyn's abdominals with her fingertips, over and over. Evyn bowed under her hand. So beautiful. "You might have to help me out."

"Doing fine so far," Evyn said thickly.

"I'm getting into unknown territory here." Wes lowered to her knees and kissed the strip of skin above Evyn's jeans. Hot, silky skin. She sucked lightly and eased both hands higher, grazing the undersides of Evyn's breasts. She'd touched thousands of bodies, but never like this. Never like this.

"God, Wes," Evyn gasped. "You make me feel so good."

"I want to touch you everywhere."

"Yes, yes."

Wes looked up. Evyn was watching her, her lids hooded, her eyes hazy. Her lips were slightly parted, a little swollen. Her breasts rose and fell rapidly. *She* had done this to her—she had stirred Evyn's body with her touch. A wave of awe and power rushed through her and her head went light. "I've never felt anything like this."

Evyn smiled crookedly. "Neither have I."

"I don't know what I'm doing."

Evyn's hands came into her hair. "Just keep doing it."

Wes rose and pulled the towel from her body. She dropped it on the floor and pressed full-length against Evyn. She kissed her again, deeper, seeking the heat she knew would warm her beyond the icy reach of the water and the terror of the dark and the years of solitude. She pulled back. "You make me warm."

Evyn laughed. "I want to make you hot."

"That too."

"I'd have a better chance if we were in bed."

"I've never done this before."

The blood rushed from Evyn's head and her stomach tightened. "Okay. Well. That's really scary, because you're really, really good. If it's all right with you, I'd like you to just keep doing exactly what you're doing."

"So would I."

Evyn took Wes's hand and tugged her toward the bed. "I want to touch you all over too. With my hands. With my mouth. Can I?"

"Yes. Please. Anything."

Evyn finally let herself look at Wes. At all of her. She'd been wrong, in her fantasy. Wes was far more beautiful than she'd imagined—her skin a tawny gold, her nipples small tan disks, every muscle sensuous and smooth. "You're gorgeous."

"Can we take your clothes off?"

"Oh yeah, I forgot that." Evyn met Wes's eyes. Now was the time for her to take back control, to lead as she always had. To pleasure from a safe distance. "Why don't you undress me." She held her breath and willed her legs to keep her upright.

"This isn't me," Wes murmured, opening the top button of Evyn's jeans. Her fingers trembled. Her hands never shook, not even when she was sliding an intravenous needle into the only remaining vein on some trauma victim, knowing if she missed, she'd lose him.

Evyn's fingers curled around Wes's wrists, gently stilling her. "Then maybe you should take a minute."

Wes looked up so Evyn could see what she knew must be in her eyes—wonder, desire, need. "I'm sorry, I said that wrong. This is more me than anything I've ever experienced—I've just never done anything without knowing what would happen next. I feel like I'm walking off a cliff."

"Let's fall together, then." Evyn threaded her fingers into Wes's hair and tugged her mouth close. The kiss was hot, urgent, hungry. "Oh yeah."

The need kindling in Wes's stomach burst into flame and she grabbed Evyn's shirt and pulled it up and off. "I want you under my hands."

Evyn moaned. She was as tremulous as a virgin, and her first time was so long ago she didn't remember—but she knew it'd never been like this. She'd never wanted so much to be taken, needed to give herself so completely. "Hurry."

"I don't want to," Wes muttered, her mouth against Evyn's chest. She kissed the slope of Evyn's breast, brushed her cheek over the tight peak of her nipple. Evyn moaned again and Wes shook inside. She took a nipple into her mouth and pushed down on Evyn's jeans.

Evyn's hands clenched in her hair. "That's so good. God, Wes, I need you to make me come."

Wes's heart leaped into her throat. She couldn't breathe around the swell of desire, and she didn't care. She'd live without air as long as she could taste Evyn. She shoved Evyn's jeans lower. "Off. Get these off."

Evyn braced her hands on Wes's shoulders and kicked her boots and pants aside. She pushed Wes back onto the bed. "More. I want your mouth on me more—everywhere. If I don't come soon my head is going to explode."

Wes stretched out on top of her, the first press of Evyn's body sending shock waves rocketing through her. She entwined her legs with Evyn's, felt the hot caress of skin against her clitoris. Leaning on her forearms, she gripped Evyn's wrists in her hands, holding Evyn beneath her. She stared into the bluest eyes she'd ever seen, fathomless and vulnerable. "You're so beautiful. I don't ever want to move."

"You better—God, you better." Evyn arched, her legs tightening around Wes's thigh. Evyn's wetness slicked Wes's skin. "I want to come, so close."

"Yes." Wes thrust, watching pleasure flow across Evyn's face. "We'll go slow the next time."

Evyn caught her lip between her teeth as she struggled not to come.

"Don't hold back," Wes murmured, pressing harder between Evyn's thighs, raking her teeth down Evyn's neck. "I need to feel you. I want to hear you. I need it. Please. Trust me."

Trust me. Wes asked for so much. Terrifying words. Evyn couldn't say no. Not now. She wrapped her arms around Wes's shoulders and pressed her breasts to Wes's chest. She brushed her mouth over Wes's ear. "Yes. Yes, please. I can't…I have to…"

"Now." Wes groaned at the pleasure flooding through her. "Now, please…With me."

Evyn cried out and buried her face in Wes's neck, losing herself for the first time ever.

When Evyn's fingers dug into her back, Wes let go. She stepped off the cliff not knowing where she would land, only knowing she had to let go or lose something more precious than safety. Soaring, tumbling, exploding, she pulled Evyn to her.

"Fall with me."

"Yes," Evyn cried. "Yes."

CHAPTER TWENTY-TWO

A t five a.m. Blair poured two cups of coffee from the urn the valet had wheeled into Lucinda's office in the West Wing. A minute later Lucinda walked in. Wordlessly, Lucinda hung her snow-dusted black wool coat on the coat tree just inside the door, draped her scarf over the collar so it hung down along the lapels, and placed one glove into each front pocket. She crossed to her desk and put her overstuffed briefcase on the floor beside her chair. In deference to the blizzard, she wore stylish brown boots beneath her chestnut pants instead of her usual low heels. The hems of her tailored pants were damp—she'd walked a ways in the snow.

Blair placed a coffee cup along with utensils and a small crystal bowl of sugar cubes in the center of the desk. Balancing her own cup and saucer—no mugs in sight—she turned one of the centuries-old stuffed chairs to face Lucinda, sat down, and took a sip of coffee. She closed her eyes for a moment of thanks. The White House kitchen made great coffee. She waited until Lucinda stirred in one sugar cube and took her first swallow. "Morning."

"When did you get in?" Lucinda set a teaspoon onto the napkin Blair had provided along with her morning coffee. "Airports are a mess, I hear."

"We caught the red-eye last night. Beat the front."

"Where are you staying?"

"Cameron's condo." Blair smiled. "I'd forgotten how much I like that place. We had some of our best fights there."

Lucinda leaned back, holding the bone china cup between the

fingertips of both hands as if the small fluted handle were too delicate to use. "I can imagine."

"Oh yeah? I never would have guessed."

Laughing, Lucinda shook her head. "So. What's on your mind?"

"You have to ask?"

"I can think of half a dozen things—but you might as well start with what's at the top of your list."

"Who do you think has betrayed my father?"

Lucinda nodded slowly, her gaze turning inward. "That's the question at the top of my list too, and I wish I had an answer for you. We don't know. We really don't."

"How bad is it?"

"We're not sure of that either—the whole picture is still coming together."

"Come on, Luce. Don't play press corps with me. You have to have some good ideas—this is the president's inner circle we're talking about."

"Believe me, I know."

Lucinda's tone was mild but her eyes flashed. She was pissed, all right. Someone—or probably any number of someones—had to have dropped the ball for something like this to even be possible. Blair said, "Okay—best guess, then."

"What we *do* know is domestic protests have escalated at every one of his public venues, and we've observed a greater presence of individuals from radical watch-list groups in the crowds. We don't publicize most of his calendar for exactly that reason—to limit his exposure to hostiles. That, combined with what we're picking up from online communications, suggests extremist factions are gaining advance intelligence."

"So he's the specific target? We're not talking about national security—we're talking about his personal security being threatened, is that it?"

"That's what we think, yes. I wish I could tell you more."

"Do you think there's going to be an assassination attempt?"

Lucinda set her cup down carefully, aware that the china was fragile enough to break if her grip was hard enough. She rested her hands on the desktop. "Probabilities are high—higher than we'd like. Yes."

Blair stood and set her coffee cup on the edge of Lucinda's desk. The icy blast of terror left her breathless. How could this happen—here, in the most advanced, sophisticated country in the world? How could they have let this happen? She paced to the wall of windows that looked out on the gardens. The carefully tended shrubs and bushes were nothing but shapeless mounds beneath snow. If she spoke now, she'd probably regret what she had to say later, and she'd learned long ago the only way to get information out of Lucinda was to keep a cool head. Lucinda was so good at what she did because she couldn't be bullied into revealing information, or pressured into using her power to influence the president's decisions, or coerced into paving the way for anyone who hoped to subvert channels. No matter that Blair had served as her father's confidant and official representative countless times in countries all over the world—Lucinda still told her only what she wanted her to know. And as much as that pissed her off, she trusted Luce like she trusted few others—and Lucinda loved her father as much as she did. Calmer, she walked back around the desk and dropped into the chair. "Does he know?"

"Of course."

"And he doesn't care, right?"

Lucinda smiled. "He told me we have plenty of people whose task it is to see he isn't bothered. He intends to do his job and let others do theirs."

Blair rolled her eyes. "Doesn't he drive you crazy sometimes?"

"Frequently."

"And you can't change him. Can you get him to change his itinerary for a while? Travel less, limit his public appearances?"

"Even if it weren't an election year," Lucinda said wearily, "he wouldn't. If we don't give in to terrorism, we can hardly give in to vague threats and uncertain possibilities."

"I take it that's a direct quote?"

"More or less. It's business as usual—which means we have to do our jobs even better."

"So you called Cam."

"I need someone I can trust," Lucinda said softly. "There isn't anyone I can name close to Andrew who I don't trust—and that's the problem. Because it must be one of them. I need Cam on this, Blair, I'm sorry."

"Why?" Blair asked, surprised. Lucinda never apologized for or qualified any decision she made.

"I know it's not what you want Cam to be doing, and you just got married—"

"Cam decides for herself what she wants to do." Blair laughed and shook her head. "Okay, to be fair, she does think about what I want, you're right—and that still amazes me. That she would do that for me."

"You're lucky."

"I know." Blair turned her wedding ring with her other hand, a comforting reminder of what she knew in her heart. Cam loved her. "All the same, she'd already decided to do this before she told me. You knew she would."

"I *thought* she would—and like I said, I know it's not what you would've wanted."

"I don't want Cam getting hurt. I don't want my father getting hurt either." Blair rose. "That means you have two people to worry about, because if anything happens to either one of them, I swear to God, Lucinda, I'll make someone pay."

Lucinda studied her steadily, her deep gray eyes unblinking. "Averill and I think the most likely source is in the military office—the duty officers know his schedule in advance and are in a perfect position to provide intel on last-minute changes, exit strategies, emergency routes—everything."

"You'll tell Cam?"

"Now that she's in town, I'll brief her formally. Is she still at the condo?"

"No, she and Paula went to the range. They're meeting me here a little later and we're going out to breakfast. I thought I'd try to catch my father. Is he up yet?"

"I imagine he's in the gym."

"Thanks. I'll go hunt him up."

"Congratulations again, by the way. The wedding was lovely."

"Thanks. It was everything I wanted, only I never knew it."

"That's the wonderful thing about love," Lucinda murmured.

"So how much time do we have before we travel?"

"He starts his first campaign sweep the first of the year."

"Oh good—I'll be able to spend my birthday on a train."

"Things have changed in the last few years," Lucinda said dryly. "We'll fly."

❖

Wes woke, twisting in the unfamiliar, too-small bed—senses alert to danger. As the remnants of sleep fled, she became aware of the body pressed close to hers. Evyn. Evyn's back was curved against her chest, her ass tucked neatly into the curve of Wes's hips. Wes's cheek rested on the pillow an inch from the back of Evyn's neck. When she breathed in she could smell the faint hint of lemon in her hair. She'd never awakened next to a woman before, and she lay very still, cataloging every sensation. The front of her thighs rested gently against the back of Evyn's, the delicate melding of skin to skin a fragile connection she didn't dare sever. Her breasts grazed the arch of Evyn's shoulder blades, her nipples electrified by the whisper of contact. The moments they'd spent making love kaleidoscoped through her mind, one after the other, in vivid breathless images. Carefully, so as not to awaken her, she slipped her arm around Evyn's waist and gently spread her fingers over her abdomen. Evyn pushed back against her, setting their bodies more firmly together.

Wes held her breath, but Evyn only murmured, "Stay," as she grasped Wes's hand and pressed it to her flesh. Wes's heart hammered harder, a wave of tenderness and unanticipated heat strobing through her. She wanted Evyn again. Her body vibrated with the urge to stroke, taste, savor. The only thing keeping her from waking Evyn was the exquisite pleasure of holding her just exactly the way they were. She nuzzled her face in the curve of Evyn's shoulder.

Evyn drew Wes's hand higher until her nipple nestled in Wes's palm. "You fit."

"Sorry, I didn't mean to wake—"

"No." Evyn turned in Wes's arms and kissed her. She stroked Wes's back, cradled her ass. "I want you too."

Excitement blossomed in Wes's depths and she groaned.

"Oh yeah," Evyn whispered, tugging on Wes's lower lip. "You tired?"

"No," Wes gasped. "God, Evyn."

Evyn slipped her hand between them, brushed her palm down Wes's abdomen. "Shoulder hurt?"

"What shoulder?" Wes ached, blood thundering in her clit, her body awakening to desire.

Laughing, Evyn murmured, "All right then," and moved her hand lower. "Here?"

"Yes." Wes held on, breathless.

"Here?"

"Yes, please. Right there." Spinning, tumbling, drowning in need.

"More?"

"Yes. Almost. Almost." Wes arched, pressure building, lungs bursting, exploding—lost in pleasure, eyes wide open and unafraid.

The next time Wes opened her eyes she was alone. She skated her hand over the place beside her where Evyn had been not long before. The sheets were cool. The air in the room was equally cool and smelled faintly of industrial cleanser. Soupy gray light trickled through the slats in the blinds. Evyn might have been gone five minutes, or an hour. Wes pushed herself up on her elbows and looked around the room.

Relief surged through her at the sight of Evyn's go bag sitting next to hers on the floor. Evyn hadn't left. But then Evyn wouldn't disappear in the night—no matter how she felt about what had happened between them, she would never walk away. She was far too responsible for that. Maybe she'd gone out because she hadn't wanted a repeat of the night before. Maybe she'd gone out to let the distance say what she didn't want to—that what they'd shared was only one night and nothing more.

The idea that the night was over, never to be repeated, sliced through Wes with unexpected pain. She didn't know what she wanted to happen next, and she had no point of reference, other than the scent of Evyn in the dark and the silky glide of Evyn's skin beneath her hands. Those memories and the clear and certain knowledge that she wanted both again were all she had. Pushing the covers aside, she climbed out of bed and grabbed her sweatpants and a heavy gray cotton pullover out of her bag. The hot-water radiator in the corner rattled but didn't seem to be throwing off much heat. Dressing quickly in the cold room, she sat on the end of the bed to put on her socks. The door banged open and Evyn hurried in, bringing a gust of frigid wind and scattered snowflakes. Her face was flushed. She wore the jeans and T-shirt from the night before. She carried a cardboard takeout tray in her right hand with two large cardboard cups of coffee and a grease-stained brown bag.

Wes wanted to kiss her. "Say it's hot and strong."

"Oh yeah. Believe it." Evyn grinned. "Thought you might be ready for this."

"I am." Wes concentrated on her socks so she wouldn't jump up and touch her. "Have you been up long?"

"No." Evyn set the tray down on the dresser. She shed Wes's jacket and draped it over the back of a lone wooden chair. Water dripped from her cuffs onto the floor. She stamped snow from her boots and kicked them off, leaving them on a square of threadbare carpet that served as a doormat. She crossed to the bed opposite Wes and held out a cup of coffee.

"Black, right?"

Wes took it. "Right. Thanks. How's the storm?"

"Dying off. The pizza place across the street doubles as a deli in the morning. There's doughnuts there too." She waved in the direction of the brown paper bag propped in the cardboard container. "Glazed. And cinnamon."

"Perfect."

"I'm having trouble making a call—I think everyone's using the cell lines. I'm guessing it will be afternoon before we can get a flight out of here. The storm is moving up the coast. Sounds like DC is getting hammered again."

"I guess I'd better try to call the unit and make sure there's enough coverage."

"Good luck. I just managed to get my neighbor across the hall to feed my cat. I couldn't get through to the House or Tom's cell."

"Well, I'm sure whichever doc is around will see that we're appropriately staffed."

"I wouldn't worry too much. They all know what to do." Evyn sipped her coffee and watched Wes pull on her socks. The bed behind her was rumpled, the sheets and blankets askew. They'd given it a workout. Thinking of the way Wes had made her come, more times in a row than she could ever remember, made her stomach clutch. The sex had been great—awesome—but the sleeping together had her out of sync. She didn't usually do that—even when she spent the night with someone, she didn't curl up with them, didn't turn to them in the night and need to be closer. Didn't need to be inside them the way she'd been crazy to be inside Wes.

"You okay?"

"I'm sorry, what?" Evyn was aware she hadn't heard a single thing Wes had said for the last few minutes. Wes looked great in faded sweats that hugged her ass and thighs. Evyn fought the urge to tackle Wes and pull her on top of her. She wanted Wes's hands on her, wanted to be under her, wanted to come for her. That wasn't her either. She was all turned around and—

"I asked if there was anything I could do—you've been taking point all morning, it seems." Wes's gaze traveled over Evyn's body, glinting with a hunger to match Evyn's.

"Probably quite a few things, but we're good for now." Evyn glanced around the clean but shabby room, searching for a way to put on the brakes. She needed to grab the controls, get her head back on straight. "At least there's TV. Hopefully it works. News okay with you?"

"Do we need to talk about last night?"

Evyn stopped on her way to check out the TV. The space between the bed where Wes sat and the dresser with the TV on top was tight. If she took two steps forward she'd be standing between Wes's legs. She mentally nailed her feet to the floor. "You don't run from the hard stuff, do you?"

"I don't see any point."

"Last night was great. If I think about it much more, I could probably scare myself, and I'd rather not."

"I understand." Wes cradled the cardboard cup between her hands and watched the coffee swirl around the rim. "If I knew enough to be scared, I probably would be too."

"So," Evyn said. "Since neither of us really scares easily, this should be simple. I don't have a problem with last night."

Wes heard the emphasis on *last night*. Sounded a lot like past tense, as in over and done. Okay. She could accept that. The pain in her chest didn't mean anything. Her turn to step up and make this simple. "Neither do I. My number one priority is to be sure we can still work together—that there's no disruption to the team."

"I don't see why what happened should interfere with anything," Evyn said quickly. Wes was giving her a graceful way out of a potentially sticky situation, just the kind of exit she usually wanted. She didn't feel all that happy about it, but her emotions were screwed up and she couldn't trust them anyhow. Better to ignore them. "We're both adults, both professionals."

"Yes," Wes said, counting on Evyn to be rational and in control. Especially now, when she didn't really feel that way herself. "We both have jobs to do. And considering the circumstances, we can't afford any distractions."

Evyn stiffened, hearing what Wes wasn't saying. "You know about the problem with POTUS."

"Yes."

"You have me on the short list of suspects?" Evyn had to ask, even as her body went cold thinking Wes might consider her capable of such betrayal.

"No, Evyn," Wes said softly, "I don't."

"Why not? You should." Evyn knew she sounded angry. She *was* angry. The whole situation made her crazy. The president was at risk, and it was her job to protect him. She couldn't do that effectively when someone she thought she could trust was a traitor. Her impotence stoked her fury. "You don't know me. A roll in the hay isn't exactly a great judge of anything."

Wes jolted. She didn't run from reality, she never had, and Evyn was making their reality very clear. Last night was a physical encounter and nothing more, and really, why would she think it was anything more. "So we keep doing our jobs."

"No reason it can't be that simple." Evyn shrugged, relieved to settle back into her comfortable pattern again. "We aren't the first two people to spend the night together and then go back to business as usual the next day. In fact, around here, it's more business as usual than not."

Wes might not have indulged in battlefield trysts, but she knew plenty did. Evyn apparently had. "No reason for last night to change anything."

"Right." Evyn quickly turned to switch on the TV. "None at all."

CHAPTER TWENTY-THREE

S enator Russo received a text in the middle of breakfast. The alert read HK1. He'd been waiting two days for this update. Setting his fork aside, he swiped his thumb over the banner alert and read the five words that sent a swell of satisfaction streaming through him. *The item is in hand.* He deleted the message, wiped his mouth with a pressed linen napkin, and said to his wife, "I'm sorry, my dear, I need to return this call. The car will be here in half an hour. You'll be ready?"

He wasn't really asking, but his wife seemed to do better with the stresses of campaigning when she could cling to the trappings of civility she'd been raised with. She wasn't fond of public appearances under the best of circumstances, and even less so now that his speeches increasingly drew protesters from some liberal leftist group or another. He'd assured her this was expected when someone with his strength of conviction and popularity engaged the people and spoke the truth. Her Southern belle sensibilities would have annoyed him more if her family name wasn't helping him to carry the Deep South.

So he played the game she needed, as long as she did as he wanted. She understood she had to be by his side during these events—he was running on a family-values platform, and she was the figurehead of his, naturally. Thus far he'd managed to keep the whole issue of his eldest daughter's absence from the campaign trail in the background. Nora had spun Jac's history as a war veteran into some very positive press while simultaneously downplaying her sexual escapades and questionable choice in partners. Since Jac had made it plain she wouldn't take part in his public appearances, that was the best they could do in terms of damage control. Fortunately, he had another daughter, a younger, feminine, wholesome daughter who didn't have any choice about participating.

"Yes, of course I'll be prompt," his wife said quickly, an altogether artificial smile failing to erase the anxious shadows in her eyes. "I'm looking forward to it."

"Wonderful." He smiled. "Wear the blue suit. It looks good on camera. And goes so nicely with your eyes."

"Thank you," she said, her attention on her plate. "I will. Yes."

He strolled toward his study, mentally reviewing his remarks for the town meeting Nora had scheduled later that morning in Nevada. He wanted to use the community forum to demonstrate his solidarity with the American people and distance himself from the recent emphasis by members of the press on his private wealth. He might live differently from most Americans, thanks to his wife's family money, but he was still one with the people. He unlocked his study door and walked in, pleased with the way things were going for the moment.

Once behind his desk, he unlocked another drawer, removed a disposable cell phone, and called Hooker. "I got your message. No problems, I take it?"

"I made the exchange for the amount we agreed upon. I'll have it tomorrow. None too soon either."

"You're certain of its authenticity?"

"As certain as I can be," Hooker said. "It's not like I'm an expert on this sort of thing. I'm mostly the courier here."

"Courier or not, I'll hold you responsible for any malfunction."

"You're not the one who'll be sitting with this stuff in his refrigerator. It gives me the creeps," Hooker snapped. "You hired me to broker the deal and run interference between the players. I fulfilled my contract. Once this is out of my hands, I'm done."

Russo clamped down on his temper. As insubordinate as Hooker could be, he had excellent contacts, he got the job done, and he was as trustworthy as any man in his profession. The election campaign was just getting started, and he'd need Hooker's services again. "You're right, of course. What news do you have from DC?"

"Not much. So far the transition hasn't been a problem."

Russo grunted, irritated by the unexpected speed with which the usually slow White House bureaucracy had replaced the WHMU chief. "The inevitable disruption may work to our favor."

"If we move fast."

"Then by all means, let's move forward." Russo glanced at his desk calendar. December was more than half over. Soon the holidays would be in full swing. "You have his itinerary?"

"Updated as of this morning."

Russo smiled. "We might want to advance the timetable."

"I just need time to brief the deliveryman."

"Very good. I'll be in touch. And nice work." Russo disconnected and locked the phone back in his desk. His plan was bold and some would say extreme, but they lived in extreme times. The American people had become complacent, with economic woes taking center stage in the public's awareness and fading memories of a terrorist attack smothering patriotism. The public needed a wake-up call, and nothing stirred national fervor like an attack at home. The time was ripe for the right leader to lead them on the path to moral redemption and renewed power. He was ready.

❖

"Please fasten your seat belts, we're beginning our descent into Washington Reagan National Airport," the flight attendant announced.

"Hey," Evyn said softly. "Wes, we're landing."

Fuzzy-headed, Wes opened her eyes and concentrated on orienting herself. Airplane. Cramp in her shoulder. Her cheek on Evyn's shoulder. She pushed up quickly. "Sorry."

"That's okay. You went out fast as soon as we were airborne. You needed the rest."

"I slept most of the morning." Evyn had booked them a late afternoon flight, and after they'd taken turns showering, Wes had fallen asleep watching CNN. She'd awakened after noon on top of the bed with a blanket over her. Evyn had covered her while she slept. Remembering that small gesture made her shift in her seat until their bodies no longer touched. She wasn't used to relying on anyone, and discovering she liked the feeling of being cared for wasn't entirely welcome. Especially when the caring came from Evyn.

"How are you feeling?" Evyn asked.

"A little stiff," Wes said, stretching out in the cramped space. She didn't want Evyn to worry—or to think she needed looking after. Evyn had done enough. "I'm okay. I think the downtime this morning really helped."

"You were shivering this morning—still chilled?"

Wes couldn't answer that question. Physically, she felt warmer— the pervasive cold that had lingered in her body long after Evyn had pulled her out of the ocean had finally disappeared, but a glacial throbbing had taken up residence in the center of her being. She ached inside in a way she never had, even when she'd been a child uncertain of the future, even when she'd been physically and psychologically depleted after weeks in the desert. The closer they came to DC—the nearer the moment when she and Evyn would go back to being only professional colleagues—the more pervasive the sense of loss. She didn't regret the decision. They couldn't work together and be anything more than colleagues, even if they'd wanted to be more. And Evyn had made it clear what they'd shared had been an isolated occurrence.

Wes had made hard decisions all her life and accepted the consequences, even when they hurt. Pain wasn't deadly—even though this hurt as much as anything she'd ever experienced. "Thanks for handling everything. I owe you."

"No, you don't." Evyn's voice shook. "I wanted to do everything I did—including last night. You know that, don't you?"

Wes covered Evyn's hand where it rested on the armrest between them. "How could I not know? You speak beautifully with your body."

Evyn caught her breath. "You always surprise me in the most amazing ways. No one has ever said anything as wonderful to me before."

"Then they weren't paying attention." Wes smiled, steadfastly refusing to think of the other women Evyn had known. Jealousy was a foreign sensation and, rationally, totally unfounded. Irrational or not, she still didn't want to imagine anyone touching her. She seemed to have lost the ability to reason when she'd first become aware of wanting to kiss her.

"Maybe *I* was the one not paying attention." Evyn searched her memory for a time she'd felt this connected—and feared it so much. She gripped Wes's hand. The lights of DC came into view. A wave of panic slid over her—she couldn't help feeling as if they were running out of time, as if she was about to lose something vital without even knowing it. "Wes—I don't want you to think last night wasn't special."

"I don't think that. Why would I?"

"I know you must think I do that sort of thi—"

"Whoa—hey. What I think is that we both wanted last night to happen."

Wes's hand was so warm, so damn perfect in hers. Evyn wanted to reverse the clock—start the last few days over. She wanted to keep Wes safe, she wanted to take her out to dinner when they weren't both exhausted, she wanted to make love with her when they weren't hurt or displaced or scared of losing their fragile connection. Hell. She wanted to date her, maybe more—something she hadn't wanted with anyone, possibly ever. "I think I fucked this up."

"No, you didn't," Wes said. "You gave me everything I needed."

The lights of the tower flashed red across the sky. The runway lights glowed brighter by the second. Another minute and they'd be on the ground. Evyn willed time to slow. She needed a little more time—when had everything gotten away from her? "We'll have to get a cab—the team will have taken the SUV back to the House. We can share one as far as your hotel, and then I'll go pick up my car."

"That's okay," Wes said. "We can head straight to the House. I want to spend a few hours at the office. I've been away more than I've been there since I've arrived, and it's time I got some things organized."

"Can't it wait until tomorrow?" Evyn wouldn't mind the few extra minutes together, but Wes was pale. "You're still looking pretty beat."

"We're coming up on the holidays. We'll be working doubles between now and after New Year's so everyone can have time off. I need to review the duty rosters and the travel schedules—and about a dozen other things."

The plane touched down and the engines whined into their deceleration.

Please remain seated until the captain has taxied to the gate and turned off the seat belt sign.

"What are you doing for Christmas?" Evyn asked.

"I'm the new guy, remember? I'm working."

"You're also the boss."

"Half the team has kids—they need to be with family."

"What about yours?"

Wes smiled. "They're used to me being away for holidays. They understand. You?"

"Ah—I volunteered to take the holiday shifts too. Good overtime, plus my sibs and I gave my parents a cruise for Christmas. They'll be gone until after New Year's anyhow."

"So we're in the same boat again," Wes said.

"Seems to happen a lot." People around them began standing and opening the overhead bins. Evyn realized she was still holding Wes's hand. She had to let go, and when she did, last night would really be over. She slipped her fingers free. The cabin lights came on full and she blinked. Passengers filed past. Wes released her seat belt and searched Evyn's eyes, questions in hers.

"So what's next?" Wes asked.

"More of the same."

"Hopefully no more water exercises."

"No." Evyn grimaced. "We're done with those. Probably keep the sims to half-days and finish up this week."

"How am I doing?" Wes didn't really expect an answer.

Evyn hesitated. "You're doing fine, Captain."

"Thanks." Wes grinned wryly at the formality. "Seems I now have quarters in a residential hotel off Dupont Circle, so I can use the extra time to move. Got the text while I was in the shower earlier."

"Need help moving?" Evyn asked.

"I'm fine—I don't have much. But thanks."

"Well, if you change your mind, let me know." Evyn said.

"I'll be in my office this evening if anything comes up." Wes pointed to the aisle as the last passengers streamed off, averting her gaze. She was a little too tired and a little too sore at heart to hide her sadness, and she didn't want Evyn to misread sadness for regret. She didn't regret a moment of their time together. "Time to go."

"Right. Don't stay up half the night working," Evyn said, stepping out into the aisle and pulling Wes's bag from the overhead compartment.

"I won't." At Evyn's skeptical look, she laughed. "Word of honor."

"I might call you to remind you of that."

"No need," Wes said, her pulse racing despite her best intentions, "but feel free to call anytime."

Evyn paused, her expression growing intent. "I'll do that."

CHAPTER TWENTY-FOUR

The cab stopped at Fifteenth and E streets, and Wes passed bills to the driver for the fare and opened her door. Evyn had spent the ride from the airport downloading mail and answering texts, and Wes had been grateful not to make small talk. She couldn't think of a thing to say that wouldn't ring false after the last thirty-six hours. "I'll see you. Take care, okay?"

"Yeah. I will," Evyn said. "You too."

"'Night." Wes stepped out and dragged her go bag out after her. The cab pulled away to take Evyn to her car. Wes didn't watch it go, although she wanted to. Instead, she hurried to the gate, showed her ID to the officer, and made her way through the quiet halls toward her office. The night had a surreal feel to it—everything was too quiet after what seemed like a constant bombardment of emotional and physical explosions for days. She nodded to the occasional valet pushing a cart on silent wheels and to officers standing post, motionless but intently alert. Suddenly craving the norm, a refuge from the chaos of her life, she detoured at the last moment and headed to the clinic area. A middle-aged man she hadn't met was making notes in a chart at the desk in the AOD's office. She recognized him from his file photo. She tapped on the door. "Evening, Colonel Dunbar."

He finished a notation, put his pen aside, and closed the file before looking up. He wore a dark blue button-down-collar shirt, a navy-and-red striped tie loosened at the neck. His expression morphed from questioning to friendly and he stood quickly. "Captain, glad to meet you finally. Sorry our paths haven't crossed before this."

"Good to finally meet you. Sorry for the circumstances."

"Damn shame about Len," he said, shaking his head. His wiry iron-gray hair was clipped military style, and his steel-blue eyes were clear and sharp. "I was on leave—my oldest daughter just got married. Couldn't believe it when I heard the news."

"I didn't know him personally, but I know it's a loss."

He took a breath. "Well, new order of the day. Anything I can help you with?"

"I think I've got things in hand, but I appreciate the offer. Anything you think I need to know, problems, questions—stop by my office or call me, anytime."

"I'll do that."

"I'll let you get back to those charts."

He gave them a morose look and sank back into the chair behind the desk. He'd already pulled the next from the stack and opened it by the time she reached the door. Halfway down the row of patient cubicles, she nearly ran into Jennifer coming out of one of the treatment rooms. Tonight she wore olive green pants, tapered and just form-fitting enough to accentuate her hips and thighs. Her shirt was cream silk and unbuttoned a tasteful distance at the throat. Her glossy dark hair was caught back at her nape with a simple gold clip. She managed to look professional and sexy at the same time. Her lips parted in a wide smile. "Captain! I didn't expect to see you back so soon."

"I just came in to get some paperwork done," Wes said. "How are things going?"

"Very well. I was just restocking after our last walk-in left." As she spoke, she brushed her fingers over Wes's arm. "Just the usual today—seasonal illnesses, a sprained knee from a stumble on the grounds, run-of-the-mill aches and pains."

"Sounds like a good day to me."

She laughed. "I guess you could say that. I prefer something with a little more action." She accentuated the last word with a squeeze to Wes's forearm.

"How did you come by this duty, then? Somehow, I see you as a field medic."

"Thank you." She colored, her eyes sparkling with pleasure. "I volunteered, actually. I thought the job was an important one, and the experience of being this close to the president is a once-in-a-lifetime thing." She moved an inch closer and her hip brushed Wes's. "And of course, I get to work with the best medical team in the world."

Wes leaned back, wanting to telegraph her lack of interest without insulting someone she'd be working with every day. She wasn't put off by Jennifer's not-too-subtle feelers—workplace assignations were common enough, even between individuals prohibited by rank. But even if she'd had a sliver of interest, she'd know better than to act on it. Yet as attractive as Jennifer was, Wes was unmoved. The memory of Evyn's body curved into hers, of Evyn drawing her close in the dark, of Evyn devastating her with pleasure was too fresh in her consciousness. She'd just sent away the only woman who'd ever made her wish she didn't always have to stand alone. She backed up, putting space between her and Jennifer. "It was good to see you again. I hope the rest of the night is quiet. Enjoy the holidays."

"I'll see you Christmas Eve." Jennifer's tone made it sound as if they'd run into each other at a party.

Wes frowned, calling up an image of the duty roster she'd reviewed several days before. "I thought you had leave."

"Oh, I did," Jennifer said dismissively. "But at the last minute my sister couldn't get away, and she's my only family. I'd just as soon work than spend the holiday in my apartment. I'd only end up cleaning." She laughed. "And my apartment isn't all that big."

"Well, I'm sorry to hear your family plans were disrupted."

"I'm not—I saw the new roster and the substitutions. I'm looking forward to working with you."

"I'll let you get back to work, then," Wes said.

"Have a nice night."

Jennifer gave a little wave and walked away. Wes went the opposite way toward her office, mentally shaking off the disquieting sensation left by their conversation. Maybe her read was off—maybe Jennifer was just friendly and outgoing. Wes didn't quite trust her assessment— she'd been off target for days. Apparently, she wasn't nearly as good at interpreting personal signals as she was at evaluating trauma.

She'd ended up in bed with Evyn Daniels and still wasn't sure how she'd let that happen. Oh sure—extreme circumstances often made people act out of character, but that was a convenient excuse and she knew it. She'd wanted to be close to Evyn and she'd enjoyed Evyn taking care of her. She'd wanted to kiss her—wanted more than that, and she'd made the first move. Evyn had put it very clearly—brief physical interludes on the job were common, and then it was back to business as usual. Maybe for Evyn that was true.

Nothing wrong with two adults sharing a few hours of pleasure and then moving on. Too bad that didn't seem to be the case for her. Even now, she couldn't forget the pleasure that filled her from having Evyn near, from knowing Evyn cared. She wanted to touch her again, wanted to be touched. She wanted the peace and certainty that steadied her when she thought of Evyn. She'd learned long ago not to want that kind of comfort, and Evyn had made her forget those hard lessons. Evyn scared her, and that was the real reason she was headed to her office alone.

❖

At the tap on her partially closed door, Wes expected to see one of the WHMU staff. She half rose when she recognized Cameron Roberts.

"Sorry to bother you, Captain," Cam said.

"No—please come in." Wes walked around her desk and extended her hand. Roberts, dressed casually in gray trousers and a black sweater, entered and shut the door behind her. Her dark eyes bore the same intense focus Wes had seen in every photo of her. Remembering her from the wedding, Wes suspected the only time her gaze ever softened was when she looked at Blair Powell. A flare of envy caught her by surprise and she quickly doused it. "Wes Masters."

"Cam Roberts. Do you have a moment?"

"Of course. Have a seat." Wes indicated the chairs in front of her desk and sat down.

"What do you make of O'Shaughnessy's autopsy report?" Cam asked.

Right to business. This was ground she understood, and after the upheaval on the personal front, welcome ground. She needed to get her head back where it belonged. "On the surface, there aren't any red flags."

"He was fifty-one. His last physical exam four months ago included a stress test. That was normal," Cam said.

"Yes. That bothers me too." Wes frowned. "*On* the surface things look straightforward. An arrhythmia, on the other hand, could account for sudden death, and there are often no precipitating signs or symptoms."

"And no way to tell on the postmortem?"

"Exactly."

"Could an arrhythmia be drug induced?"

"Of course—although the most effective way would be by injection, and he'd likely be aware of that. You suspect his death was a homicide?"

Cam shrugged. "I don't like coincidences. Len's unexpected death happening when we have a security breach is a little too convenient to ignore."

"What would be the goal? The WHMU has other capable medical team members."

"Could be something as simple as disrupting the flow so any move against POTUS would be handled less than efficiently."

Wes had used much the same reasoning when she'd agreed with Evyn they shouldn't mix business with pleasure. Considered rationally, the argument was weak. "Seems like a big risk for small gain."

"Agreed. The more likely scenario is that Len noticed something, or suspected something. Assuming he wasn't our leak and his contacts decided to eliminate him."

"Do you suspect him?"

"I suspect everyone," Cam said flatly. "Except you. But Len—not really. I've been running extended checks on every member of PPD, the WHMO, and the WHMU. Nothing turns up for Len other than a quiet affair with one of the nurses."

Wes straightened. "Who?"

"Jennifer Pattee."

"Really."

"What?"

Wes laughed wryly. So much for gaydar. "Never mind."

"Do you trust your instincts, Wes?"

"Professionally, yes." Wes thought of Evyn—she trusted her

instincts about Evyn too. Evyn was totally worthy of trust and confidence, in all ways.

"So tell me what you think about Lieutenant Pattee."

Wes hesitated, then decided her personal embarrassment was unimportant. "I had the feeling the lieutenant was more interested in female partners. I could be totally wrong in that—or maybe she's bi."

"Has she expressed a personal interest in you?"

"I thought so. As I said—"

"I'm just gathering information, Wes. As a newcomer, you're more likely to make an unbiased observation. Anything that seems off to you might be important."

"I understand."

Cam sat forward. "A puncture site is pretty easy to miss in an autopsy, isn't it?"

"Yes—very. And we won't have the tox screens back for another week or so. Without some evidence of drug administration, we don't have any reason to exhume his body. I'd hate to put his family through that."

"I don't want to do that either if it isn't necessary. I'll see about expediting the tox results," Cam said.

"Excellent."

"Could the injection go unnoticed by the recipient—say if he was distracted?"

"Possibly. Airjet injection is nearly painless."

"Peter Chang was working out with Len the day he died. He would also have been Len's most likely successor if Lucinda hadn't insisted on going outside for a new chief."

"I didn't know that." Wes tried to see Peter Chang as a traitor. She couldn't, but she didn't see anyone in the WHMU as capable of betrayal. "This is ugly."

Cam's mouth hardened. "We just have to see it doesn't get uglier."

❖

"You can pull over here," Evyn told the cabbie, pointing to a spot up the street from Louise's. She paid the fare and got out, jumping over a mound of slush at the curb. The snow had stopped but the streets were still a mess. The wind was wet on her neck—the miserable weather fit her mood. Her life had gone from orderly and uncomplicated to confusing and crazy-making overnight. Literally. Hell, she'd gone to bed with Wes Masters. Worse, she wanted to again. Right now. Her body hummed like a live wire looking to ground out on the nearest surface. If she so much as brushed a hand over herself, she'd probably come. That was a first. She'd always had great control—being sexually in charge was like being captain of the team. Calling the game, knowing just when to pull the trigger for the perfect score.

Not so with Wes—all Wes had to do was look at her and she was ready to explode. The whole airplane ride had been torture—the sweetest torture she'd ever experienced. Wes had slept on her shoulder, something Gary had done a million times. Andrea too—a smoking-hot blonde who usually worked a different shift. Andrea had also slept in Evyn's bed a few times, when they'd been coming off a detail in the ass-end of nowhere and killing time until they could get home. She didn't get hot and sweaty and ache to come in her jeans when Andrea nestled her cheek against her shoulder. She didn't long to slide her arm around Andrea and run her fingers through her hair either. Hell, she didn't want that with Louise, which was maybe why she was standing in the foyer of Louise's building right now.

She pressed Louise's buzzer. Louise opened the door and gave Evyn a curious look. "Hi. Come on in."

Feeling just a little bit foolish, Evyn followed her inside. "Sorry to drop by like this."

"That's okay. I was just about to open a bottle of wine. Are you hungry?"

"No, I don't want to put you out—"

"Don't be silly. It's no bother." Louise walked through the apartment to the kitchen, and Evyn followed, wondering why she had come and realizing what she was about to say was completely unlike her. Louise looked great in dance leggings and a tank top. She was barefoot, and her hair was loose. She was everything Evyn liked in a woman—smart, accomplished, great sense of humor, super body, and generous in bed. To make it even better, she was undemanding and independent.

So what was she doing here?

"Listen, before you pour that wine, I should probably tell you I stopped by to break our date."

Louise turned, the wine bottle in one hand and a corkscrew in the other. She leaned back against the counter and gave Evyn an appraising look. "Okay. Usually people just call."

"And I guess the excuse that I was just in the neighborhood really doesn't fly," Evyn said ruefully. She rested her shoulder on the doorjamb and ran a hand through her hair. "So, I'm feeling a little dumb here. You want me to go?"

Louise laughed. "No. I want you to stay and have a glass of wine and something to eat. How does stir-fry sound?"

Evyn's stomach rumbled and she blushed. "Well, it sounds great, but—"

"Evyn," Louise said, crossing the small space between them and kissing her on the cheek. "I think you're great. We have a wonderful time together. But we never promised anything, and I don't have any expectations."

"It's just that—" Evyn was more confused now than she had been a few minutes before. Louise must be even more bewildered. Time to stop dancing around the issue. "I'm thinking we might not be intimate again."

"Ah." Louise studied her. "It's not something I said or did, is it?"

"No, you're great," Evyn said quickly. "I'm being a total ass, aren't I? I'm not explaining anything really very well. I'm not even sure why I'm here."

"Don't apologize." Louise smiled a little sadly. "That you would come here to tell me this, face-to-face, is one of the reasons I'm sorry we have to stop at friendship."

"Ah hell—"

"But there's no law against two people who like each other being friends, is there?" Louise brushed her fingers over Evyn's shoulder. "I like you, aside from the great sex."

Evyn blushed. "It's official. I am an ass."

"Quite possibly." Louise laughed and poured a glass of red wine. "Have some of this while I cook and tell me what's going on."

Evyn sipped wine and started to relax. "I don't know what's going on. Nothing, really. That's what makes this whole thing sort of ridiculous."

"Uh-huh," Louise said, taking food from the refrigerator and pans from underneath the sleek counter. "But you're here, so why don't you start with what got you here."

"I just got back from a detail. It was a little crazy. One of my team members got into trouble." Just saying that much made her faintly sick. The recurring image of Wes sinking deeper into the water came back sharp and clear. Adrenaline surged through her blood and a coppery taste filled her mouth.

Louise glanced over her shoulder and paused in her food prep. "You sound like it was really bad. I'm sorry."

Evyn sucked in a breath. "She's fine now. It was just tense there for a couple of minutes. That sort of thing happens. It's part of the job."

"I guess it probably is. I got the sense you never really wanted to talk about it, so I never pressed. If you want to tell me more—"

"Sorry. I guess I've never really shared much of anything."

"And I never asked you to. So we're okay on that score. Go ahead—you just got back from a tough assignment. And?"

"And there's this woman…"

Louise smiled. "Isn't there always? Sometimes they really turn your head around, don't they?"

Evyn laughed. "You'd think I was new at this."

Louise regarded her thoughtfully. "Maybe you are?"

"I think you might be right." Where Wes was concerned, she sure felt like a first-timer. All hormones and insanity and hungry for more of everything. She'd kept praying Wes would lean back into the cab and kiss her good night. Yeah, right. Nuts. "Anyhow, that's kind of what this is about. This woman I'm not really involved with—not that way, I mean."

"I think I almost understand. You need to think about some things."

"Yeah—I'm sorry."

"I know. Me too—but it's okay. Really." Louise pointed a wooden spatula at the vegetables piled on the cutting board. "So—will you stay?"

"Yeah. I'm starved. And thanks."

Louise put the utensils down, motioned Evyn closer, and kissed

Evyn's cheek. "You're welcome. I like friends with benefits, but friends without benefits is okay too."

"That's good to know. Thanks." Evyn wasn't sure what she'd just done or why, but it felt right. It felt almost as good as the night she'd spent with Wes, which felt more than right. And she had no idea what to do about that.

CHAPTER TWENTY-FIVE

"You need plants," Doris Masters said, standing with her hands on her hips in the center of the small galley kitchen, surveying the adjacent living area. She pointed to the bay windows overlooking Nineteenth Street. "That window seat gets enough sunlight. A planter or two right there—"

"Mom," Wes said, "I kill plants." Behind her, Denny snickered and mumbled something about understatement.

Giving the impersonal apartment a 360-degree glance, Doris said, "A cat would be good."

"You have to feed cats," Wes said.

Her mother pointed a finger at her. "That's why your plants die."

"Better plants than a cat," Wes muttered. Her mother smiled, but Wes could tell by the glint in her ocean-green eyes she wasn't finished. Looking a decade younger than her age, with the same green eyes and brown hair shot through with burnished gold, she could have been Wes's older sister—and was sometimes mistaken for one of the sibs when they were all out together. Wes hadn't known Denny and her mother were coming, but when they had shown up a few minutes after the delivery truck brought her belongings from Maryland, she'd been glad for more than the help. Their bright, sure love helped chase away the shadows that plagued her. She'd slept poorly since the night she'd spent with Evyn. The hotel bed was big and empty and cold, and every morning she awoke lonely. She went through the days, splitting her time between exercises with PPD and clinic duties, with an empty ache inside. Evyn was friendly but reserved, and Wes didn't think it was an accident they hadn't been alone together since their return from Kitty Hawk. Evyn was avoiding her.

"Wesley," her mother said, "this isn't a temporary billet. You're going to live here for the next few years, and it shouldn't look like a hotel room."

Denny finally cut in and saved her. "Mama, give her a break. She didn't invite us down here to help, after all, and—"

"Mother's prerogative." Doris perched on the wooden arm of the tan canvas sofa. "We'll miss you at Christmas."

Wes sat next to her mother and took her hand. "I know, I'm sorry. I'd be there if I could."

"We'll miss you," her mother repeated, "and we're so very proud of you. Your other sisters wanted to be sure you knew that."

"I know. I love you. All of you."

Denny flopped down beside her and bumped her knee against Wes's. "So—on the personal front—"

Wes groaned. "Come on, Denny. Don't start."

Doris stroked the back of Wes's head and feathered the locks along the back of her neck, as if she were still ten. "There's more to life than work, Wesley."

"And there's lots of life ahead, Mom. I'm fine. Just really busy right now."

"Yeah," Denny said softly, "but are you happy?"

Wes hadn't expected the question and hesitated before she answered. Getting the third degree from her family about her personal life wasn't unusual, but after she shrugged off their good-natured queries with some standard answer, the conversation usually moved on. This time, the questions felt different, or maybe she was the one who was different. She didn't have a pat response, and the old explanations rang false, even to her. "I don't know. I've never given it much thought. My work makes me happy—"

"Satisfaction isn't happiness," Doris said.

"No, maybe not," Wes said, "but it's always been enough."

"Things change, you know," Denny said. "Don't miss the chance for more than satisfaction if it comes along."

"Okay, enough. Message received." Wes squeezed Denny's hand, kissed her mother's cheek, and stood. "You've got a two-hour drive and

I've got a ton of things to do." At her mother's frown she added quickly, "And I promised Emory I'd go out with her and Dana tonight. So I do have a social life, you know."

"Are you taking a date?" Denny asked, an eager glint in her eyes.

Wes instantly thought of Evyn. Like every time she thought of her, the memory of Evyn pressed close in the night flooded through her. Pleasure warred with pain, and she schooled her face to remain neutral. "No."

"Huh. What aren't you telling us?" Denny narrowed her eyes.

"Nothing. I'm just getting together with some friends."

"Let her be, Denny," Doris said.

Her mother studied Wes with that laser-beam look that made Wes think her mother could see inside her head. Considering all she could see was Evyn naked—moving under her, rising above her, crying out as she came—she slammed the mental door as quickly as she could. Some things her mother definitely did not need to know.

"She'll tell us when she's ready." Doris rose and gathered her things. "She always does." She kissed Wes on the cheek. "You've always done more than you were asked, and you've always been asked a great deal. They couldn't have chosen anyone better. We love you."

"Thanks," Wes said, her throat tight as she hugged her mother and sister good-bye. "I love you all too. I'll be home as soon as I can."

She had a couple of hours before she was due to meet Emory and Dana at the Black Fox. She would have canceled, but she knew Emory would hound her for her reasons. And what could she say? She was beat after a lousy night's sleep when she couldn't stop thinking about a woman who disordered her orderly world—a woman she'd be much better off not thinking about at all? No. She'd go out with her best friend and her lover and do her damnedest to put her night with Evyn in the past.

She headed to the House. Work might not be everything, but it was everything she'd always had. Work had always defined her—her goals, her sense of self, her pleasure, and often her pain. There was comfort in the familiar, and as her family drove out of the city and the loneliness seeped back and lay heavy in her throat, she needed a little comfort.

❖

The door opened behind Evyn and she didn't bother to turn around, saying to Gary, "You're early."

"For what?" Wes said.

Evyn jerked and twisted in her seat. She hadn't expected to see her—they didn't have anything scheduled. Just the night before, she'd submitted her report to Tom. The long and short of her assessment was that Wes was not just qualified, she was an excellent choice to head the WHMU from an operational standpoint. She worked well with a team, didn't buck the chain of command, and knew when to take charge when medical issues demanded. She didn't have an excuse to spend extra time with Wes any longer. "Hi."

"Hi."

Wes, in dark trousers and a pale blue shirt open at the throat, stood just inside the door, looking better than Evyn remembered, and she'd been remembering a lot. The instant her eyes had opened that morning, like most every morning, she'd thought of Wes. Wondered what Wes's day would be like, if she'd moved yet—if she needed help. If she'd call. And in her next breath, she'd remembered how she'd lain in the dark torturing herself—rekindling the fire Wes's hands had ignited in her belly, savoring the slow buildup while replaying the sound of Wes's murmurs in her ear, her low moans, the quick gasp as she orgasmed. She'd fallen asleep on the crest of her own orgasm with the memory of Wes's mouth moving over her skin, so knowing and so sure. She'd awakened ready for another and would have indulged again if her cell phone hadn't vibrated with a message from base advising her she was needed to fill in because POTUS had decided to go OTR. At the sight of Wes, the low-level arousal that she had lived with all day, every day, leaped to life. She worked on sounding casual. "Did you get moved?"

"Just this morning." Wes headed for the coffeepot, poured a cup, and gestured with it toward Evyn. "Refill?"

"I'm good."

Wes put the pot back and gathered herself. She hadn't expected to see Evyn, and the surge of pleasure at finding her there took her by surprise. "I thought you were off today."

Evyn shook her head with a wry grin. "POTUS decided to go Christmas shopping."

Wes rested against the counter and sipped her coffee.

"Something tells me that isn't your most favorite thing."

"Unscheduled trips are about our least favorite. No advance planning, lots of civilians, way too much exposure." Evyn laughed. "We like things to be orderly, controlled, planned out."

"Sounds a lot like my life," Wes said.

"Well, you know what happens when all that goes out the window," Evyn said softly.

Wes set her coffee aside. Evyn's eyes were so dark, so deep, Wes couldn't look away. The pull on her body to move closer, to touch, was nearly irresistible, and she gripped the counter to keep herself in place. "Dangerous."

"And scary."

Wes had been scared plenty in her life—scared of what would happen to her family when her father died, scared of what would happen if she didn't get a scholarship, scared of who might pay if she failed to do her job in the classroom or the field. She'd countered that fear by working harder and longer until she was absolutely certain the outcome was in her control. She didn't leave room for failure. "Sometimes being scared forces us to be stronger—better."

"Oh, no question. Nothing like a challenge to make us dig deep, find out what we've really got."

"And who we really are?" Until recently, Wes had known who she was and what she wanted. Now she wasn't so sure.

"That too, sometimes."

"This is crazy, you know that, right?" Wes murmured.

"Maybe. Probably. I told Tom you were right for the job and field ready."

"Did you." Wes slid her hands into her pockets, crossed her ankles

Evyn swallowed. "Mmm. Last night."

"So I guess I'm not a squid anymore."

"Nope." Evyn laughed.

"No more sims?"

"'Fraid not."

Wes smiled. "I'm not."

"No—I imagine you'll be glad to be done with our daily dates."

"You too, I imagine."

"Not so much," Evyn murmured.

Wes knew exactly what she should do to extinguish the possibilities that seemed to be growing without any intention on her part. She knew what to say, but she'd never been a coward. "I'm meeting friends of mine"—she glanced at her watch—"in an hour. You like jazz?"

"Sure," Evyn said, her gaze fixed on Wes's face.

"When are you going to be done?"

"My push is due in half an hour—" Evyn laughed, shook her head. "Are you inviting me to go out with you?"

"I don't know what I'm doing, but I like being with you. Pretending I don't when we're going to see each other every day isn't going to work."

"I'll come find you when Gary shows up," Evyn said. "I'm usually pretty good at pretending, but not so much with you."

Wes warmed inside. "Tonight...just so we're clear, it's just—"

"I know," Evyn said quickly. "Just friends. I know. That's good."

Wes nodded, grabbed her coffee, and left before she said anything they wouldn't be able to take back, or live with. She was halfway to her office before she recognized the ache in her middle was gone.

CHAPTER TWENTY-SIX

S o," Emory said, leaning across Dana at the table and grasping Wes's arm, "how did you meet Evyn?"

"We work together."

"I remember her," Dana said. "She was at the wedding. One of the agents."

"That's right," Wes answered while watching Evyn thread her way through the crowd toward the back of the bar. She looked great tonight, in plain dark trousers and a white shirt. More than a few people watched her pass, and Wes struggled between possessiveness and pride. Both sensations were foreign.

"She's very nice," Emory said.

"Yes," Wes said. The band was good, and the bar was packed. There hadn't been much opportunity for conversation, for which she was grateful. Emory wasn't as relentless as her mother or Denny when she wanted to know something, but she didn't let up. Her curiosity had been apparent from the instant Wes had introduced Evyn, and understandably so. Evyn was great company—sociable, funny, at ease in any situation. Wes doubted she would be as comfortable meeting any of Evyn's friends, but then she wasn't particularly comfortable in social gatherings to begin with. She hadn't had much practice. Evyn undoubtedly had, and thinking about her in a bar, comfortable, charming, connecting with other women, the twinge of possessiveness swelled to a surge of jealousy. She promptly extinguished it. She didn't have any claim on Evyn, by her own choice.

"Sexy too." Emory plucked a handful of peanuts from the bowl on the table.

"Yes," Wes said.

"When did you lose your powers of speech?" Emory asked with exaggerated politeness.

Dana cautiously eased her chair back from the table, clearing the space between Emory and Wes.

"I could use a break here, Em," Wes said quietly.

"I can see that—you're out with a great-looking, sexy, charming woman and you've been trying to pretend all evening that she wasn't there."

"That's not true." Wes could hear the testy tone in her voice and tried to dial it back. Emory was her friend. "It's complicated."

Emory laughed. "Of that, I have no doubt. Neither of you strikes me as simple. Although sometimes, I think you're kind of simple-minded."

Dana stood up, the loud scraping of her chair audible even over the music. "I'm gonna go get refills. Another drink, Wes?"

Wes eyed her half-finished beer. She'd had her hand clasped around the bottle for most of the last set, and the beer was warm. She'd feared if she let go, her hand would end up on Evyn's thigh, the hard, sleek thigh that had somehow come to rest against hers soon after they'd all sat down. The entire length of her leg tingled, as if Evyn had been sending a low pulse of energy into her for the past hour. "I'll have another Pilgrim."

"Coming up."

"So what's really going on?" Emory asked as soon as they were alone.

"I don't know, Em," Wes said, weary of pretending everything was fine and exactly the way she wanted it. "I'm still trying to sort things out."

"But there's something going on between you. That's pretty obvious. She's been watching you the entire night."

Wes stiffened. She'd been hyperaware of Evyn since the moment they'd left the White House and driven to the club in Evyn's car. They hadn't talked much, but the silence hadn't been uncomfortable. All the same, every time she looked at Evyn, she'd known the silence was masking what they both wanted to say. Even the noisy bar and the diversion offered by Emory and Dana's company hadn't diminished her awareness of Evyn next to her. Her brain registered the music, followed along in the conversations, and prompted her to answer when spoken to, but all she really noticed was Evyn—the heat of her body, the sound of her voice, the space she occupied at the table. Watching Evyn's fingers curl around her glass, all Wes could think of was the sensation of those fingers gently clasping her breast, stroking her, turning her blood to fire and her mind to a sea of pleasure.

"You're attracted to her," Emory said, making it a statement, not a question.

"Yes."

"Which one of you is throwing up walls?"

Wes laughed. "What makes you think we are?"

"Oh, come on. You're both acting as if it would be a crime to touch each other." She shook her head. "The two of you actually go out of your way not to touch when it would be perfectly natural to do so—it's so obvious. So who shot who down?"

"No one," Wes said, at a loss as to how to make sense of everything. "It's mutual—we decided not to go that route."

"What route?"

"Intimacy."

"You mean sex?"

"Come on, Emory," Wes said. "Don't make this any harder for me. You know what I mean."

"Honest, I don't. Is she married?"

"What? No."

"I know you're not."

Wes shook her head. "Can we not—"

"She's straight?"

"No," Wes said definitely. Her stomach twisted, remembering the way Evyn made love to her, so confidently, so perceptively, so powerfully. "Definitely, no."

"And I know you're not." Emory raised an eyebrow. "Are you?"

"No," Wes said, laughing despite her discomfort.

"So what's the problem? You're both available, you're both gay, and you both obviously have the major hots for each other."

"We work closely together—a personal relationship could seriously disrupt the team."

"May I say, major bullshit?"

"You don't understand—"

"More bullshit." Emory spoke without the slightest bit of heat, just calm certainty. "I know you, and I'm betting any woman you're attracted to would be pretty similar as far as this is concerned. Nothing compromises your work. I bet Evyn is the same way."

"I'm what way?" Evyn pulled out her chair and sat back down next to Wes. Her arm brushed Wes's and the tingling spread from Wes's leg into her stomach, making it hard for her to focus on Emory's inquisition.

"Totally serious and uncompromising about work," Emory said.

Evyn gave Wes a what-did-I-miss look, then shifted in her chair and regarded Emory. "Yes, I'd say that's true. Why?"

"How well do you know Wes?" Emory asked.

Wes snapped back to the conversation. She wasn't going to discuss her personal relationship with Evyn while Evyn sat an inch away. "Never mind. Emory and I were just catching up."

Evyn glanced from Emory to Wes. "I have obviously missed something pretty important here. Maybe you should catch *me* up."

"Emory is my oldest friend—she thinks that gives her certain privileges."

"It does," Emory said.

Evyn laughed. "What is it you want to know?"

"Do you really think there's anything that could make Wesley compromise her professional obligations?"

"No," Evyn said slowly. "I don't."

"That's not how you felt a few weeks ago," Wes said.

"You're right. But I know a lot more about you now than I did then."

"My point exactly," Emory said. "Experience sometimes runs counter to expectations—and proves there are exceptions to every rule."

"And sometimes," Evyn said softly, her gaze returning to Wes, "rules are just convenient shields."

Wes had the urge to get up and run, and she'd never run from anything in her life. What could be so frightening about a woman wanting to be close to her? Not just any woman. Evyn. Evyn, who had provided quiet strength, and tender comfort, and fierce passion. Evyn—who refused to be pushed away.

"Sometimes reshaping boundaries is slow work."

Evyn grinned. "I'm patient."

Wes threw back her head, laughing quietly. "How is it I've never noticed?"

"Never?" Evyn murmured.

Wes's breath caught. Evyn had been endlessly patient the night they'd made love—letting Wes lead, despite her inexperience, letting her satisfy her need to touch and taste and savor. "I remember."

"Good."

"Well," Emory said, as Dana returned, "before Wesley tells me it's none of my business, I'll butt out." She cleared a space on the table for the drinks and leaned to kiss Dana as she sat down. "But for the record, I think you two are smoking hot together."

Wes groaned and Evyn grinned.

Emory lifted a shoulder. "Just my scientific observation."

❖

Russo walked out onto the back deck of his mountain cabin. His last two public appearances and the benefit dinners that followed had been great successes. His supporters had been enthusiastic, and even his wife had managed to do her part. Now he planned to celebrate properly with Nora, who should arrive any moment. Despite the frigid air, he felt totally comfortable. The sky was clear, the stars bright points of light, the moon a huge flawless globe. Snow cascaded down the mountainside and layered the bending boughs of the pines with powdery lace. He was surrounded by natural beauty, and the brisk air stung his lungs with every breath, reminding him of the surety of life.

Nora's latest report showed his popularity growing and his strength with the electorate approaching the point where no challenger would pose a threat. Still, a substantial number in his own party found him too radical, too polarizing, and there were large segments of the Northeast and West where Andrew Powell commanded a huge following. He needed to shake up the moderates in his own party and create doubt in the hearts of the centrist liberals who might be persuaded to change allegiances if the threat to their personal safety was great enough. The time to prepare the groundwork for that shift in power was now. Certain of his course, he called Hooker.

"Hooker," the man answered.

"It's time to initiate our plans with the optimal timetable," Russo said.

"That doesn't give us a lot of time," Hooker said.

"Yes, I'm aware of that, but given the ideal location, you should have ample time to activate all the parties."

"I'll need to confirm with my contact."

"Then do so," Russo said calmly. "Unless I hear from you, I'll assume we are proceeding as planned."

"My fee just went up," Hooker said. "It's going to take a whole lot of coordinating to pull this off so soon."

"I have utmost faith in you. And if all goes as expected, you'll receive a twenty percent bonus."

"That's very generous," Hooker said.

"I hope we'll be doing business for some time."

"I'll let you know when I've confirmed with my contact."

"Wonderful. And happy holidays."

"Yeah," Hooker said, "ho-fucking-ho."

Russo rang off without commenting. The new year was going to be a very good year.

❖

"Are you coming to bed?" Blair kissed the top of Cam's head and rubbed her shoulders. "It's getting late and it's been a long day."

Cam leaned her head back against Blair's stomach and closed her eyes, enjoying the warmth spreading down her back from Blair's hands. "Have I ever mentioned I love the way you touch me?"

Smiling, Blair kissed the top of her head again. "A time or two. What are you doing?"

Cam rubbed her eyes. "Reviewing reports from this morning's security update. Looking for anything out of the ordinary."

"Why? If you think we're dealing with someone on the inside?"

"The leak may be internal, but if…" She hesitated. They were talking about Blair's father.

"It's a little late to try to shield me, don't you think?" Blair's question lacked the usual heat that accompanied any accusation of Cam being overprotective. "Lucinda briefed me and you know she doesn't sugarcoat anything. If someone is going to try to kill my father, you don't think it will be someone close to him? Someone we know?"

"I don't know a thing for sure," Cam said, wishing with everything in her Blair didn't have to be a part of this. Bad enough Blair needed to worry about her father, but Blair was going to be right in the middle of any potential attack. She was almost as much at risk as Andrew, and there was no way Blair could be convinced not to go on the trail with him.

"You're going to be there too," Blair said with her uncanny ability to read Cam's mind.

"How do you do that?"

"Practice." Blair spun Cam's chair around, straddled her lap, and kissed her with heat. They'd spent the day apart. While Cam had met with Lucinda and then gone straight into a briefing with Tom and the other agents on PPD, Blair had spent a rare afternoon with her father. They hadn't talked about security concerns. They'd talked about his reelection campaign, the major platform issues, and the role Blair would play. For a few hours she'd been able to forget the danger and the fear. The only other person who'd ever made her feel so safe was Cam.

"I missed you today," Blair said. "We're still supposed to be on our honeymoon."

Cam smiled and ran her hands up and down Blair's back. "And I am obviously falling down on my marital duties already."

Blair snuggled tighter into Cam's lap, settling her ass firmly in Cam's crotch. "Oh, I wouldn't say that. But if you're almost done, and you've still got half an hour left in you, you could see to your duties."

Cam rested her cheek against Blair's breast. "Give me ten minutes, and I'm yours."

Blair ran her fingers through Cam's hair. "All right. Have you found anything?"

"Nothing substantial, really. I'm just trolling—a truckload of munitions went missing from Fort Dix. We've got Army CID on that. A sleeper cell we've been watching in San Francisco looks like it may be waking up—I've got a Homeland Security team moving on that. An inventory irregularity turned up at a Level 4 government-funded research lab outside of Atlanta. A team from the CDC is on their way there."

"So you think someone on the inside is part of a larger group, and the attack is being orchestrated from the outside?"

"We have to be prepared for that." Cam tilted Blair's chin up and met her eyes. "We have to be prepared for anything."

Blair smoothed the frown lines between Cam's brows. "We will be. You're not alone in this—no matter what, you're never alone."

Cam wrapped her arms around Blair's waist and rose. Blair automatically locked her legs behind Cam's back. Cam kissed her. "I know. Let's go to bed."

❖

Wes kissed Emory's cheek as they stood outside the Black Fox. "It was great to see you. Merry Christmas."

Emory hugged her. "You too." She hugged Wes close to whisper in her ear. "And don't be afraid to take a chance, Wes. Sometimes, you have to."

"I'll call you soon." Wes released Emory, shook Dana's hand, and waved as they headed off toward the car. She and Evyn walked toward Dupont Circle, where Evyn had parked.

"What was that all about back in the bar?" Evyn said.

"Just the usual third degree from friends—you know, where we met, that sort of thing."

"And are we fucking?"

"Not in just those words, no," Wes said dryly. "But the intention was there."

Evyn laughed. "What did you say?"

"That it was complicated."

"I guess it is." Evyn slipped her arm around Wes's waist as they walked. Maybe it was the holiday lights on every porch and storefront or the excitement on the faces of everyone they passed that made her heart so light and filled with possibility, but she was tired of ignoring her need to really connect with Wes. "How come it seemed simple that night?"

"Because we weren't thinking past the moment?"

Evyn blew out a breath. "We weren't really thinking at all. That's not like me."

"Me either."

"So," Evyn said, "what are you thinking right now?"

Wes slowed and pointed down the block. "That my place is right over there."

"Really? Great location," Evyn said, testing the air. Wes had been calling all the shots up until now—another thing that was decidedly unlike her. She hadn't minded when they'd been holed up in that hotel room in Kitty Hawk and she hadn't had a clue what the hell was going on, but they weren't in Kitty Hawk any longer. And Wes was no one-night stand. She needed to get in the game right now.

"Yeah, close to the Metro and all that."

"So, what's the chance I could get a cup of coffee before I drive home?" Evyn asked.

"Sure," Wes said slowly before leading the way up the block toward her apartment. She shouldn't be doing what she was doing, but the tension in her chest eased with every step they took away from Evyn's car. She didn't want Evyn to leave. She didn't want the night to end. She didn't want to wake up another morning alone and questioning.

"You know we don't have to figure this all out at once," Evyn said, taking her hand.

Evyn's fingers were soft, warm, and Wes laced hers through Evyn's. "I know. I'm trying to shut my mind off, but it's tough."

"Then don't try. Some things you can't control."

"That's what's so scary."

"It's just coffee, Wes."

"Right. You're right." Wes squeezed Evyn's hand. Except what if she wanted more than just coffee?

CHAPTER TWENTY-SEVEN

Silently, Wes led Evyn to her apartment, unlocked the door, and held it wide for her to enter. She turned on a table lamp just inside the door while Evyn waited only a foot away. In the dim lamplight, Evyn's features were soft, almost blurred. Color smudged her cheeks, probably from the cold. Wes had a hard time looking away from her mouth, remembering the softness, the taste. "I'll take your coat."

"Thanks." Evyn passed her jacket to Wes and turned slightly to take in the living room and kitchen. "Looks like a pretty good place."

"My mother says it needs plants. Or a cat." Wes held Evyn's jacket in one hand, oddly unable to move.

"Mothers always think we need plants."

"Yours too?" Wes didn't know what to do with herself. She'd never brought a woman back to her quarters before. She searched her mind for the right thing to say, the right thing to do, and realized she had no idea. Evyn wasn't just any friend, and thinking Evyn might be or could be was ridiculous. She had friends. She loved Emory. She didn't want Emory to kiss her—didn't ache to see her the moment they parted. Didn't lose her concentration thinking about the way Emory tasted, the small sounds she made when they kissed. "I'll make that coffee."

Evyn moved closer and brushed a stray lock of hair from Wes's forehead. Her fingertips were warm but Wes shivered. "Why don't you take your coat off first."

Wes swallowed. Nodding, she shrugged out of her topcoat, grateful for something to do, and hung it up with Evyn's in the closet next to the door. When she turned back, Evyn was standing right in front of her.

"Coffee keeps me awake if I drink it after twenty-two hundred," Evyn said.

"It's almost zero hundred."

"I know. Honestly, the coffee was an excuse. I wasn't ready to say good night. Sorry."

Wes watched Evyn's lips move, straining to hear the words while her body flooded with the memory of soft kisses and a knowing mouth and unbearable pleasure. She pressed her fingertips to Evyn's lips, amazed when she realized she'd moved. Touched her. She hadn't meant to. "No need to be sorry."

Evyn grew silent, her eyes darkening, searching Wes's.

"I keep thinking about being with you," Wes said hoarsely. "About touching you. About the way you touch me. Remembering… everything…has been driving me crazy."

Evyn covered Wes's hand and kissed her fingertips. Drawing Wes's palm to the side of her face, she held it there, pressed Wes's fingers along the arch of her jaw.

Evyn's skin was soft, hot. Wes throbbed inside. She held her breath, held very, very still. Waiting. Searching for an answer she feared she wouldn't recognize.

"I know," Evyn whispered, leaning toward her. Inches away now. "I feel the same. I want you all the time."

Wes backed up a step. Her shoulders met the closet door and she leaned against it. Her thighs went soft and she locked her knees, forcing her body to stay upright. They should talk, but her mind was seriously disconnected. She clasped the back of Evyn's neck, fearing she might move away.

"I'm not going anywhere." Evyn smiled, a knowing, ever-so-slightly triumphant smile.

Wes kept her eyes open as Evyn slowly leaned closer, memorizing the swirling shades of blue and purple in Evyn's eyes, the flicker of her ebony pupils, the golden sparks of color that danced around her irises, like flames around the fire. She grasped Evyn's waist with both hands, pressing her thumbs into the muscles above Evyn's hips. Evyn groaned softly and excitement welled in Wes's depths. She tugged Evyn to her, but Evyn pressed her palms on either side of her shoulders, keeping their bodies an inch apart.

"Do you know what you're doing to me?" Evyn growled softly. "What I want right now?"

"I want to kiss you," Wes said.

"I want more than that." Evyn's lips skimmed Wes's. Sweet, hot, urgent. "Say yes, Wes."

"Yes."

Instantly, Evyn's mouth covered Wes's. Thought fled, instinct ruled. Wes slid her arms around Evyn and dug her fingertips into the hard muscles along Evyn's spine. A pulse pounded in her clit. Groaning, she parted her legs and Evyn's tight thigh wedged between hers. Wes arched. She wanted—needed—more too. "Yes."

Evyn took the kiss deeper. Her tongue was sweet and sure, sweeping over the inside of Wes's lips, probing lightly in her mouth, teasing her to surrender. Wes rode Evyn's thigh, hips pumping, each thrust sending spirals of pleasure twisting along her spine. She heard a whimper. Registered distantly the sound came from her.

Pulling her head back, Evyn gasped, "Wes."

Evyn's voice grated, a register lower than Wes recognized, urgent and hungry. Evyn's need made her burn. Wes twisted a handful of Evyn's shirt in her fist and yanked it from her pants. Evyn found the buttons on her shirt, impatiently worked them open, slid her hand over Wes's bare belly. Wes jerked at the sudden flash of heat. Her nipples tightened. Need gripped her like a hard hand between her thighs. She moaned. She was burning.

"Wes, God. Where's the bed?" Evyn's mouth seared Wes's neck. Her fingers slipped down Wes's belly, restlessly searching beneath the waistband of Wes's pants. "I don't want to take you against this fucking door, and if we don't find a bed soon, I'm going to."

Wes dragged her hands down Evyn's back, squeezing her ass, and thrust her hand between their bodies. She flicked a button on her pants and pushed the zipper down. "Don't move. Right here. Do it. Just do it."

Wes's command sent rockets flaring in Evyn's head, blinding her to everything but Wes. She buried her face in the curve of Wes's neck and breathed her in. Her vision tunneled. Her head reeled with the woodsy scent that seduced her to touch, to taste, to take. She panted, couldn't get her breath, couldn't find her focus.

Wes's fingers wrapped around her wrist and pushed her hand into the front of her open pants. Evyn's mind went white. Wes was wet against her fingertips, slick and hot and hard. She skated over Wes's clit, squeezed quickly, and Wes jerked upright with a strangled cry. The sharp edge of Wes's pleasure cleaved Evyn's control and her clit pumped to the brink of exploding. She pushed deeper, each stroke of her fingertips wringing another sharp cry of pleasure from Wes. The ties on her restraint unraveled and her orgasm boiled closer. "God, no, I'm gonna come soon."

Wes's nails raked her skin. Evyn cupped Wes in her palm, squeezing her, teasing her.

"Don't hold back," Wes groaned in her ear, her hold on Evyn's arm like iron.

Evyn thought she'd wear the marks of Wes's fingertips for days. The image drove her crazy. She loved Wes's urgency, her need, thrilled to the power of being wanted, being needed. She thrust deeper and Wes's other hand found her breast. Fingers closed around her nipple and she threw her head back. "Oh, Christ. Wes. You feel so good. I can't hold it much longer."

"I need..." Wes's eyes opened, impossibly green, impossibly beautiful. "I need you to make me come."

Evyn's clit twitched hard. She dropped her forehead to Wes's. "Hold me."

Wes's arms came around her waist, steadying her. Evyn pumped inside her, rolled her palm over Wes's clit. With every thrust, Wes's groans urged her on. Evyn rocked on Wes's thigh, climbed closer to exploding.

"Yes, yes. You're going to make me come." Wes rode Evyn's hand, short hard strokes. "Now, Evyn. You're making me come."

"Hold me. Wes. Please." Evyn hovered so close—so close, drowning in the sound of Wes's pleasure, on fire with the sensation of Wes pulsing around her, slick and hot. She needed to come. Needed it, needed it so bad. "Wes, please. Help me."

Wes bit her neck and Evyn came, the orgasm thundering out of nowhere.

"Oh my God!" Stunned, Evyn collapsed into Wes, her hand crushed between them, buried between Wes's legs.

"Yes. Yes. Yes," Wes groaned, flooding Evyn's fingers, coming on them again.

Evyn's breath shot out in sobs of wonder and relief. She never wanted to move. She never wanted to break the connection. She just wanted more. Her heart thundered in her chest. Her stomach rolled with need. She kissed Wes's throat, the line of her jaw, her mouth. "You're so beautiful. So amazing."

Wes's hands caressed her shoulders, her back, stroked her hair, clasped her neck. "That's okay," Wes murmured. "That's okay."

Evyn raised her head. Dazed, unfocused. "What?"

Wes brushed her thumbs over Evyn's cheek. "You're so beautiful...Thank you."

"What?" Evyn felt the tears Wes wiped away. Her tears. What the fuck was wrong with her? She looked at Wes. Wes's shirt was open, her pants around her hips. She was still mostly dressed. What was she doing? She'd just fucked Wes against a goddamned door. She didn't remember how they'd gone from keeping their distance to this. She could only remember want and need, desperate need. And now she was crying? That just never fucking happened. Not to her. She never lost control. Confusion, uncertainty, sheer panic choked her.

"Are you all right?" Wes asked, her hand cradling Evyn's chin.

What next—would Wes be asking her if she needed to process? "I'm fine. I'm not the one up against the door. *You* okay?"

The cloudy haze of pleasure cleared from Wes's eyes in an instant. Her focus sharpened, narrowed. Evyn felt naked with all her clothes on. She couldn't imagine being any more vulnerable.

"Evyn," Wes said, steady and strong. "There were two of us here. I wanted what happened to happen. Do you hear me?"

Evyn licked her lips, a little disoriented. She'd made the first move, hadn't she? She always did. What the hell happened? Where—when had she lost it? "I didn't hurt you, did I?"

"No," Wes said softly. "No. You were wonderful." Her gaze dropped down Evyn's body. "I don't think I held up my end, though. I've still got some things to learn—"

"Believe me, you don't need to learn anything." Evyn shook her head. And she was no teacher, that was for sure. "I don't usually lose it like that."

"Are you all right?"

Evyn backed up a step, tucked her shirt back into her pants. "Sure. I'm great. The sex was great—I don't guess I need to say that."

Wes zipped up, not bothering to button her shirt. Evyn looked spooked. Uneasy. Almost battle shocked. "Why don't you sit down? I really will make some coffee."

"I need to go. It's late."

"Evyn, I'm not asking—"

"You don't get it, Wes." Evyn shook her head. "I don't do serious."

"Okay," Wes said, the familiar ache settling behind her breastbone. "Is that what this was? Serious?"

"I don't know what this was," Evyn shouted. She pushed her hand through her hair, wanted to pull it out. Wanted some real pain to block the awful dread in the pit of her stomach. "No, that's a fucking lie. This was amazing. You're beautiful, sexy as fucking hell. And you make me crazy. I can't afford to be crazy."

"Tonight was my fault," Wes said.

"The hell it was," Evyn said sharply. "There's no fault here, okay? It was just…I don't know—hormones. Pheromones. Something. God, I can't be anywhere around you without wanting you."

"Which I take is a bad thing?"

"I'm sorry." Evyn looked around the room as if she had never seen it before. Her gaze settled on Wes's face. "You deserve a lot better than this—" She waved at the door. "More than a fast fuck."

Wes swallowed the pain. She didn't beg. Ever. Not for anyone or anything. "Look, let's not make this an issue, okay? We're adults, we acted on instinct, we both wanted a fast fuck, as you say. Now it's done. We're over it—we move on."

Anger flared in Evyn's eyes and Wes nearly buckled under a wave of need. She wanted Evyn naked. She wanted to be inside her. Evyn made her want things, things she'd never thought she needed, things Evyn didn't want or need from her. "If you're sure you don't want coffee…"

"No, I'm good," Evyn said.

"Okay then." Wes turned away, busied herself getting Evyn's coat, settled herself. "You're okay to drive?"

Evyn took her jacket. "I'm fine."

"Good night then." Wes opened the door.

"'Night," Evyn said softly and slipped by without touching her.

Wes turned out the light and walked to the window where her mother thought she should put a plant. Evyn was a dark shadow disappearing down the street. Now she knew. Being alone with Evyn Daniels was dangerous. She understood just how dangerous now and wouldn't make the same mistake again.

❖

Lucinda answered her phone on the first ring. "Washburn."

"I thought you might still be in your office," Cam said.

"We're two days from Christmas Eve—busy time around here."

"I know. You got a minute?"

"Where are you?"

"Outside the door."

"Come in." Lucinda replaced the phone and got up. A muscle in her back reminded her she'd been sitting too long. She rubbed it quickly. Cam walked in, closed the door. She wore jeans and a black crew neck sweater—unusually casual for her. Cam looked tired—her eyes were clear, but dark circles shadowed her cheeks. Her always carved features looked sharper, knife edged, and Lucinda realized she was seeing Cam on the hunt.

"Sorry to show up unannounced, but I didn't think this could wait," Cam said.

"You have something?" Lucinda asked.

"I don't know. Maybe."

Lucinda's breath caught on a wave of excitement. They'd all been casting in the dark for weeks, too many bits and pieces, too many fragments of facts and non-facts to shape into a coherent pattern. Directionless in the face of unseen enemies, she was left impotent and, deep inside, afraid. She couldn't afford to be afraid. Andrew refused to be intimidated, to be deterred, and she needed a clear head and clearer vision to see that he was safe. "Tell me."

"I've requested field reports on anything that might remotely be connected to a potential attack and run probability algorithms on everything I can think of," Cam said. "Another aerial assault, dirty bombs, a lone gunman, a group attack."

The matter-of-fact tone in her voice chilled Lucinda to the core. "As has Averill, I'm sure."

"Right. And neither of us hit on anything with greater than random probability." Cam paced to the windows overlooking the gardens. Her face in the cast-off glow of the walkway lights was marble smooth and stone hard. "So I started looking at everyone who surfaced in connection to suspicious events. I've got a flimsy..." She laughed and shook her head. "Whatever is flimsier than flimsy, that's the connection I've got."

"Any connection is something more solid than what we have now." Lucinda joined Cam by the windows, squeezed her arm. "You are the best there is. I trust your instincts—I trust you with Blair and Andrew. Tell me what you're thinking."

Cam rolled her shoulders, blew out a breath. "One of the technicians with regular access to a missing biocontagion at a Level Four lab outside Atlanta is from Idaho. Went to a Christian college there. So did Lieutenant Jennifer Pattee."

"So you think they might know each other?" Lucinda struggled to see a connection.

"On the surface—no. There's a six-year age difference, which means they weren't in college at the same time."

"Hometowns?"

"According to records, not the same."

"What do you mean, according to the records? You don't believe the records?"

"Here's the thing that made me look harder at the two of them— they were both homeschooled before college."

Lucinda paced around her desk. "Not so unusual in Idaho."

"No—but another point of intersection and another point of commonality. So I looked a little bit deeper—parents, siblings, other possible connectors. And I didn't find anything."

"You're right, that's not much," Lucinda said, disappointment sitting like a hard weight on her chest.

"No, what I mean is, I didn't find *anything*. Their families are off the grid."

"No record of their parents or sibs?"

"None. For homeschooled kids to go to college, they have to show GED or equivalent scores, SAT scores, and a personal affidavit." Cam slid her hands into her pockets, rocked on her heels. "That's the starting point for colleges, the beginning of a paper trail. But there's no road leading back to any place I can find."

"Are you postulating we're dealing with a domestic sleeper cell? Americans raised to carry out some long-range act of terrorism?"

Cam sighed. "I think so—yes."

"It's pretty coincidental, but I agree, there might be something there." Lucinda shook her head. "What do you advise?"

"We need to put someone on her. We need to know more about her, and we may not have a lot of time."

"Put agents on her."

"That's my plan."

"One of Blair's?"

"I was thinking we could pair one from PPD and one from Blair's detail. An insider who won't be obvious to the lieutenant, and one she doesn't know." Cam grinned, a chilling, predatory grin. "One might be a distraction and she'll miss the other."

"Fine, do that."

Cam regarded Lucinda steadily. "I wouldn't ordinarily suggest this, but I don't know what kind of timetable we're working with here. If there is any potential for a bioterrorist attack using the missing specimen, it's likely to be soon. We need as many eyes on this as we can get."

"What else?" Lucinda asked.

"Captain Masters seems to think Jennifer Pattee expressed more than a professional interest in her. Masters might be the best person to give us early warning."

"She's not a trained agent."

"No, but she's a navy captain. She's smart, she's steady. We use what we have."

"Individuals like this—extremists, fanatics—their goal is to make a point, no matter the cost. If we thwart their operation, they may opt to make an even bigger statement."

"I know. And that's a risk—and if what I suspect about Pattee is right, and she realizes we suspect her, she could become volatile, unstable. That's a recipe for disaster, but I think we have to take the chance."

Lucinda nodded. "It has to be voluntary. The captain has to agree—I won't order her to do this."

"Do you think you'd have to?"

"No, I don't think we need to order her. Will you see to it?"

Cam nodded sharply. "I'll do that. Thank you."

"And, Cam, I know this will be difficult, but don't bring Blair in on this right now. We need to keep her at a safe distance."

Cam's jaw tightened. "She might not forgive us for that."

"Let me worry about that."

"She's mine to worry about." Cam walked to the door. "And mine to protect. Good night."

"Good night, Cam." Once the door closed, Lucinda sagged behind her desk and pressed her fingertips to her eyes. She picked up her phone and made a call. "I'm sorry, were you sleeping? I need to see you. No, I'll come there."

Lucinda turned out the lights and stepped outside through the French doors and started for the residence. She thought of all those who would sacrifice everything to serve and protect, and of how many times she had asked for that sacrifice. More times than she could count, and probably many more to come.

CHAPTER TWENTY-EIGHT

At 0430, Evyn got the text from Cameron Roberts telling her she needed to be at a briefing at 0600. She'd been asleep an hour. When she got home from Wes's, she was still wired, her body still humming. She'd come out of her mind with Wes barely touching her, but the orgasm was already a distant memory and her body craved more. More of Wes. Adrenaline, that's all it was. When she got amped up during a tense training exercise or something heated up out in the field, she always got a sexual buzz. That's all it was. Adrenaline.

Whatever she called it, the burn in her blood was enough to keep her up channel surfing, with Ricochet sitting nearby, watching her warily. He didn't seem to trust her mood, because he wasn't in her lap or draped around her shoulders, where he usually perched while she chilled out. He was probably smart not to get too close because she wasn't chilling out. She was too uncomfortable in her skin to unwind. She finished the one beer she allowed herself, but it didn't settle her enough to sleep. Finally, exhaustion won out and she stretched out where she was on the couch and fell asleep in her clothes. She dreamed of running through a tangled forest, breathless, lost, pursued by a faceless menace coming ever closer. Roberts's text had awakened her, saving her from what she feared she might find—the pursuer was her and she was running from herself.

Now, after a quick shower and two shots of espresso, she was walking through the West Wing in her least wrinkled pair of black trousers and her last pressed white shirt. Staffers hurried by, already looking harried. She settled in the briefing room. There wasn't any coffee—must have been a very hastily assembled meeting. A minute later the door opened and Paula Stark walked in followed by a young agent she recognized from Blair Powell's detail, but didn't know personally.

"Hey," Evyn said, nodding to Paula. Their details often overlapped when the first daughter was traveling with POTUS. She liked Stark—she was on top of things without being super territorial.

"Hi, Evyn. This is Randy Block."

Evyn leaned over the table to shake hands with the new guy. "How you doing."

"Fine. Good to meet you." Block looked like a typical college jock—fair-haired, blue-eyed, strong jaw, good shoulders. A lot like Gary, a wholesome, all-American guy. She wondered what was going on and if Stark knew something she didn't. But she wasn't about to ask.

The door opened again and she expected Tom to walk in. She barely managed to keep quiet when Wes sat down across the table from her.

"Morning," Wes said, glancing around the table. She was wearing charcoal pants, a crisp pale blue shirt open at the throat, and a matte silver bracelet on her right wrist with some kind of intertwining pattern, subtle, understated. Sexy. Her gaze passed over Evyn's face in the same friendly but distant fashion in which she regarded everyone else in the room.

At precisely 0600, Cameron Roberts walked in. "Morning, everyone. Thanks for getting here on such short notice. I think the only one needing introductions is Captain Masters, the new chief of the White House Medical Unit."

Stark and Block introduced themselves to Wes and they all shook hands. Evyn wondered why Tom wasn't there.

"This is need-to-know," Roberts said as if reading her mind, "and I won't be giving you much in the way of details."

Evyn sat still, keeping her shoulders relaxed, preventing the tension curling around her spine from showing in her face or body. She'd learned years ago to school herself, to never give away anything, but it was hard with Wes only a few feet away. She had what she wanted—an impersonal, cordial working relationship, and she hated it. She hated that Wes would walk into a room and not seek her out first, not connect with her in a way she didn't connect with others. What the fuck was wrong with her? Why couldn't she be satisfied with the way things had always been? Why did she want things now that she'd never wanted before? Why did Wes Masters make her yearn?

Wes looked over at her as if she had been broadcasting her thoughts, and Evyn quickly looked away. She wasn't certain she could hide what she was feeling from Wes, and she didn't want her to know she regretted the night before. She regretted walking out. She regretted letting Wes think she could walk away without bleeding inside.

"We need surveillance on an individual we suspect might have ties to a domestic terrorist group that is planning an attack on POTUS."

None of the agents moved, but the air suddenly vibrated. Evyn's skin tingled and her heart rate had picked up. Her groin tightened as her senses went to full alert. Wes hadn't moved either, and she seemed completely composed. Why was she here? This was a security matter.

"We suspect the individual may have access to a biocontagion or may be a contact for someone else who does. This is where Dr. Masters comes in."

The muscles at the angles of Evyn's jaws clenched, and she had to force her teeth not to grind. What was this about? Wes wasn't trained for this.

"The individual in question is Lieutenant Jennifer Pattee, a member of the White House Medical Unit." Roberts opened her laptop and brought up an image of a woman who looked enough like Jennifer Pattee to be her sister. "We have reason to believe she may have connections to this woman—Angela Jones, although we doubt that's her given name. Jones is an employee of Eugen Corp, a private laboratory doing viral gene research. They've reported an inventory discrepancy in their Level Four lab which we believe may actually be a stolen specimen."

"The nature of the specimen?" Wes asked.

"Our understanding is it's an engineered virus—a mutant form of an avian flu virus."

"What do we know of its properties?"

"Not very much," Roberts said. "The lead investigators are stonewalling us because their work is preliminary and unreported at this point. They don't want information being disseminated prematurely, but the transformed avian virus is apparently much more highly transmissible than the natural avian virus."

"That's a problem," Wes said. "The avian flu virus has a high mortality rate, but it is not easily transmissible between fowl and humans, and not transmissible from one human to another."

Roberts nodded, her expression grave. "They won't come out and admit to this, but we believe this variant has been aerosolized and is transmissible between humans."

Wes frowned. "Then you have an agent with the potential to kill vast numbers of individuals."

Evyn shook her head. "This seems pretty complex for an assassination plot."

"On the surface, yes," Roberts said. "There are faster and more direct ways, none of which we need to enumerate here. But while assassination by gunfire is horrifying and dramatic, the public doesn't see a single act of violence as a personal threat. However, the release of a biological agent capable of killing scores or even more places the danger directly on the public itself. People will be terrified."

"And consequently," Paula Stark said softly, "the government will be distrusted and destabilized."

"Exactly."

"I don't know the lieutenant very well," Wes said. "I can't say that I've seen any particularly suspicious behavior from her."

"Nor would we expect you would have." Roberts clicked off the computer and pushed it aside. She addressed Wes directly. "If what we believe is true, these individuals have been trained since childhood to carry out specific acts of terrorism after achieving positions of power and trust. If indeed the lieutenant is part of this conspiracy, she's not going to reveal anything or do anything suspect until the attack itself is set in motion."

"What's the goal of surveillance?" Evyn asked.

"We need to intercept her when she receives the agent. Failing that, then we have to prevent the release of the contagion."

"I can adjust our schedules so I'm on duty with Lieutenant Pattee," Wes said. "Of course, that's only going to be ten or twelve hours a day."

"Yes, do that," Roberts said. "In addition, Captain, given that the lieutenant has expressed a personal interest, you might be able to observe her in less guarded circumstances."

"What?" Evyn stood before she could stop herself. She looked from Roberts to Wes and then back to Roberts. "The captain isn't trained for undercover work, which is essentially what you're asking her to do. Whatever information she might gain isn't worth the risk to her or the operation—"

"I think I'm perfectly capable of making expert observations," Wes said calmly, "and would probably recognize conditions or circumstances conducive to exchanging and transporting a biologic agent more readily than anyone else. If it's a question of asking her out to dinner or spending an evening with her or more, I'm perfectly willing."

"That's ridiculous." Evyn squared her body to Roberts. "You can't really expect her to do this."

"Evyn—" Wes said.

"It's up to the captain, of course," Roberts said, "but we expect an attack to be imminent, and we need to take advantage of every avenue of information we possibly can. I admit it's a long shot, but even the remote possibility of picking up information that would help us pinpoint and intercept the individuals involved is worth pursuing."

Stark asked, "How strong is the connection between the lieutenant and Angela Jones?"

"Loose," Roberts admitted. "But more than we have been able to find anywhere else. I want Agents Daniels and Block to work together on surveillance. The lieutenant is familiar with PPD, so Agent Daniels's presence will likely be unnoticed. And Pattee doesn't know Blair's agents at all, so Block can take the lead outside official functions. That will allow us to stagger the coverage without putting a larger detail in place. Unfortunately, we're not sure how deeply we're compromised."

Evyn was no longer a suspect, but that knowledge didn't make her feel better. All she could think about was Wes suddenly in the middle of some crazy extremist conspiracy, without backup.

"Is Wes going to wear a wire?"

"Yes."

Evyn closed her fist by her side, struggling to keep her voice even. "That'll help us monitor her. But if she's discovered with it on, she'll be an immediate target."

"You forget, Agent," Wes said softly, "I earned my rank. I can take care of myself."

"This isn't some field hospital, Wes—"

Roberts cut in. "You can leave Captain Masters's security to me, Agent Daniels. Your job is to keep the lieutenant in your sights whenever she's in proximity to the president."

"Yes, ma'am," Evyn said tightly. As much as she trusted the director—Roberts had proved more than once she was the best—she didn't plan on leaving Wes's safety in anyone else's hands. She kept her mouth shut though—she'd already revealed too much about her personal feelings. "Why isn't Tom here?"

"Need-to-know," Cam said quietly.

"I'll get to work on adjusting the schedule," Wes said.

"Good. We'll communicate by phone and text. Stay off the comm channels. Block, your contact is Stark. Agent Daniels, I'm yours." Cam glanced at Wes. "And yours."

"Understood," Wes said.

Cam stood. "Good. Let's go."

Evyn held back while others pushed back from the table. "Wes—Captain Masters—a word, please."

"Of course," Wes said as the others filed out.

The door closed, leaving them alone, and Evyn stalked around the table. "This is crazy. You know that, right? Jesus Christ, Wes."

"Evyn, we have jobs to do. There's no time for this."

Evyn gripped Wes's forearm. "Just be sure you observe and nothing else."

Wes shook her head. "Do you really think I'm in need of protection?"

The metallic taste of fear, foreign and paralyzing, blurred Evyn's focus. She took a deep breath, then another. "I know you don't. It's just—if something happens to you...I can't go there, okay?"

"Then don't. Just trust me." Wes skimmed a fingertip along Evyn's jaw. "It's okay. I like that you worry, but you don't have to. I'll be fine."

Evyn wanted to grab Wes's hand and hold it to her, wanted the warm certainty of her touch. She went very still as Wes's eyes turned that deep green they got when they were alone with nothing between them—no pretense, no fear, no excuses. Deep calm—solid and clear—centered Evyn like no amount of self-imposed control ever had. Last night she'd thought she was losing herself in Wes's eyes. Now she realized she was finding her true strength. "I'm sorry. I know you can handle this. It's just—last night. Wes, I thought—"

Wes shook her head. "Evyn, don't. You don't need to explain."

"Yeah—I do. I need you to know—" Evyn shook her head. "We've got work—I know it's not the time."

"There's always time if you need me—but I promise you don't need to worry about this."

"You'll be careful?"

"Yes. You too."

"Always." Evyn gave her stock answer, only now it wasn't just a piece of the armor she put on to compete every day in a world where she had to be the best. Now she knew she could feel and still win. "Last night isn't over. It can't be over."

"I don't want it to be either," Wes said quietly, "but I don't want to need what I can't have."

"I know I fucked up—"

"I didn't say that." Wes smiled wryly. "When this is over, we'll talk."

Not what Evyn wanted—not all of what she wanted. But she'd wait. She'd wait, but she wasn't going to let Wes forget. Or slip away. She kissed her—swift, hard. "I'm not quitting."

"Do you ever?" Wes asked.

"Never."

❖

Jennifer knocked on Wes's office door. "Hi. I got your text. I'm fine with the schedule changes."

"You'll be short and then doubling up two days in a row." Wes pulled a file folder over the report she'd been reading.

"Like I said, it's no problem. This time of year, OT is always welcome."

"Thanks. Sorry about the late notice. A couple of people have had personal matters come up—it's the season for it, I guess."

Jennifer stepped a little farther into the room, her shoulder nudging the door almost closed. "I'm glad for the excuse to spend time with you. It should be pretty quiet."

"I hear the Christmas buffet for staff is a big event." Wes thought ahead to the president's schedule—no trips planned until after New Year's. No State events during the holidays either. The largest gathering of staff and press would be in two days.

"Shouldn't be a problem." Jennifer smiled.

"Well, I'm sorry you'll be working part of Christmas Eve and Christmas Day too."

"You're in the same situation, right?"

"I'm new in town, remember? I didn't have any plans, so working isn't that much of a hardship." Wes wasn't really sure how convincing she'd be suggesting a personal interest. She didn't have a hell of a lot of practice—make that no practice—getting up close and personal with colleagues or anyone else. Except with Evyn—being close to Evyn hadn't taken any effort at all. *Last night isn't over.*

"Well," Jennifer said quickly, "like I said, my plans fell through too. Maybe that's a sign."

"Maybe you're right."

Apparently, her skills weren't as bad as she thought. Jennifer's eyes sparked, and color rose above the vee of her pale-blue cashmere sweater to her throat. "How about we catch a late dinner when our shift is over tonight. Unwind before the last-minute Christmas Eve duty."

"If you don't have any plans—"

"I don't, but even if I did," Jennifer said, her smile slow and seductive, "I'd change them. I've been hoping we'd have a chance to spend some time together."

"Then I'd like that. Tonight, then?"

"Yes, perfect."

"Shall I meet you somewhere?"

"Why don't you come over to my place for a drink after work, and we can leave from there."

"All right. That sounds perfect."

Jennifer smiled that suggestive smile again. "It does, doesn't it? See you later."

"Yes. Definitely."

Jennifer left and Wes sagged back in her chair. When she was sure Jennifer wasn't returning, she called Cameron Roberts and reported the conversation.

"Report to the briefing room before your shift ends," Cam said. "We'll wire you up."

"There's something else," Wes said.

"Go ahead."

Wes slid Len O'Shaughnessy's toxicology report out from under the file folder. Nothing had jumped out at her until she'd looked at the tissue analysis. "Colonel O'Shaughnessy had unusually high levels of potassium in his cardiac muscle. Enough to cause cardiac arrest."

"Enough for us to investigate his death as a homicide?"

"Postmortem levels might vary depending on when they were drawn—and he was given a lot of drugs during the resuscitation. This isn't hard evidence, I'm afraid."

"Your opinion, then," Cam said.

"If someone had wanted him out of the way," Wes said, "I'd say they succeeded."

CHAPTER TWENTY-NINE

B lair set her book aside when the door opened and Cam walked into the apartment. Cam looked tired, and she never looked tired. She always seemed to have endless energy and incredible stamina. The only signs of fatigue were a crease between her dark brows and a tightness around the corners of her mouth. Blair saw the stress, even though to anyone else Cam would appear as calm and centered as always. "Did you catch any sleep?"

"I grabbed a couple of hours in the ready room. I'm okay." Cam leaned over the sofa and kissed her. "Morning."

"What's going on?" Blair grasped Cam's hand and pulled her down beside her. Draping her legs over the arm of the sofa, she shifted until her head rested in Cam's lap. Blair tugged Cam's shirt from her trousers and kissed her bare abdomen. "Have you eaten?"

"Coffee and half a chocolate doughnut."

"That's not food." Blair settled back, and Cam stroked her arm beneath the edge of the threadbare USSS T-shirt of Cam's she wore to bed. The light touch was gentle and reassuring and exciting all at the same time. She never realized how much she missed Cam until she walked back in the door. The scent of her, just looking up and seeing her nearby, filled her with comfort and a peace she'd never known she wanted. "You're not supposed to deal with everything alone any longer."

Cam sifted Blair's hair through her fingers, soothed by the silky softness. "I'm not. I promise."

"But?"

"I can't help wanting to protect you."

"I know that. I love you for that. But it's a two-way street, right?"

"Yes, it is." Cam sighed. "I think we may be honing in on our leak."

"Who is it?" Blair kept a tight rein on the anger blazing in the very core of her. Disbelief and outrage stoked the flames. She wanted to strike back—and not being able to focus her rage only fueled her fury.

Cam gave her a capsule summary of what she'd reported to Lucinda. "If I'm right, there may be an attempted assault soon."

Fear licked around the edges of Blair's consciousness, but she pushed it away. "How? When?"

"I don't know. Guesses are all I have."

"Your guesses have always been good." Blair sat up and faced Cam, her knee sliding over Cam's thigh. She kissed her. "I know you're doing everything that can be done. It's not all on you."

Cam nodded. "I know. I'm just...things are starting to move and I'm preoccupied. Sorry."

"You're also not giving me much in the way of details."

Cam smiled softly. "Noticed that, did you?"

"Really, Cam." Blair shook her head. "Who told you to keep me out of the loop? Lucinda?"

A spark of humor lit Cam's dark eyes. "I'm not at liberty to say."

"Uh-huh. Okay. And exactly why aren't you following Lucinda's orders?"

The humor disappeared but the darkness remained in Cam's gaze. "Because I want you to be safe, and you can't be safe if you don't know what's going on. I think Lucinda's wrong in thinking you'll be safer if you're away from the action. We don't know what's coming, or where it's coming from, and the only way to be prepared is to hone our defenses while we work out an offensive plan."

"Meaning?"

"If your father's the target, and I believe he is, you should limit your time with him."

"That's not going to happen. If my father's the target, then I want to be with him. That means more agents, more surveillance, more protection for him."

"That's exactly what Lucinda wanted to avoid—both of you in the line of fire." Cam stroked Blair's jaw. "She loves you, you know."

"I know. So why are you telling me anything at all?"

Cam circled the back of Blair's neck, feathering her fingertips through her hair. "I'm telling you because I don't think anywhere is safer than any other place, right now. And since you won't abandon your father, you need to know what the potential threats are, to best protect yourself."

"And you know I'd kick your ass if you kept this from me."

Cam grinned again. "That too."

"So tell me what you think I need to know."

"I will." Cam kissed her, a slow exploration that melted the tension in Blair's body and settled the disquiet in her mind. "As soon as I say a proper good morning."

Blair slid her hand under Cam's shirt and stroked upward to her breasts. "Not too tired?"

"Not tired at all."

❖

Just before 1800 hours, Wes finished writing a prescription for one of the groundskeepers who had severed the tip of his little finger while attempting to clear ice from his snow blower. He hadn't been able to find the missing piece of tissue, so Wes had shortened the bone fragment beneath his nail and closed it with a local skin flap. A week of antibiotics and a protective splint ought to be all he needed. His finger would be a little bit shorter, but he should have no functional deficit. He was lucky. She walked down to the treatment area where the PA on duty with her was splinting the digit. "Here you go. Stop by in two days for a bandage change. We'll get the stitches out in a week or so. How does it feel?"

The groundskeeper smiled. "Doesn't bother me at all. Can I go to work tomorrow?"

"Is there work you can do one-handed, because I don't want you taking that splint off."

"I'll manage."

"The splint stays on."

"Yes, ma'am."

"All right, then you can go back to work." She clipped the

prescription to his chart and went back to her office to finish her notes and shut down her computer. Five minutes later she headed for the briefing room she'd been in that morning. When she walked in, Evyn was there, sorting through an array of equipment on the table.

"Hi," Wes said, eyeing the small receiver and attached wires. "What's happening?"

"The director asked me to suit you up." Evyn looked up. "You need to be wired."

Wes loved the hazy purple of Evyn's eyes, a sure sign her emotions were running hot. She hoped she was the cause—even if the timing *was* bad. Even if that turmoil in Evyn's gaze was annoyance rather than attraction. Anything was better than the indifference and distance Evyn was so adept at hiding behind. "What do you want me to do?"

"Just take off your shirt and loosen your belt," Evyn said neutrally, her attention back on the equipment.

Wes removed her blazer, folded it over the back of a chair, and unbuttoned her shirt. She tugged it from her pants and laid it with her jacket. She opened her fly and pulled up the bottom of the silk tank she wore beneath her shirt.

Evyn held up a slim black box about the size of a deck of cards, only thinner. "This audio transmitter is small enough we should be able to secure it inside the waistband of your trousers in the middle of your back. Unless you get...cozy, it won't show."

"I'm not planning to get cozy."

Evyn grew still, her expression flat and closed. "Really? How do you plan on extracting personal information if you don't?"

"People tend to relax in a social situation, even when it's not intimate. They talk about their schedules, what they plan to do the next day, where they plan to go. Any of those things might help us pinpoint a potential exchange point."

"You're right," Evyn said abruptly. "And I apologize."

Wes grasped Evyn's wrist, stilling her in mid-motion. "This morning, you said last night wasn't over."

"I remember."

"What changed overnight?"

"I know you have no reason to believe this, but I did."

"How?"

"I thought if I really connected with you, if I really let myself be open to caring about you, to letting you close, I'd lose my edge, lose control. Not be able to focus on what mattered."

"Is that what happened this morning in the briefing?"

Evyn grimaced. "Yeah, it kinda looks that way. I hope I didn't make you—"

"I said I liked that you care, and I meant it." Wes moved around the table and gripped Evyn's shoulders. "I don't want to make you unhappy."

"That's just it, you don't. The closer we are, the more I feel like myself, and that really scares me. Because if I need you for that, what happens when you're not here?"

"What happens if I don't go?"

"A whole other reason to be scared," Evyn said, her heart belying the words. She was anything but frightened by the idea of having Wes around all the time. She was exhilarated.

"I get being scared—you walked away last night, and that hurt."

"I know. And I know sorry doesn't cut it, but I am."

"I guess we're both a bit scared," Wes said.

"Yeah. And I don't like that much."

"Neither do I," Wes said, "but you're good at handling the tough jobs. So am I. We ought to remember that."

Evyn grasped her hand. Threaded her fingers through Wes's. "I will if you will."

"You've got a deal, Agent Daniels." Wes wanted to kiss her—but Evyn needed to keep focus. So did she. "Later."

"What?" Evyn frowned. "What do you mean?"

"I'll tell you when this is over."

"Then let's finish getting you wired so we can find out what the hell is going on and put a stop to it."

"Let's do that."

"Do I have to say be careful?"

"I don't mind when you do, but I promise I will be. And I'll see you at the end of the night."

Evyn's lips parted slightly, her face flushing. "I'd like that. A lot."

The tightness in Wes's belly warmed her until she was close to forgetting everything except the softness of Evan's mouth and the taste of her skin. She pulled away. "Good."

"Don't take any chances," Evyn whispered.

"Don't worry. We have unfinished business, and I plan to take care of it."

❖

"Can I get you a drink?" Jennifer took Wes's coat and hung it on a wrought-iron coat tree just inside the door of her town house.

"Scotch and water would be great," Wes said. The town house in Adams Morgan was small but impeccably restored. The hardwood floors gleamed, the walls were painted in nineteenth-century period colors, the wood staircase leading to the second floor was adorned with a hand-carved newel post and banister. The furniture and thick area rugs were understated but obviously expensive. Jennifer lived well on her military salary.

"Have a seat, I'll be right back." Jennifer disappeared through a door beyond the staircase that Wes assumed led to the kitchen. She settled on the sofa and studied the books on the floor-to-ceiling shelves opposite her. American classics for the most part, a few contemporary titles. Nothing to help define Jennifer as an individual. On the short Metro ride, Jennifer had asked about her most recent posting and how she was finding the job. The kind of casual conversation individuals getting to know each other had. At one point as they walked, Jennifer had slipped her hand through Wes's arm, an invitation or maybe a query. Wes pressed her arm closer to her body, securing Jennifer's hold, signaling—she hoped—interest. Jennifer had responded by leaning into her shoulder a little more and squeezing her arm.

"Here you go." Jennifer held out a crystal rock glass with two inches of dark amber liquid inside and sat on the sofa next to Wes with a glass of wine.

Wes sipped the scotch. Smoky, dense, expensive. "Thanks."

Jennifer sighed. "This is nice. How about I order in? There's a great little restaurant down the street that delivers quickly."

"Sure, unless you're too tired. I can go—"

"No." Jennifer pressed her palm to Wes's thigh. "Not now that I've got you here. I'll get you the menu."

"Don't bother. Order what you like—surprise me."

Jennifer smiled. "I plan to." She rose and set her wineglass on the end table. "I'll be right back."

When Jennifer returned, Wes asked, "So where does your sister live?"

"Ohio," Jennifer answered immediately. "She and her husband have a dairy farm there."

"Just you and her or a big family?"

"Just us. My parents met later in life and they're both gone now."

"Sorry."

"I was looking forward to my sister and her family coming here, but her husband's mother needed emergency gallbladder surgery. That put an end to the Christmas plans. What about you?"

"Three sisters. I would've gone home for the holidays—I generally take my annual leave at this time of year—but I'm here."

"You didn't have much notice, I guess." Jennifer cradled the wineglass in one hand, drew her legs beneath her on the sofa, and rested her free left hand on Wes's thigh.

Wes tightened automatically and Jennifer made a sound as if she were purring. Wes tried to remember the question as Jennifer's fingers stroked slowly up and down the inside of her leg. "I wasn't expecting this job, true."

"Well, I'm glad you're here." Jennifer leaned into Wes a little more. "They certainly got you on board at lightning speed."

"I'm glad it wasn't a drawn-out process."

"I guess they explained what happened to Len—the heart attack out of the blue?"

Wes chose her words carefully. Jennifer might be searching—trying to find out if Wes had any suspicions about O'Shaughnessy's death—or her questions could simply be curiosity. Somehow, though, Wes doubted it. "Nothing unusual on his post. Probably an arrhythmia."

"You just never expect it, when someone's in such good shape—" Jennifer's cell rang. "Oh, sorry. That must be the restaurant. They always forget to ask about the hot sauce." She grabbed her phone. "Hold on. Hello?"

Jennifer frowned. "I'm sorry. Let me just take this—it's a friend from out of town."

"Of course," Wes said as Jennifer rose. "Take your time."

"Hi, Tom," Jennifer said, walking toward the kitchen.

Wes hesitated, uncertain how good her audio would be a room away through the old thick walls. She got up and walked toward the kitchen, pausing outside the archway.

"Ellie told me you'd be calling. Are you in town long?"

"I'm afraid tonight isn't a good night. I think it would be awkward for me to change my plans. But if you're on a tight schedule—"

"No, no, I'm more than ready. What about breakfast?"

"There's a diner a block from my apartment. Eva's."

"Seven thirty?"

Wes registered the silence a second before Jennifer appeared in the kitchen doorway.

"Sorry," Wes said quickly. "I was looking for the bathroom."

Jennifer smiled thinly, her eyes narrowing. "Top of the stairs on your left."

"Thanks. Be right back."

"The food should be here soon." Jennifer traced a fingertip over the top of Wes's hand. "I hope you're as hungry as I am."

CHAPTER THIRTY

Evyn called Cameron Roberts. "We've got something on audio. Sounds like she's arranging a meet."

"E-mail me the audio file," Cam said.

"It's on its way." She glanced at Block, crowded next to her in the back of the surveillance van. They'd parked around the corner from Jennifer Pattee's town house, within range of the transmitter Wes was wearing but out of line of sight. Block was focused on monitoring the audio feed—he wasn't paying any attention to her. "We can't get both sides of the conversation, but the subject is coming through clear. She mentioned a mutual contact—Tom. There's no way he—"

"That doesn't concern us right now," Cam said.

She knew their priority was locating and securing the stolen biocontagion, but no way was she letting Tom become a suspect. "I just want to go on record that I'm the best one to have observed his activities, and nothing suggests he's involved."

"I appreciate that, and I'm sure he will too. We picked up the name on a few scattered communications over the last few weeks, but we haven't been able to put anything together. At this point, we're simply being cautious."

"I understand. There's something else," Evyn said. "I think she made Wes."

"Hold on. Let me listen to this," Cam said. "I'm downloading it now."

Evyn chafed in the sudden silence and switched to watching the video feed from the camera they'd mounted on a light pole halfway down the block from Jennifer Pattee's front door. If she didn't occupy her mind, she was going to drive herself crazy imagining what was going on with Wes inside that house. They didn't have eyes inside—there hadn't been time to get anything in place. So she was left to imagining Wes and Jennifer's activities by following the audio transcript on the computer next to Block. The impersonal words appeared as if a ghost were typing them, but she had no difficulty hearing Wes's voice. She knew Jennifer Pattee well enough to recognize hers too. As the words scrolled down the screen, Evyn saw Jennifer with Wes.

She'd always found Jennifer attractive but aloof, which had never bothered her because Jennifer wasn't her type. She was capable, competent, and sexy if you liked aggressive femmes, but she'd always sensed something just a little bit calculating about her. Jennifer was nothing like Wes—Wes didn't play games, didn't pull her punches, asked the hard questions, and didn't run from the answers. Wes didn't run from anything, which was why she was sitting in Jennifer's house tonight with no backup close enough to help her if something went sour. The thought curdled her stomach.

She reread the transcribed message. Even without the audio to accent the innuendo, Jennifer sounded like she was coming on to Wes. The idea of Jennifer so much as touching Wes made her want to kick down the town house door. She wasn't jealous—she was furious. Jennifer was a terrorist, and she'd do anything to achieve her goals— sleep with Len O'Shaughnessy, seduce Wes, maybe even get rid of someone she perceived as an obstacle to her mission. Right now, that obstacle looked a lot like Wes.

"Can you tell where they are?" Evyn asked, her voice sounding loud above the low steady hum of electronics.

Block said, "Huh?" and lifted the headphones from one ear.

Evyn gritted her teeth. "Can you tell where they are in the building?"

"The GPS on the transmitter is pretty specific. With the blueprints we have as reference, I can place them pretty close." He dropped the headphones back in place. "Looks like they're still in the living room."

The living room. Good. The front door led directly into the living room, so if Wes got into trouble at least Evyn could be inside in under a minute. A lot could happen in a minute.

Her phone rang, and she grabbed it off the narrow counter bolted to the sidewall of the van. "Daniels."

"It definitely sounds like a meet," Cam said. "From what we can get of the caller's voice off the enhanced audio, definitely male. Doesn't fit the scenario unless Jones handed off the stolen specimen to an intermediary."

"That would be a reasonable plan," Evyn said. "That way, Jones protects her identity and there's no link between her and the person releasing the virus."

"Except in this case, there is. Which may be exactly why they're using an intermediary. Could be they've been seen together before or fear that some other connection might come to light."

"I'll buy that. So who's the intermediary?"

"No fix on that yet," Cam said. "And we don't know how many other intermediaries might be involved. Whoever's funding this is probably many degrees removed."

"Invisible," Evyn muttered.

"Unfortunately, yes. For now, our job is intercepting the virus."

"What about Wes—Captain Masters. If Pattee gets suspicious—"

"Doubtful she'd attempt anything tonight—if Pattee was involved in O'Shaughnessy's death, she had to have planned it in advance. The captain ought to be safe tonight, but stick with her until she gets home."

"Looks like they're staying in for the rest of the evening."

"Good—that makes it less likely Pattee will pick up on our surveillance. Let me know if anything changes."

"Roger that." Evyn couldn't find anything very good about the idea of Wes being alone with Jennifer Pattee for the rest of the evening. Wes had proved she could handle herself in tight situations, only Evyn wished she didn't have to prove it in this one. She totally trusted Wes— she just didn't trust Jennifer Pattee.

"Got a car approaching...slowing..." Block sat forward and adjusted the video monitor. "He's parking right across the street from Pattee's town house."

"Food delivery?"

"Looks that way."

"Can you shoot a still remotely?"

Block fiddled with some buttons. "Ought to be able to."

"Good. Get me a shot of him and let's run it." Evyn tossed her cell back on the counter and silently sent a message to Wes, urging her to leave as soon as she could. She'd done her job—more than her job—and now it was time to let Evyn and the others shoulder the risk. Somehow, she knew if Wes received her plea, she'd ignore it. Wes didn't run, ever.

❖

Wes caught the Metro as she'd been instructed and got off at the stop closest to her apartment. She let herself in and turned on the lamp just inside the door. She was transported back to the last time she'd walked in late at night. Evyn had been with her then—moving into her, kissing her, taking her. Wes shuddered, her skin slick with nerves and heat. She pulled off her coat and tossed it over the back of the sofa. Her blazer followed, and she dropped that on the breakfast bar on her way to get a beer from the fridge. She didn't bother to turn on any more lights. She just waited.

Ten minutes later a knock came on the door and she opened it quickly.

Evyn strode in. "Are you okay?"

"Did you get everything?" Wes asked.

"They're working on the audio now, but you did good. How do you feel?"

Wes pointed to the beer she'd opened and left untouched on the breakfast counter. "Like I can't wait to get back to the clinic. How the hell do you do this on a regular basis?"

Evyn laughed softly. "I don't. I'm protection, remember?"

"Yes, but you've been in the field too."

"I never did much undercover." Evyn slid her hand around Wes's waist and tapped the transmitter. "Come on, let's get this thing off you. We need to debrief—get your impressions. We can only get so much from the audio."

"Why did Roberts want me to come back here instead of reporting directly to her at the White House?" Wes unbuttoned her shirt and pulled her tank up. "Do you really think someone might've followed me from Jennifer's?"

"No sense taking a chance. This way, to anyone watching, you finished your date and went home. Anyone following would assume you were in for the night."

"Hell of a date," Wes muttered.

Evyn carefully loosened the adhesive and removed the transmitter. "What's your impression?"

Wes sat on one of the bar stools facing out into the living room and propped her elbows on the counter behind her. "She sent a lot of mixed signals. She might have been trying to seduce me, but she was also trolling for information."

"What kind of information?"

"Mostly about Len. She's a medical person. Sudden death is something we're familiar with. But she pushed a little bit where he was concerned—maybe trying to see if we suspected foul play."

"That makes sense if she was party to his death."

"But why would she have wanted to get rid of him? Someone would take his place—if not someone from the outside like me, one of the other docs from the inside."

"My working theory," Evyn said, securing the transmitter in her jacket pocket, "is that Len started to suspect her. Maybe he overheard something. We'll probably never know, but for some reason, they wanted him out of the way."

"Then I'm no threat."

"Not unless she thinks you suspect something too," Evyn said quietly. "When you've killed once, it gets easier—at least for some people."

Evyn's eyes were cloudy, troubled. Wes took her hand and pulled her closer. "What's wrong?"

"Sitting in that van listening to you with her—knowing you were too far away for me to get you…" Evyn cupped Wes's face and kissed her. "Made me crazy."

Wes's pulse soared. Her whole life had been geared toward taking care of others—she'd learned to be self-sufficient, learned to stand alone. She'd never been so critically important to anyone before. Evyn made her feel like she mattered—right now, in this moment—more than anything else in Evyn's world. She looped her arms around Evyn's waist and pulled her in tight between her thighs. "I'm sorry if it was hard for you."

Evyn rested her forehead against Wes's. "I knew you could handle yourself—don't get me wrong."

"I think we both know we can do our jobs, no matter what."

"I do. I believe that. But part of me, the part I shoved away a long time ago so I could focus on getting where I wanted to get, that part was just a little bit scared."

"I suppose every time you're away, in potential danger, I'll be a little bit scared too." Wes kissed her. "But I'll be damn proud too."

"Wes," Evyn murmured, sliding her mouth over Wes's, kissing her throat. "I should tell you—"

"Yes?" Wes arched her neck, gave more of herself to Evyn's mouth. "What?"

Evyn groaned, her hands trembling on Wes's shoulders. "I'm falling in love with you."

Wes slipped her fingers into Evyn's hair, drawing her mouth tighter to her skin, wanting the heat of Evyn's mouth searing her flesh. "I'm so glad. Because I'm in love with you."

Evyn shuddered. "I'm not making love to you again until we're in a bed."

"I don't have plants or a cat," Wes whispered, "but I've got clean sheets."

CHAPTER THIRTY-ONE

C am turned the bathroom light off before she opened the door and walked quietly back into the bedroom. The room was filled with a soft gray haze marking the transition between moonlight and sunrise, that in-between time when night was all but gone and the day not yet born—when reality dispelled the last lingering dreams. She found the clothes she'd left out the night before and pulled on underwear, pants, and a shirt. She slid her ID into her back pocket and clipped her badge to her belt on her right hip next to her holster. Sheets rustled behind her and she turned as Blair sat up in bed. "Been awake long?"

"A few minutes," Blair said. "I like watching you dress almost as much as I like watching you undress."

Laughing, Cam sat on the side of the bed and stroked Blair's leg through the sheets. Blair was wearing another one of her old T-shirts— this one with JJRTC stenciled across the chest. A few holes peppered the front—spots she'd snagged running through the woods on one of her training exercises. She leaned down and kissed Blair. "It's pretty early yet. Are you going to stay up?"

"I've gotten spoiled these last few weeks, having you around. Knowing you weren't going to be out in the field."

"I need to be there for this." Cam settled on the bed, swung around until her back was against the headboard, and settled Blair against her side. She kissed her temple. In her new job with Homeland Security, she was riding a desk most of the time. She was a hands-on supervisor, though, and sometimes she needed to be in the field. "Your father's safety is our number one priority, but this kind of incident has the potential to terrify the nation. We'll stop it—I promise. But media containment is almost as vital."

Blair nodded. "I know. Which is why you're leading the team yourself and limiting the number of people who know the details."

"Yes." She'd put agents from the Washington field office on Jennifer Pattee the night before after Daniels and Block left to follow Captain Masters home. The other agents only knew they were maintaining surveillance on a person of interest and didn't need to know more. The intercept this morning had to be carried out by a small, select team in the know, and she needed to be there to assure the details of the plan weren't made public. Knowledge of a threat could be almost as dangerous as the event itself.

"I'm not even going to ask how dangerous you think this might be," Blair said, running her fingers over the buttons on Cam's shirt. "I already know. And I understand why you have to do this. Just be careful."

"I will be. I'll call you as soon as I can, but it might be a while."

Blair rubbed her cheek on Cam's shoulder. "Don't worry about me. Just do your job and remember, part of your job is coming back to me."

"I won't forget." Cam kissed her. "It's the best assignment I've ever had."

❖

Wes judged the time to be nearing 0430. They'd need to leave soon so Evyn could meet up with the intercept team and she could join the surveillance team and provide medical containment if necessary. She'd be in a van somewhere, safely observing. Evyn would be in the hot zone. The virus, if released, would be as lethal as a bullet, although not quite as rapid. The diner was a public place—and the agents' body armor would be no protection at all. She had nothing other than supportive measures to counteract its destructive potential—no vaccine, no drugs. Exposure could be a death sentence.

Evyn slept with her head on Wes's shoulder. She fit into the curve of Wes's body as if she'd always been there. Wes stroked the slope of

Evyn's shoulder. Her skin was soft, warm. Her breasts were firm and full, nestling against hers in a sensuous embrace. The brush of Evyn's nipple over her breast teased her clit, and she tensed with a sharp thrum of arousal. She tightened her grip on Evyn's shoulder and held her closer.

Evyn murmured and shifted above her, easing her leg between Wes's thighs. Her pelvis rocked into Wes's and the tight knot of need between Wes's thighs grew. She'd come hard the night before—the first time when Evyn had taken her with her mouth, then more slowly as Evyn had stroked her, and now she was ready again. Cupping Evyn's ass in her palm, she guided Evyn's leg to the place she needed her.

"I like waking up with you," Evyn whispered, her lips against Wes's throat. She kissed her way up and tugged lightly on her earlobe.

The tiny points of pain sent pleasure streaking down Wes's spine. She raised her hips so her clitoris rubbed against Evyn's thigh. "I like sleeping with you. I like waking up with you. I like everything about being with you."

Evyn chuckled. "Handy, that, because I plan on being around a lot."

"I think I'll need you around a lot."

Evyn propped herself up on her forearms, the first rays of morning light breaking over her face. Her eyes were blue-gray in the dusky dawn. "We haven't talked about the future."

Wes cradled Evyn's face, scooped her fingers through her hair, kissed her. "I want one."

"So do I." Evyn kissed her, exploring, teasing, tasting. She slid deeper, claiming. "I want you. Just you. I know *always* sounds like a line, but I mean it."

Wes's concentration faltered—gave way under the sensation of Evyn's mouth and hands. She pressed harder against Evyn's thigh, climbing faster. Too fast. Gasping, she pulled away. "I'm going to come soon."

"Mmm—then don't stop."

"I want—I need—to say this first. I love you. I've never wanted anyone else and I never will. *Always* sounds like the beginning."

Evyn shuddered. "I never even wanted tomorrow with anyone before. Now I want every single one of yours to be mine."

"They will be." Wes's muscles clenched and she rode the plume of pleasure higher. "I'm sorry, I can't...I'm coming for you."

"Yes. For me." Evyn scored her teeth down Wes's neck, biting gently. "Yes," she breathed against Wes's skin, hearing the startled cry as Wes's control unraveled. Her clitoris twitched, pulsed, thickened. She needed to come but she held back. She needed Wes more. "Mine. All mine. Come for me."

Wes cried out, body shattering with pleasure. She crushed her face to Evyn's neck. "Yours. Yes."

Pushing up on one arm, Evyn fumbled for Wes's hand with the other. She pressed Wes's fingers between her legs. "Touch me. I need to come for you."

Wes stroked her, slid lower, pressed inside, and Evyn exploded in her hand. "I love you," Wes whispered. "No chances today, Evyn. I can't lose you."

Evyn sighed and stretched, trailing her fingers down Wes's back—sated, supremely content. "You won't lose me, I promise. I'm here for the long term."

Wes kissed her, choosing to believe for a little while longer they could control the future.

❖

Hooker opened the minifridge tucked in the corner of his motel room and removed a small plain cardboard box the size of a ballpoint pen case. The clear plastic vial with the screw top was nestled inside, surrounded by a Styrofoam cut-out. A half-inch of milky white fluid filled the end of the tube—at least it had when he'd checked it when he'd accepted it from the woman in Georgia. He hadn't looked at it again. He didn't want to look at it, he didn't want to touch it. He wasn't superstitious, but he didn't ride around with a loaded gun and the safety off pointed at his chest, either. If all he'd been told was true, whatever was in the tube was ten kinds of deadly dangerous. He couldn't hand it off soon enough.

He placed the small, narrow box in a white plastic cooler along with a couple of cans of beer and a burrito from the minimart where he'd gassed up the rental car he'd used to drive north the night before.

Russo had pushed the timetable forward, and haste was never a good idea, but Russo lived by the polls. If the numbers showed Powell gaining in popularity, that was all that mattered to Russo—after all, he wasn't taking any risks. Hooker didn't concern himself with politics—politicians came and went as frequently as the weather shifted, and he'd never seen that whoever held power changed things very much. Money was the only true power, and Russo had plenty of that. He'd follow Russo's lead as long as the money held up.

He packed his travel bag and meticulously wiped down everything he'd touched in the motel room, which hadn't been much. He'd just arrived the night before after dark in another rental car that he'd procured with one of his aliases. He'd eaten at a fast-food place across the highway from the motel and slept in his clothes. He'd shower at his next stop. Satisfied that he hadn't left anything of himself behind, he grabbed his bag and the cooler, left his room key on the rickety table by the door, and walked out just as the sun came up. He couldn't finish this job fast enough. In five hours, he'd be at the airport headed home for Christmas Eve.

❖

Jennifer stepped out of the shower and wrapped a fluffy white bath sheet around her chest. It fell to her thighs, chasing away the slight chill in the bathroom. The temperature had dropped again, and the old town house let in a little of the night air through hidden cracks and crevices. A small price to pay for its historic beauty, except on mornings like these. She hurried into her bedroom, drying herself as she went, and dressed hastily in a navy suit, white shirt, and low dark heels. She didn't plan to stay very long in the diner and doubted the man, Tom, would want to linger, either. Twenty minutes, really, ought to be enough for two people whose only connection was a common friend to share a cup of coffee, make small talk, and go their separate ways. She'd timed the meeting so she'd finish up and arrive at the clinic at shift change, when she'd slide her lunch bag into the staff refrigerator just as she did every morning. Only today, the bag would be a little fuller. Her stomach trembled when she thought about the next step.

She wasn't frightened, she was excited. Proud to be the one to ultimately carry out the mission. Her family would be proud that she had fulfilled her destiny—that she'd learned her lessons well and had struck a blow for true freedom and independence. If she was very lucky and everything went according to plan, she might even survive. But if she didn't, she would die knowing she'd made a difference. And after all, that's what she'd been born for.

CHAPTER THIRTY-TWO

Wes sat in the van beside Block and two Secret Service agents she didn't know, watching the monitor from a camera trained on the front of Eva's Diner. She'd been watching patrons come and go since 0600. Two other video feeds—from cameras above the restroom hallway in the rear and over the kitchen door behind the counter—revealed the interior. A directional audio receiver that Block could reposition remotely from his control panel had been secured to an overhead light fixture. The place was small—a long, narrow room with eight booths against the plate glass front windows and a dozen black-vinyl-topped stools in front of the counter. At zero-seven twenty, almost every space was occupied.

Roberts had advised the diner owner who'd arrived to open the place at 0530 that the team, from an unnamed federal agency, needed surveillance to document unspecified criminal activity. The owner, a bottle-blonde of indeterminate age, was thrilled by the whole thing and a very good actress. She worked the counter and never once glanced at the cameras—or at the undercover agents posing as patrons.

Wes couldn't see Evyn, who was posted inside the kitchen with a view through the circular window on the swinging door. In order to protect the civilians, the plan was to record the exchange on video and apprehend both Jennifer and her contact outside the building in a safe zone. Wes's job was to receive the virus and supervise its transport to a secure lab. The second part of her assignment—the part she hoped she would not have to carry out—was to limit civilian exposure in the event the virus was released and oversee the treatment of any individuals who were exposed.

The other agents inside the diner posed as a businessman reading a newspaper at the far end of the counter opposite the rear exit and a young couple having breakfast at a booth just inside the front door. They blended in with the morning business crowd and neighborhood diners, and Wes doubted even someone looking for it would pick up their constant survey of anyone coming in the door.

"Here comes the subject," Block murmured, and Wes swiveled on her stool to get a view of his monitor. Jennifer Pattee, a large black leather bag over one shoulder, walked briskly up to the diner door and inside. The kitchen feed picked her up as she walked a few feet down the aisle and then slowed as if searching for someone she planned to meet. With a sudden smile, she hurried on and sat down across from a single man in a Redskins cap drinking coffee in a booth. Wes had looked at him a half dozen times and noted nothing out of the ordinary—mid-thirties, possibly older, rugged outdoor type in a flannel shirt with faint dark stubble along his jaw. He half rose as Jennifer sat, and Block adjusted the audio receiver for maximum reception.

"Hi," Jennifer said as she settled across from the man. "You must be Tom."

"And you're Jennifer. Ellie's told me so much about you."

"She hasn't told me nearly enough about you," Jennifer said. "It's great to finally meet you. I'm sorry you won't be able to stay longer in the city. I could play tour guide."

He smiled, sipped his coffee, and said nothing while a waitress approached. Jennifer asked for coffee and a plain croissant.

"Maybe next time I'm through," he said.

"That would be great." Jennifer picked at the pastry, although she didn't appear nervous. She glanced at her watch several times while her contact passed on a refill on his coffee and watched the door as other customers came and went.

"Excuse me," he said, fishing his cell phone from his pocket. "I'm expecting a message."

"Please—go ahead," Jennifer said quickly.

He checked the readout and grimaced. "I'm so sorry, a business message from a client overseas. They're available now and I have to get back to them. It may take a while. I hate to have gotten you all the way out here only to run out on you."

"That's okay—if you can get free for lunch or dinner in the next day or so, you have my number. If not, maybe I'll see you the next time I visit Ellie."

"Absolutely." He started to rise and paused. "Oh, I almost forgot…" He reached into a backpack beside him and drew out a small narrow box. "Ellie asked me to give you this. A Christmas present. She said she didn't get her shopping done in time to mail it to you."

Laughing, Jennifer slid the small box into her oversized bag. "That sounds like her. Thanks for bringing it along."

"No problem. Well—I should go."

"All right. Hopefully we'll meet again sometime soon."

He held her gaze a moment. "I hope so too. Merry Christmas."

"Merry Christmas," Jennifer said softly.

❖

Roberts's voice came over the COM. "Team one, subject is on his way out. Take him at the corner…Go."

Wes watched as two men closed in from either side and a woman stepped from a parked SUV into his path, forcing him to slow. The subject's expression went from surprised to wary, and he quickly scanned up and down the street as if considering his chances of escaping. Within seconds, the two male agents each grabbed an arm and the trio pushed him forward into the back of the idling SUV. The agents followed him in, and the vehicle sped away. The whole thing was over in less than a minute.

Wes scanned all the monitors for Evyn and didn't see her anywhere. Her mouth went dry but her pulse stayed steady. She glanced at the masks and hazmat suits stacked by the van door. Evyn knew her job, and she knew hers. No matter what happened out there, she'd find Evyn.

Inside the diner, Jennifer searched through the large shoulder bag and came out with bills that she laid on the table next to her uneaten croissant and nearly full cup of coffee. Wes wondered if she'd transferred the stolen sample to another container inside the bag. Any unnecessary handling risked rupturing the seal on the tube or, even worse, breakage.

"Showtime," Block muttered as Jennifer stood and pulled on her topcoat, slipped the strap of her black leather bag securely onto her shoulder, and strode directly toward the front door. The next second, she stepped out into the morning.

❖

"Go," Roberts said over the COM.

Evyn pushed away from the side of the diner and strode around the corner to the front. Jennifer was thirty feet away, one hand in the pocket of her coat, the other on top of her bag.

"Hi, Jen," Evyn said brightly, watching the hand on the bag. As far as she could tell, the bag was closed. She looked past Jennifer down the block, saw Paula Stark intercept a woman with a stroller and redirect her back the way she had come. The sidewalk right in front of the diner was clear—the inside team would have prevented anyone from exiting until the intercept was over and the area secured. Directly across from Jennifer, Roberts stepped out of a parked SUV.

"Oh hi, Evyn."

Twenty-five feet.

"How about I give you a ride to work."

Twenty feet.

Jennifer's friendly smile dimmed. "I'm not due in for another hour or so. Thanks anyhow."

Fifteen feet.

"I'll give you a lift home, then." And focused on shoulder bag, on Jennifer's fingers gripping the zipper along its top edge.

Jennifer glanced over her shoulder. Stark strode rapidly toward her. Her gaze cut across the street. Cam, joined by another agent, arrowed toward her. Jennifer's eyes widened.

Ten feet.

"You'll want to say yes, Jen," Evyn said, watching Jennifer's hand ease toward the now open bag. "Make this easy."

Jennifer's other hand came out of her pocket. The Sig looked huge.

"Gun!" Evyn shouted and launched herself across the last eight feet. The sharp crack split the air, heat flashed over her, and the rage in Jennifer's eyes swallowed her.

❖

Evyn went down and Wes jumped to her feet. The COM lines flooded with shouts.

Shots fired.

Agent down.

Medics. We need medics.

Wes grabbed the hazmat container, shoved the rear door of the van open, and shouldered through. Block was beside her, running. Her breath tore from her chest—shards of pain shredded her throat. Half a block seemed like an eternity. A clot of agents hovered over the prone figures. Jennifer's shoulder bag lay on the sidewalk, its contents strewn around it. The box Jennifer had received from her contact lay half in and half out of the bag.

"Get away from the bag," Wes shouted. "Everyone—back away from the bag."

Roberts materialized from the huddle of bodies and jogged toward her. "Subject is contained. We've got an agent down."

Evyn. Evyn was hurt. Wes clamped down on her panic. "The specimen could be compromised. This area is a hot zone—get everyone out, cordon off the street."

"Already gave the order."

"How is she?"

"Gunshot—close range. She's shocky."

"Evacuate her—tell them to put her in isolation. Everyone else goes into lockdown until I know what we're dealing with."

"I have to interrogate the subject," Roberts said.

"Then you'll have to do it in an isolation cell." Wes kept her focus on the bag and what it contained. Her duty, her obligation, was to neutralize that biological agent, a substance every bit as lethal as a dirty bomb and capable of killing far more. They didn't know what they were dealing with, and every member of the team had potentially been exposed. Her heart demanded she find Evyn, protect her, aid her above all others, but her duty drove her toward the open bag. Kneeling, she flipped the lid on the biohazard chest filled with dry ice and pulled on a pair of gloves. She extracted the suspect package from Jennifer's bag and dropped it into the chest. The package appeared to be intact. After stripping off her gloves and depositing them in a red biohazard bag, she donned another pair of protective gloves, pushed the spilled contents back inside the bag, zipped it, and dropped that into the biohazard bag as well. Using yet another pair of gloves, she sealed the red bag and carried it and the hazmat chest to the SUV idling half up on the curb next to her. She climbed into the back, and as the agent inside pulled the doors closed, she looked back at the group on the sidewalk.

Jennifer Pattee was facedown with her hands cuffed behind her back. Hernandez, the medic assigned to Stark's team, and Stark knelt over Evyn. Wes couldn't see Evyn's face. She stared at the plain white chest with the iridescent green biohazard sign stamped on the front resting at her feet. The SUV sped up, leaving the scene on the sidewalk farther and farther behind. Leaving Evyn behind. Wes concentrated on the job that needed to be done, ignoring the pain that made every heartbeat as agonizing as a bullet tearing her flesh. She'd had to abandon her wounded in the field again, and this time, she'd left her heart behind.

CHAPTER THIRTY-THREE

They made it the eight miles to the army research lab in Silver Spring in under twenty minutes. When Wes climbed out of the SUV with the white ice chest in her hand, three uniformed soldiers converged on her.

"Captain Masters?" the female major asked.

"That's right."

"Come with us, please."

The silent escorts led her directly through the building to an elevator and down one floor. A fortyish African American woman with short black hair and luminous mahogany eyes in a disposable cover gown and gloves met Wes as she stepped out of the elevator. The hallway in front of the air lock to the Level 4 lab was empty, save for the slowly panning security cameras mounted at intervals along the stark white corridor.

"I'm Dr. Felice Glover," the woman said. "What's the status of the specimen?"

"Contained at this point," Wes said, handing over the chest. "I don't know if we have a viable virus. I doubt it's been kept at optimal conditions since it went missing from the original lab. If the vial is compromised, widespread contamination isn't likely, but we're taking precautions."

The scientist nodded briskly. "We'll know soon enough about exposure risks. We'll scan the container for any leaks and I'll call you and Director Roberts."

"Thank you," Wes said, feeling caught up in the surreal. They were casually discussing a potentially lethal contagion while Evyn was somewhere, injured, possibly seriously. "I need to go. I'm sorry."

"I think the risk is slight, but keep the team in the vehicle until I report. It's as good as an isolation room."

"Roger that."

Wes hurried away, wondering if she'd ever find out what she'd just delivered. Her job was done—some might consider she had no further need to know. She jabbed the elevator button, rocked impatiently on her heels during the one floor trip, and strode rapidly outside. The instant she stepped out of the building, she called Cameron Roberts.

"Roberts."

"How is she?"

"We're at George Washington. The docs are looking at her now. They're saying guarded condition."

Which meant anything from walking wounded to potentially serious. "Can I talk to her?"

"They threw us all out, but she's awake—I know that much."

Relief rushed through her so powerfully Wes staggered. She braced one hand against the rough brick of the building and lowered her head, drawing a deep breath until the churning turmoil settled a little. "If they let you in to see her, tell her...Tell her I'm on my way."

"I'll do that."

"The specimen is secure."

"I had no doubt of that," Roberts said. "I'll be with her until you get here."

"Thank you." Wes jogged to the SUV and said to the agent driving, "George Washington University Hospital, as quick as you can."

"Yes, ma'am."

Wes settled in the back and closed her eyes. Her part of the mission was done, and all that mattered was Evyn.

❖

The glass door to the cubicle slid back and the curtain twitched aside. The doctor, a harried guy in rumpled scrubs and a two-days' growth of beard, walked in. He looked even more tired out of the space suit.

"I guess I'm not buggy, huh?" Evyn said.

"Your boss says only universal infection precautions are necessary, and we use those with everyone."

"Good." Evyn relaxed, the tight spring of anxiety coiled in her belly loosening. Wes must be okay if they'd determined the team wasn't at risk from the virus. "So—I'm out of here?"

"Not quite. The bullet just grazed the soft tissue at the top of your shoulder." He taped a rectangular bandage on the top of Evyn's shoulder. "You'll get some swelling in your arm and a fair amount of pain. An overnight stay and a pain pump—"

"No," Evyn said. "I'm not staying."

"I'd recommend it."

"But you're not requiring it?"

He sighed and shook his head. "Leave the bandage on for twenty-four hours. The nurses will give you a prescription for antibiotics and pain pills when you're discharged."

"Thanks," Evyn said, stretching for her shirt draped on the nearby chair. She winced at the burn in her shoulder and stopped. She didn't like being naked, but she didn't want to give the guy any reason to restrict her activities. "When can I go back to work?"

"You'll need to have a wound check in forty-eight hours—you can come back here, or—"

"That's okay. I'll see my own doctor." She almost smiled at the thought of just how true that statement was, but the pleasure faded quickly. Wes had been the one closest to the virus. Maybe she'd been exposed, but the rest of them were in the clear. She had to get out of here and find out what was going on. She needed to see Wes. "So—we're done? Thanks for everything."

He looked up from the chart. "I'd rather you see a surgeon. General medical doctors don't really have the experience to evaluate this kind of wound."

"She's not—"

The curtains parted and Wes walked in. She wasn't in uniform, but then she never needed to be to look like she was in command. Her eyes were stormy and fierce, fixed on Evyn. "I'm sorry it took me so long to get here."

"I'm okay," Evyn said immediately. "It was nothing. A scratch."

"A little more than that," the emergency physician said, studying Wes. "You are?"

"Captain Wesley Masters—chief of the White House Medical Unit." Wes glanced at Evyn. "And her partner."

"Oh, well then." He tucked the chart under his arm and pushed his pen into the ink-stained pocket of his wrinkled lab coat. "I guess you can do the follow-up."

"I think I can handle that. Thanks for taking care of her." Wes cupped Evyn's face, brushed a thumb over her cheek. The ER physician disappeared through the curtains and Wes leaned forward and kissed Evyn softly. "Now, how are you really doing?"

"I'm good. Even better now." Evyn circled Wes's wrist and pressed Wes's palm to her face to reassure Wes, and herself. "I'd feel even better with my shirt on."

Laughing, Wes plucked the shirt from the chair, and the laughter died. Blood stained the shoulder and collar. Her hands trembled. Today, Evyn had been lucky. The next time, she might not be.

"You know it always looks worse than it is," Evyn said softly.

"Right." Wes held up the shirt. "This will have to do until we get you home and into something clean."

"I'm not going home," Evyn said. "I want to get back to base for a sitrep. Roberts left a while ago to interrogate the suspects. Tom needs to be briefed, and—"

"Evyn," Wes murmured, "you've been shot, you've been given pain medication, and you need to rest. You're on sick leave as of now."

"What? You can't—" Evyn stared, her brow furrowing. "Hell, you can."

Wes said nothing, waiting for the anger and the resentment. They'd had so little time to find their personal balance and now they might never be able to. She had to pull rank—she had a duty to Evyn, to the president, to Evyn's team—she had to take care of her, no matter the cost.

"You better like cats."

"What?" Wes asked.

"Cats. I come with a cat. And if I'm going home, so are you. As least until Roberts wants you back to debrief."

"You want me to drive you home?" Wes couldn't quite grasp what Evyn was saying. "You're not pissed?"

"Sure I am. I don't get why you don't appreciate how superhuman I am. After all, I'm a United States Secret Service Agent."

Wes smothered a smile. Evyn's pupils were pinpoints. The medication was kicking in. "You are. And a stellar one."

"So—you're coming home with me, then?"

"I am." Wes held up Evyn's shirt. "This first."

Evyn slid her good arm into the sleeve, and Wes helped her thread the other sleeve over her injured left arm.

"We alone?"

"Yes."

"I take it everything's all right with the package? The doc ditched his suits."

Wes nodded. "I called when I got the preliminary from the lab on my way in. The vial is intact."

"You weren't compromised out in the field?"

"No. I'll take culture specimens from everyone to be complete, but I think we're all in the clear thanks to your quick work out there."

Evyn started to shrug, then grimaced. Her shoulder burned. "Not quite quick enough. I wasn't expecting the gun, but I guess I should've been. She's military, after all. And on a mission."

"I would've preferred if you hadn't used your body to stop the bullet." Wes carefully buttoned Evyn's shirt. She knew the risks of Evyn's job, accepted them, knew the overwhelming odds were she would be safe, but there was always the threat that she would be hurt. Wes gripped the material harder, hiding the tremor in her hands. She kissed Evyn again. "You did well, all the same."

"Huh. Maybe."

Evyn pushed off the treatment table and swayed on her feet. "I was watching the hand on the bag—I was afraid she'd pull the virus out and toss the vial into the street as a diversion. It gave her just enough time to get the gun out. Dumb rookie move."

"Instinct. That's what training is all about, right?" Wes slid her arm around Evyn's waist. Evyn might not need the support, but she needed to touch her. Needed to be sure she was alive and well and hers. "I love you."

Evyn rested her head on Wes's shoulder, holding on to her with her good arm. "I love you too. Sorry if I gave you a scare."

"You did what you had to do. I'm sorry I wasn't there for you out there."

"You were where you needed to be, doing what needed to be done." Evyn squeezed her. "Just like now. You're here when I really need you."

"I always will be," Wes promised.

"You haven't met my cat yet."

Wes laughed and softly kissed her. "Then we should go."

"Yeah." Evyn pressed her face to Wes's neck. "I want you, you know. Today. Every day. Feels good. Really good."

"I know. I'll be here."

Evyn sighed. "So let's go home."

CHAPTER THIRTY-FOUR

D errick Sullivan slipped into the parlor and signaled discreetly to Russo.

Russo smiled at the bejeweled, pencil-thin blonde by his side, grateful for the interruption. He only suffered her vacuous conversation because her husband was one of his largest campaign donors. "Will you excuse me, Mrs. Winthrop?"

She pouted slightly. "Only if you promise to return."

"As soon as I possibly can—I want to hear more about those famous racehorses of yours."

She brightened and fluttered her thick lashes. "I can't wait."

Russo threaded his way through the tuxedoed and coiffed crowd to where his aide waited just inside the door. "What is it, Derrick?"

"Sorry to disturb you, sir, but you're needed in the study."

"Dinner is being served in fifteen minutes."

"Yes, sir. Shall I tell the caterers to delay?"

"No, go ahead. I'll be there."

"Yes, sir."

Russo ignored his wife's questioning glance as he hurried out and down the hall to his study. He let himself in and closed the door behind him. Hooker lounged on a leather sofa facing the fireplace, one leg crossed over the other, his arms stretched out along the back. At least he'd worn presentable clothing, but he looked haggard—his face drawn and creased with fatigue.

"It's Christmas Eve," Russo said, "and I've got a houseful of guests. What are you doing here?"

"A problem," Hooker said. "I could use a drink."

Russo clenched his teeth but walked to the bar on the opposite side of the room and splashed whiskey into a glass. He set it on a polished mahogany table next to the sofa and made his way behind his desk. "You have ten minutes."

Hooker leaned over and picked up the drink. "The exchange was made on schedule, as planned, but the DC contact was intercepted."

"Arrested?" Russo asked, the hairs along the back of his neck tingling at the surge of adrenaline.

"Detained, at the very least."

"Can we trust him—"

"Her."

Russo rubbed his eyes and fought down the wave of anger. "You entrusted something of this magnitude to a woman?"

"Believe me, she's qualified."

"Apparently not that well qualified. What about the specimen?"

"Confiscated."

"You're telling me that all this time and money has been wasted?"

Hooker's mouth tightened. "I advised you against a plan this complex. Too many ways for it to go sideways."

"How did they find out?"

"I don't know. It's going to take me some time to get back inside."

Russo tightened his fist. "You need to see that none of this comes back on us."

Hooker smiled. "Already being done."

"And how much is that going to cost me?"

"The same as my original fee."

"The next time," Russo said, making sure the threat was apparent in his voice, "I'll expect no mistakes."

"Next time, maybe you'll take my advice and use something more straightforward and dependable." Hooker tossed back his drink and slapped the glass down on the expensive wood top with a sharp clink. "Like a rifle."

"I don't like loose ends," Russo said.

"Neither do I. There aren't going to be any."

Russo unlocked his bottom right-hand desk drawer and sorted through the cash. He relocked the drawer, walked around the desk, and handed the money to Hooker. "Merry Christmas. I'll have Derrick see you out."

❖

Blair jumped to her feet as Cam strode into Lucinda's office. "You're not hurt?"

"No." Cam kissed her quickly. "We're all okay. Evyn Daniels has a flesh wound, but she should be fine."

"And the virus?" Lucinda said, coming around to the front of her desk. "Contained?"

"All but a certainty," Cam said. "We've all been cultured, but the lab reported the vial appeared to be intact. They say the likelihood of infection is very low."

"Good news, then," Blair said.

Cam grimaced. "Not exactly."

Lucinda straightened. "What?"

"I don't suppose you have anything stronger than coffee?"

Lucinda smiled faintly and gestured to the two chairs in front of her desk. "Both of you, go ahead and sit." She walked back around to the other side. "Scotch work for you?"

"Sounds perfect."

"Blair?"

"No. Thanks."

Cam settled into the chair and leaned her head back with a sigh. Blair eased onto the arm and stroked Cam's hair. "You've been at it for hours. You need a break."

"I'm okay." Cam opened her eyes and smiled up at her. "How are you doing?"

"Fine, now that you're here. We only got a partial report from the field, and when they said an agent had been wounded, I had a couple of bad moments."

"I'm sorry, I called as soon as I could, but—"

"I know. You can't stop in the middle of what you're doing to check in with me." Blair slid her arm around Cam's shoulders and leaned down to kiss her. "So I'm just going to have to worry once in a while. I can handle it."

Cam gripped her hand. "I'll try not to make it too often."

"Deal."

"Here you are." Lucinda held out a short heavy glass filled with an inch of amber liquid.

"Thanks." Cam swallowed down half. "I don't think there's anything quite as scary as fanatics. Practically impossible to interrogate. They can't be intimidated, and when they're absolutely certain they're right—which is always—they'll protect the rest of their bunch no matter the consequences."

"I take it the lieutenant isn't talking?" Lucinda asked.

"Oh, she's talking," Cam said. "She's adamant she had no idea what was in the package, that she'd never met the man in the diner before, and she only drew her weapon because she felt threatened by Agent Daniels."

Blair snorted. "You're kidding me, right? We're supposed to believe that she thought Evyn was going to accost her? What about the virus?"

"She insists she thought she was carrying a gift from her sister. Unfortunately, the taped phone conversation from last night could be construed as supporting that story."

"Oh sure, right. How does she explain this guy passing her the vial, then?"

"She claims she's an unwitting victim in a scheme to spread the virus in the White House. According to her, the real boyfriend is still en route—and this guy hacked her e-mail to look for a cover story."

"They're smart," Blair snarled. "While it's a little outrageous, it *could* be possible."

Lucinda tapped her fingers on her desk. "What do we have for leverage to force her to cooperate?"

"Right now? Not much—the lab tech, Angela Jones, disappeared the same day the virus went missing. We've got her name and her suspected association with Jennifer Pattee. We'll work that. And we have Pattee's contact in custody." Cam set the unfinished scotch on Lucinda's desk. "And there's the other problem. He says he was hired to make the delivery yesterday—that a friend of a friend called him and offered him ten grand to meet a woman and pass her a package."

"He's claiming to know nothing of what was in the package?" Lucinda asked.

"According to him," Cam said, "he's just a messenger."

Blair jumped up and paced a step, then spun back. "Are you kidding me? What about the phone call to Pattee the night before?"

"Scripted for him. That and the conversation in the diner. He was just playing a role."

"And what did he think that was?" Blair said.

Cam shrugged. "He says he didn't care—the money was good."

Lucinda leaned back in her desk chair, frowning. "Who is he?"

"His name is Elliot Marsh—ID'd from his license. Appears to be a legit ID."

"Let me guess," Lucinda said dryly. "He's from Idaho."

"Bingo."

Blair pointed a finger at Cam. "You know it's bigger than these two. There has to be a conspiracy."

Cam nodded. "I do know, and we'll unravel it. But it's going to take time and likely mean we'll be putting people undercover."

"And in the meantime?" Blair asked. "What about Jennifer and this guy Marsh?"

"Oh," Cam said with a hard smile, "they're not going anywhere."

"We cannot allow this attack to go unanswered," Lucinda said, fixing her attention on Cam. "I want you to put together a task force and find out who's behind this. You'll head it and report directly to Averill."

Cam glanced at Blair.

"Yes," Blair said softly, taking Cam's hand. "Yes. Whoever they are, they have to be stopped."

Cam squeezed her hand. "Then that's what we'll do."

CHAPTER THIRTY-FIVE

Evyn woke to the rasp of Ricochet's tongue on her ear and the deep rumble of his purr. She didn't remember falling asleep. She only vaguely remembered the ride home. But she remembered the bright December sunlight and the fury in Jennifer Pattee's eyes. She remembered glimpsing her colleagues, her friends, closing in as Jennifer's hand dipped into the black leather bag slung over her shoulder, and she remembered the threat of death that would have followed a quick toss of a fragile vial filled with lethal virus into the street. She remembered the glint of sunlight on metal. Saw the gun come up. Pointed at her. She hadn't thought, hadn't needed to. Her body moved, conditioned and trained a thousand times over for exactly that moment.

Her mind clearer now, she knew her part in the greater picture was a small one. She'd helped stop an attack on the president of the United States. She'd done her job, the job she had wanted to do all her life. Her part was over, but the war was just starting. There were more like Jennifer and those who had conceived of the assault—at home and abroad—those who called themselves patriots and translated their fanaticism into violence. She'd keep doing her job, and the job would be more demanding than it had ever been. She didn't mind, she was ready.

Carefully, she turned onto her uninjured side, dislodging Ricochet from his spot on her pillow. He stretched, gave her the insulted look only a cat could muster, and stalked away.

Wes lay beside her, the strong planes and angles of her face softened by sleep and the morning light. Evyn touched her bare shoulder.

Warm. Warm, soft skin. Wes's mouth curved into a small smile, making her handsome face achingly vulnerable. Want and wonder stirred in Evyn's soul. She kissed her, just a light brush of lips, and Wes's eyes fluttered open. Clear spring green—innocent and vibrant and gloriously beautiful.

"Sorry," Evyn whispered.

"Not for the kiss, I hope."

"It's early. Go back to sleep."

"Mmm. Merry Christmas."

Evyn laughed. "Hell, it is!" She hugged Wes. "Merry Christmas. I didn't get you a present."

"Yes you did. I got you." Wes's arm came around her and Wes kissed her, her mouth possessive and seeking. Evyn kept her eyes open as long as she could, until the tenderness and longing forced her to surrender. She drew her leg up over the crest of Wes's hip, pressing nearer, molding to her. The brush of hot skin over her clitoris made her shudder.

"Doesn't seem right," Evyn gasped, arching her neck for Wes to feast, "that I get so much pleasure out of your present."

Wes's mouth skimmed over her cheek, along her jaw. "Be careful—shoulder. Remember your shoulder."

Evyn nipped at Wes's neck. "We've managed with a banged-up shoulder before."

Wes chuckled. "I wonder what it will be like when both of us have two good arms."

"If it gets any better, I won't survive," Evyn muttered, rocking her center along Wes's thigh. Her breasts were tense, aching, and she wanted to come. She needed it quick and hard, but she held on—wanting to hang suspended in this agonizing splendor of need and want and love for as long as she could. "God, I love you."

Wes drew a sharp breath, her arm tightening on Evyn's waist, urging her to thrust faster. "I really love waking up with you. I love how much you want me. You're so sexy. Are you always like this in the morning?"

"I don't know." Evyn's vision wavered. "I don't usually wake up with anyone." Evyn dug her fingers into Wes's shoulder, anchoring herself, pressing closer, needing every inch of her skin against Wes. Wes. Everywhere, always, Wes. Her orgasm unfurled, escaping the tethers of her control, and she kissed Wes hard. "I want to wake up with you." Her hips bucked and she buried her face in Wes's neck. "You... just you. Wes—oh God, I'm coming."

Wes kissed her eyelids, her mouth, her throat. "You're so beautiful. I could wake up like this forever."

"Stay, then," Evyn whispered, shattered with happiness.

Wes grew still. "Evyn, I didn't mean—"

"I did." Evyn drew away until she could look into Wes's eyes. She wanted Wes to see what was in her heart. Trust. Certainty. Joy. "I love you. I want to sleep with you and wake up with you as many nights and as many mornings as we have."

"I thought I knew what mattered before I met you," Wes whispered. "I thought my life was defined by what I accomplished, by what I contributed. Those things still matter, but what matters in my heart and my soul is you."

Evyn found Wes's hand and brought it to her heart. "I never let myself need anyone. I was afraid if I did, all the fears and uncertainties I kept locked away would escape. I couldn't afford to be anything less than tough and sure. But I need you, and I don't feel afraid. I'm stronger now, deep inside. I love you."

"Then I'll stay." Wes kissed her. "For all the nights and days to come."

About the Author

Radclyffe has written over forty romance and romantic intrigue novels, dozens of short stories, and, writing as L.L. Raand, has authored a paranormal romance series, The Midnight Hunters.

She is an eight-time Lambda Literary Award finalist in romance, mystery and erotica—winning in both romance (*Distant Shores, Silent Thunder*) and erotica (*Erotic Interludes 2: Stolen Moments* edited with Stacia Seaman and *In Deep Waters 2: Cruising the Strip* written with Karin Kallmaker). A member of the Saints and Sinners Literary Hall of Fame, she is also a 2010 RWA/FF&P Prism award winner for *Secrets in the Stone*. Her 2011 title *Firestorm* is a ForeWord Review Book of the Year award finalist. She is also the president of Bold Strokes Books, one of the world's largest independent LGBT publishing companies.

Books Available From Bold Strokes Books

Oath of Honor by Radclyffe. A First Responders novel. First do no harm…First Physician of the United States Wes Masters discovers that being the president's doctor demands more than brains and personal sacrifice—especially when politics is the order of the day. (978-1-60282-671-7)

A Question of Ghosts by Cate Culpepper. Becca Healy hopes Dr. Joanne Call can help her learn if her mother really committed suicide—but she's not sure she can handle her mother's ghost, a decades-old mystery, and lusting after the difficult Dr. Call without some serious chocolate consumption. (978-1-60282-672-4)

The Night Off by Meghan O'Brien. When Emily Parker pays for a taboo role-playing fantasy encounter from the Xtreme Scenarios escort agency, she expects to surrender control—but never imagines losing her heart to dangerous butch Nat Swayne. (978-1-60282-673-1)

Sara by Greg Herren. A mysterious and beautiful new student at Southern Heights High School stirs things up when students start dying. (978-1-60282-674-8)

Fontana by Joshua Martino. Fame, obsession, and vengeance collide in a novel that asks: What if America's greatest hero was gay? (978-1-60282-675-5)

Lemon Reef by Robin Silverman. What would you risk for the memory of your first love? When Jenna Ross learns her high school love Del Soto died on Lemon Reef, she refuses to accept the medical examiner's report of a death from natural causes and risks everything to find the truth. (978-1-60282-676-2)

The Dirty Diner: Gay Erotica on the Menu, edited by Jerry L. Wheeler. Gay erotica set in restaurants, featuring food, sex, and men—could you really ask for anything more? (978-1-60282-677-9)

The Marrying Kind by Ken O'Neill. Just when successful wedding planner Adam More decides to protest inequality by quitting the business and boycotting marriage entirely, his only sibling announces her engagement. (978-1-60282-670-0)

Sweat: Gay Jock Erotica by Todd Gregory. Sizzling tales of smoking-hot sex with the athletic studs everyone fantasizes about. (978-1-60282-669-4)

Missing by P.J. Trebelhorn. FBI agent Olivia Andrews knows exactly what she wants out of life, but then she's forced to rethink everything when she meets fellow agent Sophie Kane while investigating a child abduction. (978-1-60282-668-7)

Touch Me Gently by D. Jackson Leigh. Secrets have always meant heartbreak and banishment to Salem Lacey—until she meets the beautiful and mysterious Knox Bolander and learns some secrets are necessary. (978-1-60282-667-0)

Slingshot by Carsen Taite. Bounty hunter Luca Bennett takes on a seemingly simple job for defense attorney Ronnie Moreno, but the job quickly turns complicated and dangerous, as does her attraction to the elusive Ronnie Moreno. (978-1-60282-666-3)

Dark Wings Descending by Lesley Davis. What if the demons you face in life are real? Chicago detective Rafe Douglas is about to find out. (978-1-60282-660-1)

sunfall by Nell Stark and Trinity Tam. The final installment of the everafter series. Valentine Darrow and Alexa Newland work to rebuild their relationship even as they find themselves at the heart of the struggle that will determine a new world order for vampires and wereshifters. (978-1-60282-661-8)

Mission of Desire by Terri Richards. Nicole Kennedy finds herself in Africa at the center of an international conspiracy and is rescued by the beautiful but arrogant government agent Kira Anthony—but can Nicole trust Kira, or is she blinded by desire? (978-1-60282-662-5)

Boys of Summer, edited by Steve Berman. Stories of young love and adventure, when the sky's ceiling is a bright blue marvel, when another boy's laughter at the beach can distract from dull summer jobs. (978-1-60282-663-2)

Calendar Boys by Logan Zachary. A man a month will keep you excited year-round. (978-1-60282-665-6)

The Locket and the Flintlock by Rebecca S. Buck. When Regency gentlewoman Lucia Foxe is robbed on the highway, will the masked outlaw who stole Lucia's precious locket also claim her heart? (978-1-60282-664-9)

Burgundy Betrayal by Sheri Lewis Wohl. Park Ranger Kara Lynch has no idea she's a witch until dead bodies begin to pile up in her park, forcing her to turn to beautiful and sexy shape-shifter Camille Black Wolf for help in stopping a rogue werewolf. (978-1-60282-654-0)

LoveLife by Rachel Spangler. When Joey Lang unintentionally becomes a client of life coach Elaine Raitt, the relationship becomes complicated as they develop feelings that make them question their purpose in love and life. (978-1-60282-655-7)

The Fling by Rebekah Weatherspoon. When the ultimate fantasy of a one-night stand with her trainer, Oksana Gorinkov, suddenly turns into more, reality show producer Annie Collins opens her life to a new type of love she's never imagined. (978-1-60282-656-4)

Ill Will by J.M. Redmann. New Orleans PI Micky Knight must untangle a twisted web of healthcare fraud that leads to murder—and puts those closest to her most at risk. (978-1-60282-657-1)

Buccaneer Island by J.P. Beausejour. In the rough world of Caribbean piracy, a man is what he makes of himself—or what a stronger man makes of him. (978-1-60282-658-8)

Twelve O'Clock Tales by Felice Picano. The fourth collection of short fiction by legendary novelist and memoirist Felice Picano. Thirteen dark tales that will thrill and disturb, discomfort and titillate, enthrall and leave you wondering. (978-1-60282-659-5)

Words to Die By by William Holden. Sixteen answers to the question: What causes a mind to curdle? (978-1-60282-653-3)

Tyger, Tyger, Burning Bright by Justine Saracen. Love does not conquer all, but when all of Europe is on fire, it's better than going to hell alone. (978-1-60282-652-6)

Night Hunt by L.L. Raand. When dormant powers ignite, the wolf Were pack is thrown into violent upheaval, and Sylvan's pregnant mate is at the center of the turmoil. A Midnight Hunters novel. (978-1-60282-647-2)

Demons are Forever by Kim Baldwin and Xenia Alexiou. Elite Operative Landis "Chase" Coolidge enlists the help of high-class call girl Heather Snyder to track down a kidnapped colleague embroiled in a global black market organ-harvesting ring. (978-1-60282-648-9)

Runaway by Anne Laughlin. When Jan Roberts is hired to find a teenager who has run away to live with a group of antigovernment survivalists, she's forced to return to the life she escaped when she was a teenager herself. (978-1-60282-649-6)

Street Dreams by Tama Wise. Tyson Rua has more than his fair share of problems growing up in New Zealand—he's gay, he's falling in love, and he's run afoul of the local hip-hop crew leader just as he's trying to make it as a graffiti artist. (978-1-60282-650-2)

Women of the Dark Streets: Lesbian Paranormal by Radclyffe and Stacia Seaman, eds. Erotic tales of the supernatural—a world of vampires, werewolves, witches, ghosts, and demons—by the authors of Bold Strokes Books. (978-1-60282-651-9)

Derrick Steele: Private Dick—The Case of the Hollywood Hustlers by Zavo. Derrick Steele, a hard-drinking, lusty private detective, is being framed for the murder of a hustler in downtown Los Angeles. When his brother's friend Daniel McAllister joins the investigation, their growing attraction might prove to be more explosive than the case. (978-1-60282-596-3)

Nice Butt: Gay Anal Eroticism edited by Shane Allison. From toys to teasing, spanking to sporting, some of the best gay erotic scribes celebrate the hottest and most creative in new erotica. (978-1-60282-635-9)

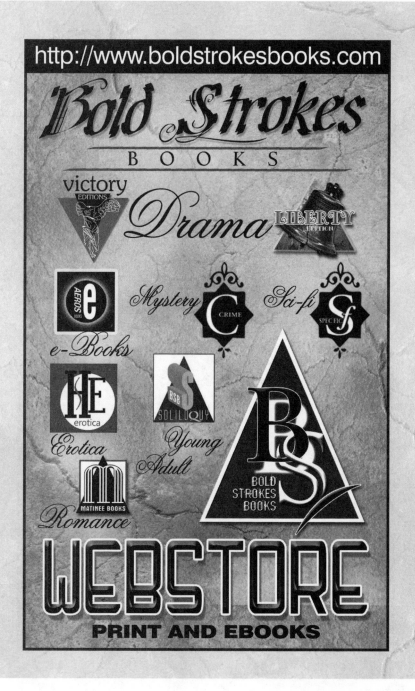